Steven Saylor is the autho[r] historical novels *Roma and* as well as the acclaimed [] mystery novels featuring Gordianus the Finder, beginning with *Roman Blood*. His fascination with the ancient world began in childhood when he saw the 1963 movie *Cleopatra* at a drive-in theater, and continued through his education in History and Classics at the University of Texas at Austin. His first trip to Rome was a life-changing event that propelled him into his 30-year career as a historical novelist. His work has been translated into more than 20 languages, and book tours have taken him to many countries, including the U.K. He has appeared on the History channel as an expert on Roman politics and daily life. With Rick Solomon, his husband of 45 years, he divides his time between Berkeley, California and Austin, Texas.

DOMINUS

A Novel of the Roman Empire

STEVEN SAYLOR

CONSTABLE

CONSTABLE

First published in the US in 2021 by St Martin's Press,
an imprint of St. Martin's Publishing Group

First published in hardback in Great Britain by Constable in 2021
This paperback edition published in 2022 by Constable

A CIP catalogue record for this book
is available from the British Library.

ISBN 978-1-472-12368-8

Printed and bound in Great Britain by Clays Ltd, Elcograf S.p.A.

Papers used by Constable are from well-managed forests
and other responsible sources.

MIX
Paper from
responsible sources
FSC® C104740

Constable
An imprint of
Little, Brown Book Group
Carmelite House
50 Victoria Embankment
London EC4Y 0DZ

An Hachette UK Company
www.hachette.co.uk

www.littlebrown.co.uk

To all the readers over the years who have chosen
one of my books to read, including this one

CONTENTS

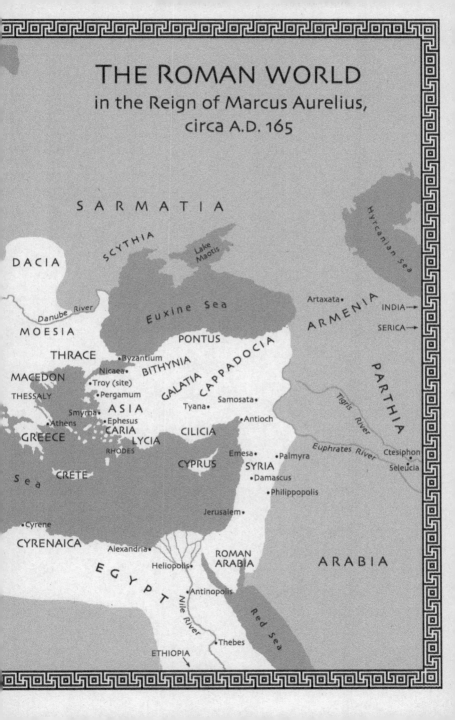

THE ROMAN WORLD
in the Reign of Marcus Aurelius,
circa A.D. 165

The Pinarii of Rome in the Imperial Period

WEARERS OF THE FASCINUM ARE IN BOLD TYPE

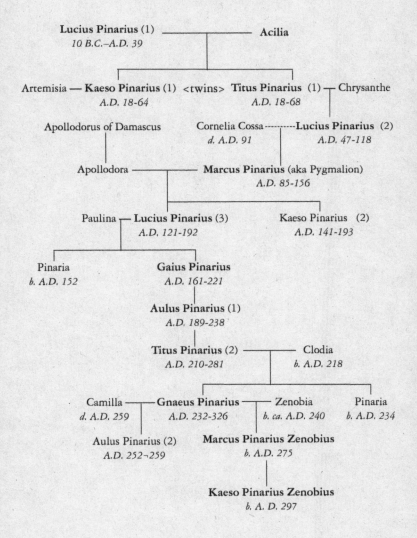

Lucius Pinarius (1) ———————— **Acilia**
10 B.C.–A.D. 39

Artemisia — **Kaeso Pinarius** (1)   <twins>   **Titus Pinarius** (1) — Chrysanthe
A.D. 18-64   *A.D. 18-68*

Apollodorus of Damascus   Cornelia Cossa ---------**Lucius Pinarius** (2)
                                                     d. A.D. 91   *A.D. 47-118*

Apollodora ——————— **Marcus Pinarius** (aka Pygmalion)
                                                A.D. 85-156

Paulina — **Lucius Pinarius** (3)   Kaeso Pinarius   (2)
                    A.D. 121-192   *A.D. 141-193*

Pinaria   **Gaius Pinarius**
b. A.D. 152   *A.D. 161-221*

                        Aulus Pinarius (1)
                          A.D. 189-238

                    Titus Pinarius (2) ——— Clodia
                        A.D. 210-281   *b. A.D. 218*

Camilla ——— **Gnaeus Pinarius** ——— Zenobia   Pinaria
d. A.D. 259   *A.D. 232-326*   *b. ca. A.D. 240*   *b. A.D. 234*

        Aulus Pinarius (2)   **Marcus Pinarius Zenobius**
          A.D. 252¬259   *b. A.D. 275*

                        Kaeso Pinarius Zenobius
                            b. A. D. 297

DOMINUS: *Latin for "Master," the word by which slaves in the Roman Republic addressed their owner; then, under the Empire, the form of address rejected by some emperors but demanded by others; then, under the Christian Church, the title by which worshippers address their god.*

PART I

THE BLOOD OF A GLADIATOR
(A.D. 165–192)

AD 165

I'm afraid our daughter might die . . .

These words of his wife rang in the ears of Lucius Pinarius as he stepped inside the Senate House, holding the hand of his four-year-old son. Surely the situation was not as bad as that, he thought. What were Pinaria's symptoms, after all? Sleeplessness, lethargy, loss of appetite, an irregular pulse, mental distraction—hardly the signs of a plague, and rather mild if the problem was an infestation by some evil spirit. On the other hand, Lucius's wife had cited a number of examples of friends and loved ones who had died from symptoms far less severe than those of their teenaged daughter, with the end sometimes coming quite suddenly. Pinaria's illness had already lasted for at least two months, despite the efforts of three different physicians to cure her. Today a new physician was coming to examine Pinaria, a young fellow from Pergamum recommended by one of Lucius's colleagues in the Senate.

But first, Lucius would begin the day as he tried to begin every day, with an offering to the goddess who presided over the vestibule of the Senate House. As he and little Gaius stepped inside and the tall bronze doors closed behind them, the goddess loomed over them, her body much larger than that of any mortal, her massive wings spread wide, one arm extended over their heads to offer a laurel wreath too big and surely too heavy for any mortal to wear. The bronze statue was painted with such skill and delicacy that the laurel leaves looked freshly picked and the winged goddess appeared ready to leap from her high pedestal at any instant. The soft light from high windows enhanced the illusion.

Little Gaius, who had never been inside the Senate House, stared upward at the statue of Victory. He made a noise between a gasp and a whimper, and grabbed hold of his father's toga.

There was no one else in the vestibule. Except for the goddess, they were quite alone. The slightest sound echoed from the marble walls.

Lucius laughed softly and touched the boy's blond curls, which gleamed by the light of the pyre that burned low on the marble altar before the statue. "Have no fear, my son. Victory is our friend. We worship and adore her. In return, she has shown great favor to us. A senator never enters this chamber without first pausing here at her altar to light a bit of incense and say a prayer. Smoke is the food of the gods, and there is no smoke sweeter than that of incense."

As he touched a bit of incense to the flame and watched it smolder, he looked up at the statue and whispered, "Sweet Victory, beloved by all mortals, bestow your favor on our esteemed emperor Verus in his campaign against the Parthians. Scatter his enemies before him. Keep safe the legions under his command. Grant them many conquests and much plunder. And when their work is done, see the emperor Verus and his troops safely home so that they may parade in triumph up the Sacred Way. I give voice to the prayers of all Romans everywhere. We all bow our heads before you." He glanced down at his son, whose head was already bowed. "And also, sweet Victory, for myself and for my family I ask a much smaller favor—that you give your blessing to my endeavor today. Let the physician be skilled and honest. Let him restore my daughter to full health." *And let him not be too expensive,* Lucius thought, but did not speak the words aloud. He did not believe in bothering the gods with trivialities.

Behind them, the massive bronze doors creaked open. The man who entered wore a toga with a purple stripe, like that of Lucius. He saw little Gaius and smiled.

"The boy's first visit, Senator Pinarius?"

"Yes, Senator . . ." Lucius knew the man only from meetings, and could not think of his name. When on official business he had a slave at hand to whisper such details in his ear, but his small retinue of servants was waiting for him outside.

"I thought so, from those wide green eyes. A senator's son never forgets his first time inside the Senate House. She's quite impressive, eh, young man?"

"Yes, Senator." Gaius had been taught always to answer his elders and to address them respectfully.

"His first visit, but far from his last, I suspect. Do you want to grow up to be a senator like your father, young man?"

"Yes, Senator!"

Lucius took Gaius by the hand and stepped aside to allow the man to make his own offering at the altar. They passed through the door, which was still ajar, and onto the broad porch of the Senate House. Father and son blinked at the bright sunshine. Below them, in the open spaces of the Forum, men stood in groups, loudly conversing. Slave boys ran about, carrying messages or running errands for their masters. After the hush inside the Senate chamber, the noise of the Forum on a busy morning was striking, and to Lucius's ears quite pleasant. The noise of the Forum was the pulse of the city, and on this morning it was neither hectic nor sluggish, but indicated the normal functioning of the grandest, most powerful, and most noble city on earth.

If only his daughter could be as healthy as Rome seemed to be on this fine spring morning!

"Will I be a senator when I grow up?" asked Gaius.

"There is every reason to think that you will. But you must be at least twenty-five years old, and you are many years away from that."

"How will I become a senator?"

"The old-fashioned way was to be elected to office, but nowadays it usually happens when one or the other of the emperors appoints a worthy candidate to the Senate. So it is always a good idea to stay on the good side of both emperors."

"Why are there two emperors? Are they brothers?"

Lucius smiled, pleased that his son was showing such a precocious interest in the ways of the world.

"Not brothers by blood; not in the same way that you and Pinaria are brother and sister. But Verus and Marcus did grow up in the same household, and the previous emperor thought it would be best if both of them took the office, so as to share its burdens, which has worked out quite well. The Empire has grown so vast that one man can hardly be expected to run it anymore. So Marcus, who is a very learned and thoughtful kind of person—a philosopher, actually—stays here in Rome and tends to laws and commerce and that sort of thing, making sure the citizens are fed and behave themselves, while Verus marches off to war. Different men are gifted in different ways. Rome is very lucky to have two such fine rulers—a thinker and a doer, if you will."

Gaius frowned. "But why aren't *you* the emperor, Father? Isn't our family the oldest family in Rome?"

Lucius smiled. "That is something we Pinarii like to say, and it may even be true. Certainly, we Pinarii can trace out roots all the way back to the founding of Rome and even further, deep into the age of legend. The Pinarii were there when Hercules killed the monster Cacus on the banks of the Tiber. It was the Pinarii who put up an altar to honor Hercules for saving the people—the very first altar anywhere in the Seven Hills. And we Pinarii were there when the deified Augustus installed the altar and the statue of Victory in the Senate House. I myself was honored to grow up alongside Marcus, years before Antoninus Pius decided to make him his heir."

"Did you wrestle him, Father?"

Lucius laughed. "Yes I did, and beat him as often as not. But to be honest, he was a better horseman and hunter than I, and a much better scholar. Not just smarter than I, but smarter than any of our tutors."

"Did you grow up with the emperor Verus too?"

"No. He's ten years younger than Marcus and I—about the same difference in years as between you and Pinaria. As a boy, Verus excelled at wrestling and hunting, too, and was not a bad scholar, though never a great lover of philosophy, like Marcus. But Verus is a fine warrior, which is something that Rome greatly needs right now, to keep the Parthians on their side of the Euphrates River, and maybe even slice off a bit of their empire, to teach them a lesson. My own brother and I are a bit like Marcus and Verus, I suppose. I've stayed in Rome, running the family business I inherited from your grandfather, while your uncle Kaeso became a warrior and serves under the emperor Verus. Oh! I think I forgot to mention Kaeso by name in my prayers to the goddess. Perhaps we should go back inside . . . but I did pray specifically for the safe return of all the troops, and that includes your uncle . . ."

Lucius could see by the boy's face that he was no longer listening, distracted by some sudden flurry of activity below them in the Forum. Ah well, Gaius was hardly old enough to listen to a senator rattle on and on, even if the senator was his father. The good thing was that the boy had curiosity and was not afraid to ask questions, and took pride in his ancestry.

"Enough talk, son. We must hurry home. I want to be there when this new physician arrives."

With two slaves to carry his various satchels full of medical devices and another to lead him to the home of his patient, Galen walked through the streets of Rome. Well into his thirties, he had traveled much of the world, including a long stay in Alexandria, and his hometown was the sophisticated metropolis of Pergamum. He was by any standard a worldly and sophisticated man. But sometimes, though he had been living in Rome for almost three years, he could still find himself agog at the sights and sounds of the world's capital. Surely Rome must be the biggest, richest, most elegant city on earth, and also the most squalid.

He had just passed through a particularly odiferous part of the Subura, filled with the smells of stewing cabbage, slave-sweat, and excrement, both canine and human, only to emerge into the bright squares between the temples and public buildings of the Forum. Here the city smelled of incense smoldering on altars, scribes' ink, warm sunshine on marble, and the tangy residue of the diluted urine used to wash to utmost whiteness the togas of senators and other prominent citizens going about their important business.

Galen and the three slaves ascended the Palatine Hill, which was almost entirely occupied by temples and imperial palaces, but not quite, as was attested by the relatively small but immaculate house tucked away on a narrow, tree-shaded street. The slave who had guided him rapped on the door and spoke to another slave inside, whereupon the broad oaken door swung inward.

As he had expected—having made a few inquiries about his prospective client—the walls of the vestibule had numerous niches that housed wax funeral masks and marble busts representing the Pinarii of previous generations. All Romans venerated their ancestors in some fashion, and the higher classes kept images of them where they would be seen every day by everyone—whether visitors, slaves, or family members— entering or leaving the house. There were two niches larger than the others, facing each other across the vestibule. In one was an exquisite bust of the handsome young god called Antinous. In his travels Galen had seen many Antinous statues, but this was a remarkable fine example, of the very highest workmanship, the marble so perfectly shaped and tinted that it seemed alive. Galen almost expected the lapis lazuli eyes to blink. The other statue was in some ways the opposite of Antinous, a full-length statuette of an old, bearded man draped in philosopher's robes.

This image, too, was familiar to Galen from the many he had seen in his travels. It was the famous sage and wonder-worker Apollonius of Tyana.

A slave arrived to escort him to a garden within the house. Galen took his two assistants with him, to take notes and to produce any devices he might need. They were trained to walk softly and to keep utterly silent, so as to be as unobtrusive as possible. He would have rendered them invisible if he could, but such a trick reached beyond medicine into the realm of magic, which Galen scrupulously avoided. Not all physicians could say the same.

Senator Lucius Pinarius was seated in a garden surrounded by a colonnaded peristyle. He gestured for Galen to sit. Galen judged Pinarius, whom he knew to be in his mid-forties, to be in excellent health. His physique was robust, his green eyes bright, his blond hair of that golden color that grows lighter with age but never turns to gray. A woman and child entered the garden. Pinarius introduced his wife, Paulina, and their small son, Gaius.

"Gaius?" said Galen, giving the boy a smile. "That's a rather old-fashioned name, not too common in Rome nowadays." His Latin had such a thick accent that Lucius had to strain to understand him. Lucius's Greek was almost certainly better than the physician's Latin, so he answered in Greek.

"We chose it in remembrance of our kinship to the greatest Roman who ever bore that name, Gaius Julius Caesar."

"Ah!" Galen nodded at this impressive assertion, but didn't take it too seriously. Romans of the old patrician class invariably claimed impressive lineage. The emperor Marcus was said to be descended from King Numa, the famously wise and peace-loving ruler who succeeded the city's bold but reckless founder, Romulus.

Glad for the implicit invitation to proceed in his native tongue, Galen switched from Latin to Greek, which he spoke with an elegant and refined accent. "Is the patient present? You all look in excellent health," said Galen.

"No. It's my thirteen-year-old daughter who is unwell. But first, tell me a little about yourself. You come from Pergamum, yes? Has the city suffered greatly from the war?"

"Normal life has been disrupted by shortages and such, but the barbarians never came within a month's march. In Antioch the situation was much more precarious. But now the tide seems to have turned, thanks to the emperor Verus and his legions."

"Do you miss your native city?"

"I do hope eventually to return to Pergamum, after the deprivations and uncertainties of war pass. In the meantime, my late father left me heir to property in Pergamum that produces sufficient income for me to travel and to live wherever I want."

"You look young to be a physician," said Paulina. "Not a gray hair on your head!"

"Nor is your husband yet gray, even though I judge him to be . . ." Galen cocked his head. "A healthy specimen of . . . forty-three years . . . ten months . . . and fifteen days."

Lucius laughed. "But—how did you . . . ?"

Galen smiled. "Just as you no doubt asked your friends about me, so I asked a few questions about you. Invariably, the first detail everyone gives about Senator Lucius Pinarius is that he shares a birthdate with our beloved emperor Marcus. That means that you, like Marcus Aurelius, were born on the twenty-sixth day of April in the Year of Rome 873."

"Are you an astrologer as well?" asked Paulina.

"No. And yes, I am younger than many of my fellow physicians. I started my medical studies very early, charged to do so by the god Aesculapius himself."

"The god spoke to you?" asked Lucius.

"Not to me, but to my father. It was his desire, when I was a boy, that I should become a philosopher. He himself schooled me in arithmetic, grammar, and logic. But in my seventeenth year, Aesculapius visited my father in a dream. The great healer of mankind told him that I should become a physician. Two years later my father died. The cause was never determined.

I had only just begun to pursue my studies, and I could not help but think: were I already the man Aesculapius wants me to be, I could have saved him! I've been trying to please the shade of my father ever since, and to catch up with my own destiny. For eleven years I studied in Pergamum, Smyrna, and at the Temple of the Muses in Alexandria."

"Eleven years of study? Impressive." Lucius nodded thoughtfully. "The last physician we consulted was a . . . how did he put it, Paulina?"

"He called himself a Thessalian Methodologist. According to him, all diseases can be put into one of two categories, *laxum* or *strictum*—conditions that expand or constrict tiny vessels inside the body."

"He also told us that no more than six months of study was necessary for any apt pupil to learn everything a physician needs to know," said Lucius.

Galen snorted. "And that is why, here in Rome, many a fellow who calls himself a physician was six months ago a barber, or a shoemaker, or a dung-collector!"

"The man charged a handsome fee," muttered Lucius.

"Unlike myself. The first time I correctly diagnosed an illness and cured a patient, I knew I would never desire to do anything else for the rest of my life. Medicine is my passion and my calling, but it is not and never will be my livelihood. I never charge for my services, having no need to do so."

Lucius liked the sound of that.

"Someone told my husband that you used to treat . . . *gladiators*", said Paulina with a slight shudder. The idea seemed to both fascinate and repel her.

"Indeed. After my studies I returned to Pergamum and was appointed chief physician for all the municipal gladiators. In some ways, my education was just beginning. The terrible wounds I sewed up, the complicated surgeries I performed! And the dissections—"

"Of humans?" Lucius said, taken aback.

"Of course not. Human dissections haven't been allowed

anywhere for hundreds of years, not since the first Ptolemies ruled Alexandria, when the physician Herophilus was allowed to cut up condemned criminals—some, it's said, while they were still alive."

Little Gaius's eyes grew wide at this detail. His parents stiffened but maintained stoic expressions.

"When I say dissection," said Galen, "I refer to the animals I've dissected, and also vivisected. The exotic creatures imported for shows in the arena at Pergamum were kept near the gladiators, so I had easy access to them. Some were quite unusual indeed, and all had much to teach me. Monkeys are the most interesting, since their insides most closely resemble those of humans."

Lucius frowned. What had wounded gladiators and vivisected animals—monkeys, indeed!—in common with a young Roman maiden who was wasting away? On the other hand, the young physician from Pergamum seemed very sure of himself; so sure, in fact, that he proceeded to put forth conditions.

"If I am to treat the patient," said Galen, "it is absolutely essential that you answer any and all questions I may ask, no matter how irrelevant or presumptuous they may seem to you. You must be completely honest with me at all times, even if you find the truth distasteful or embarrassing."

"What has my honesty to do with your ability to cure my daughter's illness?"

"A true and full picture of the circumstances is essential to my understanding."

"Do you not take my husband's honesty for granted?" asked Paulina.

Galen cocked his head and assumed the sardonic look that Lucius would come to know so well in the ensuing years. "You might be surprised at how often my patients and their carers try to mislead me, sometimes quite deliberately. For most people, bodily functions and trials of the flesh cause no end of squeamishness and embarrassment."

"Does nothing embarrass you, or make you squeamish?" asked Lucius.

"If such a thing exists, I have yet to encounter it. Shall the examination commence?"

In the privacy of the girl's room, with the physician's assistants and her parents present, Galen examined the listless, apathetic Pinaria, peering into her eyes, nose, ears, and mouth. The girl sat on her bed, wearing a long-sleeved tunic that covered her from neck to toes, her only ornament an amulet of some sort worn on a necklace outside the tunic. Both the amulet and the chain from which it hung appeared to be made of gold. She avoided Galen's gaze and when questioned about any discomfort she might be experiencing, responded with mumbles and shrugs. When her mother told her to speak up, the girl shut her mouth tightly and stared into space, her eyes bright with tears. Galen took her pulse several times, carefully noting the frequency and rhythm of the heartbeats and dictating his observations to one of his assistants, who scribbled on a wax tablet.

"I'll need to take her pulse again, an hour from now."

Lucius wondered if this was just a ruse to cadge a bit of food and wine. He could hardly host a visitor, even a physician, for an hour without offering something. "Shall we go back to the garden, then?"

"You needn't entertain me, Senator. If you have some scrolls, I should be glad to pass the hour reading."

Lucius brightened. He was very proud of the family's library. "Follow me to my study. I have a number of scrolls having to do with science and anatomy, including what I'm told are some rather rare volumes of Aristotle."

"In that case I should like my assistants to come with me, should I come across a passage worth copying."

Paulina and Gaius stayed behind while Galen followed Lucius down a short hallway and into a room lined with pigeonhole bookcases full of scrolls. The furnishings were sparse but exquisite. Lucius sat and invited Galen to do likewise. As there were only two chairs, the assistants sat on the floor, keeping still and quiet.

"I noticed that your daughter wears an amulet."

"Yes."

"I'm curious about the shape. It looks a bit like a cross, such as some Christians wear."

"I assure you it is no such thing!" said Lucius, with such vehemence that Galen was taken aback.

"Do you have a personal grudge against the followers of Christ?"

"I despise those atheists no more and no less than any other gods-fearing Roman. What makes you think I have a grudge against them?"

"Ah, you see, this is precisely why I must have full and honest replies to any question I ask. The relevance is for your physician to decide. Let me explain. What if, in fact, you were engaged in a feud with some Christians? What if they wished to exact revenge on you, or had some other malicious intent?"

"Are you saying my daughter might be the victim of some sort of spell or curse? I thought the Christians had only disdain for magic."

"Who knows what such people are capable of," asked Galen, "living as they do outside ordinary society and beyond the restraints of normal religion? In my experience, all sorts of people cast spells and curses for all sorts of reasons, or pay someone else to do so. I pursue this line of questioning because your daughter wears an amulet, intended, I presume, to protect her from something."

Lucius sighed. "That amulet, as you call it, is an ancient family heirloom—so ancient and so weathered that its original form is no longer recognizable. You aren't the first, and will not be the last, I'm sure, to remark on its resemblance to a cross. In fact it is, or was, a winged phallus."

"Ah! What you Romans call a fascinum."

"Yes. All such amulets represent the god Fascinus, the first deity known to the earliest people of Rome, older even than Saturn. Before all the other gods, there was the winged phallus that was seen to hover over the hearthfires of our ancestors."

Galen nodded. "And all these years later, you Romans put such amulets in the cribs of infants, to protect them from the Evil Eye—the malicious gaze of the envious. I am familiar with the custom."

"A rather larger fascinum is kept by the Vestal virgins, who bring it out on only one occasion, to be placed under the chariot of a commander celebrating a triumph. There, too, it deflects the Evil Eye."

"I see such charms everywhere I go."

Lucius shook his head. "The fascinum of the Pinarii is much more than a simple charm. It may in fact be the very first such amulet ever fashioned in Rome, modeled directly upon the god Fascinus, in that mysterious age before Prometheus gave the gift of writing to mankind. This is not just family lore. The emperor Marcus saw me wearing it on the day we both put on our manly togas, and took an interest in its history. He wrote a small treatise on the fascinum, drawing upon previous research done by no less a scholar than the emperor Claudius, the greatest of all Roman antiquarians."

"I had no idea," said Galen.

"But . . ."

"Yes?"

"There is . . . in fact . . . a small link to the Christians in the history of the fascinum. I had a great-great-uncle who was . . . a Christian." Lucius drew a deep breath. "For a while he wore this charm, perhaps thinking—mistakenly!—that it represented the cross upon which his so-called savior died. After the great fire, he was among the Christians arrested by Nero. The fascinum was taken from him—rescued, I should say—just before he was burned alive. It's a distasteful story, not something I would ever casually discuss. What was it you said about your patients being embarrassed or squeamish?

I suppose I feel both, thinking of that sordid episode of our family history. But now you understand why I'm so sensitive to any intimation that I or any other member of my household has any link whatsoever to the Christians, which we most certainly do not."

Galen nodded. "The fascinum didn't protect your great-great-uncle, then. Nor does it seem to be a cure for your daughter's ailment."

"Perhaps it's of no use because of her gender. By tradition the fascinum is passed from father to son. Until Gaius turns fifteen, and receives the fascinum on the day he puts on his manly toga, the amulet is for me and me alone to wear. That is the tradition. But Pinaria's ailment seems so intractable, so mysterious, I thought, perhaps, if I let her wear it . . ."

"In my experience, no amulet ever cured any wearer of any disease."

"No?" said Lucius. "I've heard of cases where—"

"The things one hears about, and the things that actually occur, are often two different things entirely. But let me correct myself. No amulet ever cured a wearer by means of some invisible, intangible, inexplicable—that is to say, magical—power. In Alexandria I encountered a boy who suffered from epilepsy, whose mother gave him an amulet to wear, rather crudely carved to resemble a crocodile, and thereupon he suffered no fits for five months. Then, through carelessness, the boy lost the amulet and straightaway the fits returned. Then his mother found the amulet, put it on the boy, and his fits again receded."

"But there you have it!" said Lucius. "It's obvious that the amulet, or whatever demon or god it represented, must have—"

"No, no. The amulet, you see, was not made of metal or stone, or carved from some common wood, but from a peony root. I carried out an experiment. I took the amulet from him, whereupon the fits returned. I found a fresh piece of peony root and had him wear that around his neck instead—and his fits ceased! It was something about the peony root that cured his epilepsy, not the amulet or whatever supernatural power the amulet was meant to represent. Why the peony root worked, we have no way of knowing, but I hypothesize it might be the action of minute particles released by the root, which the boy either inhaled or absorbed through his skin, for he was in the habit of touching it. So you see, the 'obvious' answer is not always the correct one. The skillful physician must not only learn the arts of medicine compiled over many centuries— the received knowledge of the past—but must also learn to observe, and to draw deductions from his observations."

"I see. But is medicine then just a matter of substances—of poisons and cures? Do the gods play no role in healing?"

"I never said that. Belief in magic is misguided. Genuine worship of the gods is another matter. I noticed in your vestibule, besides the busts of your ancestors, two other statues—a bearded old man and a beautiful youth. In front of both were bronze dishes in which bits of incense had been burned. The youth is the god Antinous, of course. And the old man must be Apollonius of Tyana."

"Yes, in this household we devote special worship to Antinous. My late father became the first priest of his temple at the villa of the divine Hadrian. He actually saw Antinous in the flesh, here in Rome, before the young man perished in the Nile, sacrificing himself in place of Hadrian to thwart a curse. The priests in Egypt told Hadrian that his lover had become immortal and had joined the gods. Hadrian set up temples for the worship of Antinous. I'm told that such temples are all over the empire."

"Oh yes, I've visited many of his temples and seen many images of Antinous, first in my native Pergamum, and then in Alexandria, and in Antioch, and in every city I visited on my way to Rome. I think sometimes men and women go to those temples just to stare at the god's statue."

Lucius, who missed the man's sardonic tone, nodded and smiled. "Without boasting, I can tell you that many of those statues—certainly the best of them—come from my family's workshop. The original statue, of which all others are copies, was done by my father, from the living model, at the request of Hadrian himself. My father also executed many statues of Hadrian, and then of his successor, Antoninus Pius, and many more statues of the rest of the imperial family, in both marble and bronze. Nowadays we produce an endless number of images, from life-size to trinkets, of both emperors, Marcus and Verus. The demand is greater than we can accommodate. Every Roman in the world wants an image of our beloved emperors in his house."

"You do such work yourself?" It was rare that Galen encountered any Roman of the upper classes who did anything a normal man might consider physical labor.

"Do I deign to work with my own hands, you mean? Do I end the day covered in marble dust? My father certainly did, and he taught me to handle a chisel and drill as well as any other man. But nowadays we have a large workshop and a foundry with many artisans; it's at the foot of the Aventine Hill, near the river. We also own several quarries and mines that produce the fine marbles and the metals for making bronze. I myself sculpt the most important designs and give final approval to all others, and I personally inspect the quality of every work that leaves the shop, from fluted columns to imperial portraits. Nothing leaves the workshop without my personal certification. Many is the day I arrive home with my face and hands and toga covered with marble dust, even if I never touched a chisel.

"That statue of Antinous that you saw in the vestibule was made by my father. Hadrian loved that statue. He declared it perhaps the most perfect of all the images of the young god. So great was my father's ability to breathe life into stone that Hadrian gave him a nickname—Pygmalion.

"Father also made that statue of Apollonius of Tyana, in whose honor we light incense every day at sunrise and sunset. There's a family connection there, too, you see. My grandfather was once imprisoned alongside the great wonder-worker when both gave offense to the emperor Domitian, who ordered them to be shackled and thrown to the lions. Apollonius proceeded to make a fool of the emperor, shaking off his chains and vanishing into thin air."

"I've heard that story. And your grandfather?"

Lucius, who had recounted this tale many times, especially enjoyed this part. "Grandfather possessed no such supernatural power, and was forced to face a lion in the Flavian Amphitheater, with all of Rome looking on. Thanks to the instruction and inspiration he had received from Apollonius, my grandfather stared that lion into submission. Domitian had no choice but to set him free. Thus my grandfather lived to see the end of Domitian and the rescue of the empire by Nerva, and all the good emperors who followed."

Could the story be true? Galen had grown used to hearing tall tales from the Roman elite, and this one seemed particularly far-fetched. However accurate the story, Galen was beginning to realize that Lucius Pinarius was a more important and well-connected man than he had thought.

"I know you share a birthday with the emperor Marcus. Have you known him since childhood?"

"Oh, yes. Hadrian and my father deliberately threw us together as boys. Hadrian hoped that my love of sport would rub off on Marcus, and Father hoped that Marcus's love of learning would rub off on me. We hit it off. For a long time we saw each other almost every day. I think I may be the only person who still calls him Verissimus—the nickname given him by Hadrian because he was such a truth-seeker, even as a child."

"You're close, then?" Galen had met a number of prominent men since his arrival in Rome, but never anyone with a direct link to the imperial household.

Lucius thought for a while before he answered. "I can't say we're close nowadays, though I still see him on official business having to do with sculptures and such. Were we ever close, even as boys?" Lucius shook his head. "The emperor is not an easy man to know. Even as a child, he often seemed apart from those around him. Always very thoughtful, always very precise in his speech—and quite often disappointed when those around him were not as thoughtful and precise. Not the sort to tell a joke, or do more than politely laugh at one. His fellow emperor is quite another matter. Though I've spent far less time in his company than I have in Marcus's, I always feel more at ease with Verus. Everyone does. His intellect is just as sharp—our tutors always considered him the equal of Marcus—but he wears his learning lightly. Not the type to quote Seneca, or even Homer, for that matter." He sighed. "May the gods bring him safely home! And Kaeso, as well."

"Kaeso?"

"My brother. Twenty years younger than I. The warrior in the family. Off with Verus, fighting Parthians."

"May they both come home covered with glory," said Galen.

Lucius hummed thoughtfully. "All I really know of war—real war, not just stories in books—is from Kaeso. He writes me as often as he can. He's seen more horror than glory. There was peace for so long under Antoninus, people forgot how horrible war could be."

"Yes," said Galen. "The stories I heard, before I left Pergamum! That awful business at Seleucia . . ."

"My brother was there."

"Was he?"

"Such . . . an unfortunate business. First the city was saved by the Romans, then sacked and destroyed by us. Kaeso saw it all. He says there's virtually nothing left of the city."

"And what a beautiful city it was." Galen felt a stab of homesickness, tinged with dread. If such a fate could befall Seleucia, it could happen to Pergamum as well. The Romans and the Parthians both claimed the current war was entirely justified and necessary, having been started by the other. How many tens of thousands of innocent lives had been lost? How many more would be lost before the war was over?

They both fell silent. Galen looked at nothing in particular;

Lucius looked at Galen. *Men's faces are not that hard to read,* Marcus had once told him. *It's a matter of observing, truly observing, really looking at people, not past them or through them.*

"Are you very homesick?"

"Yes!" Galen's expression was suddenly so melancholy that Lucius gave him a friendly touch on the shoulder.

"But here you are in Rome, my good fellow, safe and sound, and making a success of yourself, if what I hear is true. No other city on earth can compare to Rome. How could anyone ever wish to leave?"

"You've traveled, then?"

"More when I was younger than in recent years. Mostly on business, looking to find skilled artisans or to purchase special marbles. A number of times to Greece and Asia, also to Egypt. But no other city I've seen can compare—" He stopped when he saw that a slave had appeared at the door. "Yes?"

"You said to tell you when an hour had passed, Dominus."

Paulina joined them in the garden, and led the way to Pinaria's room.

The girl seemed in slightly better spirits than before. Galen took her pulse, then waited a while and took it again. He did this a number of times, and during the intervals managed to coax her into some mild conversation, asking about her friends and her favorite activities, both in and out of the home. All this banal talk seemed rather pointless to Lucius. Was Galen there to diagnose the girl, or to get to know her?

"So, the same tutor who taught your uncle Kaeso comes to the house to teach you Latin and Greek?" said Galen. "He must be rather old."

"No older than Father, I imagine," said Pinaria.

Lucius scoffed. "Daughter! He's twenty years older than me, at least."

Pinaria shrugged while Galen took her pulse. All this repeated pulse-taking seemed rather pointless to Lucius, as well, but he had seen other physicians do the same. They claimed to be able to read various signs and omens into the strength or weakness of the heartbeats, and their regular or irregular rhythm.

"Do you like your Greek and Latin lessons?" asked Galen.

"They're all right . . . I suppose."

"Your Greek is excellent. Better than my Latin!"

Pinaria made no response.

"She prefers her singing lessons," said Paulina.

"Is that so?"

Lucius nodded. "Pinaria is an excellent singer. By far the best in the family."

"Does she have a tutor for that as well?"

"Oh, yes. A lovely eunuch from Phrygia," said Paulina.

"Demetrius, he's called," said Lucius with a laugh. Like most Romans, he found eunuchs both exotic and a bit ridiculous. They were more common than ever in Rome, but the further east one traveled, the more frequently one encountered them.

"He's lovely," said Paulina, casting a disapproving glance at her husband. "He's able to sing ever so high, higher than some of the girls. And an excellent teacher. The lessons move from house to house. It's a way for the girls to visit each other's homes and to meet friends from suitable families."

And to see and be seen by suitors, thought Galen. It was the same in Pergamum and Alexandria. All the so-called best families moved and married within social circles exclusive to themselves, and kept a very close watch on their daughters.

"Pinaria is often invited to sing in the girls' chorus at festivals," said Paulina. "Unless she gets better, she'll miss the Hilaria."

"You talk about me as if I'm not even here!" said Pinaria. Her voice shook and she abruptly seemed on the verge of tears.

Galen smiled and reached again for her wrist. "You Romans have a very full calendar of religious holidays. All these rituals and processions and pageants—something to celebrate almost every day, in some part of the city or other. Many of your festivals remind me of the ones I grew up with in Pergamum, or saw in Alexandria, but others must be unique to Rome, I think, linked to gods and stories and customs I'm only beginning to learn about."

"Pinaria has another tutor who instructs her in the significance and history of all the festivals," said Lucius. "He comes twice a month, to talk about the days ahead. Not a Greek, of course, but a local instructor, a priest at the Temple of the Deified Julius. He's rather young, but seems very knowledgeable. We might also ask him to teach Gaius, when the boy is old enough for instruction."

"Has Pinaria kept up with her lessons?"

Paulina shook her head. "She hasn't been well enough."

"Then we must do something to make you better," said Galen "Think how pleased your parents will be when you are well enough to sing again."

Pinaria turned her face away. "I can't talk any more. What use is talking? What use is singing? I just want to be left alone. *I wish I could die!*" She yanked her wrist from Galen's grasp and buried her face in a pillow.

Back in the garden, Galen asked Lucius what other physicians had seen the girl already, and what they had prescribed. One had administered alternating cold and hot compresses on her belly and forehead, another had given her a foul-smelling herbal concoction, and the third had suggested she drink warm milk directly from a goat's udder, or if at all possible, from a lactating woman's nipple.

"You didn't try that last remedy, did you?"

"No. But only because Pinaria absolutely refused."

"Good for her! Living milk can be a powerful remedy, but not in Pinaria's case."

"What do you recommend?"

"Nothing, at the moment."

"No medicine? No procedure?"

"Sometimes watching and waiting is more prudent. I suspect I already have an idea of the problem."

"Was it her pulse? What did it tell you? What's to be done?"

"First, cease giving her any medicines previously prescribed. Keep her here in the house. Offer her simple food, and even if she refuses to eat, make sure she drinks a bit of water several times a day."

"That's what we've been doing!"

"Then continue. I shall visit again tomorrow. If I can arrange things to my liking, I think I may be able to pronounce a firm diagnosis at that time."

"You physicians, always so mysterious! Can't you tell me now what you think is the problem?"

"Absolutely not. Until he is ready to speak authoritatively, the wise physician keeps his mouth shut. That is the first thing one learns in the study of medicine."

The next day, Galen arrived in the late afternoon. He looked in on the patient, who showed no improvement. If anything, Pinaria was weaker and paler than the day before, having eaten nothing in the meantime and having slept only fitfully.

Lucius and Paulina anxiously watched him take Pinaria's pulse. "Is her heartbeat weaker today?" asked Paulina. "Is it failing?"

"It's the rhythm and consistency of the pulse that I feel for, not the strength of each heartbeat. Do you think, Pinaria, that you might be up for a visitor?"

She shrugged. "I don't feel like talking."

"Not even to your best friend? I think you told me yesterday that would be Cornelia, who lives quite nearby."

"I . . ." Pinaria seemed uncertain, perhaps confused. She furrowed her brows.

"Are you in pain, daughter?" asked Paulina.

To Lucius, it looked more as if Pinaria was frightened. But of what?

"Come, Pinaria, a visit from your best friend might cheer you up," said Galen. "I've already arranged for her to come."

"When?" Pinaria shrank back.

"Why, at any moment. Indeed, I suspect this boy has come to announce her."

"Yes?" said Lucius, turning to the young slave.

"A visitor, Dominus, for your daughter. Young Cornelia."

"Perhaps we should send her away," said Paulina. "Pinaria seems unwell—"

"No, no," said Galen. "I must insist that Pinaria rouse herself and come to the garden. Isn't that where you usually meet your friends? You told me so yesterday, when we had that lovely chat."

"But she's too weak," protested her mother.

"She can hold her father's arm, and lean on him if she needs to."

"Come, Pinaria, we must do as the physician says." Lucius saw no sense in the visit, but he had agreed to follow Galen's advice. He helped Pinaria from the bed. Her long-sleeved sleeping gown would be adequate for such a visit, he decided. Under normal circumstances, Pinaria herself would have insisted on changing into something prettier and more colorful. It was an indication of her weakness that she didn't insist on doing so. How frail the child seemed, and how thin! But her hand holding his arm was strong enough. Indeed, her fingers clenched him so hard he winced.

Cornelia was waiting in the garden, along with a slave, an older woman who had been her nursemaid and was now her chaperone. No Roman girl of Pinaria's class went anywhere without such a companion to keep an eye out for any male who might draw too close. Cornelia was warmly greeted by Pinaria's parents, but no one spoke to the chaperone, or even acknowledged her. Like most slaves, she was essentially invisible unless she had cause to speak.

Pinaria sat on a bench in the shade. Galen sat beside her, so that he could continue to take her pulse from time to time. Pinaria murmured a few words of welcome to Cornelia, who seemed flustered at first to see her friend in such a state, and then launched into a nervous, one-sided conversation, gossiping about mutual friends. When she seemed to run dry, there was an awkward silence until Galen spoke up.

"When I spoke to you earlier and asked you to visit Pinaria today, you mentioned an activity you have in common. Something about singing in a chorus."

"Oh, yes! Oh, Pinaria, we've missed you so much at singing lessons. We shall never be able to go on at the Hilaria without you! Demetrius says you have the best and strongest voice of any of the girls."

"Demetrius?" Pinaria whispered the name and looked up.

"Is that his name, the eunuch who teaches the girls' chorus?" asked Galen in a seemingly casual way as he again took Pinaria's pulse.

"You know it is," said Cornelia. "You asked me to invite him, as well."

"And did you?"

"He's waiting in the vestibule. Oh, but it was to be a surprise! Now I've spoiled it."

"I think not," said Galen quietly. "Pinaria looks quite surprised."

"And so are her parents!" said Lucius, his voice stern. "You made no mention of this—inviting a grown man to visit my daughter, and in her nightdress."

"But he's only a eunuch, husband." Paulina was watching her daughter's expression and trying to make sense of it. When had her daughter become such a puzzle to her?

"Very well," said Lucius. The physician's intrusion into Pinaria's social life seemed pointless, but he could see no harm in it. He nodded to a nearby slave. "Show the fellow in."

A few moments later, Demetrius stepped into view. Galen judged him to be younger than himself, closer to Pinaria's age, though a eunuch's age could be hard to tell at a glance; they often looked younger than their years. Demetrius had the smooth, olive complexion of a Levantine, and no beard to speak of, though his eyebrows were thick and dark. He must have been a very pretty boy, Galen thought, for he was quite attractive in the indeterminate way of eunuchs, no longer a man but not a woman, either. A scientific treatise on the physiognomy and physiology of eunuchs would make an interesting study, he thought, even as the gentle pressure of his fingertips upon Pinaria's wrist confirmed exactly what he suspected.

Should any doubt remain, it vanished entirely when Pinaria released a loud sigh and suddenly lost consciousness, her head falling forward and her limp body crumpling on the bench. Her father darted forward to catch her.

"My diagnosis is now complete," announced Galen, releasing Pinaria's wrist, crossing his arms and flashing a satisfied grin, much to the consternation of the Pinarii and their guests.

"I needed that!" said Lucius, putting down his silver goblet and wiping a bit of wine from the corner of his mouth. "Again," he said to the slave who stood by. The boy promptly refilled the goblet.

Lucius gestured to the half-full goblet in Galen's hand, but Galen shook his head. He was enjoying the familiar elation that came from not only producing a correct diagnosis, but doing so in a dramatic manner. The second rule of medicine, as one of his mentors had told him, was to remember that an unheralded and unheeded diagnosis was worse than no diagnosis at all. *You are always on a stage of sorts, expected to perform miracles, or at least to produce a spectacle. Do not let the audience down!* The glow of pleasure that resulted from a correct and dramatic diagnosis was more intense and pleasurable than any intoxication that could be attained from mere wine.

They were again in Lucius's study, surrounded by scrolls and hanging bronze lamps that were already lit, as the afternoon light was beginning to fade. The rich could afford the best and most sweet-smelling oil for burning, Galen thought.

Besides the slave, it was only the two of them in the room. In his acute embarrassment, Lucius had sent Pinaria's guests away, then carried his swooning daughter to her room, where her mother had watched over her until it came time to put little Gaius to bed.

"You're sure she'll suffer no lasting effects?" Lucius asked.

"People faint all the time, for all sorts of reasons. In your daughter's case, as you saw, she regained consciousness quickly—"

"And then began to weep, uncontrollably. I never heard such caterwauling!"

"Because her secret was out. The tears were part of the purging that can now take place, rebalancing the humors in her body, which had been thrown thoroughly out of balance by the strain of her illicit passion."

"Don't call it that!"

"Her covert infatuation, then. I think we can be certain there was never any physical contact between the two of them, nor any misconduct by the eunuch, though some are in fact capable of performing the sexual act. Like many a girl her age, Pinaria became obsessed with the most attractive person whom she happened to see on a regular basis—"

"A eunuch! What could be more absurd?" Lucius shook his head. "At least it wasn't some other man's slave with his testicles intact. By Hercules, a determined and lustful slave can get around even the most vigilant chaperone. That sort of scandal happens more often than people care to admit, and it always ends very badly for everyone concerned—the girl, the slave, *and* the chaperone."

And any baby that might result, thought Galen grimly. "There, you see—the situation could be much worse, and is certainly not as bad as you seem to think. You should be proud of your daughter, actually. By steadfastly declining to act on her desire, or even to speak of it, she turned that festering passion into suffering, insomnia, and the loss of all other appetites. Now that the boil has been lanced, she can begin to recover. It was in no way her fault. Eros is notoriously reckless. Those little arrows of his can wreak havoc even in the best families."

"Should we have married her off before this? She *is* thirteen," said Lucius. The calming glow of the wine loosened his tongue.

"You might consider doing so sooner rather than later. In the meantime, perhaps you can send her away from the city for a while, to stay with relatives, or—"

"And let her out of my sight? I don't think so!" Lucius drained his goblet and raised a finger, not even glancing at the slave who promptly refilled it. "But how did you guess?"

"I assure you, I never guess when making a diagnosis. Her pulse alerted me. Yesterday, when she and I appeared to be having a causal talk about nothing in particular, I paid close attention to her pulse. Whenever there was any mention of the upcoming festival where she was to sing, or of her singing lessons, her pulse raced against my fingertips. I thought she might suffer from stage fright. Some people become physically ill at the very thought of performing in public. But then the eunuch was mentioned, and her reaction became even more pronounced. I could only be certain . . ."—*and produce the most dramatic effect,* he thought, but did not say—". . . by observing an encounter between the two of them. You witnessed the result. I treated a similar case, in Alexandria. There, it was a lovesick wife smitten by a famous dancer, a man she'd never even met, only seen on the stage. Any time the dancer's name was mentioned—"

"A dancer? Numa's balls, that would be even worse than a slave!"

"Yet another reason you should be happy things worked out as they did."

"Ha! Another reason to pay you a very fat fee?"

"Not at all. I've never asked for payment from a patient, rich or poor. I never will. The properties in Pergamum left to me by my father produce an income more than adequate for my needs."

"Where did his fortune come from?"

"My father was a very successful architect and builder. He added the new wing to the library at Pergamum, which is second only to Alexandria."

"Ah!" Lucius nodded thoughtfully. "We have that in common. My father was not only an artist, but also a builder. And my grandfather on my mother's side was rather famous in that department. Perhaps you've heard of Apollodorus of Damascus."

"Of course! More than famous, I think; legendary. The great architect so revered by Hadrian, until . . ." He almost said it aloud: *until Hadrian put him to death.*

There was an awkward silence. Lucius cleared his throat. "No fee at all, then?"

"I ask only that you speak favorably of me to your friends."

"Ha! I can hardly do that! I have no intention of mentioning anything about this business, to anybody."

"I understand. I will be discreet, as well. Still, the day may come when you have a chance to do me some other favor."

"I certainly will." Lucius sighed and shook his head. "My dear daughter, a secret victim of lovesickness. Why did I not see it myself?"

"The thing closest to us is sometimes the thing we are least able to see, like a coin held too close to the eye; the image and inscription are no more than blurs. The practice of medicine relies greatly on the physician's powers of observation. Also upon his knowledge of human nature, and of literature and history, as well. When I diagnosed the wife who was lovesick for a dancer, I was reminded of the ancient physician Erasistratus. He was called upon to treat the son of King Seleucus, who was wasting away. Erasistratus could find nothing wrong with the young man, but noticed that he blushed in the presence of Queen Stratonice, his stepmother. Do you know the story?"

Lucius shook his head.

"Erasistratus told Seleucus that his son's disease was incurable, for he was in the grip of a love that was impossible to gratify. 'Why? Who is this woman?' asked the king. 'My wife,' replied Erasistratus, deliberately lying to see the king's reaction. 'Then you must give her up,' said Seleucus, 'for I will not have my son denied.' The physician asked, 'Would you do so even if it was your own wife with whom the prince was in love?' The king said, 'Even that!' Then Erasistratus told him the truth."

"What did the king do?"

"The king did the kingly thing, and was true to his word. He gave Stratonice to his son to wed, along with several provinces. And all lived happily ever after. Especially Erasistratus, who was paid one hundred talents—the largest fee ever given to any physician in the history of the world."

"Yet *your* service is free. Ha! But something tells me that King Seleucus had other wives to comfort him. Maybe he had grown tired of Stratonice."

Galen laughed. "You mustn't overthink the story, or you'll spoil it."

"A fine tale, indeed. Now I shall tell you one, somewhat in the same vein, if a bit more . . . indelicate." Lucius lowered his voice and leaned toward Galen. Had he not drunk so much wine so quickly, he would never have told the story. "They say that Marcus's wife, the lovely Faustina, happened to see a troop of gladiators walking by one day and fell head over heels for one of them, just at the sight of him." He laughed. "My Pinaria, pining for a eunuch, is bad enough. Imagine, the highest woman in the land, lusting for a gladiator!"

"Yes, well, when I tended the gladiators in Pergamum . . ." Galen flashed a crooked smile. "I have my own tales about high-born ladies and low-born lovers. But please, go on."

"Well, Faustina never acted on her infatuation, of course. We must give her credit for that. She is a virtuous woman, and worthy of her husband. Indeed, it was to Marcus that she confessed her intolerable fascination. He wondered if she might be pregnant, having seen her become a bit crazy during her pregnancies. But such was not the case. So Marcus called on his physicians and wise men. None was able to cure Faustina of her fascination. Her lust for the gladiator only grew stronger. Poor Marcus! His Stoicism was pushed to its limit.

"Finally, he called on Julianus the Chaldean. Many a man would have gone to the astrologer first, and the physicians last. Julianus examined the horoscopes of all concerned—not just Marcus and Faustina, but also the gladiator, who was completely ignorant of the situation. The poor fellow had no idea of the havoc he was causing in the imperial bedchamber, and no idea what was in store for him. Julianus prescribed a drastic remedy: the gladiator was to be beheaded, hung by his ankles, and drained of all his blood, whereupon Faustina, naked, was to bathe in his blood, and then, under the light of a full moon, make love to her husband. By Hercules, have you ever heard of such a ghastly cure?"

"Did it work?"

"It did. Faustina was completely freed from the passion that had caused her so much suffering."

"Perhaps not least because the man who caused it was a headless, bloodless corpse."

Lucius laughed. "I'll grant you that. But it was on that very night, so Marcus believes, that Faustina became pregnant with the twins, little Titus and Commodus. Then it was back to mothering for her, and no more lusting after gladiators."

Galen nodded thoughtfully. "The blood of a gladiator has been used by some physicians as a treatment for epilepsy. Pliny says it is most effective if drunk hot, directly from the severed throat of the gladiator, while he's still alive. There's also a love potion that involves dipping a bit of bread in the blood of a gladiator and then casting it into the house of the desired person. But to bathe in a gladiator's blood, as the worshippers of Mithras bathe in the blood of a slaughtered bull—that is new to me."

"I don't suppose the blood of a eunuch is of much use, as medicine, or magic?"

"Not that I know of."

"Good! I should hate to have made poor Pinaria . . ." Lucius blinked a few times and put down his goblet. "It occurs to me that I've been rather indiscreet. You won't repeat this story to anyone, will you?"

"Certainly not. The third rule of medicine is—"

"To be discreet?"

"I was going to say, never to cause embarrassment to the rich and powerful. That applies especially to the ruler of the Roman world, whether a Stoic or not."

It was some days later that a messenger arrived at the house of Pinarius, carrying an invitation written in elegant letters on a thick piece of parchment.

"'You are invited to witness a public anatomical demonstration by the physician Galen of Pergamum, at the Temple of Pax, sure to cause wonder in all who behold it,'" muttered Lucius, reading aloud, though except for the slave who brought the message he was alone in his library. "'Anatomical demonstration'—whatever does he mean by that? And why invite me? I seriously doubt there's anything left for me to learn about the bodies of men and women, having sculpted so many of them. But he did render his services free of charge, and Pinaria is much better, almost back to her normal self. I suppose I should go, if only to add to the numbers, especially if there's a poor turnout."

But when Lucius arrived by litter at the appointed day and time, he found a considerable crowd. The demonstration was to take place in the temple's forecourt, where a waist-high wooden platform had been set up, its shape not unlike that of an altar for sacrificing animals. Galen was busy instructing slaves who were wheeling in carts with cages, which contained pigs, to judge by the grunts and squeals. The steps of the temple served as a sort of theater, with every possible seat already taken. The rest of the crowd stood in a semicircle around the open space occupied by Galen and his pigs.

Lucius pushed his way to the front of the spectators, who yielded, however begrudgingly, to the prerogative of his senatorial toga with its purple stripe. A few other senators were there, he noticed, but most of those present appeared to be physicians or philosophers or their students. They were an argumentative bunch, and all seemed to be talking at once, mostly in Greek. From the snatches of conversations he could understand, it was all philosopher talk, quite technical and over his head, and all very loud and strident. So much for finding peace at the Temple of Pax!

Lucius quickly had his fill of their incessant chattering and was on the verge of leaving, when Galen raised his hands for silence.

"What have you to show us, man from Pergamum?" yelled a spectator.

"Yes, this had better not be a waste of my time," said another.

"Has it to do with the brain?" said another, whom Lucius recognized, a long-bearded Athenian who was reputedly one of the city's leading intellectuals. "We've already heard your foolish argument that cognition emanates from the brain. Everyone knows that Aristotle long ago determined that the brain is merely a cooling pan for the blood."

"I would love to return to that debate," said Galen, raising his voice, "but Aristotle is long dead and not present to defend his side of the argument."

"An excellent point!" shouted Lucius, thinking it only proper that he should support Galen in return for his services. This earned him some sour looks, but also a thin smile from Galen, who gave him a friendly nod of recognition, then swiftly commenced with the demonstration.

The crowd laughed at first when a squealing pig was

produced, then grew quieter when the squirming beast was tied down to the wooden platform. Galen did the tying himself, his fingers moving with great speed and dexterity. In a matter of seconds, the pig was completely immobilized.

"Now, gentlemen," said Galen, "what will happen if I strike the pig sharply on its flank with this wooden cane?"

"The pig will squeal!" said Lucius.

"Let us test that assertion." Galen struck the pig, which cried out in protest.

"But *how* does the pig squeal?" asked Galen. "We all know the answer, from our own ability to squeal from time to time, whether from pleasure or pain. The noise is made with an exhalation of air, which issues from the lungs and then passes through the throat. How might we prevent the pig from squealing?"

"Stuff its mouth," said someone.

"Cut its throat," suggested another.

Galen shook his head. "I have a much more effective method, which neatly demonstrates my theory that the controlling mechanism of the pig's voice is a particular nerve. All of you who have dissected or vivisected animals have encountered the nerves, those fibrous filaments that run all up and down every part of the body, seeming to emanate from the spine and ultimately from the brain—which is the seat of consciousness, as I do indeed assert. But if the nerve controlling the voice is severed or even sufficiently constricted, the brain's command to the vocal chords is cut off, and no squeal is produced. Let me demonstrate."

Galen produced a sharp blade and set about making a small incision on either side of the pig's neck. The loss of blood was negligible. "Now, gentlemen, I have carefully avoided cutting the carotid artery, and have only exposed the nerves that run alongside them. I will now use a very slender thread to tie off each of those nerves. The work is very fine, and requires sharp eyesight and steady fingers. I will now tighten the ligatures, just so. Now I take up the cane again, I stand back, and I *strike* the pig!" There was a whoosh of air followed by a sharp crack.

"You will observe that the pig breathes sharply in and out— *but no squeal is produced*."

A number of the spectators sat forward or jostled each other, straining for a better view.

The proponent of Aristotle crossed his arms and looked down his nose. "Can you demonstrate the same thing again, on another pig?"

"Of course. But why not do so using the *same* pig?"

"But how?"

"The production of the voice is dependent on the nerves, which relay an impulse of some sort, just as veins relay blood or the throat relays air. I interrupted those impulses by constricting the nerves, but I did not sever the nerves. Therefore, the action is reversible. Observe, as I leave the ligatures in place, but carefully loosen them . . . just so. And now, if I strike the pig again . . . like *this*!"

The pig squealed so loudly that the startled crowd jerked in unison. The Athenian gasped.

"Remarkable!" whispered Lucius.

"Should any of you still be skeptical of the nerve's function, I shall silence the pig again . . . with only a gentle tug to tighten the ligatures already in place . . . here and here . . ."

Galen then struck the pig, which again responded with silence.

"And now I shall allow it to speak once more, merely by loosening the ligatures . . ."

Again the pig was able to squeal.

Galen had certainly succeeded in producing a spectacle on this occasion—and he knew it. He was beaming with pride as he turned a full circle, surveyed the surrounding audience.

"Esteemed colleagues, had I not other demonstrations to show you, I could go on all day, silencing this pig and then letting it squeal again. Most gratifying to me is that by this simple demonstration I have actually managed to render speechless that fellow in the audience who tried to silence me with Aristotle!"

There was a chorus of laughter. Lucius looked at the Athenian, whose face was bright red.

Lucius smiled. "Something tells me," he muttered to himself, "that Rome shall be seeing more of this Galen fellow."

So impressed was Lucius by Galen's diagnosis of Pinaria's ailment, and by his public demonstration with the pig, that some days later, when a break in his management of the workshop allowed, he decided to visit the imperial residence on the Palatine, to see if he might be admitted to the emperor's presence, so as to personally recommend Galen's services. Even on the occasions when Marcus was too busy to see him, Lucius had always been turned away with the utmost respect, and a personal note of regret from the emperor had always followed. Duty was a prime value for the Stoics, and for Marcus that meant paying scrupulous attention not only to the vast enterprises of statecraft but also to the smallest details of decorum.

Modesty was also a Stoic virtue, manifested at the palace by a lack of pretense and ostentation. Hadrian had possessed a taste for costly materials and sumptuous fabrics, but Marcus preferred the simple. Everything from the well-used rugs on the spotless marble floors to the plain tunics of the busy scribes and secretaries bespoke the emperor's insistence on efficiency rather than courtly pomp.

On this day the mood at the palace was not just serious, but decidedly gloomy. Eyes were downcast, and voices were low. The air itself seemed heavy with dread. As Lucius was admitted to one waiting chamber after another, leapfrogging ahead of roomfuls of suppliants who lacked his personal connection to Marcus, he at last encountered a courtier he knew from previous visits, and asked what was the matter.

The gray-bearded man looked at him for a long moment, then finally spoke. "To anyone else I would say nothing, Senator

Pinarius, but I know your close connection to the emperor, and so I will share the unhappy news. There's an illness in the family. It's one of the twins—young Titus."

"What's wrong?"

"I don't know, but apparently it's quite serious. The matter is consuming all the emperor's attention. He spends every hour locked away with the boy and the imperial physicians. Nothing else is happening in the palace. It's been this way for two days now. Everyone is on edge. I realize no one has yet turned you away, and I myself hesitate to do so, Senator Pinarius, but I very much doubt that the emperor will be able to see you."

"Ah, but there you're mistaken! My whole reason for coming today was to recommend a particular physician—and now I find that one of the children is sick. That can hardly be a coincidence. This is the Fates at work, don't you think?"

The man looked uncertain. "All that happens is as the Fates decree. Even so, I'm not sure—"

"I came today on the off chance that the emperor might have a spare moment, but now I must *insist* that I see him. Don't just stand there, gawking. Run and tell whomever is at the top of your chain of authority that Senator Lucius Pinarius, the emperor's friend, has come to recommend the services of a very clever and highly skilled physician."

For a moment longer the man continued to hesitate—his face had the stricken look of the underling uncertain of what to do next and frightened of making the wrong decision—until Lucius clapped his hands loudly. It was a gesture he sometimes used to incite his workers when they were slow to respond, and in this instance it had the desired effect. The man scurried off.

A quarter of an hour passed. The man returned. He had regained his composure to such a degree he seemed almost haughty.

"Come along, then!" he said, ushering Lucius into the room beyond, and then down a long hallway that took them away from the imperial reception chambers and into the private living quarters of the palace. Here, too, simplicity and lack of ostentation were the rule. The quality of the mosaic floors and marble columns and painted ceilings was of the very finest, but when it came to the furnishings and carpets, any visitor would think he was merely in the house of a Roman aristocrat of unusually restrained taste, not in the home of the most powerful man in the empire.

Lucius was led around a corner, past hanging curtains, and suddenly found himself in a room so dimly lit that for a moment he could see nothing. The courtier seemed to have vanished. Then Lucius felt his hand taken in the grasp of another, and heard a familiar and very distinctive voice. From childhood Marcus Aurelius had received the finest oratorical training, and even when he spoke barely above a whisper there was something about his voice that was very mellow and reassuring.

"How sweet it is to see your face, old friend."

"And how sweet it is to see yours," said Lucius, though he could only barely perceive the sad eyes of Marcus. "I only wish the occasion were not so somber, Verissimus." Lucius used the childhood nickname, instinctively knowing it would bring the emperor a small bit of comfort. Indeed, as his eyes adjusted to the dimness, he saw a faint smile on Marcus's face. But the man's brow remained furrowed and his eyes were grim.

"Even so, the very sight of you cheers me, Lucius."

Now Lucius perceived the others in the room. Upon a bed, wearing a thin, sleeveless gown, lay Titus. Like his father, the tiny boy had a narrow face and slightly protuberant eyes. But his eyes looked lifeless, as if made of glass. His trembling lips were slightly parted. His face was drawn, the cheekbones very prominent. His arms also had a wasted look. His appearance became even more alarming when Lucius looked down to see the boy's twin, standing next to Marcus. How plump and lively Commodus looked, just as his own little Gaius or any other healthy four-year-old boy should look, his cheeks full and his eyes sparkling. With one arm the boy clung to his father's leg while he nervously sucked and nibbled the fingers of his other hand. The child's eyes darted about the room, occasionally looking up at Lucius with a plaintive expression.

Across the room stood a row of silent, grim-faced physicians, some of them holding linen cloths, others bowls, and others various esoteric implements made of bronze that glittered sharply in the lamplight.

"They say he should have darkness, to help him rest," explained Marcus. "But the poor thing simply stares into space, as if he's unable to shut his eyes—or afraid to."

"Does his illness have a name?" asked Lucius.

"None that the physicians recognize. He cannot or will not eat. He wastes away. His breathing is uneven. Sometimes there's a rattling in his throat."

"Can the physicians help him?"

"They do this and that." Marcus looked at the men across the room. Not one of them dared to meet his gaze. "But nothing seems to help."

"Oh, Verissimus! I truly think it was Fortuna who sent me here this day, wishing to bless us both. I came because a while ago I called upon a physician, a young Pergamene, and just recently I saw the most remarkable demonstration of his knowledge of anatomy."

"Yes?"

"His name is Galen—"

Lucius was interrupted by an audible snort of derision from one of the physicians across the room.

Marcus narrowed his eyes. "Galen? From Pergamum? Have we heard of this physician?" He directed the question to the man who had snorted.

"Yes, Dominus," said the man. "We have knowledge of this newcomer. And not all of it good."

"He has many cures to his credit," said Lucius.

"Because he resorts to sorcery—or so we have heard," said the man.

"No, no!" Lucius protested. "Galen is a man of good character. I personally vouch for him."

Marcus grimaced. "What would you have us do next?" he asked the physician.

"I think, Dominus, another bleeding is necessary. The imbalance of the humors persists. We have all conferred and we see no other alternative."

Marcus sighed. "Can we at least send Commodus from the room? The child is clearly distressed by the circumstances."

"No, Dominus, he must remain close to his brother. There is a special affinity between twins. The proximity of one to the other is known to be conducive to recovery."

Marcus looked down at the boy and gently touched his cheek. "Do you hear, Commodus? Titus needs you. You must be very brave."

"I *am* brave, Papa."

"Yes, you are." Marcus managed a smile. "Very well. Another bleeding." He nodded to the physicians, who moved into place around the sickbed. The one who was clearly the leader brought forth a very sharp-looking blade. Others extended bowls for catching the blood, others cloths to wipe away any drops that escaped the bowls. They pulled up Titus's gown and chose a spot on one of his wasted legs for the incision.

Lucius looked away, but from the corner of one eye he saw that Commodus was watching every step of the procedure with utmost fascination. Such an intent expression on the face of a four-year-old was somehow disconcerting. Lucius suddenly felt very out of place, and a bit peeved. His advice had been brushed aside as if his word meant nothing. Who were these physicians, that Marcus put such faith in them? From what he could see, poor little Titus was on the cusp between life and death. If the doctors were so competent, how had he ended up in such a condition? Lucius wanted very much to leave the room, at once, but to do so he would have to take his leave of Marcus, and he could hardly do so while the emperor's attention was entirely on the procedure taking place. Like Commodus, Marcus watched every movement, but with something closer to dread than fascination. What a contrast, between father and son, and the looks on their faces, as the incision was made and the blood began to flow. Titus made no protest at all, but lay inert on the bed, staring at nothing.

Suddenly, Titus gave a start. His limbs convulsed, all four at once. The bowl to catch the blood was knocked to the floor, spilling its shallow contents. Commodus jumped back, his mouth a circle, his eyes wide, staring at the splotch of red on the pale marble floor. Marcus cried out and put a fist to his mouth, his Stoic demeanor pushed to its limit.

Titus convulsed again, and then again. His eyes never blinked.

"Stop the procedure!" Marcus shouted. "Stop at once! All of you, out of the room!"

"But, Dominus, the bleeding is more indicated now than ever," the head physician insisted.

"Out!" shouted Marcus.

Lucius was aghast. He had never seen Marcus in such a state. The sight was almost as disturbing as that of the wasted, convulsing child on the bed. He turned to leave, but the emperor grabbed his shoulder.

"Not you, Lucius. Stay!"

"But Verissimus, I'm an intruder here. I'll go at once—"

"Stay! And look—as soon as the others left the room, the convulsions stopped. Is it a sign? Perhaps you *were* sent to me today by some divine power, Lucius. Perhaps I'm meant to call upon this Pergamene, this Galen, after all. Where can he be found, and quickly? Never mind, I have messengers who'll know where he is and the fastest way to fetch him. I'll send for him at once!"

Galen rushed through the narrow streets, following the imperial messenger as quickly as he could, trying not to trip on uneven paving stones. They came to a wider street. An imperial sedan was waiting. It had a seat for only one, and eight men to carry the two long poles. Galen was practically pushed into the seat, and then they were off, traveling at a run.

He sat back and tried to catch his breath. At a slower pace, the ride would have been smoother, but as it was, he was jostled violently this way and that. He had to clench his jaw to stop his teeth from chattering.

He had been summoned to the palace. That was all the messenger had told him. But why? And how had such a situation come about? He could only imagine that some terrible crisis was taking place, and that somehow his name had been put forward. But by whom? A friend? An enemy? Almost certainly the latter, for the one thing he dreaded above all others was exactly this, that he should be pressed into serving the emperor or his family under the most stressful circumstances imaginable, and that he should—unthinkable as it was!—fail, and fail utterly. An imperial relative, dead—or even worse, a dead emperor!—that was a disaster from which no physician could ever hope to recover, not in a thousand lifetimes.

The dark streets passed as if in a nightmare, barely glimpsed in the headlong rush. They came to a halt so abruptly that he was thrown from the chair onto the shoulders of the two men immediately in front of him. One of them had the effrontery to laugh as the muscle-bound runner tossed him aside, like a ball in a game, and into the arms of a courtier almost as discombobulated as Galen.

The courtier grabbed his arm with an iron grip—he was quite strong for a man with such a white beard—and rushed Galen up a flight of marble steps, into a shadowless antechamber lit by a forest of lamps, some on stands, some hanging from the ceiling. Dazzled by the light, Galen rolled his eyes up, and saw that the ceiling was gaily painted with scenes of the nymph Chelone transformed into a tortoise by Mercury. That was the sort of thing that happened to mortals who displeased a god or a goddess! What was the fate of a poor physician who displeased a Roman emperor?

Down a series of lamplit corridors they flew, and up a flight of yellow marble steps, past hanging curtains, and then into a room that seemed to him at first pitch-black. For a moment he heard nothing but his own gasping breath, but then he heard a woman weeping. A lamp was brought into the room, and then more lamps. As the darkness receded, he saw the woman. She was dressed in a very fine gown. For many a woman, even a rich one, it would be the finest gown she owned, but in these circumstances it was probably her sleeping gown. She was approaching middle age, and might have been pretty, but it was hard to tell with her face so red and tearstained, and her body wracked by sobs. Was this the empress?

Yes, most certainly it was, for the next thing Galen saw, instantly recognizable from the images on thousands of coins from the wilds of Britannia to the Parthian borderland, was the face of Marcus Aurelius.

Galen gasped, and not for lack of breath. It seemed to him he must still be asleep and dreaming, yet here he was, somewhere in the innermost recesses of the imperial house. Faustina was weeping uncontrollably. The ruler of the world was staring at him grimly. And there, just past the emperor, Galen saw how such an impossible situation had come to pass: the familiar face of Senator Lucius Pinarius, who looked as miserable as the others.

There was a little boy in the room, as well, gazing up at him with wide eyes, sucking at his fingertips. And there, on the bed, lay a second boy, the mirror image of the other, despite his pale, drawn face. Galen realized that these were the imperial twins—or what remained of them, for the boy on the bed was almost certainly deceased. Any uncertainty vanished when the emperor stepped to the bed, pulled up a sheet, and covered the boy's face. The empress wailed.

Marcus stared at the lifeless child. "And yet . . . I had . . . such hopes. Since I took on the burden of rule, nothing has been a greater comfort to me than the fact that I have another to share that burden—dear Verus, as much my brother as if we had been born from the same womb, though no one seeing us would ever mistake us for twins. Almost from—" His voice caught in his throat. He paused for a long moment, composing himself. "Almost from the moment the twins were born, I dared to hope that one day, when I should lay down my burden and pass it along, it would be to brothers—not to one man, but to two—two men who loved and trusted one another as Verus and I love and trust each other, not just brothers, but twins, true twins, my dear Commodus and my dear . . . my dearest . . . Titus!"

The empress's wailing turned to shrieks. She suddenly bolted from the room, surrounded by a vast flock of retainers and serving women, all moving to comfort her.

The emperor turned and looked straight at Galen. He felt his legs melting, but stiffened his spine and met the man's steady gaze.

"So this is Galen of Pergamum?" How strange it was, to hear his name spoken by the emperor himself. Galen was saved from making some tongue-tied response by Lucius Pinarius, to whom the question was apparently directed.

"Yes, Verissimus. This is the physician of whom I spoke."

Marcus nodded slowly, never taking his eyes from Galen's. "I should have trusted you, dear Lucius. Your coming here today *was* a sign—even if it came too late. Well, I shall heed it going forward. What fools all my physicians turned out to be! Or was there no hope from the beginning? At least poor Titus's suffering is over. In future . . ." His voice quavered. "In future, I shall call upon *you,* Galen of Pergamum, to look after the boy's brother." The emperor reached forth and laid his hand on Galen's shoulder, then looked down at the child beside him. "What do you say, Commodus? Shall I appoint this man your physician?"

"Yes, Papa," said the child, who paused from sucking at his fingers and stared up at Galen with wide eyes.

* * *

It was some months later that Lucius Pinarius, sitting in his garden, broke the wax seal on a folded bit of parchment that had come from a ship newly arrived at Ostia. The seal—a snake shaped like the Greek letter gamma—was not familiar to him, so he quickly scanned the letter to discover the sender.

"Who is it from, Papa?" asked his daughter, who sat with her mother nearby. They were both at work sewing up small tears in several of the family's garments.

"Why, it's from Galen!"

"Oh." Pinaria looked down at her sewing. Mention of the physician reminded her of the condition, or whatever one should call it, that Galen had diagnosed. Anything to do with the whole episode was distasteful to her.

Lucius was too pleased by the unexpected letter to notice his daughter's discomfort. "We were lucky to have his services. Who knew he would be leaving Rome so soon?"

"It did seem odd, especially since you had introduced him personally to the emperor. Didn't you tell me that Marcus Aurelius intended to make use of Galen?"

"Ah, that was the problem, my dear. They met under such terrible circumstances. Galen told me afterward that the experience quite unnerved him. 'Every time he sees me, he shall think of his poor, dead boy,' he said. I told him that was nonsense, and then Galen confessed to me that the idea of treating anyone in the imperial family was too nerve-wracking for him to contemplate. 'The stakes are too high,' he said. 'High stakes, high rewards!' I said. Or as my warrior brother likes to say, 'No spirit, no splendor!' But Galen would have none of it. Well, one can see his point. What if he was called to the palace to treat Commodus one day, and instead of getting better, the boy . . ."

"Touch that fascinum at your breast if you must utter such thoughts!" said Paulina. She was a firm believer in averting the Evil Eye, especially when speaking the unspeakable. Lucius dutifully obeyed.

"Galen actually confessed to me that he was relieved when he saw little Titus lying there, dead. Otherwise, had he arrived earlier, he might have taken the blame—though at the same time he insisted to me that he could have done a better job 'than those palace quacks,' as he called them. 'So which is it?' I asked him. 'Could you have saved the boy, or not?' Well, I never got a straight answer to that! And the next thing I knew, Galen invited me to join him at some shady tavern on the riverfront, for a farewell cup of wine. He was leaving Rome, and being very quiet about it. 'I never intended to stay for good,' he said. 'There's more of the world to see, and it's Pergamum that will always be my home.' 'And what happens when little Commodus has a cough, and Marcus sends for you?' I asked. And he said: 'I won't be there.'"

Lucius laughed "Ha! *I won't be there!* I never met a man so vain, but our Galen certainly has a timid streak. I still think he's some sort of genius. Well, let's see what he has to say for himself."

Lucius finally noticed the scowl on his wife's face, and his daughter's averted gaze. He proceeded to read in silence:

To Senator Lucius Pinarius of Rome, from your loyal physician and, I hope, your friend, Galen of Pergamum— Greetings from Antioch! (I have not settled here, but am in transit.)

In transit to where? Lucius wondered. Why was Galen so discreet? Perhaps he still feared a call from the emperor, who might reasonably presume that Lucius knew the physician's whereabouts—and so Galen was keeping him in the dark. Had the letter actually come from Antioch? Who could say? Lucius read on:

As my friend, and as a man who values truth and reason, I beg of you: don't let anyone start false gossip about me, or slander me, saying I left because I killed a patient or some such nonsense. Even worse would be if word spreads that I was called to the palace and witnessed the death of the emperor's son—or even caused it! Especially since the opposite is the case, and I was the only physician who might have saved the poor lad! So I ask you to divulge no details of that episode to others, who are full of jealousy and would maliciously distort the truth.

Lucius smiled. Here at last was a straight answer to his question. Galen *did* believe, at least in retrospect, that he could have done what the others were unable to do: save Titus. Like every other physician Lucius had ever known, Galen was full of bravado—especially at a safe distance. And here he was, refashioning the story of his dismal visit to the palace so as to inflate his own ego—even while asking Lucius to keep it all a secret.

Lucius put down the letter with a prickle of distaste. But then he looked at his daughter, sitting in a spot of sunshine and industriously sewing—back to her normal, lovely, calm, sweet self—and he realized just how grateful he was to Galen, and always would be.

Lucius missed the fellow. Perhaps, one day, Galen would dare to return to Rome, and when he did, Lucius would be glad to see him.

A.D. 168

Lucius was asleep and dreaming.

In his dream, it was again the day of the two emperors' joint triumph, the first triumph to be held in Rome in almost fifty years, and the first in the lifetimes of just about everyone present. Lucius himself was now forty-seven. In all that time, until Verus's Parthian campaign, there had been no wars to speak of, no grand conquests or decisive victories, no triumphs to be celebrated.

How splendid that day had been! As a senator, Lucius himself had taken part in the grand procession. The contingents ahead of him had included a great many captives in chains to represent the barbarian multitudes subdued and conquered in the war, along with painted placards held aloft depicting the cities taken, and wagons full of booty, heaped with gold and jewels. After the senators had come the two emperors, sharing a chariot so capacious there was room for every one of Marcus's children, not just Commodus but also the girls, all clustered around their father, smiling and waving to the multitude of cheering well-wishers in the vast crowds along the Sacred Way.

Feasting and celebration had followed, including gladiator combats in the Flavian Amphitheater, not one of which was allowed to end in a fatality by decree of Marcus, who appreciated the skillful display of arms but not the necessity of death as the outcome. Amid the acrobatic displays in the arena, a young boy had fallen from a tightrope and broken his neck. Some in the crowd had been amused but others were aghast, including Marcus, who decreed that thereafter all such tightropes should have nets fitted beneath them, to safeguard against future fatalities. These innovations by Marcus had not met with universal approval. Lucius had overheard one loudmouth in the latrina grumbling, "What's the point of gladiator games if no one's to die in the end? And who wants to watch some fool prance across a tightrope if there's no chance he might kill himself?"

The arena games had delivered plenty of gore and bloodshed by the end, if mostly from creatures other than human. A great many exotic animals from the Parthian border regions, including camels and wild dogs, had been chased and hunted by men on horseback. At the climax of these animal spectacles, a hundred lions were set loose in the arena at once, causing the crowd to roar with delight. To prove that the lions were man-eaters, a number of convicted criminals were forced at sword-point into the arena, with predictable results. But just as the lions were settling down after gorging themselves, archers from an elevated gallery in the arena's center rained arrows upon them. A few stray arrows went into the crowd, but no one was seriously wounded. The same could not be said for the lions, every one of which was put to death.

Relieving himself in the latrina again, Lucius happened to overhear the same grumbler, who now seemed mollified. "Well," the man bellowed, "Not a single dead gladiator and only one dead acrobat, but by Hercules, what a lot of dead lions! Hercules himself, with his mighty club, could never have killed so many!"

More celebrations had followed, including the staging of serious tragedies followed by ridiculous comedies, one of which, by a certain Marullus, caused a bit of scandal by daring to lampoon the two emperors. The comedy was ostensibly about Rome's first two kings, the bandit-warrior Romulus who was followed by the pious priest-king Numa—the first depicted as a swaggering dandy and the second as a prim, dour killjoy—but every spectator knew that the two actors were playing Verus and Marcus Aurelius, both of whom were in the audience. If either took offense, neither showed it. Indeed, the verbal wit and the sheer absurdity of the play seemed to release a deep well of laughter from Marcus. Lucius had never seen his boyhood friend laugh so hard.

Endless feasts and orgies followed, many at Verus's sumptuous new villa on the Via Clodia just outside the city, where the parties seemed never to stop. And what licentious parties they were, with every imaginable manner of carnal pleasure made available to the guests . . .

Lucius Pinarius opened his eyes, suddenly awake. For a moment he was disoriented and confused, unsure of his surroundings. A feeling of dread descended on him. This was certainly not his own bed, for he was surrounded by unfamiliar cushions and bedspreads embroidered with shimmering threads of silver and gold in strange, barbaric designs, depicting griffins and dragons and other unearthly creatures—and then Lucius remembered the story that went with the cushions, which had been taken from a Parthian nobleman's captured estate, along with a great many other exquisite and exotic furnishings, all of which decorated the sprawling new villa that was now home to the emperor Verus . . .

His head was pounding. That was because of all the wine he had drunk the night before. But why did he feel such a sense of foreboding?

Lucius heard the sound of a girl giggling, and a boy chuckling, and remembered who else was in the bed with him—the pretty young actress from Alexandria, and the even prettier young actor, both of whom had proved such congenial companions during last night's dinner. Lucius had had his eye on the two of them for quite some time, because they were always present at Verus's dinner parties, the prettiest of all the pretty young things that were invariably in attendance to amuse the emperor's chosen guests, senators and poets and wealthy merchants and other men of importance like Lucius Pinarius. Last night he had finally made his move on the pair, and they had been most accommodating, laughing at his jokes, making sure his goblet was always brimming with wine, coyly edging closer, one on each side, touching him casually on his arms and legs and then in more intimate ways, and freely allowing him to touch them in return. By twos and threes and fours the various guests and their pleasure companions retreated to more private quarters, and Lucius had been thrilled when the boy and girl each took him by the hand and led him off to a dimly lit room where the bed was strewn with glittering pillows of Parthian design.

Lucius drew a deep breath. He was at the emperor Verus's villa on the Via Clodia, in a soft, warm bed, and the boy and girl were with him. Surrounded by such splendid comforts, why did he feel so oppressed, so gloomy, so anxious?

And then, with a wrenching jolt, cold reality returned him to his senses. Try as one might to forget what was happening in the world by plunging headlong into drinking and debauchery, in the morning the reality was still there, staring one in the face like an unblinking basilisk . . .

The plague!

As soon as the triumph and its festivities were over, the parties had begun. That was also about the time the plague began, or at least when most people began to realize it. The onset of the disease was swift—fever, diarrhea, a burning in the throat. These might be taken for symptoms of some other illness, but when the pustules appeared on the ninth day—if the victim lived that long—there could be no doubt that the plague was to blame.

Even before the triumph, the imperial physicians had noticed a sudden, sharp rise in the number of deaths all across the city, but the emperors had warned them to be quiet, lest the triumph be spoiled by uncalled-for panic. The people of Rome deserved the undiluted joy of celebrating their victory over the Parthian threat.

Like most people, Lucius first became aware of the plague as a rumor, a story overheard in the Forum, and then discussed over dinner, and then made terribly real by news of the sudden death of an acquaintance or friend. Then came news of more deaths, across town, across the street, across the room— indeed, the first such death Lucius had witnessed had been that of a serving boy in his family's dining chamber.

The boy had suddenly tripped, sending a tray full of precious silver tumbling across the marble floor. Lucius had been furious—it shamed him now to remember that he had cursed at the young slave, then had risen from his dining couch and snatched a long silver spoon from the floor, intending to give the boy a sound thrashing with it. But no sooner had he grabbed the boy's shoulder and turned him face-upright than he let out a gasp and sprang backward, for the boy's eyes were rolled up and lips were flecked with foam and he began to convulse.

That was the first night he attended one of Verus's parties. He had been invited before, but had never gone, out of loyalty to Marcus, who disapproved of his junior partner's lavish entertainments. Since that first night, the parties had never stopped. Nor had the dying. Even as the death toll grew, so did the parties grow ever more debauched, the festivities ever more desperate . . .

As he had done a thousand times before, Lucius pushed all thoughts of plague from his mind and concentrated on the moment. Stoics like Marcus had long recommended such a practice—to concentrate entirely and exclusively on the present moment, and if that moment contained no physical suffering, then to be content. Why should Lucius not be happy, sharing such a lovely bed with two such lovely mortals? The boy was an actor, or so people said. Lucius had never actually seen him on a stage. The girl was an actor of a sort, too, a street mime from Alexandria. Along with all his other booty, Verus had brought back countless actors, mimes, jugglers, acrobats, flautists, and harpists, and every other sort of entertainer—so many, that some wags claimed Verus had never fought the Parthians at all, but had gone east to wage war against actors, so as to bring every one of them back to Rome in captivity. Marcus had made one of his very rare jokes about it, saying that historians were likely to call Verus's campaign "The War of Actors."

The actors in bed with Lucius seemed to be engaged in some sort of combat, to judge by all the slapping and wrestling and grunting. First she was on top, and then he was. What pretty bottoms they both had! Sadly, the two of them were far more interested in pleasing each other than in pleasing him, as had quickly become evident the previous night. They might at least *act* as if he mattered, which as actors, if not whores, they should be capable of doing. Lucius would report their unsatisfactory behavior to their master, who should give them a tongue-lashing at least, though the soft-hearted Verus was as likely to take their side as his. Last night Lucius had been content to watch the two go at it, and to pleasure himself, until inebriation and satiation at last delivered him to the arms of Somnus, in whose embrace one could find a few hours of respite from the unrelenting horrors of waking life.

Did the two of them never grow tired, would they never stop sweating and grunting? Suddenly, Lucius had had quite enough of them. "Out! Out, you two! If you must continue fornicating, then go and do it in the road, like a couple of dogs!"

As they scampered off, naked and squealing and giggling like children and dodging the pillows he threw after them, Lucius heaved a long sigh. What pretty, pretty bottoms!

Lucius dressed himself. He had no slave to dress him; the slave who did that had died some days ago, and there were no slaves in the market to replace him. Over a loose-fitting gown, suitable for lounging, he managed to throw, wrap, fold, and tuck his toga into a shabby semblance of senatorial respectability.

On his way out, crossing a small garden open to the sky, he encountered his host, looking as bleary-eyed as himself and barely decent in a blue silk tunic that had slipped off his broad shoulders to settle into something like a loincloth around his hips. Bleary-eyed, yes, but what a handsome fellow! Even the prettiest slave boy or the brawniest gladiator receded from view when Verus entered a room. A beam of sunlight sparkled upon remnants of gold dust that had been sprinkled on Verus's hair for last night's banquet, though his golden curls hardly needed adornment. His blond beard was in the new style he had brought back to Rome from the East, very long and full like those seen on Parthian statues. "Barbaric," some called it, but on Verus the cut was quite flattering.

Like the style of his beard, Verus's penchant for high living was another trait he had picked up during his time in Asia and the Parthian borderlands. As a youth he had always been very much in the shadow of Antoninus Pius and Marcus Aurelius, sharing the latter's tutors and earning from them almost as much praise for his intellect as had Marcus before him. The young Verus had never been as staid as Marcus, but nor had he been particularly extravagant or self-indulgent. His time in the exotic cities of Asia had heightened his taste for luxury, and his success on the battlefield had given him license to indulge it.

Marcus did not approve, but said nothing in public to show it. For a while, he even attended some of Verus's parties, or at least had been present in the house while they went on. He himself ate little and drank less, and participated in no debauchery, but instead tended to correspondence and caught up on his reading while half-naked dancing girls ran past, followed by tipsy senators. When his efforts to lead, or at least moderate, by example fell flat, Marcus stopped coming to the villa, but he never said a word against his younger partner.

Whatever his bad habits, it was impossible to dislike Verus. What a charmer he was, especially in his current disheveled state, grinning at Lucius and reaching up to run his hands through his tangled curls, causing a nimbus of gold dust to shimmer about his handsome face. There was something completely forthright and open about Verus. Marcus might be scrupulously honest, but there was always something reserved in his manner. His face and mood were often hard to read. Not so Verus, about whom there seemed to be nothing held back, no deceit, no hidden agendas.

"Are you leaving us, Senator Pinarius?" asked Verus, with a yawn.

"I'm afraid so, Dominus. Your hospitality has quite worn me out."

"You talk like an old man—like Marcus!" Verus laughed and slapped Lucius on the shoulder in a good-natured way.

"I hardly think so, Dominus. When I consider some of the things I got up to last night . . ."

"Was that a shudder, Senator? There's only one cure for losing one's nerve, you know, and that's to blunder headlong into the next battle. Come along with me to the baths in the eastern wing. We'll have a hot plunge and then a cold plunge and then some cakes with honey to fortify ourselves for a little gathering I've planned for the afternoon. There shall be a very talented singer from Pergamum, and a pair of dancers—a brother and sister, twins—I discovered in Antioch. After that, I've arranged for some rather brawny gladiators to wrestle a famous Greek athlete, a wiry little fellow who assures me he'll be able to pin them all, one after another. They shall wrestle in the nude, as the Greeks at Olympia do—if you like that sort of thing?"

"It's all very . . . tempting," said Lucius, and in fact he *was* tempted to stay, but not because of the entertainments being offered. In that moment, he very much wished he could be alone with Verus, sculpting him. Some trick of the morning sunlight caused Verus to glow, as if from inside. What marble could capture that glow? Lucius had sculpted Verus more than once, and though the subject himself had been pleased,

Lucius had never been satisfied with the result. Would Lucius ever be able to capture the unique quality of the man's beauty in marble or bronze—the quality he was seeing at this very moment—as his father had captured Hadrian's divine consort, Antinous?

Then Lucius blinked, and a thin cloud veiled the sun, and the moment of clarity passed. "Tempting indeed, Dominus. But I really must get back to my family. I don't mean to be ungrateful—"

"Senator, say no more. Your children—how lucky you are to have them! Especially . . . these days. You must cherish them, at every opportunity."

"Now who sounds like Marcus?"

Verus laughed. "Well, Marcus and I did have the same upbringing. I could probably do a pretty good imitation of him, if I wanted to." He smiled at the thought. "But I'm entirely sincere. Go on, then. Off with you!"

His slaves were in the outer courtyard where he had left them, along with the sedan chair on poles. Lucius stepped in, and the four of them dutifully lifted the contraption onto their shoulders. He braced himself for the unpleasantness to come.

Almost at once, as they left the immediate vicinity of the villa, signs of the plague appeared. A number of burials were taking place amid the funeral steles that lined the road outside the old, crumbling city walls. A funeral or two was not an odd thing to see on any given day, but on this morning there were more than he could count, some far from the road and others quite near, so that the shrieks and wails of the mourners grated upon his ears.

Held aloft in his chair, he could see a considerable distance, and far to one side he saw something quite shocking. A group of rough-looking men had apparently broken into what looked like a large family monument, and from its niches were removing one urn after another, and then—unbelievable!—opening the urns and emptying the ashes. For what possible purpose? As soon as the question occurred to him, so did the answer: they were making room for the newly dead, which otherwise had no proper place to be put, so quickly were so many dying. Perhaps all the family members of those in the desecrated monument were already dead, so there would be no one to object—but no, even as he watched, another group of men arrived, carrying clubs and knives, and attacked the desecrators, who used the urns in their hands as missiles. One, made of pottery, struck a nearby stone monument and exploded in a cloud of ash. The scene seemed so unreal as to be almost comic.

Lucius thought of the "war of actors," and all the lively young people Verus had brought to Rome. This abomination had also followed Verus from the East—one could call it a war over human remains, as sites for interment became so crowded people began fighting over them. Romans preferred to cremate their dead, but fuel for so many fires had become scarce, along with living humans to cut the trees and tend the flames. Even suitable urns for ashes were scarce, so that the poor were reduced to using their piss-pots! Instead of cremating them, many people were now burying their dead, as the Christians did, not from any belief that the bodies might someday come back to life, as the Christians in their lunacy imagined, but simply to be rid of the corpses and the plague that infested them. Lucius had even heard of grave robbers who dug up the freshly buried, so that new bodies could be put in the same hole. A war of corpses! Such were the horrors to which the plague had reduced the greatest city in the world.

Once inside the city proper, Lucius should have seen streets filled with people and heard the noises of city life, but all was unnaturally still. Doors and windows were shut. Balconies of upper floors were deserted. A vague sound of weeping rose and fell, muffled behind closed doors.

Even the temples were quiet, with only a few people coming and going on the marble steps. For a while every temple in Rome had been unusually crowded. Shocked and terrified at the death suddenly all around them, people called on every god they could think of, pleading for an end to the suffering. The gods did not hear, for the dying only accelerated.

As his litter passed near the buildings that housed the imperial horse guard, he received another shock. First, his nostrils were assaulted by the all-too-familiar stench of dead bodies. Then he saw that the paved public square—where the horsemen frequently showed off their steeds and practiced extravagant maneuvers to the delight of onlookers—had been completely dug up. Gone were the paving stones, and in their place was a huge pit, perhaps ten feet deep, where a mass burial was taking place. Lucius called to his litter-bearers to stop, so that he could take in the ghastly spectacle.

Most of the horsemen were from far away and had no family in Rome to grieve or to bury them, so they were being buried here, all together and all at once. Had every one of them died overnight? The gruesome work was being performed by the lowest of the stable hands—slaves who usually shoveled horse dung, to judge by their filthy tunics. Down an earthen ramp and into the pit they carried one corpse after another, all anonymous within linen shrouds, and laid them close together. Then the slaves shoveled a thick layer of plaster over the bodies. Lucius had heard that some physicians believed plaster could contain the contagion. At least it served to contain the stench.

The man directing the slaves allowed them a brief respite, while the plaster was allowed to dry for bit. From the nearby piles of linen-wrapped corpses that remained unburied it was evident what would happen next—another layer of bodies would be laid in the pit and covered with plaster, and then another layer, and yet another, until all the bodies were plastered over and the pit could be filled with earth.

Would the pit then be paved over, as if nothing had happened? Would there be no monument for the dead cavalrymen? The relentless onslaught of the plague had overtaken the ability of the living to memorialize the dead.

It had not been so at the beginning of the plague, when untimely death was still a novelty. Monuments and memorials proliferated outside the city, of course, but inside the city as well, as every family wealthy enough to do so petitioned the emperors to be allowed to set up a statue in some public place to honor some beloved and much-mourned senator or magistrate or famous philosopher struck down in his prime. Having allowed the privilege to the first few who asked, Marcus had seen no proper way to refuse those who followed, and eventually every empty spot large enough for a pedestal became occupied by a statue. A war of statues, Lucius thought, all vying for attention!

For a while, Lucius had received more business than he could handle, as his studio turned out one statue after another—so many, so fast, that he frequently ran out of marble. Eventually marble became as scarce as gold, as quarries all over the empire, one after another, were stricken by the plague. Usually, the lowly slaves in the quarries were easily replaced, but when they died by the hundreds and thousands, even the quarries were depopulated.

When Lucius crossed the city nowadays, he averted his eyes from those statues, which had appeared all over Rome in the first stages of the plague, or at least from the ones for which he was responsible. In the mounting rush, and with so much money pouring in, he had allowed his standards to slip. One statue of a senator was simply copied from the last—the same stance, hands, gestures—with only the facial features given any distinction, as his sculptors worked from wax masks of the dead. Some of the workmanship was appalling. Lucius was simply responding to the demands of his clients, he tried to tell himself, performing a public duty—but he knew that it was really greed that had gotten the better of him, along with the perverse satisfaction of being so much in demand, never mind that a plague was the cause.

It was not only the quarries that had come to a standstill. All over Italy and in every sort of endeavor there had been a sudden and severe loss of manpower. With no slaves to harvest them, crops rotted in the field. With no slaves to load the ships, cargoes sat on piers. Trade slowed to a trickle, and now one heard rumors of famine, growing closer and closer to Rome.

As Lucius gazed at the pit of plastered corpses, something Marcus once said echoed in his head. "Consider all the mortals that populated the earth before us, generation upon generation, extending back through countless centuries. All are dead, all turned to dust—so many, one wonders how the earth has room to hold them all."

Lucius called to his bearers. "Let's be off again. Quickly!"

No sooner had he escaped the stench of the pit than he saw ahead of him an unearthly sight.

In recent days, the remaining artisans in his workshop had been toiling day and night to satisfy an order that had come directly from Marcus, who specified a great many statues to be fashioned not from marble (a good thing, as there was none), but from old-fashioned terra-cotta, which was much lighter and more easily moved. These statues were to represent many different gods and goddesses, each made to human scale and depicted reclining on one elbow, as if settled on a dining couch. For Marcus, Lucius had insisted on the highest standards, despite the rush, and had overseen much of the production himself, even doing some of the painting. In the end he had been rather proud of those statues. Properly painted, terra-cotta could pass for marble, unless one thumped it with a finger. His overflowing workshop had come to resemble a house party crammed with too many guests.

Now he saw how the statues had been put to use. Overnight, scores of dining couches had been taken outdoors and arranged as if for a very large banquet. These couches were so elegant they could only have come from the imperial palace, and almost certainly from storage, since Lucius had never seen Marcus use furniture so fine. Upon these exquisitely carved and upholstered couches the reclining statues of the gods had been placed, so that it appeared as if the gods themselves had gathered for a banquet. Before each deity had been placed round tables piled high with offerings—not the coarse food of mortals, but precious incense and flowers and other aromatic substances, for everyone knew that gods lived from intangible stuff: sweet smells and smoke and the praise of mortals.

Lucius ordered the bearers to stop. He had never seen anything like it. Nor had anyone else. Having failed to end the plague with all ordinary appeals to the gods, Marcus, as Pontifex Maximus, had searched the state archives for ancient purificatory rites, and had discovered this one, which called for statues of all the gods to be placed in prominent locations all around the city, making all of Rome into a banqueting hall for the immortals. Priests would chant, people would gather and pray, and surely the well-fed gods would show their favor.

Even exotic deities had been included. Lucius himself had put the final touches to the rather fine statue of Isis that he saw reclining on a couch nearby. Her inclusion at the feast was probably due to influence of the Egyptian priest Harnouphis, who had risen to a privileged place in the imperial household. Isis was also quite popular with the citizens, to judge by the many offerings and tokens that had been piled up around her. Among the flowers and bits of cinnamon Lucius saw crude clay effigies, representations of the still-living children for whom their parents asked divine protection from the plague.

Isis would not be lonely at the banquet. Nearby Lucius saw statues of Apollo, Latona, Diana, Mercury, Hercules, and Neptune.

He called to the bearers, and hurried on.

The streets became narrower as he drew closer to his house. On doorways to either side he saw the charms that had been nailed onto many of the doors. These charms took various forms, depending on which wonder-worker had sold them to the occupants. Some doors had several such charms, from several sources. Most were made of thin, cheap metal etched with designs or letters, some more sophisticated than others. Of late, on many doors, Lucius had noticed circular tin disks, elaborately stippled around the edges, etched with letters of some foreign alphabet, and painted with a head of Medusa. Supposedly the words of the spell along with the Gorgon's glare would prevent the plague from entering. Were any of these charms efficacious? Lucius had no reason to think so, since people all up and down the street, whether they used the charms or not, continued to fall ill and die.

The Gorgon disks, he knew, came from a particular wonder-worker—or more likely, charlatan—named Alexander, who was new in the city. Lucius's brother had encountered him in the East. According to Kaeso, the man had preyed on soldiers, selling them charms that would supposedly keep them safe in battle—charms that Kaeso himself had seen on many a dead body on the battlefield. Alexander had a traveling workshop that produced amulets to ward off every evil and to cure every illness.

These were not free, of course. Alexander must have made a good living from selling them, though one would never know it to look at him, as he shambled about the city in worn shoes and tattered clothes, haranguing anyone who would stop to listen. "The humblest servant of the gods I am," he would say, "just doing what I can to help my fellow mortals."

As the bearers rounded a corner, Lucius saw the wonder-worker himself. In an open area surrounded by shops and shadowed by a few tall trees, a considerable crowd had gathered. One seldom saw such large gatherings since the coming of the plague. Alexander was not alone in addressing the crowd. A rival wonder-worker was competing for attention. Unlike Alexander, this man was dressed in the multicolored robes and high headdress of a Chaldean magus, trained to read the stars. He, too, had charms to sell. His servants were moving through the crowd, displaying little figurines that depicted various demigods and mortals, like Castor and Pollux, who had been placed by the gods among the stars. "The Gemini look down from the heavens and weep to see such suffering!" the magus cried. "Place one of these figures in every room of your home, to look after you and each of your loved ones! If you have slaves, protect them as well."

"What absolute nonsense!" shouted Alexander. "You are a Chaldean, Julianus. You know nothing at all about talismans and amulets. Stick to reading the stars! Or better yet, give that up as well, since your powers are obviously useless. Did your insight into celestial mechanics foretell the plague? Did you warn the people of what was to come? I think not! Tell us when the plague will be over, if you are able, but leave the care of the people to me!"

"You don't know what you're talking about," shouted Julianus. "My charms have successfully warded off the plague in a third of the city, while everyone knows that the houses displaying *your* amulets are the ones hardest hit."

"Then why do you see so many of my Medusa charms, all over the city?"

"Because, you fool, there is no one left alive in those houses to take them down!"

Some in the crowd laughed, but only a few. Public laughter had become a rare thing in Rome.

With more and more people gathering to watch them, the two wonder-workers hurled ever more vicious and outrageous insults at each other. "Why, they're nothing more than actors," muttered Lucius to himself. "Look at those two, all puffed up by the attentions of their audience." There was something not quite right about the situation. Were they in fact actors, working from a script? Were they colluding with each other, and only pretending to argue?

Lucius knew of only one charm that had demonstrated any power over the plague, and that was the amulet passed down by his ancestors. Through his tunic, he clutched the golden fascinum nestled in the cleft of his chest, securely attached to its necklace. Silently, he thanked the god Fascinus—and then snatched his hand away, fearful that some malevolent power might sense his thoughts and set about inflicting the plague upon his household, deliberately trying to thwart the protection of the fascinum.

Where is Galen when you most need him? he thought. All other physicians had been powerless to cure or stop the plague, but if any man could do so, it would be Galen—who might, in fact, arrive in Rome any day now. The physician's most recent letter from Pergamum brought news that the two emperors had summoned him back to Rome, not to care for the imperial household, but to accompany Verus and his legions north, where Germanic barbarians were causing trouble along the border. Another war was looming, and the Roman legions, already suffering from the plague, would have need of the very best physicians. Galen should have been flattered by the summons, Lucius thought, but in his letter he expressed only dismay. Whatever his own wishes, after his hasty exit from Rome, Galen did not dare to ignore a direct summons from the emperors.

"On, on!" cried Lucius to his bearers, but as they made their way through the spectators, the crowd grew thicker, and their progress was slow. No sooner had they passed the quarreling wonder-workers than they came upon another crowd, this one gathered to watch something in a fig tree.

The tree was in full leaf, so that hardly a branch could be seen, only a canopy of green. From the tree's uppermost reaches, a human head emerged from the shimmering green leaves. No body could be seen, only the head, but that was not the strangest thing, for the face and the bald pate were a vivid shade of red. Amid so much crimson, the wide, unblinking eyes were strikingly white. People were staring up at the head in awe. As Lucius drew nearer, he realized the head was speaking.

"This is the end!" cried the head, in a deep, sonorous voice, speaking with such a strange accent it might have been comic had the words not been so dire. "The gods have not just turned their backs on us—they have turned against us! The plague will grow worse and worse, until every mortal in Rome is too weak to stand, and then what will become of those few survivors? Do you want to know more? The end was foretold by an oracle that dwells on the most distant mountain beyond the most distant sea ever sailed by mortal men. I sailed that sea! I climbed that mountain! I heard the oracle speak and wrote down every word—a poem of nine hundred and ninety-nine lines—though at the time I could hardly imagine what it meant. I journeyed many years to come back to Rome, and the moment I arrived, the words of the oracle began to come true. But . . . there is one small sliver of hope, one faint ray that lights the dark portals of days to come. Do you want to know more? Shall I speak? Shall I recite the oracle's prophecy?"

The spellbound crowd shouted as one. "Yes! Speak!"

"A man in a yellow cap moves among you, with a bronze bowl for collecting alms. When the bowl is full, I shall speak again. Throw coins into the bowl! Make the music of silver upon bronze. I long to speak, to tell you all I know. Give alms! Give alms!"

From his high seat on the litter, Lucius scanned the crowd and spotted the yellow cap in their midst. He heard the clattering of coins tossed into the bowl.

"Well, that's another way to rob fools of their money!" he muttered to himself, though in fact he, too, was rather curious to hear what the man would say next. Then there was a commotion of some sort, and a surge of movement in the crowd, and loud cries of alarm. A group of armed Praetorians forced their way through the spectators, heading for the fig tree.

"Out of there!" cried the officer in charge. "Get out of that tree, you scoundrel!"

The eyes opened wide—a flash of white surrounded by the red face—and then the whole head vanished into the canopy of fig leaves. There followed the sounds of breaking branches and squeals of protest, and then the man was forcibly pulled from the tree. Praetorians gripped him by the arms. Lucius saw that the man was dressed in a dark robe with long sleeves. His hands had been darkened somehow. The intention was obvious: to hide his body from sight while his head appeared to float above the leaves—a simple but remarkably effective bit of stagecraft. Even Lucius had felt a shiver of the uncanny, watching him. The man's deep voice had also cast a spell, but now he was squeaking like a mouse, begging the guards to let him go.

"You there!" shouted Lucius. "Officer in charge! What's the man done?"

The Praetorian looked up, ready to bark an order, but then he saw Lucius's toga. "Good day, Senator. We are arresting this foreigner and his compatriot for falsely collecting alms. They're no better than thieves. They've been putting on this little play all over the city. This time we caught them in the act."

"But if they're merely actors, and this is a show, where's the crime?"

"Senator, surely you know that all performances of any sort must be approved in advance by the magistrates. And these fellows are no common street mimes. Did you not hear them? They're uttering blasphemy, even as the emperors are doing everything they can to placate the gods. It's sedition. When the city prefect hears his case, this scoundrel will be lucky to keep his head on his shoulders, painted red or otherwise."

"Ah, well, then . . . yes, I see," said Lucius. "But unless he's a Roman citizen, he's not likely to be granted the mercy of beheading. More likely, he'll be crucified."

The man—street mime, actor, or whatever he was—overheard, and began wailing in terror.

The Praetorians went about their business, the crowd dispersed, and the litter-bearers were able to move forward again.

What a sad, sordid place Rome has become, thought Lucius, *full of frightened people, and the tricksters who prey on people's fear.* Would the banquet set out for the gods make a difference? No one doubted that Marcus was doing all he could to save the city and its people. Lucius clutched the fascinum and whispered a prayer, asking the gods to help Marcus and to show mercy on Rome.

On a sudden impulse, Lucius gave new instructions to the bearers. More than one of them groaned aloud at the order, for they were very near his house but now would have to make a detour. It was never a good idea to get on the wrong side of one's domestic slaves, especially since the plague had made finding reliable servants harder than ever, but Lucius knew the side trip was worthwhile as soon as its objective came into view.

He called the men to a halt and stepped from the litter, for the only way to view the great arch of Marcus and Verus was on foot, making a slow circle all the way around it. The arch had been completed just in time for the triumph. On its facade were numerous sculptural reliefs depicting both Verus's victories on the battlefield and the bounty and peace of Rome under Marcus's steady hand, but by far the finest and most striking part of the monument were the two gilded equestrian statues atop the arch. Lucius's father might have created greater works of art—his many images of Antinous, or the fantastic quadriga atop Hadrian's mausoleum—but on his own, since he had been in sole charge of the workshop, these were Lucius's masterpieces. His Marcus, seated so serenely yet so commandingly on his steed, was nearly as grand as Hadrian in his chariot, and his Verus, likewise mounted on a charger, was almost as handsome as Antinous. To see these two statues shining golden in the lowering sun gave him a moment of respite, a brief, bright memory of the order and beauty that had existed in Rome only a short while ago, and might yet exist again, especially with two such fine emperors to lead her out of darkness.

When Lucius at last arrived home, he ordered a ration of wine for the bearers, which earned him a cheer louder than their previous groans. He made his way through the house, to the garden.

Pinaria looked up from her sewing. His daughter was still not married, alas, and was not soon likely to be, given the dearth of suitors caused by the plague. Young Gaius looked up from the board game he was playing with his uncle Kaeso and gave his father a smile. Kaeso, too, looked up, but did not smile. With his creased brow and grave expression, how old he looked for a young man of twenty-seven! In all the months he had been back from the wars with Verus in the East, Kaeso had not smiled even once. Nor had he spoken much. Kaeso mostly brooded. From the few comments he had made, it seemed the experience of war had not been a good thing for Kaeso. He would only allude vaguely to things he had seen and places he had been, never giving details.

At least the silly board game he was playing with Gaius— some nonsense to do with throwing dice and avoiding the jaws of a Nile crocodile while rescuing a kidnapped princess— seemed to be providing Kaeso with a bit of distraction.

Absent from the garden was Lucius's wife, who had died not from the plague but suddenly and without much suffering a few months before the plague arrived. How singular and without parallel had seemed Lucius's grief in the days after Paulina died, until so many others began to die. How he still missed her, every time he stepped into this garden! How he still missed his father, who also had died of natural causes, long before the plague.

The plague had so far taken no one from Lucius's family, and hardly any of his slaves, a fact that would seem quite remarkable, indeed inexplicable, were it not for the obvious explanation—the protection of the fascinum. If he knew of a way to multiply its power and share it with others, he would do so gladly—and not charge for the favor, like those so-called wonder-workers.

The board game was suddenly over. Gaius, who had won, seemed quite pleased with himself. He went off to do something else. Pinaria also gathered up her sewing and headed elsewhere, pausing as she passed her father to whisper,

"He's in a very foul mood today," by which she meant her uncle Kaeso.

"But how can you tell?" Lucius whispered back.

Pinaria rolled her eyes. The gesture reminded him of Paulina. He sighed.

"You don't sound very happy for a man who's been just back from the villa on the Via Clodia," said Kaeso, idly fingering one of the wooden dice.

The comment stung, for Lucius had just been thinking that if Paulina were still alive, he wouldn't be wasting his time at Verus's orgies and making such a fool of himself—a forty-seven-year-old senator mindlessly cavorting with actors young enough to be his grandchildren, who barely disguised their contempt for him.

"You know you're perfectly welcome to come along, if you wish to see for yourself," said Lucius. "Verus himself has told me so."

Kaeso turned up his nose. "I saw more than enough debauchery in the East with Verus. How he maintains such a voracious appetite for it, I can't imagine. Boys, girls, wine—he could never get enough."

"Perhaps resorting to such behavior was his way of coping with the stresses of war. And now it's how some of us cope with the plague. Not everyone is as resolute a Stoic as our *other* emperor."

"Thank the gods one of them has some decency and common sense!"

"Oh, Kaeso, you sound very old for a man your age. Why, when I was twenty-seven, I was serious about my work, to be sure, but still—"

"When you were my age, you hadn't been to the places I've been to . . . or done the things I've done . . ."

Lucius held his breath. Was Kaeso finally ready to talk about the mysterious experiences that weighed so heavily on him? Lucius was not sure he was ready to listen.

"I was there," said Kaeso quietly, staring at the wooden

die between his finger and thumb. "I was there at the very beginning."

"The beginning of what?"

"Of all *this*."

"Kaeso, I don't understand. What are you saying?"

Kaeso was silent for a long time, so long that Lucius began to feel a bit relieved, thinking the moment of candor must have passed. Then Kaeso spoke, in a strained voice that seemed to come from a person Lucius had never met.

"The plague! You must have heard where and when it began."

Lucius cleared his throat. Where was a slave when one needed a cup of wine? They all seemed to have vanished, as if frightened by Kaeso's voice. "Well, like everyone, I've heard various rumors, but which of them is true, I couldn't say—"

"In Seleucia. That's where it began."

"Yes, I've heard that said. But you served directly under Verus, and Verus wasn't there. He told me himself that he was far away when all that . . . when all the trouble in Seleucia . . . took place."

"And so he was. But I was one of the men he sent to check on the behavior of Avidius Cassius and his men. It was Cassius in charge of 'pacifying' the city of Seleucia. The city had already surrendered. The city fathers were cooperating with the Romans, doing whatever they were told. So there was never any need for . . . violence. But Verus had a bad dream, or so he said, and he feared that Cassius might let the situation get out of hand. It's always a delicate matter, when soldiers occupy any city, no matter whether the city is friend or foe. Soldiers . . . take liberties. Citizens take offense. Even a small dispute can suddenly erupt into . . ." Kaeso's voice trailed off.

"We don't have to speak of this . . . if you don't want to," offered Lucius. Truly, he was parched. Should he yell for one of the slaves? Perhaps not. Kaeso's demeanor demanded his complete attention.

"No, now is the time," said Kaeso. "I have to speak of it. I *will*." He was quiet again, as if summoning his courage, and then proceeded, speaking calmly and evenly, without emotion. "I showed up in Seleucia just after the violence began, so I can't say how it started. But it was like a raging fire, spreading everywhere at once, out of control. It was like . . . do you believe in evil spirits, Lucius? Do you believe mortals can be possessed by such spirits?"

Lucius shrugged.

"It's a common belief in that part of the world, more common the further east one goes. Perhaps they're right. Because the things I saw Roman soldiers do that day . . . the look on their faces . . . the complete lack of mercy . . . the things . . . that I myself did that day. The atrocities . . ."

"Are you saying an evil spirit possessed you?"

"I don't know. I can't explain it. Before that day . . . and after that day . . . I couldn't imagine myself—I, Kaeso Pinarius, a Roman, a man, a mortal—doing the things I did that day."

"Would you . . ." said Lucius, speaking very quietly. "Would you care to join me in drinking a bit of wine?"

Perhaps he spoke too quietly, for Kaeso seemed not to hear him. "If you ask them, people here in Rome will say, 'Yes, I know what happened in Seleucia.' But it was worse, so much worse, than anything they can imagine. They have no idea. The slaughter and the bloodshed, the gore, the mutilations, the murders . . . not just of men, but of women—of course, women!—and children, little boys and girls younger than your Gaius! Every time I see him, I think of those little boys and girls in Seleucia. And you wonder why I no longer have a taste for Verus's debauchery?"

"But surely it's not the same thing—"

"And the blasphemy! The things that were done in temples, right in front of the gods. What were we thinking? Did we think we could do such things, and the gods would look away?"

"Yes, I heard that temples were looted," said Lucius.

"Not just looted, though that was bad enough. Rape and murder! Priestesses stripped naked and tortured. I was there . . . I was among the Romans that day, that hour, that moment, in the temple of Apollo . . ."

"Yes, yes, I've heard of this," said Lucius quietly. "That the plague was somehow unleashed from a temple in Seleucia. They say a golden casket was found, assumed to be full of treasure, and the priests warned the Romans not to open it, but they did—"

"A golden casket?" cried Kaeso. "Yes, that makes for a pretty picture, such as might grace a pretty story. Like Pandora's box, or urn, or whatever it was."

Lucius was rendered speechless by the sudden scorn in his brother's voice.

"No, the plague was unleashed only on the following day. Verus arrived. He was appalled. He was stunned. But what was Verus to do, except make the best of the situation? The survivors of Seleucia were to be enslaved. You could hardly let them loose in the world, free to plot revenge on Rome. And the temples, already desecrated—even the gods had fled from the city, surely—the temples might as well be looted of whatever treasures they possessed. Statues, paintings, objects of silver and gold—the accumulation of many lifetimes of worship. The coins and such were to be distributed among the soldiers—as if to reward them for what they had done! The larger items were to be presented to Rome's allies in the region, tokens of Verus's generosity. But the very best things, the most precious, those were to be put in crates and carted back to Rome.

"But we had to hurry! Fires had broken out all over the city, set accidentally or on purpose the previous day, and the fires were spreading out of control. Verus ordered me to oversee the collection of the statue of Apollo in the temple. I asked him not to send me—no, that's not true, I told him I *couldn't* go back into that temple, and he lost his temper—something he never does—and he very sharply told me to do as I was ordered.

"When I set foot inside, it was like a place I had visited in a dream—a nightmare. Surely the things I remembered doing had never happened, could never have happened—but there was the blood and gore on the walls . . . there was the naked body of the priestess, lying crumpled, twisted in a horrible way . . . and there was the statue on its pedestal, and my men with their pulleys and ropes, and I had my orders.

"The men removed the statue and carried it outside. The pedestal had moved, and I saw something curious. I called back the men and had them shift the pedestal, and sure enough, underneath it was a trapdoor. The opening to a secret treasury, I thought! How pleased Verus would be if I had uncovered something really spectacular.

"And then—truly, it was like something in a play!—out of nowhere a priest appeared. He must have been very well hidden the previous day—who knows what secret rooms were in that temple? But for some reason, he suddenly showed himself. He must have seen us, watching through a peephole. He saw, and couldn't stay hidden, couldn't keep quiet.

"He ran toward me, screaming that I mustn't open the trapdoor. What an old fool, I thought. How did he propose to stop me? By words alone? Even before he reached me, one of the men raised his sword and struck him down. The blade sliced into his neck, almost cutting off his head. A fountain of blood erupted from his neck. Blood was everywhere! One of the men slipped in it and fell.

"And like a fool, like an idiot, I did exactly what the priest told me not to do. I gripped the handle of the hatch . . . and I opened it."

Kaeso fell silent and stared into space, a look of horror in his eyes.

"And then?" whispered Lucius.

"And then—it was as if a wound had opened in the earth and a howling, foul-smelling wind blew out. The hatch opened onto a void, not man-made but lined with rock. It was deep, endlessly deep—later, men tried to plumb the depth, and never reached the bottom. A great chasm, a festering wound, full of stench and horror. Strange, winged creatures flew out, and wasps the size of my fist, and other things . . . nameless things . . . too horrible to talk about.

"And . . . carried on that rushing wind . . . was the plague. That was how it came into the world. There and then, in that ruined temple of Apollo. Later I was told that the opening had been closed ages ago, long before the temple of Apollo was built, by Chaldean magi using all their secret knowledge to seal it up. And I—Kaeso Pinarius—I opened it. I let loose the pestilence. I polluted the whole world!"

He began to tremble, so violently that Lucius rushed to him and held him. "Oh, Kaeso! Surely not! Something horrible happened, I have no doubt, but the idea that you could possibly—"

Kaeso drew ragged breaths, almost weeping. "The very next day, the first Roman soldiers fell ill outside Seleucia. The very next day! Only a few, and the sickness spread slowly at first. But from that day on, there were more and more reports of soldiers falling ill. First a handful, then scores, then hundreds. Of the men who served directly under me, not one is still alive. And when Verus returned to Rome, the plague followed right on our heels, striking every city we passed through."

Lucius was aghast. He tried to keep the expression from his face, lest Kaeso should see and become even more agitated. What was he to make of such a story? Kaeso could hardly have imagined the whole incident, but what had really happened, and what did it have to do with the plague?

"Brother, I'm glad you finally told me this. I can see how heavily it's been weighing on you. Galen says that sometimes just talking about an affliction can make the sufferer feel better."

"An affliction? You think I'm cursed?"

"No, I never said that! I think something happened . . . something truly awful . . . but it may have nothing to do with the plague. As philosophers says, coincidence does not necessarily imply causation—"

"Which do you think I need, then, a physician or a philosopher?" Kaeso laughed. It was a hollow, horrible sound.

"Everyone has heard of the sack of the temple in Seleucia, or some version of the story," said Lucius. "And yes, there are people who say the impiety of Roman soldiers caused the plague. But other people have other ideas. Some blame the Chaldean magi who supposedly sealed up that hole. The Chaldeans guard their wisdom too jealously and keep too many secrets. What they practice has nothing to do with Greek or Roman religion, yet suddenly their influence is everywhere. Even Marcus has come to rely on them."

"If only Marcus had been there, and had consulted his Chaldeans before the sack of Seleucia," said Kaeso. "Perhaps it could all have been avoided, all the horror—"

"And others say the Christians are to blame for the plague, because they refuse to honor the gods."

"Christians? Are there really enough of them to have angered the gods so much?"

"They were blamed for the great fire under Nero, and there were fewer of them back then. And fewer still, after Nero flushed out and burned as many as he could. Yet their numbers have steadily grown since then, especially in the East. Some say the emperors need to follow Nero's example, to put Rome right with the gods and stop the plague."

Lucius held his breath, fearing that Kaeso would counter with the embarrassing fact that a great-great-uncle of theirs had been among the Christians burned by Nero—and had been named Kaeso. But his brother said nothing. He turned away and began to pace back and forth across the garden.

Poor Kaeso! How great must be his guilt and shame, that he had been driven to entertain such a notion, this preposterous idea that he and he alone had unleashed the plague the moment he opened that hatch in Seleucia. Was such a thing even possible? Marcus might know. He was Pontifex Maximus, after all, so in theory no one on earth knew more about religion than he did. But how could Lucius ever raise the question without telling Marcus the whole story?

Galen, too, might have an opinion. Why was he not yet back in Rome?

Through the wool of his toga, Lucius touched the fascinum. Should he have allowed Kaeso to take it with him when he went to war, to protect him? The idea had briefly crossed his mind before Kaeso set out, but Lucius had said nothing, and as it turned out, Kaeso had no need for its protection, for here he was, back from the battlefield, unscathed.

Or was he? This terrible notion that tormented Kaeso was a sort of wound. Perhaps Galen would know how to treat it.

The alternative—that his own brother, driven by bloodlust and greed, had singlehandedly unleashed so much suffering and death into the world—was simply unthinkable.

Lucius hurried across Rome, answering a summons from Marcus.

The litter arrived at his destination and Lucius quickly stepped out. He allowed one of the bearers to adjust his toga, and then he hurried up the steps of the Hadrianeum, the temple consecrated to the divine Hadrian, one of the most beautiful in Rome. Painted panels in the vestibule depicted Hadrian on his many travels, often accompanied by Antinous. Here were images of the pyramids in Egypt, the temple of Zeus at Olympia, the Parthenon in Athens, and many more places. Hadrian had traveled more than any of his predecessors, taking advantage of the Pax Romana to visit almost every part of the empire.

Lucius came upon Marcus, who was wearing his purple toga and staring up at the panels with a wistful gaze. As far as Lucius knew, Marcus had never ventured out of Italy.

Marcus turned his gaze to Lucius. He sighed. "It is never a good thing to feel envy, and the wise man avoids it altogether, but sometimes I feel rather envious of Hadrian. All the places he traveled, all the wonders he beheld! Sometimes I feel a bit envious of Verus, for his travels to Greece and Asia, though I most certainly do not envy him the battles he's fought and all the bloodshed he's seen."

"Nor do I envy my brother for his travel," said Lucius quietly.

Marcus sighed. "Yet, at the same time, I'm relieved that I have *not* been obliged to travel. Even with all my endless duties here in Rome, I still find time for peaceful contemplation in a garden, or for quiet reading, or for conversation with the many philosophers who reside in Rome. Let's hope it stays that way, with Verus traipsing off to see the far edges of the world while I am allowed to remain here in Rome, where the world, whether I like it or not, comes to me."

"The ravages of the plague must weigh heavily on you, Verissimus."

Marcus Aurelius smiled sadly, comforted by the sound of the pet name Hadrian had given him so long ago. "Along with the plague that kills, there is another plague, if that I may call it, of charlatans and false prophets and tricksters who take advantage of the situation."

"Indeed," agreed Lucius. "A man can hardly set foot outside his home without encountering such scoundrels. Not long ago, I saw one of them arrested, a fellow pretending to deliver oracles—from a fig tree, if you can believe it!"

Marcus nodded. "I am aware of the incident."

"Are you? Such a petty matter hardly seems important enough to merit your attention, Verissimus."

"Nevertheless, the case was brought before me, and I tried the matter myself."

"Did you? Well, I presume the fellow was summarily crucified, or strangled, or received whatever penalty the law prescribes."

"No."

"No?"

"Perhaps he deserved to die, but I did not deserve the burden of inflicting such a punishment. There is enough death already in the city—in the whole world, for that matter. I let him go."

"Unpunished?"

"He was placed on a ship and sent back to his native city—where, I can't remember—and barred from ever stepping foot in Italy again."

"Verissimus, truly you are merciful."

"Don't say that quite yet—not until you've heard my request."

"A favor? You know, Verissimus, I am only too happy—"

The emperor quieted him with a wave of his hand. "Among those I spoke of—charlatans, false prophets, tricksters—are these people who call themselves Christians. They are not only impious, but absurdly proud to be so. Absurdly happy to die, as well. They seem to consider torture and public execution by the state to be a sort of stage performance, with themselves as the leading actors, each striving to outperform the others. What show-offs! 'Look at me, hanging from a cross, and yet I grin and sing—applaud, applaud!'" Marcus shook his head. "It behooves every man to face death with equanimity, but not with such deluded vulgarity. Impious *and* vainglorious. They set my teeth on edge."

"The Christians are not the only people who make a show of death," said Lucius. "Remember Peregrinus the Cynic, who died so famously when we were boys? At the end of the Olympic Games one year, he announced he would die at the next Olympics, four years later. When the day came, a huge audience gathered and Peregrinus delivered his own funeral oration. 'One who has lived like Hercules should die like Hercules'—talk about vainglorious! And then, while everyone watched, he climbed onto the pyre and set himself aflame! They say people could hear him screaming in Athens. No one knew if they were witnessing a tragedy or a comedy!"

Marcus responded with a long face. "The only reason that idiot's death was noted here in Rome was because Peregrinus had lived here for a while and had gathered something of a following, until his attacks on the emperor became so strident that Antoninus Pius had him thrown out of the city. What a farce that was—a campaign of abuse staged by an angry Cynic against the mildest emperor who ever lived! Before he became a Cynic, Peregrinus was a Christian for a while. Did you know that?"

"I had no idea."

"Yes. Went to Palestine to live among them, until he made himself so unpleasant that even the Christians drove him off. Then came his sordid sojourn here in Rome, followed by his fiery and pointless death in Greece." Marcus heaved a long sigh. "But Lucius, you've distracted me from my reason for calling you here."

"Pardon me, merciful one. I gather some particular problem regarding these Christians weighs upon you?"

"Yes, a bothersome matter, having to do with a Christian in the city named Justin. He's not especially troublesome, and you know the precedent that was set by Trajan: unless a complaint is lodged by a reputable member of the community, it's better to take no action against any given Christian."

"Ah, yes," said Lucius, remembering Trajan's formula. "'Ask not, tell not.'"

"Exactly. But in fact, a complaint *has* been lodged against Justin, by—wouldn't you know it?—a Cynic. A fellow called Crescens claims that Justin steadfastly refuses to recant and worship the gods, and that he aggressively recruits naive young Romans into his cult. Crescens and Justin are neighbors. It seems they obsessively watch each other's comings and goings, like a pair of old gossips. Crescens further alleges that Justin's impiety—and that of his fellow Christians—is what stirred the gods to bring about the plague."

"Does he, indeed?" said Lucius quietly. "But surely this is a matter not for the emperor, but for the city prefect."

Marcus nodded. "Which post, this year, happens to be occupied by my beloved old teacher, Junius Rusticus. Reviewing the case, Rusticus came across material that he sent along to me, saying he thought I might be interested. There's nothing surprising about the Cynic, but there's a bit more to this Justin fellow than you might think. Among the documents Rusticus compiled is an old letter Justin submitted years ago to Antoninus Pius when he was emperor. Also included in the salutation of the letter are the two heirs apparent at that time, Verus and myself. I don't recall ever seeing this letter, or hearing it read. Indeed, I doubt very much that it ever reached the attention of Antoninus. But the letter has been in the imperial archive year after year, as if patiently waiting for just the right moment to come to my attention. A peculiar chain of events, don't you think? And you know I don't believe in 'mere coincidence.'

"Like most such letters, this one opens with a great deal of fawning and flattery, but then proceeds with astonishing self-confidence. Justin is no—'ignoramus' is not quite the word I want. The old Latin word 'paganus' is better. Justin is no 'paganus,' no peasant or backward country bumpkin. At some point in his life, before he became a Christian, he made a serious study of philosophy. The difficult case he puts forward—rejecting a thousand years of Greek wisdom and extolling Christianity as the only true belief—is sometimes quite clever, and deeply felt, I have no doubt. But what a nerve the fellow has, to set about lecturing the emperor, like a father lecturing a child! Such people have no idea, none whatsoever, of the challenges one faces, every hour of every day . . ."

Staring up at a painting of Hadrian, Marcus seemed to grow distracted. At last he continued. "Anyway, Justin's letter vexed me. *And* it amused me. I feel as if I've met the fellow, and though I can't say I like him, I don't relish the idea that he should be tortured and executed. It would hardly be proper for me to meet with the man, but, as a personal favor, would you be willing to do so, Lucius?"

"Me, Verissimus?"

"Yes, you, Senator Pinarius. There is no more levelheaded fellow in Rome than you. Read Justin's letter, and then have a talk with him. Talk also with Crescens, his accuser. The man is a Cynic, so who knows if he can be believed? I don't want an official report from some clerk. I want the impressions of a man I know and trust. Meet with the two of them. Then return and share your thoughts. Will you do this for me?"

Lucius could hardly refuse.

The small, crowded cell in which Lucius found the Christian was just as dank and foul as he expected, with only a small, barred opening high in the wall to admit air and light, a few crude benches for the only furniture, piles of straw for beds, and a single large bucket to receive the urine and excrement of the dozen or so prisoners. But the Christian was not the wild-eyed troublemaker he had expected. Justin had unkempt hair and a long beard, and he was rather filthy and foul smelling, to be sure, but who would not be after several days in such a place? His manner was quite sedate—almost too calm, Lucius thought, for a man facing torture and death.

Justin also looked vaguely familiar, but Lucius couldn't imagine where he might have seen him before. Perhaps if the man were washed and groomed, Lucius might recall.

The guards released Justin from his shackles and allowed him out of the cell so that Lucius could interview him in a setting more suitable for a senator. This room was also dank and malodorous, but at least it had chairs and was reasonably private, with two armed men standing in the doorway, watching.

The explanation for Justin's calm manner quickly became evident. The man believed absolutely that he was right about everything (meaning others, including the emperors, had to be wrong), and that he would be proved right in the end—not merely at the end of his own life or the end of an age, but at the end of the whole world, which would conclude with fiery, eternal punishment for all who did not think exactly as he did, and the reward of eternal life (presumably a happy one) for himself and his fellow Christians. This end of the world,

Justin believed, was likely to occur any day now. Indeed, in his opinion, the plague was very likely the first warning that the final days of mankind were swiftly approaching.

"But let it not come today," said Lucius. "I am expecting the arrival of a friend from Pergamum."

He meant this to be a joke, but Justin took him seriously. "I would say the same thing, Senator, but for a different reason. If the end were to come now, today, at this very moment, then my martyrdom would be taken from me. But listen to yourself, Justin!" The man had the peculiar habit of addressing himself by name, as if there were two (or more?) of him present. "What a shameful thing to say! To long for martyrdom is to commit the sin of pride. Who are you, Justin, that you think yourself worthy to wear a martyr's crown in paradise?"

"Are you saying that if the end of the world occurred right now, you would be disappointed because you would then *not* experience the many hours of torture and the shameful death that very likely await you in the days to come?" Lucius hated to speak so bluntly, but the man's demeanor demanded candor.

"You see through me, Senator. Justin is a vain fellow who somehow fancies himself good enough to join the company of the fearless men and women who suffered and died for their faith, who shall dwell in the company of Our Dominus in the hereafter, ceaselessly singing his praises and basking in the warm glow of his endless love."

"Is that how you imagine it? It seems to me it's your dominus, as you call him, who is the vain one, demanding to be ceaselessly praised. Why should this master of the universe care if you praise him or not? Does the praise give him sustenance? In that case, he seems no different than the other gods."

"There are no other gods."

"How can you say such a thing? Do you really think that Jupiter and Mars and Minerva do not exist? What of Venus? Surely every man has felt the power of Venus in his youth."

"I never said those beings do not exist," said Justin. "But why do you call them gods, and think them worth worshipping?

Their behavior is petty, selfish, vile, and repulsive—hardly what one expects from the highest and holiest power in the universe."

"You mock the gods?"

"What sort of god would turn himself into a swan and ravish a poor, unsuspecting woman, betraying his own wife, and not for the first time but the hundredth? Yet Jupiter did so with Leda, committing not only rape and adultery, but bestiality!"

Lucius winced. "Gods are not constrained by the moral strictures of mortal society."

"His bestiality did not stop there. Your Jupiter then turned himself into an eagle and flew off with pretty little Ganymede, and after having his way with the poor boy, Jupiter turned him over to the other gods to be their 'cupbearer'—in other words, their toy, to do with as they pleased. What a lecherous bunch!"

Lucius was speechless. He had always found the story of Jupiter and Ganymede a beautiful tale. Certainly it had inspired much great art.

Justin took advantage of Lucius's silence to continue his argument. "You say Our Dominus is vain because he demands the love and worship of his children, but what sort of god—a being worthy of worship—would lure a poor mortal into a musical contest, and then, when the mortal inevitably lost, not merely boast of winning, but hang the wretch from a tree and flay him alive? Yet that is what you would have me believe took place with Apollo and Marsyas. Now, that is not only vanity at work, but wickedness and spite. The screams of poor Marsyas were sweet music to Apollo! If these so-called gods of yours actually exist, they are more powerful than mortals, obviously, but in no way divine. They are not gods but evil spirits who delight in human suffering. Yet I do not condemn the Romans for their wrongheaded religion. I would save them from it! Just as an innocent man or woman may become possessed by an evil spirit, so the empire of Rome is possessed by these wicked beings, who not only oppress you but delude you into worshipping them. Rome must be exorcised of these spirits—Jupiter and Hera, Venus and Mars, and all the rest! Cast out the demons, I say!"

Lucius shook his head in dismay. "I think I should end this interview immediately, before you utter even more impiety." He stood and turned toward the doorway, then stopped and looked back. "Wait a moment. *Now* I remember where I've seen you! You were present at one of Galen's anatomical demonstrations. Yes, it was that first time I saw Galen prove that a pig's ability to squeal is dependent on a particular nerve."

Justin smiled. "I remember attending such a demonstration. I've been known to mingle on occasion with the physicians and philosophers outside the Temple of Pax. Arguing with them sharpens my wits."

"Does it? When my friend Galen makes some startling assertion, he follows it with a demonstration of empirical proof. Can you prove any of the impious things you say?"

Justin sighed. "I wasn't much impressed by your friend's crude anatomical demonstrations. I suspect he trained that poor pig to squeal or not to squeal on command. The squealing of a pig is anything but miraculous!"

"Galen never said it was a miracle. Quite the opposite. The whole point—"

"Do you know about the Christian Peter and his wonder-working contest with the wicked magician Simon Magus, here in Rome?"

Lucius was confused by the change of subject. "What? When was this?"

"Long before our lifetimes."

"I've never heard of this Peter and Simon, or of any contest."

Justin laughed. "What a city this is, where people are blind to miracles in their midst, yet make a fuss over a physician and a squealing pig! Peter did something truly miraculous. Without cutting into them, mind you—without even touching them—he made animals to utter *human speech*. Those who witnessed were astounded, and Simon Magus was made to look a fool."

Lucius bit his tongue. What was the use of arguing with such a man, at once so clever and so obtuse? Talking animals! Why did Christians make up such ridiculous stories about themselves and their exploits? Was it any wonder they attracted the hostility of decent citizens? Lucius hurriedly left the squalid room and did not look back.

But as he stepped into the street, leaving the stench of the prison behind, Lucius could not help but feel sorry for Justin. It seemed wrong somehow that such a mild fellow should be subjected to torture and execution, and not for anything to do with what he said, but because he refused to burn a bit of incense to the gods. Touch a flame to the sweet-smelling stuff, and Justin would be released at once. How absurd it seemed, that Justin would not submit to an everyday ritual that would save his life!

Or was the incense test itself absurd, as the determinant of life and death? Galen had once said that true impiety lay not in refusing to burn a bit of incense, but in doubting the perfect order of the universe. Justin would no doubt say he believed in perfection, but Lucius would never understand his point of view.

Lucius met Crescens at the place of the Cynic's choosing, which happened to be the baths closest to Crescens's home. Perhaps it would be a good thing, Lucius thought, to interview the man in easy, informal surroundings, where the Cynic might be more candid than cagey.

Lucius had never been to the small establishment before, and was expecting something far nicer. He had never stepped foot in such a tawdry bathing establishment in his life. There was not a painting to be seen, and the few statues were very poor copies hewn from inferior marble and painted in gaudy, slapdash fashion. Venus would be appalled to see such an image of herself, though Lucius thought it unlikely the goddess had ever passed this way. The place had a strange smell and was dimly lit, which was probably not a bad thing, judging from the filthy state of the tiles and the grout.

Like all the baths in Rome since the plague struck, however grand or humble, this one was largely deserted. An entire wing seemed to be closed, either because there were not enough patrons, or because there were not enough slaves to keep all the furnaces and waterworks in operation. Many people preferred to stay at home unwashed, fearing contagion, either from other people, or perhaps from the water itself.

Fortunately, in the part of the baths that remained open, the plumbing and heating were in good order. Indeed, the hot pool was almost too hot. That was where he found Crescens, who looked surprisingly like the man he was persecuting, having the same unkempt hair and ragged beard as Justin, and the same unwavering, beatific facial expression. No matter where the conversation led, Crescens seemed infinitely pleased with himself and the universe.

Lucius decided to be frank from the start. "I didn't think Cynics believed in bathing," he said, settling into the pool with a sharp breath as the steaming water lapped at his privates.

Crescens shrugged. "Earth, air, fire, water—I am equally at home in any element, and equally disagreeable in all."

"Even fire? Like your fellow Cynic, Peregrinus?"

"So! You are not a complete ignoramus after all, despite that toga with a senator's stripe I saw you wearing on your way in."

This was the kind of insulting talk typical of Cynics. Lucius was determined to avoid distractions and to stick to the subject. "You've lodged a very serious accusation of impiety against your neighbor Justin. Is there some animosity between you?"

"Do I take offense at living in close proximity to such an *atheotatous* fellow?" This was a bit of Greek meaning "most atheist of atheists." Lucius had heard other philosophers apply the word to Christians. "I certainly do object! Such gross impiety is likely to draw the wrath of Jupiter himself upon Rome, and where do you imagine the Father of Gods will strike first? A thunderbolt cast upon Justin's balding head is likely to set my own humble abode aflame, and me and my boys with it."

The natural riposte, of course, would be to remind Crescens that he had just declared himself at home in fire, or perhaps to ask what boys he meant, but Lucius refused to be drawn into pointless queries or debates. He was about to speak again when the boys referred to suddenly appeared, making three large splashes as they jumped into the pool in quick succession. A pair of older patrons at the far side of the pool sputtered and grumbled, but Crescens greeted the newcomers with a wide grin. He was missing several teeth, and those remaining were various shades of brown and yellow.

"And here they are, my trio of delights! Senator Pinarius, meet Chrestos, Callinicus, and Hilarion. Truly, they are the three cleverest boys in Rome!"

Lucius judged them to be about his own son's age, though their swaggering, smirking demeanor was hardly childlike.

Crescens patted each of them on the head. "What is it the Christians' man-god says of his followers? 'They toil not. Neither do they spin.' Ah, that's my boys. Such layabouts. Yet somehow—it's a most remarkable thing—they always have a few coins between them, as if they can somehow make money from the mere fact of being pretty. I'm sure I don't know where it comes from, but I do welcome the sesterces they contribute to help Uncle Crescens pay the rent and buy the wine."

Lucius had little doubt about how the "nephews" made their income, but it was not his concern. "You do realize that Justin faces torture and execution?" he asked. The Cynic began speaking before he was finished.

"One of my boys is even named Chrestos—that's Greek for 'good,' you know—which he certainly is, and which also sounds awfully like the Greek *Christos,* don't you think? But when I pointed out this happy coincidence to Justin—oh my, he threw such a fit!"

"You make a good living off these boys, then?" Lucius saw no point in being subtle.

"I? Certainly not. I myself own nothing. Well, next to nothing—only a staff to lean on and a leather pouch to hold my meager assets."

Chrestos raised an eyebrow. "Oh, your assets aren't *that* meager."

Callinicus grinned. "But he does keep them in a leather pouch."

"Most of the time!" Hilarion giggled.

This was not at all the interview Lucius had in mind when he agreed to meet at the baths. "Do these boys pay for your admission to this place?"

"Certainly not! To cover such basic expenses, I myself earn a poor pittance, as do most philosophers, by giving public lectures in the gardens adjoining the baths, to those rare Romans who are philosophically inclined. My latest talk, and very popular it is, is titled 'The Christians in Rome: Threat or Menace?'"

Lucius chuckled, despite himself. Like all authors rewarded with a laugh, Crescens was delighted. He clapped his hands. "There! How much less stuffy you look, Senator. We are all allowed to laugh at life, you know. Laughter costs nothing. The Christians never laugh. Never! What dour people they are. And so backward, so ignorant of even the rudiments of life. 'Boy-lover,' Justin calls me, as if that were an insult! Well, I can hardly deny it. Only Hadrian ever loved a boy more than I love these three scamps. Justin calls them my 'little Ganymedes'—as if that, too, were an insult, comparing me to Jupiter—except that I have three Ganymedes to Jupiter's one! Just another example of Justin's impiety, for which his ignorance and his rude disposition offer no excuse."

"I thought you Cynics were oblivious to insults."

"To insults, yes. To blasphemy, no. I am a Cynic, Senator, not a Stoic. Stoics are forbidden to complain. We Cynics do little else!"

"Perhaps you're jealous of Justin."

"How so?"

"It occurs to me that Cynics and Christians compete in poverty, as other men compete in wealth or power. And like the wealthy and powerful, you, too, must be susceptible to jealousy. Is Justin poorer than you, more austere, more wretched? Does that make you jealous of him?"

"Preposterous! *He* is jealous of *me*."

"Justin says you are a corrupter of youth."

"Also preposterous! Does the gardener corrupt the flower, or the farmer his apple tree? I merely bring my boys to fruition, in accordance with the natural order of the universe, as ordained by the gods, and bless them for it! Justin is the corrupter of youth, luring impressionable young minds from the proper worship of the gods, leading them into the crime of impiety, and delivering them to the just punishments of our emperor."

Lucius grunted. "Yes, Justin does have a small but ardent following. A few of his fellow Christians were arrested along with him. They happened to be in his room at the time of his apprehension, taking part in some Christian ritual."

"Ah, yes, that weird cannibal rite they practice—stomach-churning, I call it. How any boy could be lured into such atheism—though, if the boy is young and innocent enough, vulnerable to all and any nonsense . . . never realizing, until too late . . . it will be the death of him . . ." Crescens's sardonic cheerfulness abruptly ended. His grin became a scowl. His eyes lost their sparkle.

"He's talking about Mopsus," said Chrestus, in a low voice.

"Don't even mention him!" snapped Crescens.

"Why not?" asked Lucius.

Chrestos leaned toward him and whispered, "He can hardly bear to hear the name spoken aloud, ever since Mopsus died—"

"Was *executed*, you mean!" cried Crescens. The word seemed to curdle in his throat. He swallowed hard and blinked back tears. "For the crime of impiety—for refusing to honor the gods—because that foul Christian, that *atheotatous* corrupter of youth and hater of all that is beautiful, that hideous spider

Justin drew that poor boy into his web, and so filled his little head with horrible ideas that Mopsus felt compelled to make an example of himself, to become a martyr for that wretched death-cult."

"Justin lured away one of your boys?"

"Seduced his spirit! Poisoned his mind!"

"Turned him into a Christian, you mean. And then the boy made a public show of his atheism and got himself arrested, and ended up . . ."

"Dead!" wailed Crescens. Without the barbed armor of his Cynicism, he was like a turtle without its shell, exposed and vulnerable and not pretty to look at. His sharp features and defiant posture softened into a mass of fleshy wrinkles. He looked like any other old man long past his prime, gray and befuddled and sad.

"So the grudge *is* personal, between the two of you," said Lucius, but he did not wait for a response. He had had quite enough of such tawdry surroundings. He would have to take a long soak at his regular bathing establishment to wash himself free of the place.

Justin would not budge.

Lucius saw him again and tried to reason with him, to no avail. There was no reasoning with a mortal who believed the whole world was wrong about everything, and only he and a handful of others were right—and not merely right but absolutely sure of their rightness because of an imaginary authority that could not be questioned.

Under the circumstances, Lucius could hardly recommend leniency, especially since a substantial part of the citizenry blamed the Christians for somehow starting the plague, or for making it worse by their intransigent impiety.

"No mortal can defy the laws of both gods and man and expect no consequence," said Lucius when he met with Marcus.

"Yes. They will have to be executed. As Pontifex Maximus, considering the very loud and active complaint against Justin and his friends, I can endorse no other judgment."

Lucius frowned. "Do you remember that hoaxer in the fig tree?"

"Oh, yes."

"You showed mercy to that fellow. You merely banished him, saying there was enough death in Rome already. Must Justin be put to death?"

Marcus sighed. "The hoaxer was nothing more than a petty criminal preying on gullible fools. These Christians are something more sinister. They not only mock the gods, they mock their own punishment. They set an insidious example. It is a good thing, to have no fear of death. But to yearn for suffering and death is perverse. In Justin's case, the law must follow its course."

On the night before Justin's trial, Lucius dreamed that he was in a noisy, crowded place, amid a throng of spectators, and a man bound to a stake was being set on fire. Lucius was horrified, and wanted to escape, but instead the crowd pushed him closer and closer to the burning man. He felt compelled to look up at the victim, but the smoke and flames obscured his face. Was it Justin? Then, through the murk, he saw a glint of gold. The man was wearing the fascinum! This was the long-ago Pinarius who had been a Christian, who was turned into a human torch by Nero while all of Rome looked on and jeered.

Lucius woke with a start. He sat bolt upright, covered with sweat.

He had been wavering about attending the trial of Justin, thinking of excuses not to go, but now he had no choice. Not to do so would be cowardice.

Unable to go back to sleep, he started the day very early, but even so he ran late. Every simple act, even putting on his shoes, seemed to vex him and slow him down.

When he finally entered the examination chamber in Trajan's Forum, the torture and questioning were already well under way. Against one wall, in shackles and with armed guards watching them, stood Justin's fellow Christians, waiting their turn to be questioned. On a low dais sat the city prefect, Marcus's white-haired old mentor, Rusticus. Nearby sat a scribe who was recording the proceedings, using Tironian shorthand. In the center of the room, stripped to a loincloth, was Justin. His hands were tied behind his back. The rope binding his wrists was attached to a hoist manned by several rough-looking brutes. They seemed to be enjoying their work, certainly more than Rusticus, who looked quite exasperated.

"Very well," the prefect snapped, "hoist him up again!"

The brutes went to work. Justin was drawn upward until he stood on his toes with his arms bent backward and raised behind him. The pressure on his shoulders must have been excruciating, yet Justin showed no expression. But if his face was his to control, his body was not. Sweat erupted from every pore, drenching him. His bladder was loosened. His loincloth grew wet and streams of urine mingled with the sweat running down his skinny, naked legs. The torturers grunted. Lucius turned up his nose. Rusticus sighed.

"Let me make very clear to you, Justin," said the prefect, "exactly what will happen if you continue to refuse to burn incense to the gods. Once my questioning is over, before sentencing, a hook will be inserted through both of your cheeks. That is to prevent you from uttering curses against the emperor. After sentencing, you will be taken to the place of execution where a crier will announce your crimes while these brutes take turns lashing you with a whip. This will happen in public, where people are free to watch and make comments, to jeer and insult you and gloat. There are plenty of people in Rome nowadays, frightened and angry because of the plague, who will come to watch you die. They will pelt you with stones, rotten fruit, or whatever comes to hand. Quite often, feces, human and otherwise, are thrown at the villain."

"I do not fear the opinion—or the waste—of other mortals," said Justin, in a hoarse whisper.

Rusticus shrugged. "A bit higher, then."

Justin was hoisted upward. His toes no longer touched the floor. He hung suspended in space. Lucius was appalled. How did the man keep from screaming?

"And in the end, finally, mercifully, you will be beheaded," said Rusticus.

"I—do—not—fear—death!" Justin said, gasping between each strangled word.

"But that is not *quite* the end. There is the aftermath. Your separated head and body will not be buried or cremated—I forget what you Christians prefer. Burial rites are not for those who mock the gods. Your remains will be handed over to the citizens, who will be allowed to do whatever they wish. Your head will be kicked through the streets, and your carcass dragged by long poles with sharp hooks. They'll head for the Tiber, where they'll toss your mangled remains into the river, like so much garbage. It is an unseemly business, in my opinion, but it is sanctified by long tradition. By making yourself an enemy of the gods, you are an enemy of Rome, and no respect whatsoever will be shown to your corpse. Do you understand? Can I persuade you to relent from your impiety?"

This seemed to give Justin pause. He grunted. His lips trembled. Then he gasped and fervently shook his head.

If Lucius recalled correctly, the Christians believed that after death their mortal bodies would come to life again and be transported to some wonderful place. But what sort of body would Justin have to resuscitate? What would eternal life be like in such a ruined vessel?

What strange ideas these Christians had!

"I can hardly believe you attended the execution," said Kaeso. "That sort of spectacle is aimed at the very lowest creatures of the mob, the kind of lowlifes who need to be reminded every now and then of the consequences of crime and impiety."

Lucius had just described to his brother the beheading of Justin and several of his cohorts. "And yet, they seemed to find it rather entertaining," said Lucius, his voice a bit shaky.

"Who, the Christians?"

"Is that a joke, Kaeso?"

"Well, you said they went to their punishment singing."

"So they did, some with more bravado than others, though all the singing stopped pretty quickly once the scourging began. The song itself was actually rather pretty. 'O holy glory, O joyful light, the sun has set and comes the night, but the stars shine brighter than day . . .' Something like that, a sort of chant to their god—or is it gods? One is the son of the other, I think, except they're actually identical, and their mother was a virgin." He shook his head. "It's all quite confusing."

"It confuses even the Christians," said Kaeso. "I saw quite enough of their squabbles in the East. They're constantly at war with each other about this or that fine point of their religion—as if any of it mattered, since it's all made up. All that yelling alarms their neighbors, who then complain to the magistrates, who then have no choice but to set in motion the whole ugly business of interrogations and executions. Really, they bring it on themselves."

"They do seem to crave this martyrdom, as they call it, this horrible self-destruction. With so many people dying from the plague, you'd think life would be more precious to them."

"Enough talk of Christians, brother. Right now there's a greater threat to Rome than antisocial atheists, or even the plague, and that's the barbarians up north." Kaeso was busy sorting through and packing his few belongings. "We did a good job, putting out fires on the Euphrates, but now there's trouble along the Danube River—Langobardi and Obii invading Pannonia, gold mines in Dacia under attack, on and on. The generals up north have called for both emperors to lead us into battle. My comrades here in Rome say we should have set out long ago, but both emperors kept dragging their feet, Marcus because he thinks the city will need him until the plague abates, and Verus because—well, because Verus is having too good a time at his villa!"

"In the Senate they speak of logistical problems and shortages. There's a great deal of death and disorder in the legions, because of the plague."

"You'd think the gods would make soldiers immune from sickness, so as to grant them the chance for a nobler death in battle," said Kaeso quietly. He buckled the leather satchel he had been packing. "Well! I for one have had enough of the city. I shall be glad to get back to the real man's business of war."

Lucius raised an eyebrow.

"Intending no insult to you, Senator Pinarius," said Kaeso, with a feeble laugh. "It's just that I'm hoping . . . that I'll have the opportunity . . . to vindicate myself." He grimaced. "To shake the shame I've felt, every day since that slaughter in Seleucia."

Such talk made Lucius uneasy. Was his brother hoping to die in battle? Had Kaeso come to desire death, as Justin and the Christians desired it?

"If the danger is so very grave, brother, then perhaps . . . you should take this." Lucius reached into his tunic, pulled the necklace above his head, and held forth the fascinum.

Kaeso stared at the lump of gold for a moment, then shook his head. "No, you're the elder son, Lucius. Of course you must keep it, to give to little Gaius when he comes of age, and for him to give to his firstborn. Besides, I'll be in no greater danger than you will be here in Rome, surrounded by death on every side. I'd rather fall in battle than die of plague." He reached out to touch the fascinum and lowered his voice. "And if what I believe is true . . . that I unleashed this accursed plague, at Seleucia . . . then no power on earth—not even the fascinum of our ancestors—can protect me from whatever suffering I deserve."

The words sent a chill through Lucius. He closed his fist around the fascinum and uttered a silent prayer.

A.D. 169

"Who will bid on this rare treasure?" cried the auctioneer on the Rostra, holding up a pair of ornate goblets. "Made of solid silver, and decorated with splendid images of satyrs and maenads at their leisure. The emperor Marcus says he finds these vessels too precious to drink from, yet too exquisite to be melted down. You need have no such qualms, if today you make them yours. Who will bid?"

Lucius and Galen were some distance from the auction platform, strolling between the rows of open tents in the Forum of Trajan, where imperial treasures were on display, tended by imperial clerks and armed guards.

"What do you think?" asked Lucius.

"What a spectacle of excess and greed," muttered Galen.

"The imperial collections? Or the people bidding on them?"

"Both! I mean, really, what could this possibly be good for?" From a table displaying jewelry, under the baleful gaze of an armed guard, Galen picked up a ring made of silver clasping a huge lump of topaz. "The stone is as big a baby's fist. Much too large and cumbersome for the hand of a child or even a grown woman, and any man would look ridiculous showing off such a gaudy stone."

Lucius, who was almost certain he had seen the ring in question on one of Verus's fingers during a banquet at the villa, coughed and cleared his throat. Galen returned the ring to the table. The guard never blinked.

There were indeed many extravagant objects being auctioned—vases carved from murra, clothing made of silk, and jewels of rare size and perfection. Some were going for a steep price, but others were being snatched up at a bargain. There were also a great many common household items on offer, and these also were in great demand, simply because they came from the imperial household. As Lucius had noted of an ivory claw on an ebony stick, "I suppose the new owner can boast, 'Marcus Aurelius himself might have used this to scratch his back!'"

Galen was finally back in Rome. First he had gone to Aquileia, where Marcus and Verus were marshaling their forces in preparation for the march northward. But an outbreak of plague had so devastated the troops that the emperors suspended the military campaign and headed back to Rome. While the emperors hurried back, Galen and the surviving legions made the journey from Aquileia to Rome with excruciating slowness, their journey delayed by a great deal of suffering and death. Almost an entire legion had been lost, and not a battle had been fought. In the meantime, hordes of barbarians were crossing the Danube, meeting no resistance.

"A harrowing ordeal," Galen had called the journey from Aquileia to Rome, "the likes of which I hope never to experience again." His skills had been useless against the plague. When Galen finally reached Rome, he at once called on Lucius, and only then learned the terrible news: the emperor Verus was dead, the cause uncertain. "If only I had been present," Galen had told Lucius, "I'd at least have been able to diagnose him!"

Marcus had conducted an enormous public funeral for Verus, with every man in Rome wearing black, and every woman in white, as was the custom when an emperor died. Marcus was in a grim mood, not only bereft of the man who had been like a younger brother to him, but now facing the prospect of waging the impending war entirely on his own.

At Lucius's insistence, Galen was residing at the house of the Pinarii. Kaeso was also back in Rome. He had come to the auction with Lucius and Galen, but had wandered off on his own. Lucius searched the crowd and saw his brother some distance away, listlessly perusing a table of bronze lamps. Lucius went to join him.

"Do you see something you want, brother?"

Kaeso grunted. "What a depressing spectacle."

"But a necessary one. Or so Marcus thinks. He's desperate to raise money. It's this economic crisis brought on by the plague. The treasury was forced to debase the currency, and then—"

"You know I have no head for money matters, Lucius. That's for you senators to worry about."

"Not just senators. Soldiers have to be paid—"

"It's the debasing of the army that I worry about," said Kaeso, with sudden vehemence. "This plan to conscript gladiators into the legions is lunacy."

"But as Marcus says, better they spill blood fighting for Rome than fighting each other in the arena."

"And not just gladiators, but bandits, and convicts, and even slaves."

"There is precedent for such conscriptions—"

"Not since the wars against Carthage, hundreds of years ago."

"And is this war not as important, and the situation not as dire? The loss of manpower in the legions has to be made up somehow."

"And now I hear that Christians are allowed to serve, even if they refuse to burn incense to the gods before battle, along with the other soldiers. What sort of madness is that?"

Lucius sighed. "The implications were discussed at length in the Senate. One idea is to keep them in units to themselves, so as to avoid giving offense to the more pious soldiers, and also to prevent their atheism from contaminating the others, if that is the right word."

"How can they be soldiers if their man-god forbids them to kill?"

"If not suitable for fighting, they can at least do heavy labor—cutting trees, laying roads, building forts. That will allow the regular soldiers to save their strength for killing barbarians."

Kaeso shook his head. "The Christians are a bad lot. They'll disrupt discipline and lower morale. The drawbacks far outweigh any value they might bring to the war effort. What if the gods take offense, and turn their backs on Rome? Did you discuss that possibility in the Senate House?"

"I'll admit that allowing Christians into the military is an experiment—"

"A risky experiment, likely to go awry. Too risky, if you ask me. Not that the Senate ever listens to soldiers."

Lucius cleared his throat. "Speaking of the gods, on that table over there I saw two very small but very fine bronze statues, one of Antinous and another of Apollonius of Tyana—small enough to take with you on campaign. Shall I bid on them, Kaeso? I would be honored to make a gift of them to you."

"Don't bother," said Kaeso curtly. "I mostly worship Mithras nowadays, as do many of the soldiers."

"Oh? I see." Lucius had heard of this fervor of the troops for the god Mithras, whose cult was of neither Greek nor Roman origin, but from somewhere further east. Kaeso said nothing more about it. The worshippers of Mithras put great store in keeping secret their initiation ceremonies and rituals. That, he suspected, was part of Mithras's appeal to military men like Kaeso, who tended to regard themselves as aloof from the rest of the citizenry.

From the corner of his eye, he saw Galen walking swiftly toward them. The physician's expression was grim. Lucius sensed he was bringing bad news. A perceptible wave of dismay was spreading through the crowd.

"What's happened?" asked Lucius.

"Another of the emperor's sons has died."

Kaeso drew a sharp breath. "Commodus?"

"No, his younger brother, Annius. They say the boy had a tumor of some sort, and the physicians felt obliged to cut it out, and now the boy is dead. If only I had been there . . ."

It was curious, thought Lucius, that Galen had fled Rome rather than be called on to treat the imperial family, but now seemed confident that he could do better than the best of Marcus's physicians.

"Now Commodus is the only male heir remaining," said Kaeso. "That boy's life is priceless, invaluable—unlike any of this rubbish." He gestured dismissively to the glittering objects around them.

It was some months later, in the middle of the night, and with no explanation, that Galen was summoned to the imperial residence. The litter sent by the palace was large enough for two, and the messenger indicated that Lucius was to come, as well. Awakened from a sound sleep, Lucius threw on his toga, stumbled out the door and into the litter, and they were on their way.

"What do you think it could be?" asked Galen fretfully.

"I don't know," mumbled Lucius. "I asked the messenger, but he insists he has no further information. But, since the death of young Annius, I think Marcus has lost faith in his personal physicians."

"So this might be it," said Galen gravely. "A summons to actually treat one of the family."

"Perhaps. Or perhaps it's only one of his clerks or secretaries."

"In the middle of the night?"

"Yes, it does seem to be an emergency of some sort. Probably not the plague, as no one has yet found a treatment for that. And there seem to be fewer cases of late."

"Only because there are fewer people left in Rome to catch the damned plague!" said Galen. "Sweet Athena—what if it's Commodus? What if the boy is sick? Failure would be catastrophic. But if I succeed . . ." He shuddered. "Oh please, let it be injury, not illness! Injuries are at least straightforward."

Lucius tilted his head. "I can't believe my ears. You've just wished an injury on the emperor's heir."

"I did no such thing!"

Lucius laughed, and yawned, wishing he were back in his bed.

As it turned out, it was not Commodus who needed treatment, nor Faustina, nor any of the emperor's daughters. It was Marcus himself, as a grim-faced attendant informed them on the quick walk to the private quarters of the palace. By the flickering torchlight, Lucius saw Galen turn white. They were left alone for a moment while the courtier went ahead to announce them.

"By Hercules, the emperor himself!" whispered Lucius.

"Indeed." Galen's voice was flat.

"A successful outcome will make you one of the leading physicians in Rome."

"Yes. It would also mean that I'll have to go along with the emperor when he heads north again."

"And would that be a bad thing? Such a rare honor—"

"If you had seen the horrors I saw, on the march from Aquileia to Rome—and that was without a battle! I don't know how your brother does it."

"He's a remarkable soldier, to be sure. Just as you are a remarkable physician."

"Am I, really?"

"Of course. That's why you're here."

"But how did I get here? A few successful cures, some impressive demonstrations—which are hardly more than sleight of hand, mere tricks. Do I really know more than anyone else, about anything?"

"Galen, this sudden attack of modesty is unlike you."

The courtier returned and escorted them to a crowded chamber just off the imperial bedroom. The space was hung with costly fabrics and brightly lit. The murmur of men conferring in low voices fell silent as all turned to stare at the newcomers. Among those present Lucius recognized several prominent philosophers and senators, and also some of the wonder-workers who were currently vying for Marcus's favor. Lucius recognized the eminent astrologer Julianus the Chaldean with his long beard, and the shaven-headed Egyptian priest Harnouphis, who likewise was said to attain wisdom by studying the sky.

The attendant showed them through another door and into the adjoining room. This room, too, was crowded, but with men of a more menial sort, household servants and the emperor's personal slaves and freedmen. Marcus was sitting up in bed, looking very weak and pale. He allowed Lucius to take his hand, and then nodded toward Galen.

"We will talk later, dear friend. It's this one I want to see."

Lucius stepped back, but before Galen could take his place, Marcus urgently gestured to one of the slaves, who rushed forward with a silver vessel into which the emperor loudly and convulsively proceeded to vomit.

Lucius wrinkled his nose, but Galen, suddenly sure of himself, reached for the vessel after Marcus was done and set about inspecting the color and texture of the contents. Perhaps they yielded some clue, for Galen hummed and nodded shrewdly. He proceeded to query Marcus about the nature and duration of his symptoms, and what cures had so far been prescribed. He also took Marcus's pulse several times, and felt his forehead for fever. The interview went on for quite some time, mostly in voices too low for Lucius to follow, interrupted twice more by urgent calls for the silver vessel, followed by Galen's careful inspection.

At last Galen turned to some of the attendants and requested that they fetch certain herbs and other substances, including warm water and dried oats.

"Do you mind," said Marcus weakly, "if a few of my regular physicians come in to observe?"

"Of course not," said Galen with a smile. He seemed completely recovered from his attack of self-doubt.

Soon the ingredients arrived, along with the physicians, who looked on with varying degrees of skepticism as Galen set about concocting first a tonic for Marcus to drink, and then a material compounded of oats, herbs, water, and wine, which had the consistency of wet mortar.

"That is the poultice?" asked Marcus.

"Yes, Dominus."

"And it must be applied on the mouth of the stomach, you say?"

"Yes, Dominus. Three times a day, until you are completely recovered. I shall apply it myself."

"Very well. Help me, will you?" He gestured to a couple of the younger, stronger slaves.

While Lucius and everyone else in the room looked on, the emperor pulled up his bedclothes, baring his lower half, and rolled over to assume a position on his hands and knees on the bed. He lowered his head and raised his buttocks. The slaves, one on each side, pulled his buttocks apart, whereupon Galen proceeded to apply the poultice to that part of the body which Greek physicians called the mouth of the stomach, but which Lucius would have called the anus.

"It feels . . . rather . . . soothing," said Marcus, his voice muffled by pillows.

"Yes, Dominus, that will be the theriac beginning to work. Its effects can seem almost magical. It is rare and costly stuff. I wasn't sure the imperial pharmacy would have an adequate supply on hand, but as it turns out, they do. Still, I will want to ascertain exactly what formulation the chief pharmacist concocts, as recipes do vary, and I have my own ideas as to which formula is best for which ailment. Theriac was also in the tonic I had you drink."

"Was it?" said Marcus, his speech slightly slurred. "I've

heard of theriac, but I've never taken it before. Yes, I do feel something . . . a bit . . . magical, as you say . . ."

Finished with applying the poultice, Galen stepped back and looked at his work with satisfaction. Heads bobbed up and down as the physicians in the room appeared to register cautious approval. Lucius was about to speak up, to offer soothing words of encouragement to Marcus, but before he could open his mouth there came from the pillows a low, buzzing rumble, the kind of snoring that accompanies a deep sleep.

"The patient is resting quietly," Galen announced.

"What is this theriac? I don't think I've heard of it," said Lucius, on the litter ride home.

"Probably because it's frightfully expensive, and difficult to make. Or rather, finding all the ingredients can be difficult, for there are many of them, and some are hard to come by. From what I understand, it's been kept as a standard remedy in the stores of the imperial palace ever since the time of Nero, whose physician Andromachus devised his particular recipe, basing it on the remaining evidence for the lost 'universal antidote' against all poisons devised centuries ago by King Mithridates of Pontus."

"Ah, yes, this does sound familiar. Theriac is made from the cooked flesh of a snake, is it not?"

"Snake flesh is one ingredient, yes, boiled and then dried and powdered and cleansed of its poisonous properties, but there are many other ingredients. The theriac known in my native Pergamum is a bit different from the one here in Rome—it contains more cinnamon and less poppy juice. There are more than sixty other ingredients—"

"Sixty!"

"Each specially prepared and added in precise order and in exact proportions. The effectiveness of Roman theriac as an antidote to a number of poisons is well attested, as is its efficacy as a remedy for snakebite, spider bites, and scorpion stings."

"But Marcus is suffering from some disturbance of the bowels, not a spider bite."

"He also suffers from insomnia, which can exacerbate other conditions. Nero's physician called his particular recipe *galene*, 'tranquility.' It is known to have a soporific effect. I'm going to recommend that the emperor continue to take theriac for a while, at a dosage I shall prescribe. We can't have the ruler of the Roman world missing his rest."

"What if it works too well? What if he oversleeps? Marcus likes to be up at dawn, ready to get to work."

"If theriac makes him drowsy in the mornings, or clouds his mind, as it can do, I shall adjust the dose accordingly."

Called back to the palace some days later, Lucius and Galen found Marcus fully recovered, and full of praise for Galen and his treatment.

"The theriac has done wonders for my sleeplessness," he said. "I suffer from insomnia especially when traveling—one reason I resist doing so. As soon as possible I must head north to join the legions mustering along the Danube. I worry that I won't be able to sleep at all."

"Then I would advise Dominus to take the theriac daily, if necessary. It can only do you good. Why, I would take theriac myself every day, if I could afford it. The ingredients and the difficulty of preparation make it very costly, one reason the only substantial store of the medicine anywhere in the world is to be found here in the palace. But since it is here, surely Rome's emperor should avail himself of it."

"You must of course come with me when I head back to the front."

Galen's smile faded. He cleared his throat and looked askance. "Dominus, I must inform you that I have received a divine sign which indicates that I should *not* leave Rome."

"A sign?"

"Last night I had a very troubling dream. Early this morning I went to the Temple of Aesculapius to pray for the health of the emperor, and also to seek an interpretation of the dream. My special relationship with Aesculapius goes back to my youth, when he indicated to my father that I should become a physician. I have always sought for and followed his loving guidance. The god's priest saw in my dream a very clear sign that Aesculapius wishes for me to remain in Rome."

Marcus said nothing for a long moment. He looked steadily into Galen's eyes. Finally he nodded. "Ah, well, then, if that is what Aesculapius desires for you, I won't go against the god's wishes. Perhaps it's for the best. Commodus is still too young to come with me on campaign. Perhaps Aesculapius wants you in Rome because he foresees that my son will have need of you."

Lucius looked sidelong at Galen, whose face was a blank. His friend had in fact gone out very early that morning, and had mentioned to Lucius a visit to the Temple of Aesculapius, but had said nothing about a dream or an omen. Lucius knew that Galen wanted very much to stay in Rome, or at least not to go with Marcus to the front, and now he had his way. But the alternative was to look after the emperor's heir, with all the prestige—and terrible risk—entailed by such a grave responsibility. What was the old Etruscan adage? *Out of the pot and into the fire!*

Marcus thoughtfully tapped a finger against his lips. "But who will compound the theriac for me?"

"I can do that myself, Dominus, here in Rome, and send you fresh batches as needed," offered Galen. "It would be impractical to carry all sixty-odd ingredients from camp to camp. Better to make it here in Rome where fresh, potent stores of even the rarest and costliest ingredients, such as cinnamon, are regularly replenished in the imperial vaults."

"That makes a great deal of sense," said Marcus. "As physician to Commodus, you'll have full access to the imperial pharmacies, of course, and the authority to order whatever ingredients you need, and to compound and store whatever medicines you deem necessary, in the amounts you deem appropriate. And more importantly, Commodus will have you close at hand. Good! The welfare of Commodus has been much on my mind. Indeed, it was regarding Commodus that I wanted to see *you* today, Lucius."

"Me, Dominus? I'm no physician."

"Let us take a walk. Just you and I, old friend."

They left Galen in the reception room and strolled through an elegant garden decorated with statues of gods and emperors. "Do you remember," asked Marcus, "when you and I were boys, and Hadrian still lived?"

"Of course, Verissimus."

"What an extraordinary time! What extraordinary men! What minds! A great, glittering generation, perhaps the greatest generation that has ever lived on earth. But now, Hadrian and his generation are gone—hardly a one of them still lives. When you and I and our generation die, there will be no one living who actually knew them. Hadrian will be only a story, and then, in time, he will be only a name among other names in a list of the emperors who came before and after him, and eventually even that list of names will be forgotten. His generation has vanished, as all men vanish. We too will exist for a time, and then we will not exist, to be remembered for a while and then remembered no longer, utterly forgotten."

"What a thing to say, Verissimus! Especially with the war looming. What have those Chaldean astrologers been telling you? Or is Harnouphis the Egyptian putting such morbid thoughts in your head?"

"Don't blame that lot! They have only good predictions for the war. I'm optimistic. Eventually—inevitably, if the favor of the gods for Rome holds fast—all the bloodshed and horror that are about to be unleashed will end, and the empire will have a new province that stretches all the way to the frigid northern sea. The Roman province of Germania will be a bulwark against further invasions, and maybe even a new source of wealth for the empire. Who knows what gold and silver may be slumbering under the earth up there, as yet untapped by the primitive natives who've never seen a coin, who barter with horses and slaves and fur? But . . ."

"Yes, Verissimus?"

"I do worry for Commodus, especially with the plague resurgent. Yes, resurgent, I say, for I've just received a batch of reports from all over the empire, terrible news of yet another wave of illness and death, just when the plague finally seemed to be subsiding. I worry so much for Commodus that . . . I have a rather extraordinary request to make of you."

"Of me? What is it, Marcus? You know you have only to ask."

The emperor took a deep breath, and seemed unable to look Lucius in the eye, a most peculiar thing for Marcus, whose gaze was always so steady. "It has not escaped my notice that the entire household of the Pinarii, even many of your slaves, are seemingly immune to this plague."

"It's true, we have been spared when others have not." Lucius frowned, wondering where this might lead.

"And why is that? What makes your household different from all others? I can think of only one thing—that amulet you wear around your neck, your family's fascinum."

Lucius felt a sinking sensation. He said nothing.

"Do you remember, Lucius, long ago, when I myself researched the Pinarii and their amulet? I consulted the files kept by Claudius, who was a mediocre emperor but an outstanding antiquarian. His evidence indicated that the fascinum of the Pinarii may be the oldest known such amulet— perhaps even the original, and if that is so, a thing of great power. I think Claudius was right."

Marcus paused. Now it was Lucius who averted his gaze and remained silent.

"Lucius, I ask this favor not as your friend, but as your emperor. I speak to you not as my friend, but as a Roman. Will you allow Commodus to wear the amulet? All other talismans—all those charms prescribed by Alexander and his lot—have been shown to be worthless. I understand the sacrifice I ask of you—as a friend and a Roman, and as the patriarch of the Pinarii—but the stakes could not be higher. If the plague continues, if the war goes badly, if I die, the future of the empire itself will depend on the survival of Commodus."

No! Lucius wanted to shout. *Not that! Never that!* He took several deep breaths to steady himself. When he answered it seemed to him that someone else was speaking. "As a loan, you mean?"

"Of course. I know your family's tradition, that the fascinum is passed from father to son when the son comes of age. I would ask for Commodus to enjoy its protection only until that day, when your Gaius turns fifteen and puts on his manly toga, and the fascinum becomes his to wear."

"But . . . Gaius is only eight."

"Yes, the same age as Commodus."

Seven years! thought Lucius. *You ask too much!* But again he breathed deeply, calming himself. The coming war would demand sacrifices of everyone. Families would lose sons and fathers. People would go hungry. Some might even starve if the state of the economy grew worse. The Stoics believed that a virtuous man must recognize his duty and submit to it. Was this his duty? Marcus clearly thought so. But to give up his birthright to another man, even to Marcus—had any of his ancestors ever agreed to such a thing?

Appalled, he heard himself say, quietly and evenly, as if agreeing to some entirely reasonable request, "Very well, Verissimus, let it be as you ask. I give it to you freely. I only hope that it will be as beneficial to Commodus as it has been to me and my loved ones." He took hold of the thin chain, raised it over his head, and offered the fascinum to Marcus.

It was only as it left his grasp that he felt the full enormity of what he had done. He became lightheaded and a veil seemed to drop before his eyes.

It was some moments later that he came to his senses.

Marcus was smiling, looking years younger, and somehow Galen had rejoined them, and they were heading somewhere in the palace.

They passed a succession of armed guards, who all made obeisance to Marcus, but it was only when they arrived that Lucius realized where Marcus had led them.

Sunlight was scarce in the room, admitted by only a few narrow windows set high in the walls. Small torches were given to each of the three men by the doorkeeper who admitted them. The flickering flames were reflected countless times by objects large and small arrayed on shelves all around them. The torches were like small suns, and the points of light like stars amid the darkness, but more colorful than stars, reflected off items of gold and silver and jewels of every color imaginable.

This was the imperial treasure room, the chamber where the most cherished and valuable items owned by the emperor and his family were kept. Lucius had been in this room a handful of times, but only long ago when he and Marcus were boys.

Galen's face lit up and his eyes grew almost comically wide. "I thought the state had been obliged to sell the imperial treasures," he said. "But the items I saw being auctioned were mere trinkets compared to these."

"Some of the lesser imperial treasures were auctioned, yes," said Marcus, his voice low and almost reverent, as if they were in a temple. "The greatest treasures still reside in this room, objects of such value or veneration that they could never be sold for any price. The only one I know of that could possibly serve as collateral for the fascinum of the Pinarii is this." He handed his torch to Lucius, so that both his hands were free.

Lucius looked at the fascinum in Marcus's right hand, which looked small and crude and insignificant compared to the magnificently wrought objects all around, and then at the thing in Marcus's left hand. "What is it?" he asked.

It was a clear crystalline stone the size of a hazelnut, pointed at either end. When Marcus held it between his finger and thumb and raised it to the light, it shone with an almost unbearable intensity, as if it captured the gold and red firelight of the torches and then cast it back, magnified many times over.

"It is called a diamond," said Marcus. "This is the largest one known to exist."

"Where did such a stone come from?" asked Galen.

"Some say from India, though others say from a land beyond Egypt and Ethiopia. It is the hardest of all stones. The diamond can break any other stone, but no other stone can break it. It is the King of Stones. Thus Nerva named this specimen when he added it to the treasury. Since then, every emperor has presented it to his chosen successor. Nerva passed it to Trajan, Trajan to Hadrian, Hadrian to Antoninus Pius, and Antoninus Pius to me. So you see, Lucius, though not as old as your fascinum, it nonetheless possesses great value as an heirloom—but would be of no value whatsoever, a mere rock, if my son should die. Better, for now, that you have the King of Stones, Lucius, to hold in trust, while Commodus wears the fascinum."

Marcus held forth the diamond. Lucius took it. The stone felt very cold and heavy on the palm of his hand.

"All gemstones are said to possess certain powers," said Galen. "Some have curative properties. I wonder what power this magnificent stone possesses."

Not the power to avert the Evil Eye, thought Lucius, or else Marcus would not have seen so many of his sons and daughters die, one after another.

Lucius turned to see that Commodus was suddenly with them, in the treasure chamber. Marcus must have sent for him.

"Would you do it, Lucius?" asked Marcus. "It would be more proper that way, I think." He handed the fascinum on its thin chain to Lucius.

Still awkwardly clutching the diamond, Lucius did what was asked of him—by his friend and emperor, by duty, by fate. He placed the chain over Commodus's head. The talisman settled against the boy's tunic. Lucius stifled an impulse to snatch it back.

Commodus looked down and touched the fascinum with his fingertips. He flashed a crooked smile.

Marcus gave Lucius a kiss on each cheek, which Lucius returned. They had not exchanged such a kiss of friendship since they were boys. Then Lucius and Galen were shown out, while Marcus and Commodus and the fascinum remained in the treasure room. Lucius clutched the diamond in his fist, but it gave him no comfort.

A.D. 173

Young Commodus had just returned to Rome from a visit to the front.

The sight of the emperor's twelve-year-old son in their midst, an unusually good-looking boy quite at home on horseback, had bolstered the morale of the troops. The trip had also given Commodus a taste of life in the camp, and some experience of the battlefront, if not of actual combat. As important as these other reasons, the visit had provided some relief for the emperor's loneliness and homesickness. Marcus missed both Rome and Commodus very much.

Kaeso had been among the select officers who escorted Commodus back to Rome, and it was at his invitation that Lucius and young Gaius found themselves in the gardens of a small but very elegantly appointed gymnasium secluded deep within the palace. Lucius had been to the complex a few times, always at the invitation of the late Verus, who had personally overseen the decoration of the luxurious baths and the adjoining courts for exercise and leisure. Colorful marble columns and fine statues were everywhere one looked. Dazzling mosaics were everywhere underfoot. These baths were a sort of monument to Verus and his extravagant taste. Marcus would never have made such an expenditure, or seen the point of it.

The three Pinarii bathed, exercised, and stretched, then received massages from three very exotic-looking young males. Kaeso said they came from somewhere beyond the Indus River, from the lands never conquered by Alexander. How they had ended up in Rome was anyone's guess.

As the Pinarii relaxed in the garden, sipping a very good wine mixed with spring water (with Gaius's portion being the most dilute), Kaeso suddenly began to talk about his experiences at the front. Neither his brother nor his nephew had asked him to do so. He began spontaneously, and the words came quickly, as if they had welled up inside him and needed to come out.

Kaeso used many Germanic place names that meant nothing to Lucius, who consequently was never quite sure where any of the actions took place. In his mind, Kaeso's stories blurred together into a miasma of bloodshed and illness and deprivation. No wonder Galen had been so determined to wriggle out of his deployment!

Gaius seemed fascinated by his uncle's every word, but Lucius was only half-listening when a familiar name caught his attention.

"What was that you just said, about Harnouphis? Do you mean the Egyptian priest in Marcus's retinue?"

"Yes, the very same. It was Harnouphis who saved the day. Well, Mercury, actually, but it was Harnouphis who called on the god."

"I'm sorry, I still have water in my ears. What was this about?"

Kaeso looked exasperated and made no reply, but Gaius, who had been hanging on his uncle's every word, was happy to repeat the story.

"It's about the Rain Miracle, Papa. I've heard about it— well, everyone has, I imagine—but I had no idea *you* were actually there, Uncle Kaeso, and saw it with your own eyes."

"I was a witness," said Kaeso quietly.

Gaius eagerly continued. "The Roman soldiers had taken

refuge in an abandoned fort, and were hemmed in on every side by the enemy, who greatly outnumbered them. The fort had no water, and the soldiers had no way of getting any water—there was a river nearby, but the enemy held it—and the sky was blinding hot without a cloud in sight. The Romans grew weaker and weaker, until they were half-mad from thirst, and the Germans closed in, bringing up a tall siege tower on wheels. The soldiers manned the barricades, but they were almost certainly doomed."

"And *you* were among them, Kaeso?" said Lucius with a gasp.

Gaius laughed. "No, Uncle Kaeso was with the scouting party and saw the situation at the fort from a hilltop some distance away. And it was Uncle Kaeso who rode as fast as he could back to the emperor's camp, and told him what was happening. But all the legions were engaged elsewhere, and there were no men to spare who could go to the rescue of the surrounded Romans. So the emperor called on his advisors, both the military men and the sages and priests, and they were all useless, except Harnouphis the Egyptian, who seemed absolutely certain that he knew what to do."

"In such circumstances," said Kaeso, "it's often the man who seems most sure of himself who carries the day. Sometimes that can lead to disaster . . ."

"But not in this case," said Gaius. "Harnouphis set up an altar, and carried out a ritual—"

"And by no means a traditional Roman ritual," said Kaeso. "Except for the priest's Egyptian assistants, none of us present could understand a fraction of what was said and done."

"And then Harnouphis called upon—what did he call the god, Uncle Kaeso?"

"Thoth, who is the same, so Harnouphis says, as the Roman Mercury."

"So why not simply call on Mercury?" asked Lucius.

"I don't know," said Kaeso. "But whatever he did, and however he did it, Harnouphis obtained the intended result.

I rode as fast as I could back to the vantage point. What happened next took place very quickly."

"As you would expect, from winged-footed Mercury!" said Gaius.

Kaeso nodded. "Indeed. Mercury was the messenger, but only Jupiter could have caused such a storm. The cloudless sky was suddenly black. Clouds rolled over us, like a huge door closing over our heads, with a crash that unleashed thunderbolts that lit the sky and fell all around us, shaking the ground beneath our feet.

"A rain fell such as I had never seen before, a hard, drenching rain. The thirsty Romans trapped in the fort caught the rain in their shields and drank their fill. They told me afterward that no water ever tasted so sweet.

"And it came about that the same storm that saved the Romans destroyed the barbarians. Their wooden siege tower was right up against the wall, deploying a battering ram, when it was struck by lightning and set aflame like a torch. The rain did nothing to quench it. The barbarians inside were set afire. I saw them leap from the tower—at such a distance, they looked like cinders flying from a burning log. But I could hear their screams, even above the noise of the storm.

"All the other barbarians were terrified. They turned and fled back to the river. And then, in the blink of eye, the river became a raging torrent. The barbarians were swept away, sucked under the waves, drowned—hundreds, maybe thousands of them, dead in a matter of heartbeats. I never saw so many men die all at once."

"It served the bloodthirsty savages right!" said Gaius.

Kaeso shook his head. "No, nephew, you shouldn't speak of them that way. They are the enemy, most certainly, and barbarians, ignorant of Roman ways and Roman religion, but the great majority of them are no more bloodthirsty than we are. It's not a thirst for blood that drives them, but a need for land to pasture their herds and to raise crops and feed their families. Entire tribes of these people are on the move, not just warriors, but also old men, women, and children, pushed to desperation by other barbarians who've taken their land and driven them into ours. What they thirst for is a place to live. Unfortunately, that drives them into Roman territories that are already occupied."

"Your uncle is right," said Lucius. "Some of these people the Empire can accommodate—after negotiation, and an understanding of the terms—but too often they force their way in, and the only possible reaction from Rome is to strike back with all our might and regain control of our borders."

Kaeso nodded grimly. "But their numbers are so great, and their determination so fierce, the result has been warfare on a scale surpassing anything in Rome's history. The fighting is much bloodier than anything I experienced under Verus in the East, fighting the Parthians—gigantic battles, massive desolation, terrible suffering. I said they weren't bloodthirsty, but that's not entirely true. I have witnessed things, in the heat of battle, things so savage and cruel I could scarcely believe my eyes—and I'm no newcomer to bloodshed. Yes, the barbarians are sometimes savage and even bloodthirsty, but so are the Romans. I've seen atrocities committed by both sides. Things you'll never read about in those Greek novels you enjoy, Lucius, or even in histories. Things that are never discussed on the floor of the Senate House."

Taken aback, Lucius had no reply.

The uncomfortable silence was broken by the appearance of Commodus, along with the slave Cleander, his companion since his childhood. These two young men were roughly the same age as Gaius. In a letter delivered by Kaeso to Lucius, Marcus had proposed that Commodus and Gaius should become friends, as Marcus and Lucius had been paired by their elders when they reached the age to hunt and wrestle and race.

The three boys moved away from their elders to another part of the courtyard. Commodus turned to Gaius and gave him a long, hard look. "Father says we two must now be friends," he said. "What do you think, Cleander?"

"I suppose he'll do."

"Shall we wrestle, Pinarius?"

"If you wish," said Gaius.

"Let's all strip, then, the way the Greeks do it. Cleander, you can be gymnasiarch and referee us." Commodus quickly pulled off his tunic and loincloth and kicked off his sandals. Nestled in the cleft of his chest was the golden fascinum on its necklace. Gaius caught a glimpse of it and lowered his eyes. His father had explicitly told him not to mention the fascinum, and to take no notice if Commodus was wearing it.

Gaius was a bit awed by the other boys. Cleander was rather skinny and not much to look at, and a slave, but he exuded a worldly self-confidence far beyond his years, while Commodus was strikingly good-looking and had a strong, wiry physique.

Commodus easily won three matches in a row. Gaius had never met a boy so strong and agile.

They competed in a footrace, the length of the courtyard and back, which Commodus won by several strides.

He also beat Gaius at archery. Gaius thought himself fairly competent, having been taught to shoot by his uncle Kaeso, but Commodus's marksmanship bordered on the uncanny. He hit the center of the target every time.

While they rested, Gaius asked Commodus about his visit to the front. "My uncle was just telling some amazing stories."

"Oh, I have stories to tell. You've heard of the Rain Miracle?"

"Oh, yes! Uncle Kaeso—"

"You uncle may have observed from a distance, but I was actually nearer to the field of battle. So close, I could smell the barbarians. They exude a very particular stench, you know. Sort of like Cleander."

Cleander smirked and made a rude noise with his lips. Clearly, he was used to being the butt of his master's jokes.

"Uncle Kaeso says it was Harnouphis—"

"What, that simpering imbecile? Yes, I know he's taking the credit, but that story is as fake as his magic spells. It was I who brought about the Rain Miracle."

"You?"

"Yes. With a little help from *this*." He reached up to touch the fascinum glittering in the cleft of his sweat-glazed chest. Now that Commodus was inviting him to do so, Gaius took a closer look.

"I know what that is, of course," said Gaius cautiously.

"My father thinks it fends off plague, but I've found it useful for all sorts of things."

Was it the fascinum that gave Commodus such skill at wrestling, running, and archery? Gaius felt a twinge of jealousy, staring at the little lump of gold.

"When I realized the dire situation of those thirsty Romans trapped in that fort, I prayed to this talisman to save them. I'm certain that Hercules heard me, and he interceded with his father Jupiter to send the rain."

"Hercules?"

Commodus rolled his eyes. "I see I know more about this amulet than you do, never mind your family's claim to it! I do listen sometimes when my father speaks, and he says that this fascinum may be one of the oldest—perhaps *the* oldest—such talisman in all of human history, dating back to the very first Pinarii, who lived amid the Seven Hills before Rome became a city. And what are you Pinarii famous for?"

"We put up the first altar beside the Tiber," said Gaius.

"Yes, the Altar of *Hercules*. So there must be some link between your family's talisman and the god whom they were the first to worship, don't you think?"

"The fascinum embodies Fascinus," said Gaius, "a god even older than Hercules—"

"Yes, quite literally a penis with wings. Did you ever see such a thing?"

"No. But have you ever seen Hercules?"

"Only in glimpses, sometimes, when I look in a mirror." This seemed such an odd remark that Gaius wondered if Commodus had misspoken. He glanced at Cleander, who was standing slightly behind Commodus. The slave's expression gave no indication that anything unusual had been said. "Anyway, it was Hercules who heard my prayer for rain, and Hercules who answered it."

Gaius remained skeptical. "But you weren't actually present, were you? You weren't trapped with those soldiers in the fort. Surely your father would never have put you in such danger."

"I most certainly was there!" insisted Commodus.

Cleander, still behind Commodus and unseen by him, slowly shook his head and seemed hardly able to keep himself from laughing—a clear denial of what his master was saying. Gaius was confused. His father had told him that the emperor Marcus was the best and most honest of all the mortals on earth, so how could it be that Marcus's son would lie about something so important? And how could it be that a slave of the imperial household dared to contradict and even mock his master, doing so literally behind his back?

"But enough about the fascinum," said Commodus. "Did you bring the collateral, as I asked? Cleander, you did send my message to Gaius ahead of our meeting?"

Cleander stepped forward and nodded.

Gaius looked over his shoulder at his uncle and father, who were some distance away. "Yes, I brought it, but Father mustn't see. He's told me never to touch it." He walked to his clothing and reached into a hidden pouch, then returned to Commodus and held forth the diamond.

"Pretty," said Commodus, taking it in his left hand. "And heavy!"

"Are you left-handed?"

"Of course. Did you not see how I hold the bow? All the best archers shoot left-handed. All the best gladiators are left-handers, too."

"Gladiators?" Archery and wrestling were suitable pre-occupations for the highborn, but Gaius's father disdained any interest in gladiators, and so did the emperor Marcus. What could Commodus know about gladiators?

"Can it do magic?" asked Commodus, staring at the diamond.

On this subject, Gaius was actually quite knowledgeable, thanks to his father, who had taken an interest in the matter since becoming custodian of the King of Stones. "The diamond prevails over all poisons and renders them powerless," Gaius said. "It dispels attacks of madness, and drives groundless fears from the mind."

Commodus stared at the glittering stone, fascinated. "Yes, someday it shall be mine—my inheritance. But to wish for that would be to wish my father dead. I'll tell you a secret, Pinarius. That's the one and only thing I fear—my father's death. Of course I shall take his place someday—the Fates have seen to that, killing off all my older brothers. But not yet. I'm not ready!"

"Of course you're not," said Gaius with a laugh. "You're only twelve. Even Nero was sixteen before he succeeded Claudius. It will be years and years before you become emperor. Antoninus Pius lived to be seventy-five. Your father was forty before he became emperor."

"Yes, you're right. It's a long time away. Still, one day, this pretty thing *will* be mine!" Commodus held up the stone so that it captured dazzling pieces of sunlight. A bit reluctantly, he gave it back to Gaius. "I worked up a sweat! Shall we go inside and take a cold plunge, and then a hot one?"

Gaius had already had enough bathing that day, but his father had made it clear that he wanted Gaius to get along with Commodus, so he nodded and followed the two other boys. He would like to have squealed when he jumped into the cold pool, but neither of the others did so, so he stifled the impulse. After the cold plunge, the hot pool provided another shock, and though Commodus and Cleander quickly sat in the steaming water up to their necks, Gaius could not help but hiss and hesitate as he lowered the more delicate parts of his anatomy into the pool.

Commodus laughed. "Do you think it's hot, Pinarius? I don't. Tepid, I would say. Not nearly warm enough to resettle my humors after that cold plunge." He shook his head and frowned. "My humors feel all out of balance. I'm shivering!

What incompetents are running this place? You there!" he called to a nearby slave, who came running. "Bring me the bathkeeper in charge of the furnace. Fetch two of my bodyguards, as well."

"I don't know what you're complaining about," said Cleander. "The water's quite hot enough. I wouldn't want it to be any hotter."

Gaius was thinking the same thing, but he would never have dared to contradict Commodus as boldly as did Cleander. What sort of master was Commodus, to allow a slave to speak that way? There was a great deal he admired about Commodus, but there were other things about the boy that puzzled him.

The bathkeeper, a paunchy slave with soot on his face, soon arrived, followed by a pair of armed men. The two soldiers were part of Commodus's traveling retinue, comrades of Kaeso, who had introduced them to Gaius and his father when they first arrived at the palace.

"What do you think you're playing at, you old fool?" demanded Commodus. "Can you not see that we're freezing in this pool?"

"But Dominus, this is the hot pool," said the bathkeeper cautiously.

"Is it? Then why am I so cold? Don't just stand there, you idiot. Stick your hand into the water and test it!"

The bathkeeper dropped to one knee and reached into the pool. Before he could speak, Commodus lunged toward him and splashed him in the face. There was nothing playful about the gesture. Commodus looked furious. The bathkeeper instinctively skittered back, then went rigid, not sure what to do, but ready to be splashed again if that was what Commodus wanted.

Gaius looked at Cleander for some indication of how to react. The other boy kept his mouth shut and moved out of range, so Gaius did likewise.

"Guards!" shouted Commodus. "Take this useless slave and throw him into the furnace."

The two guards looked dumbfounded for a moment, then moved in unison to seize the sodden, sputtering bathkeeper by the arms and pull him to his feet.

"If he lacks enough fuel to stoke the furnace, then let his body fuel the fire instead. Do as I tell you, at once! In a few moments, I expect to smell roasting flesh!"

The bodyguards dutifully removed the bathkeeper, who began to wail and blubber but was too timid to resist.

Commodus stepped out of the pool. He clutched himself and shivered, even though steam rose from his glowing flesh. "Cleander, fetch a cloth—no, one of those sheepskins from the pile over there. Dry me off, at once! Rub me until I'm warm again!"

Cleander brought the sheepskin and wrapped it around Commodus, whose teeth were chattering. "And where are you off to, Pinarius?" he asked.

"I need to . . . to relieve myself."

"Then piss in the pool, like everyone else."

"No, I have to . . ."

"Whatever! Off with you, then. Cleander, wrap another sheepskin around me."

As Gaius left the chamber, he grabbed a sheepskin from the pile, then hurried after the two guards and the bathkeeper.

"Publius," he called, keeping his voice low. "Isn't that your name?"

The guard stopped and looked over his shoulder. "What do you want, young Pinarius?"

"You can't burn the man alive."

Both guards looked at Gaius, and then at each other. "We don't really have a choice," said Publius. "In the absence of his father, Commodus has full authority to—"

"Burn this, instead!" Gaius thrust the sheepskin at them. "It will smell like burning flesh, or close enough. Commodus is ill, can't you see? He needs a physician. He won't follow you all the way to the furnace room."

"And if he does?"

"I'll see that he doesn't."

The guards looked dubious.

"I know! I'll fetch my uncle Kaeso. He knows how to handle Commodus, doesn't he? And I'll have my father send for the physician."

The soldier looked at him shrewdly. "You take after your uncle, boy. Hard as nails, that one, but he has a soft spot, like you. Alright, then. We shall burn the sheepskin . . . and hope for the best."

"But there'll be no screaming," objected the other soldier.

"We'll say we throttled the slave first, and then burned his corpse." Publius smiled. "And *that* is why I am a rank above you." He tapped his skull. "Quick thinking! As for *you*," he said, releasing his grip on the weeping slave, "go very far away, very quickly, and do not come back."

As it turned out, the slave had only to hide for a short while, because Commodus became delirious with fever and later remembered nothing of the incident. The onset of such a fever, so quickly, was alarming to everyone, not least Galen, who was summoned to deal with the matter. The fever explained why Commodus had behaved so viciously, or so Galen said. Gaius was not convinced.

Whatever cure was prescribed by Galen, it must have worked, for Commodus was almost entirely recovered, if still a bit weak, within a few days. At the behest of his father, Gaius paid a visit to the patient, who remained bedridden at Galen's insistence. As always, Cleander was also present.

"I think I was hallucinating that day," said Commodus. "I'm almost certain that you had the head of a fish, Pinarius."

Cleander laughed, but Commodus seemed quite serious.

"It's a good thing Galen was here to look after you," said Gaius. "My father says he's the best physician in the world."

"Maybe," said Commodus. "But I don't think it was Galen who cured my fever. I think it was *this*." He reached into his tunic and pulled out the fascinum. "I've grown rather fond of it. I like it better than that diamond. What diamond ever cured an emperor's son, or caused anything like the Rain Miracle?"

Gaius looked at the shiny little nugget of gold for just an instant, and then looked elsewhere, and decided it would be best not to repeat to his father what Commodus had just said.

A.D. 180

At almost fifty-nine, Lucius was feeling his age on this chilly March day as he left a special meeting at the Senate House. His son awaited him in the vestibule. Lucius wore his senator's toga, and Gaius, now nineteen, wore the armor of an officer in the legions and sported a thin but neatly trimmed beard.

Lucius paused at the Altar of Victory to light a bit of incense. He looked up at the statue of Victory. Black wreaths hung from her shoulders. From the assembly chamber, the whispering of the senators was like the sighing of the sea, pierced by the sound of men openly weeping.

The grim news had arrived that day from Vindobona on the Danube River. Marcus Aurelius was dead.

By force of old habit, as he had done so often in times of anxiety or stress, Lucius reached up to touch the fascinum at his neck—but it was not there. Nor was Gaius wearing it, despite the fact that he had come of age some years ago. Commodus was still in possession of the Pinarii's amulet. Even after more than ten years, Lucius sometimes still found himself searching for it with his fingers, and finding only a void.

On the way home, walking through the Forum, they ran into Galen. Before anyone spoke a word, the looks they exchanged made it clear they had all heard the terrible news.

"Of course, I can't help but wonder," said Galen, "if I had been there, could I have saved him?"

Lucius tilted an eyebrow. How many times over the years had Galen said such a thing? If only Galen could be present everywhere at once, it seemed, no mortal would ever have to die.

"The messengers dispatched to the Senate say he grew very ill very suddenly and died the next day," said Lucius. "At least the Fates granted him a speedy death."

"As we were leaving the Senate House," said Gaius, "I overheard a couple of senators saying he might have been poisoned."

"They should keep their mouths shut!" snapped his father. "And so should you, young man. That kind of talk is dangerous. And completely unfounded."

"But inevitable," noted Galen. "There are always such rumors, when any rich and powerful man dies. But who in this case would have had a motive? Certainly not Commodus. The lad's barely nineteen and hardly champing at the bit to take his father's place—though now he must find the strength to do so."

"Let's hope he proves ready for the challenge," said Lucius. The thought made him uneasy. Again he reached for the fascinum that was not there.

"Oh, but I almost forgot!" said Galen. "The first copies of my new book are ready at the shop, on the Street of the Sandalmakers, and one of them is reserved for you, as always. Do you have time to go there with me? Of course you do! Come along and I shall inscribe a copy to you and your family, with all best wishes for perfect health—in which case you will never need to read the book."

In the years since his return to Rome, Galen had written and published a great many works. This important and time-consuming labor was one of the ways he justified himself when asked why he had never gone to war with the emperor, or followed Commodus when he went to serve under his father.

"No one can say I've wasted my time," he would say. "There's so much to recount, so many cases to discuss, so much scientific knowledge to record—and so much nonsense to debunk!"

His latest was titled *On Prognosis*, in which he looked back on his first arrival in Rome and recorded a number of his more memorable cases, including his treatment of both Marcus Aurelius and Commodus.

The proprietor of the bookshop gave Galen an effusive welcome and told him that requests for copies of the new work were flooding in.

"Is the demand greater than usual for one of Galen's works?" asked Lucius.

"Yes, indeed, Senator Pinarius. It's because the author mentions his dealings with the late Marcus, blessed be his memory, and with Commodus, blessed be his reign. Anything to do with the imperial family is always guaranteed to sell, and with today's awful news, people are hungry to read anything to do with the beloved Marcus. Any memory of him is precious, since there shall be no more."

Even a rather dry account of placing a poultice on the emperor's anus? The question popped into Lucius's head but he did not speak it aloud.

"Of course," the shop owner went on, "there has always been a great appetite among readers for anything about Marcus, ever since he was a young man, even before he was emperor. People adored him. But you know that already, Senator Pinarius, with your workshop turning out all those thousands of images of him, for people all over the city to put in some place of honor in their houses, no matter how humble or great. I sell such images here, as well." He gestured to a row of niches in the wall, each of which contained a little statue or bust, varying greatly in size and quality but all depicting Marcus at various stages of his life, from beardless boy to wise elder. "People worship him, if not as a god then as a demigod or a divine hero, a demon as the Greeks call them, like Hercules or Achilles, a savior to call upon in times of need or to lavish with gratitude when things go well. I'm sure some of these images must have come from the Pinarius workshop."

"Only the very best ones, I should imagine," said Galen with a smile.

What a good mood he was in, despite the day's terrible news, thought Lucius. Galen was this way every time he had a new treatise come out, a happy author with a new book to show the world. His prolific writings had made him famous, not just in Rome and his native Pergamum, but all over the empire, wherever books were sold and read. At home, Lucius had a bookcase in which every niche was filled with a scroll by Galen. To be sure, of all those many words, Lucius had read only a fraction. Galen's work tended to be bit too detailed and technical for his taste.

The bookseller handed Galen a scroll that had the crisp edges and inky smell of a brand-new book. As Galen handed it to Lucius, he read the expression on his face. "This one is quite different from my others, I promise you. Not dry at all. Full of name-dropping and gossip, just the sort of thing you'll love."

Lucius responded with a lopsided smile. As the bookseller could attest, he did have a taste for scandalous imperial biographies and romantic Greek novels.

When they returned home, Lucius and Gaius and the entire household put on black robes of mourning. Incense was burned before the images of Antinous and Apollonius of Tyana, and prayers said in memory of Marcus, beseeching the gods to give special help to Rome in the uncertain days ahead.

Lucius should have been recalling fond memories of Marcus, but instead he found himself able to think of only one thing: the absent fascinum.

In the year that both Commodus and Gaius turned fifteen and put on their manly togas, the fascinum should have been returned to the Pinarii. That was what Marcus had agreed to. That was what he had promised.

As the toga day of Gaius had approached, Lucius had greatly looked forward to the return of the fascinum so that he could hold it once again, if only briefly, before ceremoniously handing it over to his son. But when Lucius asked for the fascinum, Marcus refused to return it. He explained, in a lecturing, condescending way, that as the war raged on with no end in sight, and as Commodus assumed greater responsibilities, his son's safety was more vital than ever, even as the danger to him grew. Marcus had insisted that Commodus keep the fascinum, which had successfully protected him so far. It was for the good of Rome. It was a sacrifice the Pinarii must be willing to make.

Not long after his birthday, Commodus had been named consul—a bit hubristically some thought, as no Roman except Nero had ever been elevated to such a high office at such a young age. Then Commodus was given the title Augustus, essentially making him joint ruler, as Verus had been, and legally establishing him as Marcus's successor, despite his youth. Commodus was also soon married. To commemorate that event, coins were issued and lavish spectacles were staged.

As for Gaius, he was given a minor rank in the legions and assigned to accompany Commodus to the front, to be part of his entourage, a friend and companion of the Augustus. Marcus had told Lucius, "Your son will at least be *close* to the fascinum at all times, if that gives you comfort."

When an uprising by an upstart general required the emperor's response, not only Marcus and Commodus, but also Faustina and much of the imperial court made a months-long excursion to the eastern provinces. Kaeso remained with the troops containing the Germans, but Gaius accompanied Commodus, and returned with wide-eyed tales of exotic wonders. The upstart general was defeated and killed, but on the way back the imperial family suffered a terrible casualty: Faustina fell ill and died in Antioch. Marcus bore her passing with Stoic fortitude, but Commodus was distraught at the loss of his mother, especially in a strange city so far from home.

When the imperial court returned to Rome, a torrent of gossip about Faustina was unleashed, including alleged infidelities with everyone from sailors and shopkeepers to the late emperor Verus. The old story resurfaced that Faustina had bathed in a gladiator's blood to fend off an illicit lust, afterward making love to Marcus under a full moon and conceiving Commodus in the process. There was even a rumor that Marcus, discovering that Faustina had been in league with the upstart general, poisoned her. Lucius dismissed such wild rumors. Why was it so, when a famous person died, that so many people felt compelled to fabricate malicious lies?

Now, after a reign of nineteen years, Marcus was dead. Gaius had arrived with the advance party that rushed to Rome to bring the news. Commodus was heading back from Vindobona at a slower pace, accompanying the ashes of his father so that they could be interred in the mausoleum of Hadrian. Upon his arrival, Commodus would be hailed as sole emperor by the Senate. There had been no emperor so young since Nero, who ascended at an even younger age, sixteen. Even Caligula (whose birthday, the last day of August, Commodus happened to share) had been twenty-five—old enough, since the days of Augustus, for a man to be made a senator, but still too young, Lucius thought, for any man to be made sole ruler of the empire. Even so, having been raised by such a wise father, Commodus was sure to do a better job than Nero or Caligula.

And also, now that Commodus was to be emperor, surely he would hand over the fascinum to Gaius, its rightful owner, who had been such a loyal friend to him. Lucius imagined that Commodus would be eager to trade the tiny, much-worn amulet for the glittering diamond which for so many generations had marked by its bestowal the transmission of power from one emperor to the next, a sign of the abiding trust between each ruler and his chosen successor, an acknowledgment that the recipient was truly worthy of the honor. Now the King of Stones would mean everything to Commodus and the fascinum would mean nothing, thought Lucius. But when he mentioned this to Gaius, his son only nodded vaguely and said nothing.

The long period of mourning was over. The ashes of Marcus Aurelius had been properly interred. He had been deified by the Roman Senate, which established a cult and priesthood to honor him. It was proclaimed that his spirit had ascended to the heavens, where he now dwelt with the gods. He would now be called the Divine Marcus.

Despite what many senators and military officers believed— that Rome's latest victories over the Germanic tribes were so tenuous they could hardly be called victories—Commodus decided to commence his reign with the celebration of a triumph.

Lucius, along with his fellow senators, marched down the Sacred Way at the head of the procession, then took a seat in the viewing stands to watch the rest of the parade—the glittering booty of barbarian treasures, the wagons full of captured arms, chained captives representing all the many tribes that had been defeated, and then, at last, the conqueror himself, Commodus, driving the ancient ceremonial chariot that had been used by countless generals and emperors before him.

The handsome new emperor looked very relaxed as he held one arm aloft and nodded to either side, acknowledging the cheers of the crowd. He seemed neither intimidated by the occasion nor too impressed. Commodus was the first emperor to be born heir to the throne—"born in the purple" as it was called in countries that had kings and royal dynasties—and he seemed completely at ease, behaving as if he had been emperor all his life. Even seen at a distance, Commodus's appearance was impressive. His physique was youthful and muscular, like that of Apollo or Hermes, and his fair hair shimmered like a halo. For this occasion, in imitation of the late emperor Verus, Commodus had sprinkled his hair with gold dust that sparkled in the sunlight.

How comparatively nondescript Gaius looked, dressed in armor with his helmet under one arm and his shield on the other, following after the chariot in the imperial retinue. Lucius could remember when the young men were children and seemed not so very different from each other. The gods had shown great favor to Commodus.

Why, then, thought Lucius, did Commodus insist on keeping the fascinum as his personal talisman? Why did he need it any longer? Commodus was undoubtedly wearing it at that very moment, under his purple toga. This fact struck Lucius with painful irony, because he knew that beneath the triumphal chariot, unseen, there was a much larger golden phallus, an object of ancient veneration kept by the Vestal virgins and placed by them under the chariot each time it was used in a triumph. A man celebrating Rome's highest accolade was the object of every eye in the city, beloved and praised but also a target of envy and perhaps even spite. The Vestals' fascinum was specifically intended to ward off the Evil Eye as the conqueror rolled down the Sacred Way. With such a powerful talisman now protecting him, why must Commodus keep the heirloom of the Pinarii?

After the procession, which ended with sacrifices and ceremonies atop the Capitoline Hill at the Temple of Jupiter, the streets were filled with revelry and feasting. Accompanied by his entourage, Commodus took a leisurely stroll among his subjects, smiling and waving. At the sight of him, men shouted, "Ave Commodus! Long live Commodus!" Boys and girls screamed and jumped with excitement. Women swooned.

Later that day, as shadows lengthened, Lucius attended a private reception for the emperor held in a magnificently appointed room in Trajan's Forum. Marcus had preferred simple surroundings, but Commodus had a taste for luxury and ornament.

Among the hundred or so people present were Gaius, who had taken off his armor and put on his best tunic, and Cleander, who seemed never to leave Commodus's side. One of the new emperor's first acts had been to make Cleander a freedman and to grant him an official role in the court. Commodus, Cleander, and Gaius were conspicuously the youngest men in the room, which was filled with senators and magistrates.

A hush fell as Commodus stepped onto a dais and Cleander gestured for everyone to be silent.

Commodus seemed as relaxed in this prestigious company as he had been all day. "The era of constant, costly war, which has gone on for most of my lifetime, is over and done with. My triumph today marked the end of that age and the beginning of another. A philosopher-king and a warrior-king—my father was both, one by nature and the other by necessity. I intend to be neither. I will be my own man. Papa listened to advisers who insisted the Germans must be pacified once and for all and that a new province or two should then be established to contain them. With that as his goal, he fought on and on, year after year, battle after battle. But I tell you, more war in the north would only be a waste of men and treasure. It is time now to declare peace, and to enjoy the fruits of peace.

"My first order of business will be to decommission all those gladiators Papa drafted into the legions and put them back in the arena where they belong."

His audience responded with some quiet laughter and scattered nods of approval.

"Dear Papa! Do you remember how he used to behave in the imperial box at the Flavian Amphitheater, writing letters and conferring with clerks and completely ignoring the gladiators, because he found their combats so distasteful—and wanted us all to know it! And the rules he imposed, having gladiators fight with wooden swords. As if people should be happy to go home at the end of a long day at the arena and say, 'Oh, what terrible bruises those gladiators inflicted on each other!' Really, I don't think he understood the whole point of death in the arena—not just the thrill of bloodshed but the deep satisfaction such a death gives the audience. Poor Papa saw enough blood and gore and severed limbs fighting the

Germans, I suppose, but your average Roman, here in the city, is starved for such sights. Well, I shall give it to them!" He grinned. "To his credit, Papa did put on some impressive hunts in the arena. That time he had a hundred lions killed by archers all firing at once—I was only a boy of five at the time, but I never forgot that spectacle, and the awe that fell over the spectators. Well, I shall do better than that. I myself shall shoot a hundred lions—yes, all by myself."

Some in the crowd laughed nervously, and a few even dared to scoff. Lucius grimaced, for no emperor had ever, or could ever make such a public spectacle of himself, lowering his dignity to take part in the arena games for the amusement of the mob.

Commodus mistook the pained reactions of his listeners for skepticism. "You don't think I can do it? Ask Gaius Pinarius here how good an archer I am. He's been on many a hunt with me over the years, in the Roman countryside and up north as well. That's all those endless forests up there are good for, all the game. Once, on horseback, I shot a boar through the eye at a hundred paces. Isn't that so, Gaius?"

"Yes, Dominus. I counted the paces myself," said Gaius, looking acutely uncomfortable. Lucius could tell his son had drunk more wine than he was used to, and had not expected to be called on to speak in public.

"But I shall not neglect the honors due to my father," said Commodus. "The blood of a hundred gladiators would not please him—but I know what would." He turned his gaze on Lucius. "Many a time, Senator Pinarius, I heard my father praise the work of your father—I mean in particular the column your father helped to erect in honor of Trajan, only a few feet from this room. A long relief sculpture winds around it, from bottom to top, that shows in picture the whole story of the Dacian War. Trajan's statue stands atop the column and his sacred remains are interred in the base. 'A masterpiece like no other,' Papa called it. 'The greatest work of art ever produced in all the history of Rome.' He said those very words. I suppose that praise was just a bit backhanded, since he didn't include Greece along with Rome. Well, there's nothing here in Rome or anywhere else that can compare with the statue of Jupiter at Olympia, or the Athena of the Parthenon, is there? Made all of gold and ivory, those statues. Chryselephantine, they call that sort of sculpture. Perhaps I should have you make a chryselephantine statue of my father, as large as the statue of Olympian Jupiter."

Lucius winced. A gigantic, ostentatious statue was hardly the sort of monument that would be pleasing to the shade of Marcus Aurelius. Commodus continued to stare at him, awaiting a response. Lucius cleared his throat. "Only Nero ever dared to make a statue of himself on such a scale—I mean that statue of the Colossus by the amphitheater, which was changed to be a statue of Sol after Nero's death. Surely such precious materials, on such a scale, are suitable only for portraying the gods."

"Do you think so? Maybe you're right. A column—that's the thing! Come with me, Senator Pinarius. Let's take a look at Trajan's Column. You, too, Gaius. You shall put away your sword and take up a chisel again, like Cincinnatus going back to his plow. Cleander, come along as well."

They followed Commodus out of the room, to a staircase that took them to an upstairs gallery. Here, a terrace surrounded and provided a close view of the column, which was enclosed in a courtyard with ground-floor libraries on either side. Lucius had visited this viewing gallery many times to admire the magnificent work of his father and grandfather and their workshop. The meticulously painted spiral relief depicted every phase of the Dacian War, from beginning to end. Trajan's conquest of Dacia, especially his acquisition of the country's legendary gold mines, had marked a high point for the empire.

"You shall design and build a second column for me," said Commodus, "in honor of my father, to celebrate his triumph over the Germanic tribes. I have no interest in waging wars myself, but I don't mind celebrating the wars of my father. He was every bit as great a general as Trajan. Trajan had more rapport with his troops, I imagine—the common touch— but Papa made up for any lapse in leadership with a complete focus on whatever task lay before him. Unlike Trajan, he never allowed himself to be distracted by dancing boys! Or girls, for that matter. Dear Papa, what a dour fellow he was. But a great general—as the world must never forget. Imagine all the splendid scenes you can depict, captured upon a column for all time. You must include the Rain Miracle, of course. To picture that scene, you can use myself as an eyewitness."

Gaius fought an impulse to roll his eyes. He had learned long ago that Commodus was prone to exaggeration and outright invention. His participation in the Rain Miracle, by calling upon the fascinum and invoking Hercules, was a complete fantasy, but Commodus had repeated the story so often that he seemed actually to believe it. If anyone should be consulted an expert on the Rain Miracle, it was Uncle Kaeso, who knew all the details and had witnessed it with his own eyes.

Lucius was not thinking that far ahead; he was too taken aback at the very idea of creating a second column. Trajan's Column had already been done. Why copy it? The very idea was hubristic. He tried to think of some way to decline the commission without giving offense.

And yet . . .

Such a column—more than a hundred feet tall, with hundreds of images from the war, including of course the Rain Miracle—such a column would constitute the single greatest commission for the Pinarii since the giant quadriga atop Hadrian's tomb. It would be a huge engineering challenge, never mind that it had been done once before, and not without hazard—Lucius's father had often spoken of the near-catastrophe involving a building crane that collapsed and very nearly brought down Trajan's Column with it. Such a project would allow Lucius to create a great work of art to honor his childhood friend, the man he had been privileged to call Verissimus. And, if the Pinarii were properly remuner-ated, a commission on such a scale, executed over a number years, could also make the family not just rich, but very, very rich . . .

"Here, let's go up inside the column, to the very top," said Commodus.

Accompanied by Cleander, a secretary to take notes, and a pair of messenger boys, Lucius and Gaius followed Commodus down to the courtyard and then into the base of the column, with its shrine to Trajan and his wife, Plotina, and then up the dizzying spiral staircase, lit every so often by tall rectangular openings.

Lucius had been to the top of the column a number of times, but not for many years. The bird's-eye view of the city, open in all directions, took his breath away. Higher still, above their heads, loomed the gilded, larger-than-life statue of Trajan, forever gazing out on the magnificent Forum he had built with Roman blood and Dacian gold.

Commodus saw him peering upward. "Just such a statue must be made of my father, to put atop his column." Commodus returned his gaze to the city below, and to the roof of the distant Senate House. "And now that I think of it, there must be *another* gilded statue of my father, to place before the Senate House, perhaps posed thusly." He struck an exaggerated pose with upraised hands, like a flamboyant actor in Plautus's *Swaggering Soldier*. Never in his life would Marcus Aurelius have assumed such a ridiculous pose. Gaius actually laughed out loud, but immediately covered his mouth and coughed.

Holding the pose, Commodus called to the secretary. "You there, hand your stylus and tablet to Senator Pinarius, so that he can make a sketch for reference." The slave hurried to obey, and Lucius set about drawing, his teeth on edge.

"Quickly, just a sketch. Your emperor is far too busy to play artist's model. Done? Good. Another thing, that wonderful equestrian statue you made of Papa some years ago . . ."

"Yes?" The statue was one of Lucius's proudest achievements, the single most recognizable image of Marcus anywhere in the city.

"A masterpiece, to be sure, superb in every detail. But even that splendid work could use an improvement."

"Yes?" said Lucius uneasily. Marcus and even Verus, in his extravagant way, had been paragons of good taste who always respected Lucius's judgment, but Lucius was not at all sure what to expect from Commodus.

"That equestrian statue was made to celebrate one of Papa's triumphs, and yet, there's no indication of triumph in the statue itself."

"No? He rides a charger, he has his hand raised, as if to greet his loyal troops, his expression is that of a confidant but merciful conqueror—"

"Perhaps *too* merciful. Should there not be another figure in the piece?"

"Another figure?"

"Yes, a cowering barbarian trapped beneath the horse's upraised hoof. Domitian had a statue like that, and he hardly conquered anybody."

Lucius drew a sharp breath. He knew well the equestrian statue of Domitian, and in fact had used it as a model for the statue of Marcus, but Domitian's inclusion of a downtrodden foe had always struck him as superfluous and a bit vulgar. He had never considered including such a motif in the statue of Marcus, and Marcus had not requested such a motif. It would be impossible to add such a figure at this point, anyway, as he was quick to point out. "There's no room for such a figure. The space beneath the hoof is not large enough. To fit it in, the foe would have to be quite out of scale, practically a dwarf—"

Commodus clapped his hands and grinned. "All the better! The German foe shall be depicted as a sniveling dwarf beneath my giant father and his mighty steed! Cleander, you come from some mongrel barbarian stock, do you not? Perhaps you could model for the dwarf. Kneel down, hunch your back, bring your face to the floor and put on a cowering expression. Don't just stand there, do it!"

Lucius thought the emperor could not be serious, but Cleander, used to the whims of his master, adopted the humiliating pose without hesitation. He had been obliged to put up with much worse from Commodus over the years, and had learned to make the best of it.

"Yes, that's perfect!" said Commodus. He gave Cleander a playful kick on the buttocks, as if to drive home his satisfaction. "There, Senator Pinarius, sketch that!"

"There's no need, Caesar. I shall remember the pose. And if needed, I shall ask a slave, not a Roman citizen, to assume the posture."

Gaius drew a sharp breath, thinking his father had gone too far, but Commodus perceived no rebuke. "Alright, then, Cleander, back on your feet. But I'm sure you see, Senator Pinarius, that my idea will improve the statue, not just thematically, but aesthetically as well. It shall be both more impressive and more beautiful than before. My old tutor Onesicrates said that unforeseen 'accidents,' undesired and perhaps even detested by the artist, sometimes actually improve a work of art, and here is just such an example. Write that down, scribe. Today your emperor Commodus added more genius to a work already of genius, and all to honor the shade of his departed father."

He smiled at Lucius, oblivious of his discomfiture. "Thanks to me, Senator Pinarius, in future you will have many opportunities to put all those long-dead Greek sculptors in the shade. The great column, more statues of my father and of myself—and who knows what other assignments I'll have for you? My mind is always at work, you see, conceiving wonderful, beautiful, spectacular things."

Commodus gripped the railing and gazed out at the city, a joyful look on his face.

Suddenly, Lucius felt the perfect moment had arrived to offer Commodus the diamond. Lucius had carried it on his person all day, hoping for such an opportunity. He pulled it out and extended his arm. The jewel flashed in the sunlight.

"Dominus, I feel the moment has come when I should return to you the King of Stones. You are emperor now, and this is yours to hold in trust for your successor, as emperors have done since the time of Nerva."

Lucius looked past Commodus to Gaius, expecting to see a smile on his son's face, but instead Gaius looked appalled. That he was a better judge of Commodus than his father was demonstrated the next moment. Commodus took the diamond, frowned at it, and then tossed it away, as one might discard an apple core. The diamond plummeted over a hundred feet, landing with a sharp crack that echoed around the courtyard between the two libraries. Lucius clutched the rail and looked down to see that the diamond had actually cracked a paving stone.

For a long moment Lucius stared at Commodus with his mouth open. "You refuse it?"

"Of course not. That stone is mine and always has been, or at least since the day Papa made me Augustus and officially his heir." Commodus peered over the rail. Directly below, a librarian, hearing the noise, had emerged to inspect the cause. He spotted the diamond and picked it up, looked at it, and then gazed up in wonder, perhaps thinking the stone had fallen from the sky. At once, the man saw Commodus peering down at him. Even at such a distance, Lucius saw all color drain from the librarian's face.

"I did that simply to get your attention," said Commodus. "It seems to have worked. Now, Senator Pinarius, and you as well, Gaius, go down all those stairs, fetch that stone, bring it back to me, and then be on your way. You were thinking to trade it for *this,* weren't you?" He reached into his purple toga and pulled the fascinum into view. "Well, that shall never happen. This little amulet means a great deal to me. It's kept me safe through plague, battle, boar hunts, storms at sea— even an earthquake in Alexandria, when a wall fell on two slaves behind me, squashing them like bugs, while I was spared. The fascinum must continue to keep me safe now that I'm emperor, threatened from all sides by the scheming, lesser men. The Evil Eye of the envious is always trained on one such as I." He looked sidelong at Gaius, then smiled broadly. "Both of you, do as you are told. Go fetch the diamond, bring it back to me, and then be on your way." He turned his back on them and gazed out at the city.

As Lucius moved to obey, he heard the emperor muttering under his breath. What was he saying? He seemed to be turning his own name into the name of a city, and testing the sound. "Commodopolis . . . Commodiana? Commodiana . . . Commodopolis? Both sound pleasing, but which is better?"

Every downward step was galling. Father and son did not look at each other. The perplexed librarian, waiting at the foot of the statue, handed them the stone and then quickly vanished. It was perfectly intact, unharmed by the fall. Every upward step, taken in silence, was harder than the one before.

The glittering diamond, pressed into Commodus's hand, seemed to spark a kindred fire in his eyes. Now he possessed both diamond and fascinum, and the Pinarii had neither. This was surely not what Marcus had intended.

With one hand, Commodus had granted the Pinarii commissions that would last for years and bring them much income. But with the other hand, he had taken back the diamond, leaving Lucius empty-handed. This might have been a day for rejoicing. Instead, it had become one of the worst days Lucius could remember.

"Gaius," said Commodus, "you are dismissed from your various duties in my entourage, so that you may assist your father full-time. The two of you and your artisans have much work to do, if we are to turn this into a city worthy of my name."

A.D. 192

"I think I've finally figured out how the mind of Commodus works," said Gaius.

"Impossible," said his father. "I'm ancient—more than seventy years old, and thank the gods for granting me the longevity they gave to my father and his father as well ... though neither of them lived past seventy-one! But what was I saying?"

Gaius smiled. His elderly father's mind had a way of wandering. "That you are ancient."

"Ah, yes," said Lucius, remembering his point. "Nothing in all my seven decades has prepared me to comprehend the mind of our young emperor. Young, I say, but his youth is no excuse. He's the same age as you, Gaius. You're over thirty, and *you* put aside puerile frivolity long ago. You have your own son to raise now. But the mind of Commodus follows no plan. His ideas for ruling the state are completely incoherent, and thus beyond comprehending."

"Not exactly," said Gaius. "Certainly, he has no deep ideas or clear political program, but he *is* consistent, and I shall tell you how. In every situation, when a choice is required, I think he must ask himself: 'What would my father do?' And then ... he does the *opposite*. Marcus fought the Germans, again and again. Commodus, against the advice of all his father's generals and diplomats, is determined *never* to fight them. Marcus made a point of asking senators for their counsel. Commodus spurns and humiliates the senators at every opportunity. Marcus in his last speech in Rome, which turned out to be his farewell, proudly noted that he had not put a single senator to death, while Commodus . . . well, I've lost track of all the senators, and the imperial relatives, and all the others who've been executed on the emperor's orders. In trivial matters, it's the same. Marcus despised banquets, Commodus loves them. And remember what Marcus thought of gladiator shows? He made them fight with wooden swords, lest the loser bleed! Commodus demands bloodshed at every match. In private, he trains as a gladiator himself—oh, yes, Father, with my own eyes, on trips to the imperial residence, I've seen him outfitted as a secutor, with shield and sword and a golden helmet. I hear he's quite good as a gladiator, a match for anyone he trains with, which I can believe. Commodus was always a splendid athlete, strong wrestler, superb hunter. No one can draw a bow with greater strength, or throw a spear with more force, or shoot an arrow with truer aim. They say he's just as good with a trident as he is with a sword.

"So there you have it. Commodus makes himself in every possible way the exact *opposite* of his father. It's not a philosophy, but it *is* a kind of discipline. It keeps him consistent. You can't call him erratic or unpredictable. Just imagine what Marcus would do in a given circumstance—and then expect his son to do the opposite."

They were in their large new workshop on the Esquiline Hill. Their old studio on the Aventine had become too small to accommodate all their ongoing projects and to house the many artisans, both slave and free, whom they kept hard at work every day. Attached to the workshop was a sprawling new house where father and son lived in different wings. Selling their old family home on the Palatine had allowed them to buy a very large property on the Esquiline and rebuild it to accommodate all their needs. The new neighborhood lacked the quiet refinement of the Palatine—indeed, they were surrounded by considerable squalor—but they now had room to spare.

Lucius and Gaius were conversing in a relatively quiet corner of the workshop. The big room hummed with activity. There was the steady clanging of hammers striking chisels, as well as shouted orders, animated conversations, and the occasional burst of laughter. After a long winter, the days were at last growing longer, which provided more sunlight to work by. The lingering chill in the air was unnoticed by the more lowly slaves who were in constant motion, moving blocks of stone, fetching tools, or sweeping up wood shavings and marble dust.

Drawings and scale models of the spiral sculpture for the column were scattered all around. The engineering challenge of the column had proved even greater than Lucius anticipated. Apollodorus of Damascus, his maternal grandfather, had been the genius behind the erection of Trajan's Column, with the assistance of Lucius's father, but both of those men were long gone, and Lucius had been frequently stumped in his attempts to duplicate, let alone surpass, that structure.

Also slowing their progress was a severe recurrence of the plague, which had killed half of the artisans. His friend Galen had lost his entire household of slaves, even though Galen had carefully concocted and administered the only cure anywhere in the world that had been reported to work, a combination of cow's milk from Stabiae, earth from Armenia, and the urine of a young boy. All of Galen's slaves had been given the cure. All had died.

But at last the column was standing, surrounded by scaffolding, and the work of decorating it with the spiral relief depicting scenes of the war was progressing nicely. Looking at one section of the sculpture, Lucius wondered what Apollodorus and his father would have thought of it. Trajan's Column was made while the emperor it honored still lived, designed expressly to please him. It told a story from beginning to end:

the conquest of Dacia and its rich gold mines was Trajan's greatest achievement. But Marcus was no longer alive to critique depictions of his war, and the story told by the sculpture was not so clear-cut. Lucius had based the images on conversations with the officers who were at the battles, including his own brother, Kaeso, and he had tried to be true to their bloody, sometimes horrific accounts.

Kaeso was away from Rome, as he usually was. Now a grizzled veteran, he had risen in the ranks and commanded the legions in Britannia, where savage barbarians had dared to venture south of the great wall built by Hadrian. Commodus's desire to have no more wars had been thwarted by this breach in the empire's seemingly endless frontier.

The emperor's enthusiasm for the column had waxed and waned. Work on the vast project had frequently been sidelined by sudden demands from Commodus, who seemed to spend his days thinking of new statues he would like to see, mostly of himself. These had included one of Commodus as an archer with drawn bow, presumably in imitation of Ulysses when he slew the interlopers in his home, except that this archer was placed directly in front of the Senate House, aiming at the entrance. The message was not subtle. Lucius had not been aware of the planned placement until the very day the statue appeared in public. The first time he saw it, entering the Senate House, he had been mortified, and for days afterward had been unable to look his fellow senators in the eye.

The latest statue, just finished and still in the workshop, portrayed Commodus as Hercules with a club over his shoulder. It was not for public display, but destined for one of Commodus's private gardens, the Horti Lamiani on the Esquiline Hill. "There I can look at it from time to time," Commodus had said, "to remind me of who I am, and my true place in the world. The statue shall be my mirror, you might say." The emperor's identification with Hercules had become a sort of mania. At times, he seemed literally to believe that he *was* Hercules. At least the Pinarii had no need to embellish the statue's beauty so as to flatter its human model. Year by year, Commodus grew more handsome, and also more muscular, thanks to his rigorous regimen of athletic training. Many people said he was the handsomest man in the city.

"I'm not sure, son, that your analogy of opposites is entirely accurate," said Lucius. "Is Commodus mainly driven by a desire to undo his father's work, to make himself, perversely, into a sort of anti-Marcus? Surely there's more method than that behind his madness."

"I never said he was mad!" said Gaius with a nervous laugh. He and his father were already speaking more boldly than they should, even with their voices low and the constant hubbub of the workshop around them.

"His *seeming* madness, then, because however we define his behavior, it *does* have method," said Lucius. "It's precisely because Marcus waged constant war against the barbarian tribes that Commodus can now enjoy a respite of peace on the northern frontiers. And there's good reason for Commodus to be suspicious of others, even those closest to him. His father had a much easier time of it, from the outset. Marcus was much older when he became emperor than was Commodus, more established, more mature, more sure of himself. And Marcus was *not* surrounded by scheming siblings and conniving cousins! Poor Commodus was emperor barely a year when his sister Lucilla and her circle hatched that plot to kill him. They nearly succeeded."

"What a farce that was!" Gaius flashed a wry smile. "I'd say the would-be assassin behaved like a comic actor on a stage, but I've never heard dialogue that stiff in even the worst play." He mimicked the infamous moment when Lucilla's stepson (and lover), Claudius Pompeianus Quintianus, botched the whole plot by blurting out his intention too soon. He drew his dagger, rushed up to Commodus, and then, instead of striking at once, paused to announce his intentions: "Look! See what the Senate has sent to you!" The assassin was seized before he could deliver the blow. Lucilla had been exiled to Capri, and later killed.

Even more theatrical had been the attempt on the emperor's life by the ex-soldier Maturnus, a sort of Spartacus figure who incited a following of fellow ex-soldiers, bandits, and other desperate types to wreak havoc in the countryside. Maturnus and some of his henchmen entered the city during the Hilaria, when costumes and disguises were part of the festivities. Dressed as Praetorians, they attempted to infiltrate Commodus's private bodyguard and murder him. But they were easily apprehended, then publicly whipped and beheaded as part of the festival, lending a macabre air to the usually lighthearted Hilaria.

"Someday, someone will write a play about the emperor's narrow escapes," said Gaius. "But will it be a comedy—or a tragedy?"

"If we may return to my point, son: Marcus never put a senator to death, because Marcus never had *cause* to do so. No one can say the same about Commodus, whose life has been repeatedly threatened, virtually from the start of his reign, back when the two of you were hardly more than boys. It's no wonder he's so suspicious, and so often resorts to violence. And to add to his problems, this horrendous recurrence of the plague, just when we thought it was gone for good. Two thousand people are dying every day in the city. So Galen says, and he should know."

"And yet Commodus seems to be immune, and people have noticed," said Gaius. "He tells people that his secret is to withdraw every so often to his estates at Laurentum, so named for all the laurel trees. His physicians hypothesize that the lovely scent fills the nostrils and allows no ingress to whatever foul matter in the air causes the plague. As a result, you see desperately frightened people all over Rome dousing themselves with prophylactic perfumes, and filling their houses with choking clouds of incense, thinking a sweet smell will ward off the plague."

"At least the smell of perfume serves to cloak the stench of corpses," said Lucius grimly.

"Meanwhile, you and I know what *really* protects Commodus, or at least what he thinks protects him—the fascinum of the Pinarii. He never speaks of it to anyone, keeps it a secret, for fear an enemy might steal it and leave him defenseless."

Which means that he has no intention of ever returning it. Both thought it. Neither said it.

"And then, to follow plague, famine," said Lucius, as if to change the topic to something less distressing. It seemed to Lucius and many of his colleagues in the Senate that the food shortage had been a direct result of the plague, because it disrupted trade and agriculture, but a wicked rumor had spread among the populace to the effect that the famine was entirely manmade, due to the incompetence of Cleander, the right-hand man who was practically running the state while his master spent his days practicing archery or sword-fighting or racing chariots on his private track. Others said that the famine was deliberately manmade by conspirators in the imperial bureaucracy who wanted to get rid of Cleander. Rome had been torn by riots, with huge loss of life as soldiers were ordered to kill citizens—an atrocity that in all his years Lucius had never known to happen in the city. To stop the chaos, Commodus finally had Cleander put to death and then threw his corpse to the mob to be mutilated. A massive purge of the state bureaucracy followed. Many magistrates and senators had been put to death. Commodus became even more feared and hated by the Senate and even more secretive and withdrawn.

The Pinarii were among a handful of people who had regular contact with him, thanks to his ongoing demands and his oversight of their work. Lucius liked to think that he and Gaius were immune from the havoc Commodus had wreaked on others—accusing senators of conspiracy, stripping them of property, and exiling them to rocky islands or putting them to death. As long as Commodus was impressed by their work, and wanted more from them—and as long as they knew when to keep their mouths shut—Lucius and Gaius would be safe. So Lucius told himself.

The thing that would most help Commodus, he thought, would be to sire a son. That might put an end to the schemes of his rivals and nervous family members. But after more than ten years as emperor, Commodus remained childless.

Lucius looked about them, at models and drawings of the column, and sighed. How he would love to devote himself to the project full-time! But now Commodus had come up with yet another, quite literally colossal, diversion, his most audacious idea to date . . .

The foreman of the workshop appeared and cleared his throat to get their attention. "Dominus, I've assembled the men, the ones you want to go with you today."

"Very well," said Lucius. "Let's be off."

They left the workshop with a large entourage, all on foot, including Lucius, who at seventy-one was proud that he could get about as well as any other man. The party headed to the Flavian Amphitheater, where some of the Pinarii's other workers were already gathered at the feet of the Colossus, sketching, taking measurements, and assembling materials to erect massive scaffolding.

It was Nero who first erected the Colossus, in a courtyard of his Golden House, as an image of the sun god Sol, giving it Nero's face. At great effort and expense, Hadrian had enlisted a previous generation of the Pinarii to move the statue closer to the Flavian Amphitheater, in order to make way for his enormous Temple of Venus and Roma; it remained a statue of Sol, but the face had been remodeled so that it no longer looked like Nero. Now Commodus had ordered the whole gigantic statue to be refashioned so that it would no longer depict Sol, but Hercules.

The Pinarii stood at the base of the statue, staring upward. "When he says Hercules, we may presume he means himself, just as Nero expected his Sol to look like Nero," said Lucius. "So how in Hades are we to set about making this big fellow into Commodus-cum-Hercules?"

"Obviously, the golden sunbeams radiating from the head

will have to go," said Gaius. "A pity, as they're so striking when seen from a distance."

"But removing the gilding will hopefully supply the gold we will need for the new pieces," said his father.

"In place of sunbeams, we'll need to add a lion-headed cowl. Hercules's club could touch the ground—that would give the structure additional support. And if it's to resemble Commodus, it will need a beard, and a narrower nose than it has now. How soon does the emperor want the job done?"

"He's quite insistent that it must be ready to show in time for the Roman Games in September," said Lucius.

"It's going to require a great deal of gold and silver, and many hours of bronze-smelting, and enormous manpower." Gaius, who had taken over most of the practical management of the family business, seemed to be adding sums and filling out ledgers in his head. "The imperial finances are already strained, thanks to circumstances no one can blame on Commodus—war in Britannia, plague, famine. What will this cost?"

No sooner had they given instructions to the artisans and laborers for the work that needed to be done that day than a messenger arrived with a summons from the emperor. They followed the messenger, Gaius with a capsa full of rolled drawings and plans slung over his shoulder. They both expected to be taken to the Palatine palace, but instead they were conducted to a vast complex on the Caelian Hill, not far from the Flavian Amphitheater, where gladiators lived and trained.

A keeper unlocked a barred gate for them. They followed the messenger down a long corridor and emerged into a sunlit gallery that overlooked a large sandy court. Scores of gladiators were exercising or training with wooden swords that made a constant clacking noise.

"The smell of an arena—sweat and dust and sand baking under sunlight. Don't you love it?"

They turned to see that the messenger was gone and in his place was the smiling figure of Commodus. But this was not the Commodus-as-Hercules of the marble statue they had just finished, or the Commodus that Gaius had been sketching from memory as ideas for the reimagined Colossus. His beard was gone. So was most of the hair on his head. He was very casually dressed in a simple short tunic that showed off his brawny arms and his long, suntanned legs.

He saw them both staring at his cropped hair and reached up to run his fingers through it. "It's called a 'gladiator cut.' Very simple, very practical. It makes me feel more at home in this place." He stepped to the railing of the gallery and looked down at the sandy arena. "I could stand here and watch them train all day," he said. "I know the name of every man down there, how many times he's fought and with whom—and how many kills he has to his credit. I can spend hours setting up imaginary matches, moving those fellows about in my mind like tokens on an Egyptian game board. Well—if we stand out here I'll only be distracted, so let's go inside."

On the opposite side of the gallery was a row of cubicles. Commodus showed them into one of the small, dusty rooms equipped with a few pieces of rustic furniture.

"Is this how they live, the imperial gladiators?" asked Gaius. "How many in a room? I see only one cot for sleeping."

"That's because I'm the sole occupant."

"This is . . . *your* room?" asked Lucius.

"Why not? I need somewhere to rest when I'm tired from training. I sleep better in this room than anywhere else. Over on the Palatine, the magistrates and clerks are constantly after me to approve of this or that expenditure, or I have to dress up and put on a show for visiting dignitaries. Here, I can relax and be myself. The keeper at the gate knows not to allow any of those nattering bureaucrats inside. And if some insistent clerk should dare to slip into my sanctum, I'll throw him into the arena and let the gladiators kill him for sport."

Gaius and Lucius sat on a crude bench. Commodus stripped off his tunic, which was drenched with sweat. Wearing only a loincloth, Commodus displayed the body of a well-muscled athlete in his prime, the sort of physique that sculptors searched for when making a statue of Mars or Apollo, or of Hercules in his youth. He tossed his tunic onto a small table, atop a wooden sword.

"Have you been . . . training? With the others?" asked Lucius.

"What else? An hour or two of hard exercise down in that arena, and all is well with the world. But I need to find better gladiators, or better trainers. I'm twice as fast as any man down there, and as strong as the strongest. And much smarter, which goes without saying. None of them can pose enough of a challenge for me."

Nestled between his hairy pectorals glimmered the golden fascinum. Commodus saw that Lucius was looking at it, even as Gaius was trying not to do so. Commodus touched it. "It's kept me safe through years of plague and from countless assassins. Now it's my amulet for good luck when I'm in the arena. That's why I've never lost!"

"Surely the emperor's skill is the reason for his victories," said Lucius, dismayed that Commodus had found yet another reason to keep the fascinum.

"Even the best gladiator needs a bit of luck from time to time," said Commodus. "But I see that capsa you've brought. Have you something for me to look at?"

Gaius produced the preliminary drawings and plans for the transformation of the Colossus. Commodus sat on the cot and pored over them.

"These are not bad, not bad at all. But as you can see, the statue must now have short hair, and it should remain clean-shaven, like myself."

Lucius thought of the newly completed Commodus-as-Hercules statue back in the workshop. Would Commodus want that to be redone, as well? The emperor mistook the pained look on his face for one of disdain for the surroundings, and laughed.

"Not every man feels at home around so much sand and sweat. But don't think I've abandoned the life of the mind.

People say I don't like books. Not true! I just don't like *boring* books. I'm a more avid reader nowadays than ever before. In fact, I have quite a nice little library here in my gladiator's cubby."

He reached into a basket and produced a scroll with ornately carved and gilded handles.

"That must be quite a book, to justify such an elegant scroll," said Gaius.

"Oh, it is. This is a copy of my father's private war journal, a daybook where he recorded his thoughts while he was stuck in darkest Pannonia. *Marcus Aurelius, to Himself,* I call it."

"I had no idea such a work existed," said Lucius, feeling a poignant thrill at being near such a venerable relic.

"Papa had a remarkable mind, that's for sure. In a lifetime of consorting with philosophers, he never met a man more brilliant than himself. This book is philosophy, of a sort, but *not* boring, at least not to me. Reading it, I sometimes get the uncanny feeling he's in the room with me, looking over my shoulder. But it's not cheerful reading, I can tell you that. Here, listen to this: 'Consider the court of Augustus—wife, daughter, descendants, ancestors, friends, physicians, and sacrificing priests—the whole court is dead. Then think of the death not of a single man but of a whole family, like that of Pompey, and the words engraved on their tombs: "The Last of His Line." Think of all the pains taken by their predecessors to leave an heir, and yet, in the end, someone must be the last—and another whole race of men is made extinct.' Just a bit morbid, eh? What a glum fellow Papa was! But I've turned out rather differently, don't you think? The exact opposite of Papa, some say."

"Do they?" said Gaius, casting a sidelong glance at his father.

"Might I borrow it?" asked Lucius, awestruck at the idea that Marcus had recorded his innermost thoughts.

"You may keep it," said Commodus, handing him the scroll. "That copy is my gift to you. I had a number of copies made, mostly for family members. Some of them think I don't appreciate my father, but that's not true. The column with the statue of Papa on top will demonstrate to the whole world my reverence for him."

He leaned toward them and lowered his voice, as if confiding a secret. "But, to be perfectly frank, when it comes to books, I prefer *The Golden Ass*."

"The version by Apuleius?" asked Gaius.

"That's the one! Most novels are so boring, nothing but far-fetched love stories and totally fabricated travelogues, but this one, by this Apuleius fellow, is sheer delight! You almost believe he really *was* turned into an ass and then back again! I wish my tutors had given me books like that when I was a boy, instead of the scribblings of all those long-winded Sophists! But the writer I most admire is Lucian of Samosata, the satirist. Do you know him?"

"Actually I met him once, briefly, here in Rome," said Lucius. "Galen introduced us."

"Really? Well, I envy you that, Senator Pinarius. I just read Lucian's diatribe against Peregrinus the Cynic, the one who burned himself to a crisp in front of the crowd at Olympia. The book is hilarious! Lucian is merciless. Have you read his exposé of that charlatan, Alexander? Scathing. It does make you wonder a bit about Papa's judgment, his habit of turning for advice to sages and mages and priests like Harnouphis. In his piece on Alexander, Lucian writes about the time Germans were spotted across the Danube, and for some reason Papa sought the advice of Alexander, who declared that two lions must be driven across the river, whereupon the sight of them would terrify the Germans into disbanding."

"Lions?" said Gaius dubiously.

"Well, wouldn't you know, there happened to be a pair of lions at Carnuntum, or Aquincum, or some place with an arena for gladiator shows, and Papa saw to it that the beasts were carted up and brought to the riverbank, then floated on a barge halfway across, then forced into the water. The soldiers on the barge threw stones to drive the poor creatures to the far bank. The lions were in a foul mood when they stepped onto German territory, roaring and growling, and quite ready to eat any man they saw. But the Germans didn't run away in terror. They'd never seen a lion, you see, and thought they were just some sort of shaggy dog. They took up clubs and went for the lions. The beasts fought back, and some Germans were indeed killed, but by then there was no turning back, and the Germans didn't stop until they'd beaten the poor lions to death. Then they skinned them, ate the flesh to acquire their ferocity, and made the hides into trophies. What a fiasco! And all because people like Papa could never see what a complete fraud Alexander was."

This sort of talk made Lucius acutely uncomfortable, and he would have liked to change the subject, but Commodus was not finished.

"Then again, perhaps you can't blame Papa. Diplomacy never worked with those barbarians. Lying backstabbers, every one of them. The Romans were at a low ebb, short of men, and Papa was at his wit's end, ready to try anything to avoid open warfare. Oracles and sacrifices and wonder-workers served him well on other occasions. He always thought it was Harnouphis who pulled off the Rain Miracle using Egyptian magic, when of course we know it was actually *this*." He fondled the fascinum. "I can't wait to see your depiction of the Rain Miracle on the column. And of course you must *not* depict the slaughter of those two lions by the Germans, though it might make for a striking image. What a waste of lions!"

"I don't think Papa ever read Lucian; not dull enough for his taste. It's ironic, don't you think, that the two best writers of my lifetime should have been my father . . . and Lucian. Yet two men could hardly be more different. Imagine if the two of them had met! Where is Lucian these days? You, scribe!" A slave, posted outside the doorway, quickly appeared. "Take a note: I believe that Lucian of Samosata, the satirist, resided for quite some time in Athens, where he was able to support himself by his writings alone, no mean feat. Is he still alive? If so, let's see if he might accept a sinecure. Well, of course he will. No one ever turns down an imperial posting that pays handsomely and requires no work. I'm sure we could find Lucian a cushy and lucrative imperial appointment in whatever city he might desire. Alexandria, perhaps? They could use more of his sort. Alexandria must have the largest population of charlatans and false prophets in the world, just waiting for a fellow like Lucian to make mincemeat of them. But here I am, doing all the talking. *Have* you read Lucian, Senator Pinarius?"

Lucius answered slowly. "I have."

"You have no comment?"

"To be sure, Dominus, I am . . . less enthusiastic about Lucian's work than you are."

Gaius gently elbowed his father. "You must admit he's awfully funny."

"And sometimes . . . impious, I would say. After I read the piece in which he scoffs at the divinity of Antinous, I put down the scroll and never picked it up again."

"Where does Lucian do that?"

"*Assembly of the Gods.* Oh, he doesn't refer to Hadrian and Antinous by name, he talks of Jupiter and Ganymede, but his meaning is clear. Frankly, I had rather read Galen. Heaven knows, there's so much of him to read, on such a wide array of topics, not just medicine but also philosophy, and the language of the Athenian theater, and—"

"Galen?" Commodus made a rude noise. "Please! It's enough that I must submit to his finger down my throat or up my rectum every now and again. Don't ask me to wade through one of his endless treatises! I'd sooner swallow a dose of that foul medicine he had Papa taking every day. Theriac! Poor Papa said it steadied his nerves and helped him sleep at night. If I want to doze off, I don't swallow viper's guts, I just drink more wine. Surely by now Galen has written enough treatises. What might we do to keep him busy and stop him from writing more? I could send him off to Britannia to patch up the soldiers. Scribe, take a note—"

Lucius groaned on his friend's behalf. The last thing Galen desired or deserved was to be sent to a war-torn backwater.

"Perhaps . . . instead . . . it would be better to put Galen to work looking after the imperial gladiators. Who better than Galen to keep them at the peak of health and fitness? In his younger days he was a physician to gladiators in his native Pergamum."

Commodus tapped his beardless chin. "Yes! Why did I never think of that? There are physicians on staff here, but none of Galen's caliber. As he began his career, so might he end it. Perhaps, after one of these fellows dies in the arena, I might allow Galen to dissect the body. You know he would love the chance to slice up a human body, instead of yet another pig or a monkey."

"*Human* dissection?" The idea was so appalling, so against all standards of decency, that Lucius could hardly believe what he was hearing.

"Why not?" Commodus lowered his voice. "Once, during the war—I tell you this in strictest confidence—some of his physicians talked Papa into letting them dissect a dead German. It's true! Big fellow, thick-skinned and hairy as a boar, covered with a wiry red pelt. Killed with an arrow through the head, so the body was perfectly intact. No one was allowed to watch, except Papa. And me—after I begged him to let me watch. Once they cut open the body, the physicians squabbled so much about which organ was which, and what belonged where, Papa became disgusted and told them the procedure was pointless, and he never let them do anything like it again."

Commodus abruptly sat forward. "Or—why wait until one of them dies? Can you imagine old Galen's excitement if I allowed him to *vivisect* a gladiator? Strap the big fellow down and then let Galen have at him with his scalpels and hooks and pincers and chisels? Now *that* would be a spectacle to behold! You know those tricks he does, making a pig squeal and then making it silent and then making it squeal again, simply by pressing on a nerve? Imagine a demonstration like that—but with a human. Could it be staged in the arena, do you think, for an audience? Ha! Perhaps I should offer Galen a senator to vivisect, instead of some poor gladiator. Yes, that's a lovely idea . . ."

Lucius felt his mouth go dry. He stared at the emperor, unable to tell whether he was serious or not.

"Listen to me ramble!" said Commodus. "All this book talk. It's because I can't discuss such things with that lot." He nodded toward the arena to show that he meant the gladiators. Lucius realized that the clacking din from the arena had stopped. He thought he heard the neighing of a horse. "Hardly any of them can read. Some don't even speak Latin. With them, the level of discourse never rises above 'Helena with the huge breasts,' or 'Chrestos with the tight bum.' Mention the word 'philosophy' and they only scowl. But they *are* religious. They never fail to join me when I offer incense at the altar of Hercules. Good men. Pious men. Not a Christian atheist among them." Commodus looked thoughtful, then grinned. "But I brought you here for a reason. I have something to show you, something really quite special."

He abruptly rose and left the cubicle, not bothering to put on any clothes besides his loincloth. Lucius and Gaius followed him down a flight of stairs, then through an open gate and onto the sandy arena. The practice period was evidently over, for no gladiators were to be seen.

But the arena was not empty. While they had been talking with the emperor, a number of horse-drawn vehicles had been driven into the arena. The drivers were all dressed alike, in bright green tunics, and the teams of horses were superb creatures, every one of them tall and muscular and gleaming white in the sunshine. The vehicles themselves were quite unlike any that Lucius had ever seen before, beautifully designed and crafted and very ornately outfitted with sumptuous leather upholstery and gold-plated hardware.

"This is my private fleet of wagons and chariots and carriages. What do you think of them?" asked Commodus. "As an artist, I mean. I designed them myself. By which I mean I told the builders and engineers exactly what I wanted and how I wanted it done. See here, on this open-air carriage, how these bronze steps appear with a simple touch on this lever, and then with another touch, they retract out of sight. Ingenious, don't you think? No more of that nonsense of having a slave carry wooden steps, and having to call him to put the steps down, and then he never puts them in quite the right place, and you lose your footing, and it's all a tragedy, for the slave, anyway. Instead, pull the lever, and the steps fold out. Push the lever, and the steps retract."

"Ingenious!" said Gaius, with genuine enthusiasm. "But why is this here?" He referred to a stack of folded sailcloth at the back of the carriage.

"That, Pinarius, is the retractable top. In good weather, one prefers to ride in the carriage with the top down, to feel the breeze and to take in the scenery. But if there should be rain, or if the sunshine is too hot for the fair-skinned beauty with you, you have only to pull on this cord, and the top unfolds, rises up and over—you attach the cord securely here—and there you have it: the vehicle and its passengers are now nicely protected from the elements."

"That is *too* fine!" said Gaius. Hearing his son gush, Lucius wondered if a mania for fancy vehicles was a trait of the younger generation.

Commodus proceeded to show them one vehicle after another, all of them outfitted in unique and extraordinary ways, and clearly at great expense. There were adjustable awnings, seats that fully reclined ("For sleeping?" Lucius asked, at which Commodus and Gaius both laughed), and a device with gears attached to the axle that could calculate how many miles one had traveled, and, by further consultation of an hourglass, at what rate of speed.

Commodus insisted on taking them for a few turns around the arena in the most elaborate of the chariots, which had straps to hold all three of them in place and all sorts of leather compartments, though what a charioteer would need them for, Lucius could not imagine. The vehicle was designed not just for show but also for speed, as Commodus proceeded to demonstrate by driving the horses faster and faster. "See how it hews to the sand, even at speed?" shouted Commodus. "A lesser chariot would tip over and crash into the wall!"

When at last the ride was over, Lucius unstrapped himself and staggered from the chariot feeling not just queasy but profoundly disconcerted. Commodus was over thirty now, yet he seemed to care more about fancy carriages and fast chariots than about the state of the Roman frontiers or the sufferings of Rome's citizens. Lucius found the emperor's passion for gladiators and chariots to be in extremely bad taste, if not downright dangerous. All through his twenties, Commodus had grown increasingly withdrawn and suspicious of those around him, and now he seemed to have let go of all inhibition, losing himself in a frivolous regimen of athletic training, racing, hunting, and mock-combats.

Commodus saw his expression. "I used to see that very look on Papa's face. Cheer up, Senator Pinarius! So, Gaius, what do *you* think? Is this the chariot I should use to make my entrance at the Roman Games in September?"

Now Gaius frowned. "I hardly think a chariot would fit the private passageway that leads to the imperial box."

"Of course it wouldn't, you fool! I mean to enter directly into the arena, dressed as a charioteer and taking a few turns on the sand at top speed, for everyone to see. The people will love it!"

Lucius was appalled. "And the senators?"

"Who cares what those old farts think? If they scowl at me, I shall raise my sword and shake it at them, then watch them whimper and wet themselves like frightened slaves."

"Your . . . sword?"

"Of course I'll be carrying a sword, Senator Pinarius, since I am to fight in the Flavian Amphitheater."

"In . . . the arena? With . . . gladiators?"

"Of course. Why do you think I sleep and eat with these fellows, and train for hours every day? It's not for the sparkling conversation! Come the Roman Games, I intend to put on a performance the people of Rome will never forget."

"But, Dominus . . . in public? In the Flavian Amphitheater?"

"I shall demonstrate my prowess with the bow, as well." Commodus mimed pulling a bowstring with his left hand, holding the imaginary bow with his right. His shoulder and arms bulged with muscles. "I shall stand atop a raised platform in the center of the arena, and below me, wild beasts of every sort will be unleashed, one by one. Like Ulysses dispatching the suitors of Penelope, I shall shoot the creatures, one after another—scores of them, hundreds of them!—while the people look on and marvel. I shall allot myself one arrow for each kill. I shall need no more than that."

This will not end well, thought Lucius, but he kept his mouth shut. He looked at the fascinum nestled between Commodus's brawny pectorals. Of its protective power, he had no doubt; Commodus's survival was proof. But could the fascinum save Commodus from himself?

Lucius and Gaius were atop the column, inspecting the area where the massive new statue of the Divine Marcus was to be put into place using a giant hoist. The day was clear but blustery, with strong gusts of wind. They both happened to be clutching the guardrail to steady themselves when the earthquake struck.

At first, neither of them understood what was happening. They thought the sudden shaking was due to the wind. But not even the strongest wind could make the column shiver and tremble in such a way. Lucius let go of the rail with one hand and clutched his chest, searching for the fascinum that was not there.

The platform pitched and swayed beneath their feet like a ship on a stormy sea. The tremor seemed to last an eternity, and then was over.

The column still stood. It seemed undamaged. As their terror subsided, both felt a thrill of elation.

"The column stands!" said Lucius. "A good omen, don't you think? Sent to us by Neptune, maker of earthquakes?"

"Or simply an indication of your engineering skills, Father. Or both!"

Father and son laughed, more loudly than was called for. Both were a bit amazed that they were still alive.

It was Gaius, whose vision was sharper than his father's, who first spotted the plume of black smoke in the direction of the Forum. He pointed. His father squinted.

"It's very near the Temple of Pax," said Lucius quietly.

Even as they watched, the roof of the temple caught fire. Amid so much flame and smoke and at such a distance, it was hard to tell what was happening, but most certainly the Temple of Pax was engulfed in flames—and the wind seemed to be spreading more flames toward the Palatine Hill, with its jumble of temples and closely crowded imperial structures.

Between faraway buildings they caught glimpses of people fleeing, antlike at such a distance, and heard echoes of screaming, crackling flames, and falling bricks. Eventually they saw, heading toward the flames, the helmeted and uniformed vigiles, the brigade of firefighters founded by Augustus.

The vigiles went to work around the perimeter of the flames, bailing water, hoisting ladders, and firing a huge jet of water from a wagon with a water tank. Lucius and Gaius were spellbound. Eventually they dismissed the workers, then continued to watch the horrifying spectacle from their perch atop the column.

They heard a commotion directly below them, and gazed down to see the arrival of a very ornate vehicle, its gold-plated hardware gleaming in the sunlight. It could only have been one of those owned by Commodus. Marcus had banned the use of carriages within the city, but Commodus did the opposite, flaunting his use of the vehicle.

They saw the emperor step out of the carriage, using the

retractable steps he was so proud of. He glanced upward at them, then entered the base of the column.

He must have run up the spiral stairway, yet when he stepped onto the platform he was not at all out of breath. He rushed to the railing without saying a word. His staring eyes flashed red and yellow, reflecting the distant flames. His reaction was hard to make out. He seemed appalled, to be sure, but also thrilled.

"Has there ever been such a fire since Nero's day?" he whispered.

"Surely it won't spread as far as that," said Lucius. "The fire of Nero went on for days. Huge parts of the city were burned to ashes. As far as I can see, this fire has destroyed only a small part of the Forum, and some of the Palatine—"

"I shall have to rebuild the city, as Nero did," said Commodus, not listening.

With what money? Lucius wondered. The Temple of Pax and the heavily guarded treasury buildings adjoining it held a huge amount of both state and private wealth. Gold and silver might not burn like wood, but vessels valuable for their antiquity and workmanship would be destroyed, gems would shatter, and coins would melt.

"Or rather," Commodus said, "I shall build a new city and name it for myself, as Romulus did. Yes! You must make a new statue, Senator Pinarius. Of myself, in the guise of Romulus when he yoked the oxen and plowed the sacred furrow to mark the boundary of his city. What does a plowman wear, I wonder? Never mind, I should be depicted nude, I think. As naked as the unadorned hills of Rome before Romulus clothed them in brightly painted temples and gleaming palaces. And I shall name my new city . . . Commodiana!"

Lucius stifled a groan. Yet another statue of Commodus, yet another distraction! At least Commodus was not asking to be depicted as Nero. But to assume the guise of Romulus was almost as alarming, considering the way the founder ended— cut to pieces by senators who hid the remnants so well that no trace of him was ever found.

The fire raged for days, and was finally extinguished by a torrential rainstorm that caused landslides on the Seven Hills and flooded the Tiber.

In the middle of the Forum, at the charred, soggy ruins of the round Temple of Vesta, a crowd had gathered. Lucius and Gaius met Galen, who had only just arrived in the city that morning, returning from what had been planned as a long, restful retreat at one of his estates in the countryside. Galen appeared weary and haggard. *How old we both look!* thought Lucius.

When the Temple of Vesta burned, and its walls collapsed, the famous Palladium, the wooden image of Venus brought to Rome from Troy by Aeneas, had been exposed to view. Normally only the Vestals and the Pontifex Maximus ever saw it, kept as it was in the inner sanctum of the temple. Amazingly, the wooden image was unharmed. The eternal hearthfire at the temple's center was also exposed to view. Even the torrential rain had not extinguished it. Crowds had been gathering each day, finding places to stand amid the rubble, to gaze at these rare and remarkable sights. A cordon of Praetorian Guards kept people from getting too close.

As the three men watched, a procession arrived on foot, led by Commodus, dressed in the sacred robes of the Pontifex Maximus, followed by the Vestals. They filed past the Praetorians and mounted the temple steps. While Commodus stood before the eternal flame and the Vestals chanted, temple slaves carried the Palladium down the steps and loaded it onto a bier, covered it with a linen shroud, and carried it off, presumably for safekeeping until the temple could be rebuilt. The Vestals and Commodus followed after them. The crowd was awed by the solemnity of the ceremony.

"I must admit," said Galen, "Commodus makes a striking figure as Pontifex Maximus. So tall and handsome, with such a confident bearing."

Lucius made no comment.

The three men took a stroll through the ruined parts of the

city, past piles of blackened brick and charred timber, fallen columns, patches of impassable mud and pools of water choked with ashes. They came upon what remained of the Temple of Pax, which was unrecognizable amid the rubble and filth.

"I was away from Rome when it happened, planning to be gone for quite some time," said Galen quietly. "In my absence, to keep them safe from burglars, I stored my most precious possessions—including all my journals and notebooks, and my entire library—in the guarded storerooms at the Temple of Pax. I was told the building was fireproof because only the doors were made of wood. But when the doors burned, cinders must have been blown inside, and the contents caught fire. Then the roof collapsed. Everything was lost. All of it, completely and totally incinerated! I had been planning, on my return, to have a complete set of copies made of all my writings, to be sent to Pergamum, so there would be duplicates in cities far apart, to guard against exactly this kind of catastrophe. But too late!"

"But there are so many copies of so many of your books, in many cities," said Lucius.

"That's true of my more popular books, yes. But some of the burned volumes were the only copies I knew of. Lost now, forever! And my personal library has also been lost, which included recipe books for thousands of medicines. I spent a lifetime building that collection! And it wasn't just my library that was destroyed. Imperial collections on the Palatine also burned, libraries nearly as great as those in Alexandria and Pergamum. Those collections housed thousands of titles, including some that were very rare, even unique. Not long ago, browsing in a musty little room that smelled of mouse droppings, I came upon a work by Aristotle that I'd never heard of—I don't think anyone alive even knew it existed—a lovely little treatise about all the different colorations of living creatures. Yet there the scroll was, tucked behind some others on a dusty lower shelf, untouched and forgotten for decades, perhaps for centuries. If only I had thought to have a copy made! Now that book, too, may have been lost forever, for who can say if there was another copy in any other library in any city on earth? Books are so precious, and yet so fragile! All the library catalogues and lists were also burned, so we don't even know what was lost."

"It seems unthinkable that so much human knowledge can vanish overnight," said Gaius quietly.

"I'm surprised you can keep your wits at all, after such a loss," said Lucius. "The Divine Marcus would be proud of your equanimity."

Galen sighed. "Not everyone is so stoic. I was back in town less than an hour when I learned that a good friend of mine, the author of many a learned study of the ancient playwrights, committed suicide. He'd lost his entire life's work in the fire. He couldn't bear it! And now, to discover that this is all that's left of the Temple of Pax—this utter devastation! The place where we're standing was the center of intellectual debate in Rome, where all the best thinkers came to argue and show off and steal each other's ideas."

"I remember watching you conduct your famous experiment on the vocalization of pigs, on this very spot," said Lucius.

Galen managed a sad smile. "It would be hard to overestimate the total loss and the impact the fire will have on so many people in Rome, from this day forward." He shook his head, then gripped Lucius's arm. "Do you smell that?"

"What?"

"I smell it," said Gaius, sniffing the air. "It's very odd."

"Not just treasures of gold and silver were kept at the Temple of Pax," said Galen. "This was also the storehouse for the imperial supply of theriac, and many other precious substances, including a huge store of cinnamon. That must be what we're smelling now, the charred and sodden remains of all those herbs and distillates and rare concoctions. How strange it smells!"

"It's the loss of so much treasure that worries me," said Lucius. "The Senate meets to discuss the crisis tomorrow. Not just a huge store of wealth has vanished, but also ledgers and property deeds and records of loans, all completely destroyed—a boon to debtors, but utter ruin for lenders. We are almost certain to experience a financial panic."

"And yet, our emperor seems oblivious of the situation," said Gaius, lowering his voice, though no one else was near them. "He insists that he will rebuild 'Commodiana,' as he calls the city, on an even grander scale than before."

"And the lost libraries? How can they be rebuilt?" asked Galen.

"I've seen the list of structures that have priority," said Lucius, "and libraries are not among them. The building that Commodus cares about most is the Flavian Amphitheater, of course, and that was unscathed."

"Which means," said Gaius, lowering his voice even more, "that the emperor's debut as a gladiator at the Roman Games can proceed as planned."

The month of September had come. Lucius and Gaius stood once again atop the Column of Marcus. But they were not alone: the gigantic statue of Marcus Aurelius had only that morning been hoisted up and placed atop its pedestal, crowning the monument. Below them, winding up the column, every piece of the spiral frieze was now in place. The column was still surrounded by scaffolding, to allow the painters to do their job, painstakingly tinting and coloring every surface of the frieze.

Commodus had insisted that the column be ready for dedication by the end of the year, and the Pinarii and their workshop had made phenomenal progress over the summer, partly because the emperor had left them alone to work in peace, for Commodus himself had been obsessively training for hours every day, not only as a gladiator but also practicing with hunting weapons, having imported the finest Mauritanian spearmen and Parthian archers to be his instructors.

Gazing up at the larger-than-life image of Marcus, with his serene countenance, Lucius felt a stab of heartsickness. How he missed his old friend, Verissimus! Even with the ravages of plague and the often desperate war years, the reign of the Divine Marcus now seemed a golden age compared to twelve years of Commodus.

Despite the hatred he had sown among the senatorial class, Commodus was still quite popular with the common people, who actually seemed to admire his bottomless vanity and his eccentric behavior, however crass and inappropriate it seemed to men like Lucius. Born and raised in the most privileged and elite surroundings, Commodus had nothing whatsoever in common with the lowborn, yet they seemed to see in him themselves made large: he behaved just as they imagined *they* would behave, if they were rich and powerful and ruled the world.

Excitement about the Roman Games had been building for months. Commodus promised to present hundreds of creatures from the far ends of the earth, some never before seen in Rome. He himself, in the guise of Hercules, would take aim at these animals and slay them with arrows and spears. Causing even more excitement was the remarkable news that the emperor himself would engage in combat with the best gladiators from all over the empire. One could truly say, without exaggeration, that no such spectacle had ever been seen in Rome, or anywhere else. All of Italy was abuzz. People had traveled to Rome from the most distant provinces, and even from foreign lands. Commodus had already succeeded in one goal: to make himself the chief topic of conversation not just in Rome, but also across a great part of the world.

Lucius and Gaius descended the column. Lucius took the steps very slowly, feeling stiff in all his joints and slightly lightheaded, and very much a man in his seventies. In the workshop that had been built on the site, slaves helped them to hurriedly put on formal dress. Like his father, Gaius now wore a senator's toga. In his latest list of new men to replace those executed by the state, Commodus had made Gaius a senator.

With an entourage of bodyguards and attendants suitable for a pair of senators, they joined the crowd that was heading for the amphitheater. As senators, the Pinarii's attendance at the Games was mandatory.

Outside the amphitheater they met with Galen. He had grown to despise Commodus, and had no interest in the emperor's athletic pursuits, but he could not resist attending the Games so as to have a firsthand look at all the exotic animals to be hunted and slaughtered, while they were still alive and moving. Commodus had agreed to allow him to dissect any of the carcasses that interested him. It was an opportunity not to be missed.

Before they entered the amphitheater, all three men paused to gaze up at the towering Colossus, the statue that had once depicted Nero, then Sol, and now, thanks to the ingenious designs of the Pinarii, had been transformed into Hercules with the face of Commodus. This Hercules was left-handed, like Commodus, and thus held his club in his left hand. Enormous amounts of gold and silver had been required to gild the statue to the emperor's satisfaction. The result was so gaudy that Lucius was actually a bit embarrassed by it. What a contrast there was, between this overbearing Hercules and the serene statue of Marcus atop the column. And yet, from the surging crowd all around them, Lucius heard only exclamations of delight and admiration.

"Have you ever seen anything so glorious?"

"How huge it is!"

"Is the emperor really that handsome? Is he really so muscular?"

"And is his club *really* that big? It touches the ground!"

"How extraordinary, how beautiful! It's a wonder of the world! Only in Commodiana can one behold such marvels!"

Commodiana was now the official name of the city on every piece of legislation leaving the Senate. The crowd had come to use the word with a more specialized meaning, to refer to a certain state of mind, a way of looking at the world. Galen and the Pinarii still lived in Rome, one might say, but the thrill-seekers who craved the blood and gore of the arena and who gushingly admired what they called the emperor's style and panache were living in Commodiana.

Would the same crowd praise the Column of Marcus as effusively, once it was finished and ready to be dedicated? Lucius doubted it. A Stoic emperor atop a ribbon of grim war scenes could hardly compete for attention with mighty Hercules, the colossal emperor.

"Shall we go in?" said Lucius, with a feeling of dread.

The Roman Games lasted not one day, but several.

Lucius would later remember those days like a sort of fever dream, so bizarre yet so starkly real were they. The audience was first treated to a spectacle of comic mimes, tumbling acrobats, and trained animals, and then, with a swelling murmur of excitement, to the arrival of Commodus as he drove one of his absurdly ornate chariots onto the sand of the arena, wearing the scanty outfit and tight leather cap of a racer for the green faction. He rapidly gained speed, and at the end of a full circuit, jumped onto another moving chariot, changing places with its driver as neither team of horses slowed down. This daredevil stunt he performed not once but several times, to the delight of the spectators, each time showing off another vehicle from his collection. Women in the stands pretended to swoon or even to orgasm, and so did a number of men.

The final vehicle was an outrageously ornate carriage that Commodus drove quite slowly, so that all could feast their gaze upon it. It was not only gilded and set with gemstones, but had a canopy of dozens of polished silver mirrors set at all angles, so that they cast dancing reflections of sunlight all over the amphitheater, dazzling the spectators. Commodus himself could hardly be seen, so blinding was the light of the mirrors, brighter than any star, a rival to the sun itself.

When the carriage disappeared, a loud murmur filled the amphitheater and did not die down until some minutes later when Commodus and his lover Marcia appeared in the imperial box. The emperor had changed out of his racing gear. He and Marcia were identically dressed as Amazon warriors in loose, belted chitons that left one breast bare.

"Why an Amazon?" Gaius muttered under his breath.

"He's Hercules, don't you see?" Lucius answered. "Not *our* Hercules—not the hulking herdsman who killed the monster Cacus and saved the little village by the Tiber. This is Hercules when he was commanded by the Oracle at Delphi to serve Queen Omphale for a year, dressed as a woman. There are temples in the East where Hercules is worshipped in female dress. Commodus presents himself as the lover of Marcia, but also her fellow Amazon, an incarnation of the oracle-bound Hercules."

"Though he's not any sort of warrior at all," muttered Gaius. "But the crowd—do you see, Papa? They're laughing and cheering. They love it! Who could have predicted *that*?"

"Commodus," said Lucius.

With Commodus and Marcia presiding, more acrobats flooded into the arena, performing ever bolder and increasingly dangerous feats, climaxing with a tightrope that was stretched between the very highest tiers of the amphitheater, so that the walkers were high above the audience. No tightrope had ever been strung so high. Nor was there any net to catch the walkers if one should fall. Once again, Commodus was the opposite of his father, undoing with a vengeance one of the most humane of his father's innovations. The crowd screamed with excitement. They wailed and shrieked when one of the walkers staggered wildly on the rope. Some thought it was intentional, and laughed—until the man lost his balance and plummeted to the sand far below. The sound of impact was sickening. For a moment, shocked silence reigned. Then Commodus began to clap, as if to praise the dead man's showmanship, and the audience broke into wild applause.

"Bet you can't do it again!" shouted a wag in the crowd, which sent a ripple of laughter around the amphitheater. Commodus heard the jest and smiled.

"If that poor fellow had fallen just a few steps earlier," noted Lucius, "he would have landed right in the stands. People would have been killed."

"Don't let Commodus hear you say that, Papa, or he'll insist they work it into the act."

Just as Commodus had promised, one by one, hundreds of animals were released into the arena. Just as he had promised, standing with spears, a bow, and a quiver of arrows on a raised platform that projected from the imperial box, Commodus slew every one of them, not once missing the mark. Even the senators were in awe.

And, just as he had promised, Commodus himself took part in the gladiator contests in the arena. Until that day, the very idea of a Roman emperor setting foot on the sand had been unthinkable. The separation between the lofty personages in the gold and purple imperial box and the dusty arena below, populated by desperate mortals and doomed animals, was so vast as to be unbridgeable, until the moment when, with a blaring fanfare of horns, a series of metal steps suddenly unfolded from the imperial box and descended all the way to the sand of the arena. The retractable steps of Commodus's carriages had been adapted and expanded for use on a far grander stage.

Commodus reappeared in the imperial box, now dressed as Hercules in a genuine lion skin complete with the fanged head for a cowl, and, except for plates of armor strapped over his limbs and across his chest, wearing very little else. Attendants rushed to equip him with a sword and shield. A crier announced that the combats would not be to the death, but only until the first blood was drawn.

Surely the fights would be staged, at least to some degree, or so Lucius had presumed. Commodus would never endanger his dignity, much less his life, by subjecting himself to real danger. Or would he? The combats were very convincing. If Commodus could make himself into the world's strongest spear-thrower and keenest archer, why not the best gladiator, as well?

But when Lucius looked more closely, he perceived that certain handicaps were imposed on the gladiators. Their swords were shorter than usual and seemed to be quite dull, their shields were smaller, and their armor very thin.

Commodus bested one opponent after another. Sometimes the combat ended quickly, with Commodus merely nicking his opponent, though in one instance he sliced a gash across a man's arm that spurted such a fountain of blood that the gladiator suddenly vomited and then fainted. The crowd was delighted. Other combats lasted longer, and ended only when Commodus forced his opponent to the ground, stepped on his throat, and inflicted a token scratch with the point of his sword.

Making the proceedings all the more unpleasant for Lucius were the childishly simple, obsequious chants the senators were made to recite, lavishly praising the emperor and his prowess. These ditties were written on thin wooden tablets and distributed to all the senators by Praetorian Guards who then kept close watch, ready to arrest any senator who failed to comply.

Commodus, Dominus, worthy of all praises!
Hercules our hero, what a mighty sword he raises!

If the senators tended to mumble their lines, the common citizens needed no encouragement to take up the chants and repeat them. They seemed genuinely to love Commodus's performance, some of them vehemently so. They invented vulgar, bloodthirsty chants of their own—in every crowd there was always a clever Clodius with a knack for spinning verses on the spot—urging Commodus to not merely wound or kill his opponents, but to cut them to pieces and chop their heads off.

Commodus basked in the attention of the multitude. All of Rome was in the amphitheater, and every eye in the amphitheater was fixed upon him.

The admiration of the crowd flagged only once, when one of the gladiators, a left-hander like Commodus with the appropriate nickname Scaeva, took umbrage at whatever handicaps had been imposed on him, threw down his helmet and sword, and refused to fight. While the gladiator stood with arms crossed, Commodus became furious and ordered that Scaeva be put to death.

"And not the quick and honorable death-blow deserved by a defeated gladiator!" shouted Commodus. "You shall be crucified, like the lowest criminal, right here in the arena, a slow death, so you can linger and suffer while the games go on in front of you!"

The crowd began to boo.

Lucius had never seen or even imagined such a thing—Romans booing an emperor. It was an indication of the degree to which normal conduct had been degraded, largely thanks to Commodus himself, for if the emperor could play gladiator, then why shouldn't the mob jeer if they wished? Commodus was taken aback, but then turned the incident to his advantage by granting Scaeva an imperial pardon on the spot, to the delight of the crowd. How swiftly their mood could change, thought Lucius. Unlike the mob, his fellow senators had remained stonily silent throughout the episode, as shocked and mortified as he was.

Scaeva responded by spitting on the ground. Then he picked up his shield and raised his sword in the air, to an uproar of cheering as he made his exit. He was never to be seen again.

Commodus returned to the imperial box. Then gladiators fought each other, to the death. In his long lifetime, Lucius had never seen so much blood and viscera on the sand. At one point Commodus descended once again to the arena. He inserted his hand into the torn chest of a dead gladiator, and drew out his hand covered with blood. The moment was so appalling and strange that the crowd fell silent. From high above, Lucius could hear the faint sound of awnings flapping in the breeze. He remembered the story Galen told him at their first meeting, about Commodus's mother bathing in the blood of a gladiator. Even Marcus had believed there was some magical property in doing so.

Then Commodus smeared the blood on his face. The crowd gasped at the sight. Clearly Commodus had planned the moment, because a chariot appeared in the arena. Commodus took the reins and circled the arena, slowly, raising his bloody hand to the crowd. For a full circuit there was only an awed silence. Then people began to cheer, and Commodus drove faster, then faster still, circling the arena at full speed, so fast that at times his outer wheel rose from the ground, and all the while with only one hand on the reins and the other held aloft. He was not only a spectacular archer and spearman, and a competent gladiator, but showed himself to be a superb charioteer, in complete control of his steeds at every moment.

The bright red blood on his face focused every eye upon him, and its symbolism drew on the deepest traditions of Rome. Long ago, beginning with Romulus, commanders in a triumph had painted their faces red for their sacred procession through the city. The Flavian Amphitheater, not the Sacred Way, was the venue Commodus deemed appropriate for his triumph. The blood on his face was a primal symbol of a victory not just over mortal enemies, but over death itself.

If this was the high point of the games, the low point came when a flock of ostriches was driven into the arena, and Commodus appeared in his Amazon costume, followed by attendants carrying the various weapons of his arsenal. The ostriches made a strange clucking noise and ran about in constant panic while a circle of beaters made escape impossible and drove them back toward Commodus. Some he killed using a bow and arrow, some with a spear at a distance, some he jabbed to death, and some he knocked about with the broad edge of a sword before delivering a death blow. The effect was comical, and intentionally so—the slaughter of the ostriches had been scheduled at a point when usually mimes in outlandish costumes amused the crowd with pratfalls. The amphitheater roared with laughter. Commodus was delighted.

Eventually, only one ostrich was left. The exhausted creature cackled and flapped its useless wings as Commodus closed in, raised his sword, and with a single blow sliced off its head. The body of the ostrich continued to run wildly about, headless and spurting blood from its neck, until it tripped over its own head and tumbled in a heap of feathers on the sand. The crowd went wild with excitement. Even the beaters doubled over with laughter.

Then with his right hand Commodus picked up the ostrich head and held it aloft. Blood and bits of gore dribbled from the dangling neck. With his left hand he pointed his bloody sword at the senators in the stands, grinning at them and slowly shaking his head. The sight was at once ludicrous and terrifying. Some senators sputtered with laughter. Some stared stonily back at Commodus. Some went pale with fear.

Was the emperor deliberately issuing a threat, or was he only clowning? Either way, it seemed to Lucius that the gesture was incredibly reckless. No man was invulnerable. Even Achilles was undone by his heel.

Then, amid the sweat and dust on the emperor's chest, Lucius saw a glint of gold, and was reminded that Commodus wore the fascinum.

It was the next-to-last day of the year, and the festival of Saturnalia was in full swing. Slaves and masters changed roles, extravagant gifts were exchanged, and at night people gathered under the starry sky with tapers and candles to dispel the winter darkness and sang ancient songs to Father Saturn.

But amid that day's universal celebration, Lucius and Gaius were busy working, overseeing the dismantling of the scaffolds that for months had surrounded the Column of Marcus Aurelius. Lucius had promised the emperor that the grand project would be finished by year's end, and he was determined to meet his deadline.

As more scaffolds were removed, more of the brightly painted spiral frieze was lit by the white winter sunlight. The sight was stunning.

Kaeso, back from Britannia, was with his brother and nephew to watch the gradual unveiling. His horrific tales of combat and atrocity had influenced many scenes on the column. It was altogether a somber work, a testament more to truth than to glory, and a greater work of art, Lucius thought proudly, than the Column of Trajan.

It was Kaeso's version of the Rain Miracle that was depicted in the frieze. Lucius and Gaius had gone over the details with him many times. Their depiction was also inspired, like so many sculptures, by poetry. To depict the Rain God, Lucius drew on Ovid's description of Notus: "Forth flies the South-wind with dripping wings, his awful face shrouded in darkness, his long beard heavy with rain. Water flows in streams down his frosty locks. Dark clouds rest upon his brow. His long wings drip with dew. With huge hands he kneads and squeezes the low-hanging clouds. He claps! The thunder is deafening, and dense clouds pour endless rain."

"So the emperor hasn't seen it yet?" asked Kaeso.

"Not in its entirety," said Lucius.

"Commodus promises he'll come on New Year's Day to see the finished column," said Gaius, "as soon as he's performed the annual induction of the two new consuls and the other magistrates. If he's satisfied, he'll choose a propitious date for the dedication. It's going to be the high point of Papa's career." He beamed at his father, then went to oversee some of the workers, leaving Lucius and Kaeso alone.

"Will you have more work to do tomorrow?" asked Kaeso.

"No, the column is truly finished. Tomorrow Gaius and I will sleep late for the first time in months, and finally take a

Saturnalia holiday on New Year's Eve. Then it's back to work on New Year's Day, when Commodus and the new consuls come to inspect our work."

Kaeso lowered his voice. "The troops in Britannia are a bit confused by the emperor's theatrics, or at least what we hear about them. The emperor as Hercules—that, they like. The emperor as Hercules in Amazon clothing—not so much. And renaming the city Commodiana—that smacks of hubris."

"Here in Rome, Kaeso, my fellow senators hate everything he does. But the citizens adore him."

"Do they?" Kaeso lowered his voice even more. "The only sure way I know to gauge the temper of the people of Rome is to watch the mime shows you see on street corners, where the performers beg for alms and scamper off before the authorities can nab them. I saw such a show just today, a bit of Saturnalia fun, about a gladiator with a crown, a veritable king of gladiators, who uses his left hand for everything, including masturbation—just like his idol, another gladiator who's nicknamed Scaeva."

"And what was the plot of this mime show?"

"Well, when it comes time for the combat between the gladiator-king and Scaeva, the king takes fright. He says that two left-handers can't possibly fight. Instead, he orders his minions to crucify Scaeva, who's hoisted up on a cross. But as soon as the king turns his back, Scaeva gets loose and comes down off the cross. He picks up his sword and skulks closer and closer to the king. The children and the simpletons in the crowd yell at the king, 'Look behind you! Look behind!' But the king thinks they're cheering him, and takes one bow after another. Meanwhile, Scaeva sneaks closer and closer and raises his sword to stab the king in the back—then thinks better of it and runs off. The crowd cheers his escape—and the vain king thinks they're cheering for him. To end the play, a narrator tells the crowd they have just seen the story of Scaeva, the *genuine* left-handed gladiator, not the pretend one, the only mortal ever known to survive a public crucifixion—except of course the man-god of the Christians. The jab at the Christians gets a big laugh, of course, since we know they detest blood sports, and then the mimes end the play and go through the crowd asking for donations."

"At least people laughed at the expense of the Christians," said Lucius.

"Oh no, brother. They were laughing at the emperor."

"Perhaps the column will give them something else to think about—the emperor's father. Everyone loved and respected Marcus Aurelius. And everyone knows that the pacification of the northern barbarians, which the column commemorates, was his greatest achievement. Had the times been right, had there been no plague, Marcus could have been another Trajan."

"And then Commodus could have been another Hadrian?" Kaeso scoffed.

Lucius shook his head. "Only with you, little brother—and only out of earshot of the workers—would I ever talk so freely."

"Not even with your son?"

"Gaius has his own relationship with the emperor, from when they were young. He also has children of his own. Rightfully, he puts their survival above all else. So I try to avoid putting my own negative thoughts into Gaius's head, for fear he might repeat them at precisely the wrong moment."

Kaeso sighed. "Is the problem simply that Commodus became emperor too young? Or was he never fit for the role? Nero wanted only to be an actor, they say. And Commodus wants only to be a thrill-seeker, with flashy chariots and shiny swords and all the allure of being a gladiator with none of the danger. Nero and Commodus both would have been happier leading a different life. Neither of them should ever have become emperor."

"Yet the gods allowed it."

"Your friend the Divine Marcus is the one who allowed it. And now . . . will Commodus end as Nero ended?'

"No one wants that, Kaeso. Four emperors in a single year followed Nero, and a very bloody civil war. If Commodus were to die, who would be fit to replace him? He's killed all the decent, competent men appointed by his father, and replaced them with worthless sycophants."

"*You're* still alive, Lucius."

"And there are many who would call me a sycophant, or worse. Do I not glorify the emperor with every statue I make? Whatever his faults, Commodus has given the Pinarii constant work, and rewarded us handsomely."

"After Nero, it was a military man who finally took control," said Kaeso quietly. "Is there a commander alive today, anywhere in the empire, who could equal Vespasian? That's the question."

In the middle of the night, Lucius was awakened by a tapping on his forehead. Kaeso softly whispered his name. Lucius left his slumbering wife and followed his brother to the library, which was lit by a few flickering lamps.

"Commodus will never see the finished column," said Kaeso.

"What do you mean?" asked Lucius, but in his chest he felt a sinking sensation.

"Commodus won't live to see the new year."

"What are you saying, Kaeso? How do you know this? Are you involved in some sort of plot?"

"Yes."

"Oh, Kaeso! What are you thinking?"

"If I want to see the new year myself, I have no choice. Only an hour ago, I was shown a list that was taken from the emperor's bedchamber."

"What sort of—"

"A list of names—enemies and rivals. Commodus intends to begin the year with another purge. Anyone he imagines might pose a threat will be arrested and executed. Pertinax is on the list, which is madness, because he's probably the best Roman general still alive."

"And?"

"My name is on the list, too."

"Oh, Kaeso! Are you sure this list was authentic?"

"Absolutely. My choice is to flee Rome tonight . . . or else take action."

"And my name?"

Kaeso made a rude noise that Lucius took for a laugh. "No, brother, your name is *not* on the list, and neither is your son's. The fact that you could even imagine such a thing is proof of how terrified we've all become."

"Why are you telling me this?"

"To get you and Gaius and the rest of the family out of harm's way, should something go wrong. Get out of Rome for the holiday. Go to one of your country estates. Or better, to the estate of someone you trust, where you might not readily be found."

Lucius thought for a moment. "Galen has a place in Campania . . ."

"No, not there! Not . . . Galen."

Lucius was startled. "Is Galen on the list?"

"No. But . . ."

Lucius gasped. "Is Galen part of the plot?" No one in Rome knew more about antidotes, thought Lucius—or more about poisons. No one knew more about Commodus, his diet and habits and physical constitution, having been his lifelong physician. Galen would know the poisons to which Commodus would be most susceptible, and exactly when and how they might be most effectively administered.

"Galen is a healer, not a killer. But . . . is that it? Is it to be by poison?"

"I can tell you no more. But tomorrow you might want to be away from the city and safe, no matter what the outcome. Even if we succeed, matters may spin out of control."

"What does that mean?" said Lucius.

"Think of what happened after Nero. No one could see the future. No one was safe. Many good citizens died before the bloodshed finally stopped."

"What makes you think this plot will succeed, when so many previous attempts have failed?"

"Because this time the deed will be done by those closest to him."

"Who could be closer than a sister? Yet Lucilla failed. First she was exiled. Now she's dead."

"Closest to him physically, I mean. In closest proximity, within his private quarters, when he bathes, when he sleeps."

"Will you tell Gaius, too? We had a long day. I assume he's fast asleep in his wing of the house."

"He's your son. I leave it up to you, to decide what Gaius should be told."

"And if this plot *does* succeed? Will you restore the Republic?"

Kaeso snorted. "You attend the Senate, Lucius. You've told me how they dawdle and bow to Commodus. Do you think your fellow senators are up to the challenge of ruling an empire? Hardly! If you ask me, Pertinax should be the next emperor. Marcus Aurelius thought highly of him. I know him well, and he's certainly my choice. He's also here in Rome— and *not* part of the plot, which will be to his advantage. But he might not accept."

"Who else, then?"

"Some think Septimius Severus. He's a fine general, certainly, but his greatest support would come from Africa, where he's from, and right now he's posted to the opposite end of the empire, in Upper Pannonia, keeping the northern barbarians at bay. Better to have a claimant here in the city, on the spot."

"If neither of those men, then who?"

"If not Pertinax . . . or Severus . . ."

"Yes?"

"My name has been put forward by some."

Lucius felt a sudden chill, even as his face turned hot. Who would have dared to imagine it—a Pinarius as emperor? And yet, if Commodus were to be removed, it might happen. The Pinarii were as ancient as any family in Rome. A Pinarius had been one of the three heirs of Julius Caesar, though it did the fellow little good in the end. Since then, the Pinarii had experienced their share of bad fortune, but what family in Rome had not? Kaeso had commanded troops in Asia, the German front, and Britannia, earning wide respect, rising high enough in honor and distinction to earn a place on Commodus's list of rivals to be eliminated. At fifty-one, he was also the right age, still young enough to have the stamina required—considerably younger than Pertinax, who was well into his sixties—yet mature enough to possess the gravitas that Commodus had never attained, and never would.

"All hail Kaeso Pinarius!" Lucius whispered slowly, thinking aloud. "Dominus . . . Caesar . . . successor to the Antonines . . . founder of a new imperial dynasty? Or one could say *restorer* of the dynasty of Julius Caesar, given our blood kinship with him."

"Believe me, it's not something I desire," said Kaeso. "But only the Fates know what lies ahead."

Lucius returned to bed, but did not sleep. As the sun rose, he decided that he would not leave Rome. If the assassination succeeded, whatever followed, he would need to be in the city to look after his workshop and his home and all his other interests. And if the plot failed, he would only draw attention to himself by having fled, and the distance of a day's journey would not put him beyond the wrath of Commodus.

He resigned himself to a long, anxious day of waiting for news, one way or the other. He decided not to tell Gaius about the plot—better that his son should know nothing, and go about his business as usual. After a frugal breakfast, Lucius walked down the long hallway to Gaius's wing of the house. Their plan for the day was to relax for a few hours at the baths, eat a leisurely meal, and then host a small New Year's Eve party with close friends.

But Gaius was not to be found in any of the public rooms of his wing. Lucius saw one of the slaves, an old fellow who had been with the family a long time, but whose name Lucius could never remember.

"Is your master still abed?"

"The master rose early. But he's not here. A little while ago, an imperial messenger arrived, with a summons to the palace. The master was going to put on a toga, but the messenger said he shouldn't bother, and to come at once."

"What nerve! Imperial messengers had better manners when the Divine Marcus was alive. So Gaius set out for the palace alone, without me?"

"As the messenger requested. The master only just left. I was about to come and tell you."

What did it mean? Had Kaeso been arrested, and the plot revealed? If so, why was only Gaius summoned, and not himself? Perhaps it was some concern to do with the Column of Marcus. But again, why summon only Gaius and not himself? What was he to do now, follow, or stay put? Lucius paced anxiously, paralyzed by indecision.

Gaius, meanwhile, was being carried aloft in a litter sent by Commodus. Like all the emperor's vehicles, this one had a number of luxurious features. The upholstery was of very fine leather, and there seemed to be hidden compartments everywhere. There was also a long wooden tube through which the passenger could speak directly into the ear of the chief litter-bearer, which seemed to Gaius a needless innovation, unless one was too hoarse to shout orders at the slave.

They were headed not toward the Palatine, where the refurbishment of the fire-damaged imperial quarters was not complete, but to the Caelian Hill, where Commodus had taken over an old villa adjacent to the gladiator training facilities and made it into his imperial chambers. Gaius was puzzled by the unexpected summons, but was more irritated than anxious. He would almost certainly feel underdressed without his senatorial toga, wearing only a simple long-sleeved tunic. He should have made the messenger wait, but the man insisted that he come immediately, just as he was.

When they arrived, the messenger handed Gaius off to a courtier, who escorted him past a number of Praetorian Guards and then passed him to another courtier, this one a young eunuch whose brief, gossamer tunic made Gaius feel overdressed. Clearly they had passed from the official chambers into the more private and informal recesses of the villa, for none of the slaves he passed, male or female, seemed to be wearing much of anything. Were they not cold, he wondered, then realized that the floors seemed to be heated, like the floors of a bathing establishment. Marcus Aurelius had been famous for enduring harsh winters in Pannonia, but for Commodus, all must be comfortable and opulent and luxurious.

Gaius was shown into a small but elegantly furnished room, where he found Commodus attended only by his Master of the Bedchamber, Eclectus, and his lover, Marcia. Eclectus looked a great deal like Commodus, and had many of the same mannerisms. It was like Commodus, Gaius thought, to choose companions who were mirrors of himself. About Marcia, Gaius knew little except that she was strikingly beautiful and rumored, oddly enough, to be a Christian. Gaius would never have guessed. "You can't tell by looking," people said of the Christians. You never knew who might turn out to be one.

There was wine, unmixed with water, despite the morning hour, and some rambling conversation that to Gaius seemed quite pointless but to Eclectus and Marcia must have been quite witty, since they kept laughing. The wine went to Gaius's head, and without quite knowing how, he found himself alone with Commodus in the emperor's private bath, a sumptuous room with elaborate mosaics on every floor, wall, and ceiling, dominated by a gilded statue of Hercules on a pedestal in the center of the heated pool. From certain angles the demigod appeared to be walking on water. Commodus seemed to be quite drunk and determined to become more so, holding a brimming cup of wine in his left hand, sitting naked on submerged steps at one corner of the pool with water lapping at his brawny chest.

Gaius, not invited to enter the pool, sat on a plushly upholstered couch nearby. A female slave, naked except for copious strings of pearls, pressed a large and rather heavy goblet of wine into his hand and then vanished. Gaius at first thought the cup, made all of silver and gold, was in the shape of a horn, then realized it was in fact in the shape of a very lifelike, erect phallus, pointing downward. He looked for a place to set the cup aside, but as the goblet had no base there was no way to put it down without spilling the contents. Nor was there a slave present to take it from him.

He saw that the cup held by Commodus was quite similar, though not as large. Gaius had heard of these cups, and had dismissed the tale as mere rumor, but here was the proof in his hand. The goblets were said to be modeled exactly on the anatomy of Commodus and a few of his closest confidants. To be offered such a cup was presumably a great honor. To have such a cup modeled on one's anatomy was an even greater honor.

The cup made him think of the fascinum. As always, Commodus was wearing it on a chain around his neck. Commodus caught him looking at it, and reached up to touch it.

"What do you say, Pinarius, shall we make a fair trade, so you can be done with envying my little amulet? You shall never have it back, but I tell you what: you can keep that goblet. One phallus for another, eh? And not just any phallus. That's *my* penis you're holding. Well?" Commodus stared at him, demanding an answer.

"I . . . I don't know what to say, Dominus."

"Then never mind! I'll have that goblet back when you're done with it. But that's not why I called you here, Pinarius. There will have to be changes made."

"Changes, Dominus?"

"Changes to the column."

"But . . . you haven't seen it yet."

"Yes, I've been preoccupied with other matters and I've failed to give it the attention I should have—a mistake on my part, if what I've been told is true."

"And what is that?"

"For one thing, I've been told that I do *not* appear in the images representing the Rain Miracle. Is that true?"

Gaius squirmed on the couch and cleared his throat. "I assure you, Dominus, our sculptors worked from the descriptions of actual witnesses—"

"Stop that! I summoned you, and not your father, precisely because your old man has a way of talking around a subject until I forget what I wanted to say. My father was good at that, too. By Hercules, what a lot of words he spewed in his long, miserable lifetime. Words, words, millions of words—all amounting to rubbish. I say: talk less, live more! There, I have just dictated my book, *To Myself.* Short and to the point." He drank from his cup and then raised it, gesturing that Gaius should do likewise. Gaius put the goblet to his lips but only pretended to take a sip. He suddenly felt quite sober, and very nervous.

Commodus's speech was slurred, which was only to be expected since he was drunk. But why did he look so pale? His brow was beaded with sweat. That could be due to the hot bath. But the hand that held the cup was unsteady, sloshing drops of wine into the water. Was the emperor ill?

"I know why you left me out of the Rain Miracle," he said. "You did so deliberately! This is the revenge of the Pinarii, because of *this*!" He pointed to the fascinum nestled between his pectorals. "My guarantor of good fortune! This amulet protected me from the plague, year in and year out. It kept me alive when those closest to me did everything they could to see me dead! You'd like to take it back from me, wouldn't you? You would rob your emperor of his protection. Admit it!"

Gaius sat speechless. Commodus drank more wine, and gestured that Gaius should do the same. As Gaius raised the cup to his lips, a horrible thought occurred to him. What if Commodus was not ill, but had been poisoned? Was there poison in the wine?

"Drink, Pinarius! You ungrateful swine!" shouted Commodus.

Gaius pressed the cup to his lips but could not bring himself to drink.

"Drink, I said!" Commodus stood up in the water, and started to step from the pool, but then seemed to lose his balance and fell back, splashing water across the mosaic floor. Perhaps he was only very drunk, after all, thought Gaius. Then he saw a movement from the corner of his eye and gave a start.

"This is ridiculous!" shouted Marcia, who seemed to appear from nowhere. "The poison would have worked by now if it was going to. Giving him more is *not* the solution."

Eclectus was also in the room. "You're right. He must have taken an antidote beforehand. Theriac, perhaps."

Gaius stared dumbly at the two of them. His hand was clenched tightly around the phallic goblet. He had a sensation he had not experienced since he was a child, when he sometimes fancied that he was invisible and no one could see him as long as he sat very still.

"Make it happen!" shouted Marcia.

"Yes, do it! *Now!*" screamed Eclectus.

Another person was suddenly in the room, a tall, muscular young man. Gaius had seen him before, in Commodus's entourage. Narcissus was his name, a powerful athlete, one of Commodus's wrestling and sparring partners. He looked pale but determined, swallowing hard as he slowly approached the pool, which Commodus was again attempting to exit. Narcissus hesitated for a moment, then made up his mind. He knelt by the pool, grabbed Commodus by the neck, pulled him half out of the water, and then began to strangle him.

Commodus flailed and struggled, but his resistance was

feeble. Still half in the water, he kicked wildly, splashing water all over Gaius, who sat as still as a statue on the couch.

"Don't drown him!" cried Marcia.

"And don't break his neck!" added Eclectus. "It must appear to be a natural death. It will be much easier that way."

To Gaius, sitting motionless, the gruesome act seemed to take a very long time. Weakened though he was, Commodus nonetheless possessed tremendous will. He did not die quickly. The slow strangulation was excruciating to watch.

Afterward Gaius would wonder if he should have acted. But what could he have done? He was outnumbered and without a weapon, in an unfamiliar place, unable even to put down the goblet in his hand.

At last, Commodus was dead. His naked body lay limp and crumpled on the tile floor, with bits of steam rising from his wet flesh. Narcissus released his grip. He stood, slipping awkwardly on the wet floor. He was breathing hard and shaking, blinking his eyes, looking as if he might weep.

Gaius's hand began to tremble, so violently that wine spilled from the cup. Impulsively, he cast it away, into the pool, where it fell to the bottom. The red wine dispersed like blood in the water.

"What about this one?" said Eclectus, staring at him. "He saw everything. What shall we do with him?"

Narcissus drew back his shoulders and looked grimly at Gaius, then stepped toward him. Gaius raised his hands and drew back on the couch.

"No," said Marcia. "Don't hurt him."

"But he'll talk," said Eclectus. "He and his father owe everything to Commodus."

"I know what will buy his silence." Marcia walked to the corpse and squatted beside it. She took the chain from Commodus's neck, then rose and brought it to Gaius. She dangled it before him. He stared at it. He had not seen the fascinum so close in many years.

"This is yours, is it not?"

Gaius nodded. He reached for it, but she held it back. "You must never wear it in public. Do you understand? All Rome has seen it, worn by Commodus. No one must ever see it again."

Again, Gaius nodded.

"And also . . . you were never here. Do you understand? You saw nothing, know nothing. And that is because . . . ?"

"Because . . . I was never here," Gaius said hoarsely. "But what do you intend to tell people? Even with no witnesses, you can't hide a thing like . . ." He looked at the corpse.

Eclectus flashed a grim smile. "We've been working on the exact wording of the official statement."

"Yes," said Marcia, "how does the final version go?"

"'Commodus, your emperor, is dead. The cause was apoplexy. The emperor was responsible for his own death. The blame falls on no one else. Time and again those closest to him urged him to adopt a safer and saner course, yet he paid no attention. You know the way he lived his life. Now he lies dead, choked by his own gluttony. The end he was destined for has met him at last.' There, Pinarius, what do you think of that? Credible enough? Even if the senators don't believe it, they'll want to. He has no supporters left in the Senate, except perhaps for a handful who profited from his excesses—like you, Pinarius."

"What about the citizens?" said Gaius. "Many of them still—"

"The rabble are capable of believing anything. The ones who actually thought Commodus was a god—immortal Hercules returned to earth!—will see how wrong they were. And the ones who thought that an emperor could be a gladiator—well, they can hardly be surprised that such a rogue met an early death."

Gaius stared at the fascinum dangled by Marcia, then seized it. Touching it, he felt a sudden awe. There was a rush of physical sensation as well, a tingling all over his body. He put on the necklace. He touched the fascinum where it lay against his chest, unseen beneath his tunic.

"How Commodus loved that worthless little trinket," said Marcia. "He told me all about it—how old it is, how he came to have it. How powerful he thought it was! But I wouldn't put any faith in it, if I were you. It certainly didn't protect him today."

"What do you know, you ignorant bitch?" snapped Gaius, suddenly overcome by conflicting emotions. "You know nothing! Are you a Christian, as people say? A hater of the gods?" He sprang up from the couch, clutching the fascinum, and stared at the corpse. He trembled. He hated Commodus for keeping his birthright from him. He was furious at the cold-blooded murderers. He was angry at himself for having been a virtual slave of Commodus, and equally angry to find himself indebted to the man's killers.

"Go now," said Marcia, her face ashen. "While you still can."

Eclectus glared at him. Narcissus fought back tears.

Gaius stifled his rage and ran from the room.

He pushed aside the courtiers in the outer rooms and walked past the Praetorian Guards, out of the villa. Heading home, he passed through crowds of laughing, drunken Saturnalia revelers. They could not yet know what had happened, but it seemed to Gaius that all of Rome was celebrating the death of Commodus.

Commodus was dead! He saw it happen with his own eyes, but still could hardly believe it. Even more amazing, the fascinum was his, at long last! How pleased his father would be. Losing himself in the throng of drunken revelers, Gaius felt giddy, filled with a sublime sense of well-being, an elation far beyond the intoxication induced by wine. Commodus was dead and the fascinum had come back to the Pinarii.

On this day, the gods had smiled on him, and on Rome. From this day forward, Gaius felt certain, the world could only become better and better.

PART II

THE WOMEN OF EMESA
(A.D. 194–223)

A.D. 194

Gaius and his five-year-old son, Aulus, stood before the funeral monuments of the Pinarii outside the city, amid the multitude of graves along the Appian Way. With them was Galen.

Two monuments stood side by side. They held the ashes of Gaius's father and uncle, and had only recently been finished and put in place. The task of designing them had fallen to Gaius. The monument for his father was very elaborate, with a bust of Senator Lucius Pinarius recessed in a deep niche, surrounded by relief carvings depicting many of his sculptural works in miniature, prominent among them his masterpiece, the equestrian statue of Marcus Aurelius—without the downtrodden barbarian later added at the insistence of Commodus. There was a long inscription, as well, praising his long tenure in the Senate and his great service to Rome.

Like his father and grandfather before him, Lucius had not lived past the age of seventy-one. After the murder of Commodus, Gaius had hurried home and told his father what he had witnessed, and showed him the fascinum. Lucius had been elated, but had ordered Gaius to tell no one else. It would not be prudent to allow the household of the Pinarii to stage a celebration on the day the emperor died. That very night, in the early hours of New Year's Day, Lucius died in his sleep, with a smile on his lips. It was as if he had waited for that singular event, the restoration of the fascinum, and then had let go of his spirit.

Lucius's well-timed departure also spared him from the violence and chaos that followed, including the death of his beloved younger brother.

The monument for Kaeso was much plainer, with only a bust that showed him in a toga, not in military dress, and a very brief inscription. Considering the circumstances of his death, Gaius had thought it best that his uncle's monument should draw no attention to itself.

Gaius burned a bit of incense before each of the monuments and poured an offering of olive oil and wine. After this formality, little Aulus was allowed to sit on the grass, where a caterpillar attracted his attention.

"What do you think becomes of the dead?" asked Gaius.

Galen, well into his sixties and having seen so much illness and suffering, had given much thought to the question. "I believe that some singular unity informs all creation, that there exists a kind of world spirit that extends through all space and time, the full reality of which we mortals can only vaguely grasp."

"Since my father and his father were devoted followers of Apollonius of Tyana, I was raised to believe in such a universal spirit as well," said Gaius. "And I believe in an afterlife—at least for some mortals. Great rulers, like Marcus, become divine after death, and live among the gods. Great heroes, like Achilles, or great sages, like Apollonius, also continue to exist after death, but they stay closer to the world of the living. They become demons—spirits lower than gods but worshipped by mortals who call upon such demons to guide and protect them. But is there an afterlife for us ordinary mortals? If so, what might it be like?"

"On that question, the philosophers differ," said Galen.

"Indeed they do," agreed Gaius. "Some, like Marcus, seemed to think the afterlife hardly matters."

"Marcus epitomized a particularly Roman virtue, if we may call it that," said Galen, "the idea that *this* life and *this* moment are all that matter. Anything that follows can only be a place of dim shadows to which the wise man gives little thought, knowing that what most matters is his existence here and now, and the duties a man owes to the gods, to his family, and to the state."

"Is there no individual soul, then?"

"I think there must be. But I can't claim to understand the essence of the soul. The soul is immortal and incorporeal, yet we find it coexisting with the body, and it is possible that it works through the medium of the natural activities of the body. So long as the body retains its sensible temperament, it does not die, and it remains coupled with the soul."

"By temperament, you mean . . . ?"

"The constitution of the body is continually changing from a state of vigorous heat and moisture toward coldness and desiccation, until, by old age, it dries up entirely and loses all heat. When coldness and dryness are all that remain, the soul can no longer perform its particular activities and itself grows weaker, just as the body does. Life is then extinguished through the extinction of the soul." He shrugged. "To the physician, treating disease, it doesn't matter whether the soul is mortal or immortal, nor does it matter whether its substance is corporeal or incorporeal, or whether its substance is contained in the cavities of a living creature, or spread throughout its fundamental parts, or inhabits every minute particle of the body. Personally, I believe the soul inhabits the brain, and the brain is therefore the chief instrument of the rational soul."

"I suppose I tend toward what you call 'Roman virtue,'" said Gaius, gazing eye to eye with the bust of his father. "I believe that what truly matters is this life, this existence, this world's calling to duty, honor, virtue."

"The opposite view, and perhaps the reason that Romans in particular, like Marcus, judge them so harshly, would be that of the Christians," said Galen. "If I understand correctly, they think that this world is of no importance whatsoever, that this is merely a sort of staging area for some other, far better existence, a place of perfect bliss, which can be known to mortals only *after* death, and then only to those mortals who accept a certain very specific and very narrow set of beliefs. And about the exact nature of these beliefs, the Christians squabble among themselves endlessly, engaging in mock-philosophical debates that would make any true philosopher cringe, since what they argue about is merely smoke and mirrors."

Gaius nodded. "And the further east one goes from Rome, the more elaborate and intricate, and even preposterous, become the native religions. Uncle Kaeso once related to me the details of some eastern religion he had encountered, supposedly revealed in a blinding flash to a self-proclaimed prophet who then wrote down in exquisite detail all the dozens of levels of existence, all of which intersected with each other in very complicated ways, rather like a house of many stories with countless chutes and ladders and trapdoors—none of which can be proven, or even in any way observed, of course. Reason means nothing when the worshippers are completely reliant on the revelations of the prophet."

He glanced down at his son, who had abandoned the caterpillar, expecting to see the boy looking bored or distracted, but instead Aulus was watching them intently, listening to every word.

"All I really know is that once my father lived, and now he does not. Once he was here among us, and now he is not." Gaius returned his gaze to the monuments. So it was, too, with his uncle Kaeso, the brave warrior, the tireless defender of all that was Roman, a man who helped to bring about so much change in the city, but who did not profit from it in the end . . .

With Commodus dead, the situation at first looked promising. Pertinax, innocent of the murder plot, was pressed by senators to take the throne. He could hardly be called a second Marcus Aurelius—who could be?—but he had been a part of Marcus's inner circle, and at the age of sixty-six was far more experienced, reasonable, and mature than Commodus had been. His assumption of imperial power marked an immediate return to sane and sober leadership, and many Romans breathed a sigh of relief.

Though widely disbelieved, the official version of events maintained that Commodus had died of natural causes, so no one was punished. But not everyone was glad to see Commodus dead. Palace courtiers and the Praetorian Guards who had received Commodus's special favor bitterly resented his sudden death and suspected foul play.

The Senate issued a long decree denouncing all the follies and crimes of Commodus, calling him "more savage than Domitian, more foul than Nero." There was an immediate and thorough elimination of Commodus's images all over the city, beginning with the archer aiming his bow at the Senate House, which was pulled down and smashed with hammers that very day. Gaius had been heartsick to see so many splendid works by the Pinarii shattered or melted down. At least his father had been spared from witnessing the destruction.

Most spectacular was the beheading of the Colossus. In the rush, no special planning took place. A team of slaves with tools was dispatched to climb up and crudely cut off the head of Commodus-as-Hercules. With a wrenching scream of broken metal, the giant head plummeted a hundred feet to the ground, where it burst into jagged shards that badly wounded several spectators and killed one of them on the spot, beheading the poor man, ironically enough. The Senate decreed that a head of Sol with a crown of sunbeams should be restored to the Colossus. For that task, Pertinax turned to Gaius, following the logic that those who had altered the Colossus once might be trusted with the complicated job of changing it back. The project was tedious and more than a little daunting, especially without his father's guidance, but at least it was keeping Gaius busy.

If his father had been spared from seeing the demolition of so many of the Pinarii's creations, he had also missed the joy of seeing the Column of Marcus Aurelius formally dedicated at last. Never mind that the towering monument depicted so much horrendous suffering and bloodshed, or that it had been commissioned by Commodus; Pertinax saw the column's dedication as an opportunity to look back on the reign of the stalwart Marcus, and to look forward to his own tenure, informed by the same values. From such a perspective, the reign of the unwarlike Commodus could be seen as a depraved but temporary aberration.

There had been a public auction of Commodus's private goods, not only to raise much-needed money for the treasury, but to expose the full decadence of his lifestyle, including his sumptuous clothing and jewelry and, of course, his fabulous collection of carriages. Bidding had been fierce to acquire items of his personal gladiator gear, especially his gem-encrusted armor and golden helmets. Less popular, despite their costly materials of gold, silver, and precious stones, had been the emperor's collection of phallic-shaped goblets reputed to represent exact likenesses of Commodus and his circle of favorites, including the slave Commodus had nicknamed Onos, Greek for "donkey."

A new day had dawned in Rome, a return to the sound government of the past.

But early on, Pertinax alienated the Praetorian Guards by trying to rein in their wild behavior. Under Commodus, the Praetorians had become undisciplined and arrogant and often abusive of citizens, blatantly engaging in rape and theft without fear of punishment. Determined to put a stop to such lawlessness, Pertinax disciplined a few disobedient Praetorians with harsh corporal punishments and heavy fines. Hardly three months into his reign, some disaffected Praetorians decided to murder Pertinax.

The assassins stormed into the palace. Messengers alerted Pertinax. The new emperor did not flee, or even send his own bodyguards to confront them. Instead, he calmly strode out to meet them, found an elevated place to stand, and began to orate, as if they were misbehaving schoolboys who simply needed to be shown the error of their ways. The soldiers were infuriated by his condescension. They not only murdered Pertinax, but also beheaded him—the first time such an atrocity had been committed against a Roman emperor since the loathsome Vitellius.

The Praetorians rampaged through the palace, killing a great many imperial courtiers, including Eclectus, Commodus's treacherous chamberlain, who had been allowed to keep his post under Pertinax. Eclectus was the first of the assassins of Commodus to die—but not the last.

There followed perhaps the most shameful moment thus far in the history of Rome. Having done away with Pertinax, the Praetorians decided that they, not the Senate, would choose the next emperor, and not by merit or rank or blood, but by auction. They contacted the two men most eager to succeed Pertinax and told them that whichever of them offered the largest payment to each soldier would become emperor. The winner of this auction was Didius Julianus, a political enemy of the dead Pertinax, who told the soldiers they could call him Commodus, to their delight.

What had the empire of Marcus Aurelius come to?

The short reign of Julianus was chaotic from the start. At the horse races to celebrate his ascension, a mob of citizens rushed the stands of the Circus Maximus and claimed the seats reserved for senators, then hurled insults at Julianus in the imperial box. The Praetorians were ready to slaughter every citizen on the spot, but Julianus kept them in check, not wanting to begin his reign with a bloodbath. He acted as if nothing was amiss. The races proceeded without the attendance of the outraged senators. Having no places to sit, they stalked out in disgust.

The people despised Julianus and the Praetorians. The Praetorians despised the people. The Senate despised everyone else, especially Julianus, and everyone despised the Senate in return. Julianus's hold on power became even more tenuous when word arrived that two rivals, each commanding an army, were heading toward the city from different directions. In his slightly more than two months as emperor, Julianus's only accomplishment was a declaration of what everyone already suspected, that Commodus had died not of natural causes but by murder, and the apprehension and summary execution of two of the leading participants in the plot, Commodus's lover, Marcia, and the city prefect, Laetus.

Gaius's uncle Kaeso somehow escaped Julianus's net, as did Narcissus, the hulking young athlete who strangled Commodus while Gaius watched. So did Galen—if in fact Galen played a part in the poison plot. About this, Gaius had never directly questioned Galen, and Galen had never offered any information. Gaius nonetheless had come to suspect that Galen supplied poison to Kaeso, who then supplied it to Marcia and Eclectus. What an irony, that a poison provided by the world's foremost physician proved useless! In the end, brute force had been the solution. The participation of Galen, if indeed he played a part, had been ineffective and unnecessary.

And now, the one man who could have told Gaius the truth about Galen—his uncle Kaeso—had been silenced forever, the last of the conspirators to be punished, not by the short-lived Julianus but by the man who succeeded him . . .

When Pertinax accepted the throne, a relieved Kaeso had shown his nephew the short list of men whom the plotters had considered as possible successors to Commodus. Among them (along with Pertinax and Kaeso himself) was the prominent general Septimius Severus, who had risen steadily through the ranks of the various magistracies, proving his political skills, and had shown himself equally adept as a commander on the battlefield.

Counting against Severus was his exotic origin. He had been born in the province of Africa with Punic as his first language, and he still spoke Latin with a distinctly African accent of the sort often played for laughs by stage comedians. It was hard not to smile when the man pronounced his own name as "Sheptimiush Sherverush." His wife was even more exotic, a Syrian from the city of Emesa, where the males of her family held the hereditary priesthood of the sun god Elagabalus, whom the Emesenes believed to be greater than all other gods.

Gaius, betraying his patrician roots, had scoffed at the idea that such an uncouth outsider could ever become First Man in Rome, the successor of titans like Augustus and Marcus Aurelius. But when Severus arrived at Rome with his army, declaring himself the avenger and successor of Pertinax, Didius Julianus was quickly murdered and a shaken Senate declared Severus emperor.

After the very short reigns of Pertinax and Julianus, and with yet more military claimants to power looming on the horizon, many thought the reign of Severus might be equally short-lived. But Severus was bold and confident from the start. With his own troops to back him, he dismissed the unruly and arrogant Praetorian Guards, the source of so much trouble for emperors and citizens alike, and replaced them with his own loyal soldiers. He not only deified Pertinax, but declared that Commodus, too, had been a god. He also claimed that Commodus had been his brother, because Severus, too, was a son of Marcus Aurelius, and thus was his legitimate successor. Everyone in Rome knew that this was a metaphor at best, but in state records and inscriptions all over the empire, Severus's descent from Marcus became a legal fact, which made him no longer an African upstart but the heir of a long and illustrious line of rulers.

Like Marcus at the outset of his reign, Severus promised that no senator would ever be put to death without a fair and open trial. But as brother of Commodus and friend of the murdered Pertinax, he could not let their deaths go unavenged. Severus first tracked down Narcissus, the athlete who had strangled Commodus, and threw him to lions in the arena, where he was eaten alive for the amusement of the audience. This was the punishment that Hadrian had decreed for parricides, and wasn't any man who murdered his emperor a father-killer?

But Severus did not stop with Narcissus. He proceeded to arrest and put to death a number of men, including senators, on the grounds that they had played a part in the murder of Commodus or Pertinax or both.

Among those men—and guilty as charged, as Gaius knew—was Kaeso Pinarius.

Offered the honorable option of suicide, Kaeso had ended his life at home in a hot bath with his wrists cut, attended only by his wife. Kaeso had forbidden Gaius and even his own children to be present, wanting to limit, as much as possible, any taint of guilt by association. His funeral had been a quiet affair. His plain monument was so fresh from the Pinarius workshop that little drifts of marble dust still nestled in the recesses of the chiseled letters.

Gaius stood before the monument, still shaken by Kaeso's death, his nerves frayed by the constant violence and wrenching uncertainty of recent months. He had been in suspense every day since the murder of Commodus, fearful that his long connection to him would put him in peril, or fearful for the opposite reason, that his uncle's part in the plot would bring down all the Pinarii. Both friends and foes of Commodus might yet see fit to eliminate him.

For one thing he was thankful: his presence in the room when Commodus was strangled had never been made public. Even in rumors, he was never mentioned. This miracle Gaius could only ascribe to the return of the fascinum, which never left his person, firmly attached to a chain around his neck.

Now Septimius Severus was away from Rome, headed east to deal with a rival claimant to the throne. With the emperor gone, Gaius had thought himself safe at last. But very early that morning, an imperial messenger had arrived at his home.

Gaius held the rolled message, which was tied with a purple ribbon and sealed with wax impressed with the imperial emblem. Gaius had not yet dared to open it, waiting until he could stand in the presence of his father's shrine, with his son present and with Galen to advise him.

"Are you ready now to read it?" asked Galen quietly.

Gaius took a deep breath, then managed a crooked smile. "Perhaps it's about the Colossus. That could be it, don't you think? Since the day Pertinax hired me to restore it, no one in the palace has said a word to me. There's a rumor among the work crew that Severus, being such an outspoken admirer of his so-called brother, will sooner or later make us stop what we're doing and restore the statue as it was before—with a head of Commodus as Hercules!"

"I hardly think that's likely," said Galen.

"No, I suppose not." Gaius broke the seal. He unrolled the message and read aloud, forcing himself to speak the words slowly and steadily, occasionally frowning or drawing a sharp breath.

"'We have been reviewing the plans you submitted (to our predecessor the Deified Pertinax) for the restoration of Sol. It occurs to us that the sunbeams emanating from the god's brow are much too short. They should be twice as long. We realize that this change may pose an engineering challenge, but we are assured by those familiar with your work that you are competent to solve any problems that may arise. Also, we wish to receive from you an estimate of the increased amount of gold necessary to gild these larger sunbeams, so that we may calculate the cost thereof. You will come to us at the palace this afternoon.'"

Gaius stared at the message. "So it *is* about the Colossus." He heaved a long sigh of relief. "But I don't understand. Severus is gone from Rome. Who dictated this message? Whom am I to meet?"

Galen raised an eyebrow. "It's *she* who summons you, of course. Domna, the empress. She's in charge of the city while Severus is off to war. Did you not know? Have you not met her yet?"

"No. Have you?"

"Certainly. I've met the whole household. Domna wanted the services of the best physician in Rome, and that of course is myself. But she's a very busy woman. It's taken a while for her to turn her gaze to you. But why so crestfallen, Gaius? You should welcome the summons. Domna knows and cares about your work and intends for you to continue. Good news, my boy!"

Gaius smiled. At the age of thirty-three, he was hardly still a boy, but Galen would probably always think of him that way. "But . . . to make the sunrays so much longer at this stage is impossible—"

"Domna says otherwise."

"What does *she* know about it?"

"Lower your voice," whispered Galen, though the closest people were travelers on the road some distance away. "As a matter of fact, Domna knows quite a bit about the sun god, Sol—or Elagabalus, as the Emesenes call him."

Little Aulus spoke up. "The Emesenes worship a *rock*, don't they?" He cocked his head to one side and looked dubious.

"Why, yes," said Galen. "In the sanctum of the Temple of Elagabalus at Emesa there is a very large black stone said to have fallen straight from the sun to the earth, many hundreds of years ago. It was still smoldering when it was retrieved by the awestruck locals who decided to worship it, and who thus became the first priests of Elagabalus—the ancestors of Domna. So goes the legend. Elagabalus is not the only example of stone-worship, which has a long tradition in the East. In Greek we call such a sacred stone a baetyl."

"Baetyl," Aulus repeated, enjoying the exotic sound of the word.

"Greek and Roman images of the sun god are quite different from those of the Emesenes," Galen continued, "but it's not surprising that the daughter of the high priest of Elagabalus in Emesa should have an opinion about the Colossus of Sol here in Rome. Whatever its form, it depicts the deity she worships above all other."

"But seriously—they worship a black stone?" said Aulus, still skeptical.

"We have such a sacred stone right here in Rome," said Galen, "installed in the Temple of Magna Mater, brought from Pessinus in the days when Rome was in a life-or-death struggle with Carthage. Some think it was the installation of that stone that tipped the scales in Rome's favor."

"Like this Elagabalus, Magna Mater is a deity of distinctly foreign origin," noted Gaius, "and with a very strange priesthood—fanatic worshippers who literally castrate themselves."

"What is 'castrate'?" asked Aulus, frowning.

"Something you need never worry about," said his father, tousling the boy's hair.

"We Greeks were the first to make bronze and marble statues of the gods, worthy to be put in temples," said Galen. "When we first encountered you Romans, you were still worshipping crude images made of terra-cotta. Keep in mind that the black stone of the Emesenes was made by no mortal at all, but came directly from the fireball of the sun. Everyone who sees it is rendered speechless with awe—so they say."

"I want to see the stone," said Aulus.

"Perhaps you will," said Galen, "should you visit Emesa one day. Now you'd better hurry, Gaius. You have a meeting at the palace with our Domina."

"Is that how I'm to address her? As 'Domina'? As if I were her slave?"

"How else? Ever since Domitian, our rulers have been addressed as 'Dominus.' Why should it be different with a woman? As it is, her given name is very close to 'Domina,' but only by coincidence. In her native tongue, which derives from Phoenician, 'Domna' means 'black.'"

"And is she?" asked little Aulus.

Galen smiled. "Browner than you, probably, but hardly black; no more so than the emperor's rival in the East, Pescennius Niger, despite his name."

"And why does she write in the plural?" asked the boy. "'*We* have been reviewing . . . *We* realize . . .' Has she two heads?"

"I suspect," said Galen with a laugh, "that the plural implies that she speaks both for herself *and* for her husband, having been given his full authority to make decisions in his absence. That 'we' might even presume a certain *equality* with him."

Gaius snorted. "Domna, Domina, whatever. No woman will ever rule Rome! Still, out of respect for her husband, I shall address her as you suggest. But I shall have to disabuse her at once of this crazy notion of changing the sunrays of the Colossus at this late stage of reconstruction. Or is she one of those women impossible to lead to reason?"

Galen suppressed a smile and shrugged. "You'll soon find out, my boy."

Gaius arrived at the palace bringing with him a pair of secretaries to take notes, one skillful at drawing, the other at shorthand. He was shown to a part of the Palatine palace rebuilt since the fire, and unfamiliar to him. Commodus had virtually abandoned the Palatine, living with his gladiators at their barracks. All three emperors since his death had conspicuously chosen to reside at the Palatine, even if some parts remained unfinished, as if the address itself conveyed legitimacy. Some rooms of the palace did in fact date all the way back to Augustus.

Gaius was shown into the audience chamber, where Domna sat on the throne that would usually be occupied by her husband, wrapped in a purple stola that covered her from head to foot. She was younger than Severus, in her thirties, about the same age as Gaius, while Severus was close to fifty. She had a long face, very large eyes, and a small mouth. She was not pretty but plain, and her unblinking gaze was slightly unnerving. Her skin was somewhat dark, but her hairstyle was the most strikingly foreign thing about her. Her hair was parted in the middle and on either side descended in a series of finger-sized waves, covering her ears completely and drawn into a bun at the back of her neck. It was surely a wig, thought Gaius, for what mortal could sit still long enough to have her hair so elaborately styled?

Domna was attended by numerous secretaries and courtiers. Also in the room, seated to one side on the dais, was Domna's older sister, Maesa. She had a larger nose than Domna, sharper cheekbones, and smaller eyes; her piercing gaze was even more unsettling. Her husband was serving with Severus in the East. According to Galen, Maesa wielded considerable power in the imperial household, essentially acting as her sister's second-in-command while Severus was away from Rome.

Gaius was announced by a courtier. A secretary handed Domna a wax tablet scribbled with notes. She gazed down at it, reading, then set the tablet aside and cleared her throat. Her Latin had an odd but not unpleasant accent. For a moment Gaius panicked, thinking he would not be able to understand her. It would not do for him to ask her to repeat herself. He concentrated and listened closely.

"I have called you here for three reasons, Senator Pinarius. Firstly, as I indicated in my message, there must be changes to the Colossus of Sol. This is essential and not a matter for discussion. Do you understand?"

She gave him such a fierce look that Gaius abandoned any intention of opposing her demands.

"Yes, Domina."

"You should understand that my husband, your Dominus, is a very enthusiastic and pious convert to the worship of Elagabalus, who is the one god above all other gods. As our father, the god's high priest, taught us, 'He is as high above other gods as those gods are above mortals.' For political reasons, the emperor chooses to call the god Sol Invictus, a name already known to soldiers all over the empire, and to make images that conform to Roman traditions. So be it. But understand, Senator Pinarius, that when you work on the Colossus, you render worship to Elagabalus Most High."

"Elagabalus Most High!" cried her sister loudly. She rolled her eyes upward, and raised her hands and shook them in the air. "As high above other gods as those gods are above mortals!"

Gaius was startled by the outburst, but none of the courtiers reacted. No doubt they were accustomed to these affirmations. What was it about these adherents of eastern religions that made them want to worship *one* god rather than *many*? Jews, Christians, and now these two sun-worshipping sisters! One of the glories of Rome's empire had been the addition over the centuries of countless gods and goddesses to her pantheon. As the empire grew, claiming new provinces and new populations, new deities were encountered as well, new priesthoods were assembled, new temples were built, new statues were made. More gods made Rome more pious, more powerful. The worship of more gods, not fewer, was the very hallmark of civilization. It was only the most ignorant, the most unsophisticated, unlearned, untraveled people who thought their local god must be the best and highest and only god worth worshipping. What had Marcus Aurelius called such a person? *Paganus,* an old Latin word meaning an ignorant rustic, a country bumpkin. Yet here was the most powerful woman on earth, as paganus as you please, apparently leading the emperor down the same narrow path, determined to winnow the delight of worshipping many gods and settle on just one.

But Domna was speaking again. Gaius had to listen closely to decipher her accent.

". . . a new commission," she was saying, "which is to be an equestrian statue of the emperor, based on a dream he had before he came to power. In that dream, he was in the Forum along with a great multitude, and Pertinax appeared riding a very fine steed. But the horse grew restless and threw Pertinax off, then galloped to Septimius and scooped him onto its back, at which the multitude cheered. That dream, sent by Elagabalus, foretold his rise to power, and so it came to be. We have seen the equestrian statue of Marcus Aurelius that was made by your father, a great masterpiece. You will give form to the dream of Septimius Severus. This statue will be your chance to surpass your father."

Was he to show poor Pertinax as well, thrown off the horse and lying crumpled on the paving stones off to one side? "I doubt that I could ever surpass my father, Domina, but I shall do my best to equal him."

"Well said. You are a dutiful son. And finally, the third reason I called you here." She made a flourish with her hand. A tall figure stepped from the crowd of courtiers. He was young and elegantly dressed in a tunic and cloak proper to a tutor in a great household. Domna now spoke Greek, with no hint of a Syrian accent. Indeed, her Greek was more polished and elegant than Gaius's. "Let me introduce you to my young friend, Philostratus of Athens. Shall I tell you a secret, Senator Pinarius?" She crooked her finger and leaned forward. Gaius dared to step closer. "He is only twenty-four!" She sat back. "Yet anyone who reads his work would think him a sage of seventy. Precocious is my young friend, Philostratus of Athens. They say he was the brightest student of Antipater of Hierapolis, until the student surpassed the teacher. Now he teaches Latin and Greek to my two sons. He even ventures to correct my Greek, when I make an error."

The young man smiled and bowed his head. "Domina, you never do!"

"True. I said that merely to flatter you. But I speak truly when I say that Philostratus is as talented a writer as you are an artist, Senator Pinarius. Have you read his work?"

"I'm sorry to say I have not, Domina."

"But I am most certainly aware of the work of the famous Pinarii," said Philostratus. "I have seen a few—too few, alas—of your statues of Commodus that survived, most of them outside Rome, but also of course your father's remarkable bust of Commodus as Hercules holding a club and wearing a lion's head for a hood. People will marvel at that statue for as long as Rome exists, I think. And the equestrian statue of Marcus, which our Domina mentioned. And of course, the great Column of Marcus that was so recently dedicated. I sometimes engage in a certain verbal exercise, the description of paintings, which can be most challenging—how to convey in words the colors and shapes our eyes apprehend in an instant, and also the deeper meanings that occur to us when we gaze at a great painting. But how much harder it would be to describe a sculpture, especially a sculpture of such exceeding complexity and size and power as the Column of Marcus, depicting so many stirring episodes! It would take many poems, a whole book of poems, even to begin the task."

Gaius took an immediate liking to Philostratus, despite a certain fussiness about the young Athenian's speech and mannerisms.

Domna turned to her sister. "I think these two may hit it off."

Maesa muttered something in their native language. A few of the courtiers sniggered. (Later, one of them, drawn aside by Gaius and given a small gratuity, would tell him what she said: "Next thing you know, they'll be sucking each other's cocks." Apparently, Maesa slipped into Phoenician dialect whenever she wanted to say something vulgar, which was rather often. "That one curses like a centurion," said the courtier. "She makes even the emperor blush.")

Domna wrinkled her nose but otherwise ignored her older sister. "I have a reason for introducing the two of you, beyond the fact that you both have such promising careers ahead of you. At my request, Philostratus has begun work on a book about Apollonius of Tyana. Ah, I see your face light up, Senator Pinarius. It is my understanding that one of your ancestors knew the great wise man, and became one of his most devoted followers here in Rome. It is said that the two of them conspired to outwit the impious emperor Domitian."

"I think it was Apollonius alone who did the outwitting," said Gaius.

"There, you see, that is precisely why you must get to know Philostratus, and vice versa, so that you can share with him the exact, authentic details of your family's dealings with Apollonius, so that Philostratus can weave them into his narrative."

"This is to be a biography?" asked Gaius. "I thought only emperors and kings were worthy of those."

"Why not philosophers?" said Domna.

"Indeed," said Philostratus.

"And perhaps even women?" said Maesa.

This last notion clearly went too far for Philostratus, who ignored it. "Biography, philosophical treatise, novel?" he said. "I'm not sure what posterity will call my book about the sage of Tyana, yet I can see it quite clearly in my mind's eye, glittering with wit and brimming with wisdom, a book quite unlike any other."

Domna clucked her tongue. "That is a Platonic ideal of a book, not a real book—which is what I'm paying you to write. Such a book is greatly needed by the world, so that all people everywhere may become acquainted with Apollonius of Tyana."

"You are a follower, Domna?" asked Gaius.

"I am. Just as Elagabalus—Sol Invictus, if you wish— outshines all other gods, so the guiding light of Apollonius outshines that of any other mortal who ever lived. His every utterance, and every story about him, is more precious than gold. And yet, all I know of Apollonius is a patchwork of legends and secondhand tales. So I think a book is needed, to capture once and for all time the man and his teachings. Such a book might change the world, I think."

Philostratus nodded.

Domna inclined her head to Gaius. "I am told that you and your family have a shrine to Apollonius in your home, Senator Pinarius."

"We do."

"So do my sister and I. In our shrine there is a statue of the sage, and also a staff and a cloak that belonged to him."

"Precious relics!" cried Maesa, raising her hands. "Sacred relics of the wise man!"

"We brought them all the way from Emesa," said Domna.

Easier to transport than a giant black rock, thought Gaius.

"Would you like to see the shrine, Senator Pinarius?"

"I would."

There followed a great deal of ceremony as various courtiers departed from the chamber following some predetermined order of rank, while others formed a cordon to escort the empress and her attendants, including Gaius and Philostratus, out of the room and down a series of hallways. These elaborate proceedings were something new to the palace, at least in Gaius's experience. Commodus had not bothered with such formalities. Perhaps this was how things were done in Emesa.

Domna was at the head of the party, followed by her sister, with Gaius and Philostratus close behind them. Suddenly, ahead of them, two little boys, screaming with laughter, careened around a corner and came racing toward them. Gaius thought they looked about the same age as little Aulus. They skidded to a halt, barely avoiding a collision with Domna, who abruptly stopped, as did everyone else in the party.

The two little boys were red-faced from laughing. "Mother!" cried one of them, looking up at Domna, so that Gaius realized they were the emperor's two sons.

The rowdy boys were followed by two flustered, angry teenaged girls who looked so alike, and so much like their sharp-featured mother, that Gaius knows at once they must be Domna's nieces, the two daughters of Maesa. The two sets of siblings were first cousins, and they clearly did not get along. This was not surprising. Even the imperial family was, after all, a family, with many of the same dynamics that existed in households everywhere.

"What is going on?" demanded Maesa of her daughters.

"They're behaving like monsters, Mother," said one of the girls.

"Malicious little monsters!" said the other. "They were rooting through my jewelry box and stole a very delicate brooch with pieces of colored glass and copper, the one that's shaped like a peacock. I told them to give it back, but they say they'll break it before they let me have it."

"But you can't touch us!" said the bigger of the boys, clutching the brooch to his chest. "We're the sons of Severus, and no one on earth has the right to touch us except the emperor himself!"

"And your mother!" said Domna, so sternly that the boy's stubborn lower lip began to tremble. "You will return the brooch to your cousin at once."

"You'd better do it!" said the smaller of the boys. An array of rebellious, sulky expressions played across the face of his older brother, who at last seemed ready to obey as he turned toward his cousin and held forth the brooch. With a triumphant smile, the girl reached out to take it, but at the last moment the boy threw it against the floor, where bits of colored glass shattered against the polished marble.

The girl let out a scream, and then began to weep. Her sister moved to comfort her. Their distress seemed only to encourage the little boy, who proceeded to stamp his foot on what remained of the brooch.

"Now you've done it!" said his little brother.

"Because I'm not a coward, like you."

"I am not a coward!"

"You're both little monsters!" said the girl comforting her sister.

"You mustn't call them that," said Maesa.

"But it's what they are, Mother. Horrible little monsters good for nothing but making us miserable."

"Boys, you *will* apologize," said Domna.

"But I'm not the one who took it," said the smaller boy.

"But it was your idea," said his older brother.

Suddenly all the members of the imperial family seemed to be talking at once—the boys squabbling, the girls expressing outrage, their mothers demanding order. Finally Domna clapped her hands and they all fell silent. She turned to a pair of courtiers and ordered them to escort the children away. The boys were taken in one direction and the girls in another.

"And find someone to sweep up this mess," she ordered, pointing the end of her elegant sandal at a bit of shattered glass.

As they proceeded toward the shrine of Apollonius, Gaius attempted to assume a properly pious demeanor, but he could hardly keep from laughing.

Later, at the house of the Pinarii, Galen arrived as a dinner guest. While they relaxed in the garden, drinking wine and nibbling roasted pine nuts, Gaius told him everything about his imperial audience.

"To think, that a woman with such lofty philosophical pretensions should have produced two such ill-behaved children!" Gaius shook his head.

"But they're only little boys, after all," said Galen.

"So is Aulus, but I would be appalled if he ever behaved in such a way, especially in front of other people."

"Yes, but Aulus is not an emperor's son."

"All the more reason one might expect those two boys to be better behaved, to have more self-control, even if they're only five or six. Marcus Aurelius was never like that, not even as a child. So my father always told me."

"I think that Marcus Aurelius must have been as exceptional among boys as he was among men. And we are now ruled not by Marcus, but by Septimius Severus. Considering his political canniness, and his skill on the battlefield, Severus is likely to be our emperor for quite some time—long enough, perhaps, for one of those little boys to grow up to succeed him."

"As Commodus succeeded Marcus? When I think of the savage behavior of those two boys—'malicious little monsters,' as their cousins called them—and the impulsive way the older one destroyed that trinket rather than return it, in spite of his strong-willed mother, and in front of everyone . . . well, the idea of such a child as emperor is a sobering thought."

A.D. 204

A crier in a bright yellow tunic, attended by boys waving colorful cloth streamers, strode down the street, announcing a forthcoming celebration. "The likes of which," he shouted, "no one alive has seen before, nor will ever see again!"

"How can he make such a claim?" asked Aulus, peering out a window at the motley procession below. "I've never seen these so-called Saecular Games before, but I'm only fifteen. Who's to say I won't live to see the next Saecular Games?"

They were in the upstairs room of the workshop. On a long summer day, the room could become very warm, but the open windows provided the best light for drawing. Aulus had shown himself to be an excellent draftsman. Even now, he was making a quick sketch of the herald and the boys with streamers.

"The Saecular Games take place only once every hundred and ten years," explained his father. "The last were held in the time of Domitian, when your great-great-grandfather wore the fascinum and knew Apollonius of Tyana. I wasn't around for those Saecular Games, and I surely won't be here for the next. Nor will you, my son, unless you live to be a hundred and twenty-five."

"Why every hundred and ten years?"

"Because that is thought to be the longest possible length of a human life, and thus the schedule makes true the claim—any given man will see only *one* in his lifetime, if indeed he sees one at all. Thus the old joke: An athlete loses every competition at the Saecular Games, but he is comforted by a friend who tells him, 'Cheer up! I'm sure you'll win at the *next* Saecular Games!'"

Aulus groaned. His father told terrible jokes.

"And because they are so rare, those who stage them feel obligated to make the Saecular Games truly memorable. It's a rare opportunity for an emperor to celebrate his reign."

In fact, Septimius Severus had much to celebrate. After successfully putting down Roman rivals in both Asia and Gaul, and winning the greatest victories in the East since Trajan— not only sacking the Parthian capital Ctesiphon but adding the rich city of Palmyra to the empire—Severus had taken a valedictory homecoming tour of his native Africa with the sixteen-year-old co-emperor, Antoninus. Back in Rome at last, Severus was in the mood to stage an expensive, extravagant, truly once-in-a-lifetime spectacle to celebrate his reign and the restored well-being of the empire.

Along with plays and chariot races and athletic contests, the Saecular Games would be marked by ceremonial sacrifices on various nights at different temples and sacred sites all over the city, each ceremony overseen by the emperor himself and attended by a chorus of boys and girls to sing the ancient hymns, including the famous song composed by the great poet Horace when Augustus revived the Games, which had lapsed during the civil wars of the old Republic. Because he was blessed with a splendid singing voice and had not yet put on his manly toga, Aulus had been chosen for the chorus, which was a great honor.

For the last month, he had spent many hours rehearsing with the chorus. Among the other singers, despite having only a passable singing voice, was the emperor's younger son, Geta, who was the same age as Aulus.

Gaius dismissed the workers. He and Aulus spent the last hour of daylight at the baths, washing off marble dust, then went home and changed into suitable tunics for dinner. Gaius welcomed two friends he had not seen in some time, Galen, who at seventy-five seemed quite old, and Philostratus, who at thirty-four seemed very much in his prime. Before dinner, everyone gathered in the vestibule and lit incense before the shrine of Apollonius of Tyana. Everyone conversed in Greek, in deference to the native tongue of the guests, and also because Gaius felt that Aulus did not speak Greek often enough and could use the practice.

Over dinner, they gossiped about the imperial family. Aulus had his own unique insights, having befriended Geta and having listened to his complaints. Geta was jealous that his brother, older by only a year, had been made co-emperor at the age of ten. Antoninus would serve as his father's partner at the upcoming sacrifices, while Geta was literally to be relegated to the chorus. Domna, who frequently attended and on occasion took over rehearsals of the chorus, expended a great deal of energy keeping peace in the household. Mother, father, and sons all had domineering personalities. This created conflict but also a certain dynamism. No one could call the Severans boring.

All four had spent time not only in Rome but also on campaign, including Domna, who was called "Mother of the Camp." Severus seemed to rely on her for political advice and even for military strategy.

"They say there's been no woman her equal since Cleopatra," said Philostratus.

"Ah, Cleopatra!" said Galen. "Always the standard against whom any strong female is compared."

"And not always as a compliment," noted Gaius, "since Cleopatra was the enemy of Rome, and came to a bad end."

"Better comparison to Cleopatra than to Agrippina!" said Aulus, whose tutor had recently assigned him Suetonius and Tacitus on the reign of Nero.

Talk turned to business matters. Gaius and his workshop had at last finished the equestrian statue of Severus that Domna had commissioned years ago. Gaius proudly believed it could stand comparison with the renowned equestrian statue of Marcus, his grandfather's masterpiece. Renovation of the Colossus of Sol had been finished and dedicated long ago, and the great Arch to mark the emperors' victories over Parthia had been dedicated the previous year.

"For Parthia, Severus deserved to celebrate a triumph," said Galen, "but alas, his gout had taken so severe a turn that he couldn't possibly stand upright in the chariot for the duration of the parade."

"Will he be able to stand for the ceremonies at the Saecular Games?" asked Aulus.

"We must pray that he will. The affliction waxes and wanes."

"But we were speaking of the new equestrian statue of Severus," said Philostratus. "I've just finished my composition commissioned by Domna, a brief discourse in Greek that I will read to a private gathering of the imperial family before the dedication of the statue."

"Father says you're the best writer in Rome," said Aulus. Galen frowned. He had come to consider himself not only a physician and scientist but also a philosopher and, if he were frank, the greatest living master of the Greek language. Aulus didn't notice the old man's reaction. "Why didn't our Domina also ask you to write a hymn for the Games, as Augustus asked Horace?"

"The answer is simple, Aulus," said Philostratus. "First, I am not a poet. Second, I write in Greek, not Latin. Imagine a Greek hymn sung at the Saecular Games of Rome!"

"How goes your biography of Apollonius of Tyana?" asked Galen, a bit maliciously, since they all knew that Philostratus despaired of ever finishing it.

"It plods along. The research is never-ending, but I've finished a few chapters to show Domna that I progress. If anything, she's more enthusiastic than ever. She says that my book is something the world sorely needs right now, to remind people of the greatest of all the wonder-workers who ever lived, and to acquaint them with the source of his marvelous powers, the singular, universal spirit that underlies all existence, and is most clearly manifested to mortals in the life-giving rays of the Sun."

Galen cleared his throat, sorry now that he had asked, but Philostratus wasn't finished.

"There are so many fools and charlatans and cults nowadays that prey on the gullible and the ignorant, turning them away from philosophy and true religion. As Domna puts it, 'Who would waste his time bowing down to the mean-spirited storm god of the Jews, or adoring the imaginary wonder-worker-on-a-cross worshipped by the Christians, if he could be made aware of the marvelous story of Apollonius of Tyana, and emerge from the shadows that obscure true wisdom into the full light of the Sun?'"

Gaius nodded. "Well put! Except from sheer ignorance, what man would worship a local storm god above the one and only Sun that shines on us all? What rational person would revere a convicted criminal above the most beloved and miraculous of all wise men? I came across a Christian writing recently that I found particularly offensive. I would never have bothered to read such trash, except that a friend who knows of our direct family connection to the Rain Miracle, via my uncle Kaeso, thought I should know about it.

"A certain Tertullian claims that it was the prayers of Christian soldiers to their god that brought about the Rain Miracle and saved the Roman army, and further, that the proof of this can be found in a letter written by Marcus Aurelius himself, wherein he openly credits the Christians. Now, if Tertullian means the letter Marcus wrote to the Senate to report on the Rain Miracle, Marcus said no such thing! I actually went to the archives to read it myself. In the letter Marcus states what everyone knows: it was the prayer of Harnouphis the Egyptian and the piety of the Divine Marcus that saved the Romans that day."

"Not to mention wing-footed Mercury and the storm wrought by Jupiter," said Galen, stating the obvious.

Gaius nodded. "You know, Commodus tried to take credit for the Rain Miracle, too, though no one ever believed him, and now these Christians want to do so. It's quite horrible how an event so remarkable, so singular, so *beautiful,* must inevitably be tarnished by latter-day opportunists with their own agenda and no respect for the truth!" He took a deep breath. "I apologize for my outburst of emotion. I suppose it's because thoughts of the Rain Miracle bring to mind Uncle Kaeso, whom I still miss so very much. Dear Uncle Kaeso would have given this Tertullian a kick in the balls! But now I descend to vulgarity, so let's change the subject. What else are you working on?"

Philostratus pressed his fingertips together. "There is a—a dream project, shall I call it?—a work I will call *On Heroes,* about the afterlife of Achilles and other Greek heroes who attained immortality and live on in the mortal realm as demons—it's good that we're speaking Greek, for I think there is no exact Latin equivalent for that word. When a mortal calls for help in times of distress, and no god or goddess hears and responds, that beleaguered mortal may turn to a demon, like Achilles. I myself on numerous occasions have called on Protesilaus. The hero has never failed me."

Philostratus saw the blank look on the face of Aulus. "When the Greek fleet landed at Troy, Protesilaus was the first man to leap ashore, despite the prediction of an oracle that the first Greek warrior to touch land would be the first to die. Protesilaus was bold and fearless. He killed four men in combat before he himself was slain by Hector. Thus he became the first Greek to die, fulfilling the prophecy. He is not as famous as Ajax or Achilles, to be sure, but he is a powerful and trustworthy demon, nonetheless. Perhaps, Aulus, your tutor should assign more Homer and less Tacitus."

"That would be fine with me!" said Aulus. The others laughed.

"Many people, when they are sick, turn for help to a demon rather than a physician," said Galen. "That is, if they can afford to do so. As you know, I've never charged a fee for my services, but the priests who keep the shrines of heroes invariably demand an offering if one wishes to sacrifice at an altar or to sleep overnight on temple grounds, seeking guidance from a dream. Consulting demons can be quite expensive."

"I'll tell you what's expensive," said Philostratus. "Theriac. Yet everyone seems to be using it, and everyone swears by it. It's said to be good for every ailment."

"And even better if you have no ailment," quipped Gaius, who had once tried theriac and had found it quite intoxicating.

"You know, theriac used to be quite rare," said Galen. "It was available only to a select handful, like the Divine Marcus— who consumed it voraciously, as if it were a food. Now theriac is everywhere, though I suspect much of the stuff that passes for theriac is counterfeit, or made from inferior recipes. Real theriac alleviates pain and induces a restful sleep. It also relieves loose bowels."

"Causes constipation, you mean," said Gaius, with a grunt.

"That *can* be a side effect," said Galen.

"No wonder so many people in Rome walk about looking so glum nowadays," mused Philostratus, "if they're all taking theriac!"

The three days of the Saecular Games began at sundown with a distribution to all the citizens of torches made of pitch and brimstone. The smoke from these torches purified the city, fending off plague and illness. The light illuminated temples and altars where nocturnal sacrifices were made to the deities of the underworld. Black hogs and milk-white lambs were slaughtered by priests and offered to the gods.

For all the citizens to be out on a warm, starry summer night was strange enough; to see the city lit by thousands and thousands of torches was truly magical. Surely the gods, no matter how high they dwelt, could see the lights of Rome that night. Gaius felt a welling of religious fervor that he had not experienced in a long time. Rome was truly the center of the world, he thought, and the sacred rites and ceremonies of the Roman people, so numerous and complicated and ancient, practiced century after century, were the most pleasing of any on earth to the gods, who continued to bless the city, its people, and its empire. The spectacles, feasts, plays, and races in the days ahead would be produced on a scale no other city in the world could match, but it was the religious rites that were the essential core of every Roman festival. These moments of animal sacrifice, observed with pious devotion and scrupulous attention to the minutest details, exemplified the everlasting bond between the citizens and the priests, between the people and the gods, between the living and their ancestors and the generations yet to come.

Gaius reached up and touched the fascinum where it nestled under his toga. In another year, he would be passing it on to Aulus. How quickly time passed!

The next morning, men and boys attended a sacrifice of white bulls to Jupiter, while at the Temple of Juno women and girls witnessed the slaughter of white cows and heifers. They all came together at the Temple of Apollo, where the boy singers stood along one side of the temple steps while the girls stood on the other.

On the porch of the temple, looking out over the vast crowd, sat the imperial family. They had planned to stand, but the emperor's gout was acting up, so all were seated.

Senators stood at the front of the crowd. Gaius Pinarius was in the front row, with an unobstructed view of the singers, including Aulus, who stood next to Geta. Poor Severus, he thought, looking up at the imperial family. At fifty-nine the great general and statesman had become a gouty old man who could hardly stand, reduced to resting on his laurels.

The Terror of the Senate—his promise to kill no senators had frequently been broken—had become the beloved and avuncular Father of the Fatherland. Next to him, Domna, at forty-four, was more demanding and domineering than ever. On this occasion as on others, she had intruded on the ceremonies and was taking part to a degree never previously allowed to a woman. Her older sister, Maesa, sat beside her, along with her two daughters, young women in their twenties now with senators for husbands. Gaius thought of the first time he had seen them, angry and tearful over the theft of a brooch, and smiled.

At the right hand of Severus sat one-half of the cause of the girls' vexation on that occasion, young Antoninus. Like his father, he was dressed in imperial purple. The little hellion was now a sixteen-year-old, a man by law, and deemed by his father ready to take on a share of the imperial burden. Antoninus certainly exuded a fierce energy, with his flashing eyes and brooding good looks.

Nearby, on the steps, standing next to Aulus, was young Geta, looking a great deal like his brother, but a year younger, and thus relegated to the boys' chorus. He was not as intense and somber as Antoninus. There was still something of the mischievous boy about him.

At that very moment, in fact, Geta was whispering something to Aulus, and both of them were staring at Antoninus, ignoring the city prefect on the temple steps who was making a rather long and boring speech.

"At home, we don't call him 'Antoninus' anymore," Geta whispered.

"What, then?" Aulus whispered back.

"Father started it. He calls him 'Caracalla.'"

"Do you mean to say 'Caligula'?" asked Aulus, hoping to get a laugh, but Geta only grunted.

"No!" he whispered. "It's a kind of cloak worn by Gauls. You'd recognize one if you saw it—stupid-looking thing, reaches to the ankles. At home, Antoninus wears hardly anything else. He'd be wearing a caracalla now if Father didn't insist on a purple toga in public, which I think looks even stupider on him. But you're right, it does sound a bit like 'Caligula.' That name came from a common soldier's boot. 'Little Boots'—such a harmless name for a boy who turned out to be such a nasty viper." He gave his older brother a baleful stare.

"'Caracalla' sounds harmless, too. Rather euphonious," Aulus whispered, using a Greek word he had learned from Philostratus. "'Caracalla'—why, it's almost musical. But sweet Apollo, there's our cue!" The city prefect had finished his speech, the chorus master had taken his place, and the hymn was beginning.

As they sang, the boys kept one eye on the chorister master and the other on Caracalla, as he would henceforth be known.

Earlier, as everyone had been taking their place for the ceremony, Domna and the other women of the family had come over to say a few words to Geta and Aulus, wishing them a good performance. Caracalla had been with his mother, but had said nothing. As the imperial party turned away to walk up the steps, Geta and Aulus had performed a move they had practiced in advance, Aulus pulling back a fold of Caracalla's toga while Geta dropped something inside. The maneuver had gone perfectly. No one saw or suspected a thing.

"Life-giving Sun," the boys sang, "who brings forth the day and hides it away, born each day anew, yet ever the same . . ."

Seated stiffly upright next to his father, Caracalla suddenly began to squirm. His movements were so slight at first as to be almost imperceptible, but it was the very thing the two boys had been watching for. Caracalla's fixed, sullen expression was interrupted by a quivering of his chin, rapid blinking, a sudden grimace.

"May you never, Apollo," the boys sang, "as you span the whole world, bringing everywhere light, behold any sight greater than Rome!"

Aulus strove to keep singing, desperately trying not to laugh. Beside him, Geta began to giggle, and raised a hand to cover his mouth. While they watched, Caracalla, with the eyes of all Rome upon him, sat as stiff as a statue but turned bright red while a large spider crawled out of his toga, down one arm, and across his trembling hand. He swallowed hard and clenched his jaw. Very slowly he turned his head and fixed on the boys a gaze of pure malice.

Aulus felt a chill go up his spine, and fell silent. But Geta, staring at his furious, red-faced brother, could not stop giggling.

A.D. 217

On the first really warm day of spring, Gaius, Aulus, Philostratus, and Galen all agreed to meet at the recently opened facility that everyone was calling the Baths of Caracalla—the nickname by which the emperor was commonly known by everyone from family members to fishmongers. The late Severus might have been first to use it, but the name had quickly spread among soldiers along the Rhine and Danube when the young emperor ruthlessly put down a barbarian uprising, and then through the general population. Admirers and detractors alike called the ruler of the empire Caracalla.

Gaius had even sculpted the young emperor wearing his namesake garment. He and Aulus paused as they passed the statue, which stood on a pedestal in the vestibule of the new baths. No one could miss it. It was an unusual, even daring work, for Caracalla seemed to be glowering at all who passed. That was the expression the emperor had insisted on. This portrait, and countless others—sculptures, coins, medallions—marked Caracalla's deliberate break from the aloof images of the philosopher-emperors of earlier generations. His close-cropped haircut was that of a common soldier, and his pugnacious scowl was so realistic that all who saw it felt threatened. He was certainly not a philosopher, nor a wastrel, would-be gladiator, like Commodus, but a true warrior, like his father, a rugged soldier-emperor. Severus had wanted statues that made him look like Hadrian or the Divine Marcus. Caracalla wanted statues that looked like no one but himself.

Like his father, he had proven to be quite ruthless. Severus, ill and dying while campaigning with his son in Britannia, had decreed that Caracalla and Geta should rule jointly. Perhaps he imagined they would be an ideal pair of rulers with complementary temperaments, like Marcus Aurelius and Lucius Verus; but this was the wishful thinking of a dying man. "Keep peace between you, shower money on the soldiers, scorn all others," he had instructed them. But there was no peace in the palace as the two brothers and their factions squared off, despite Domna's desperate attempts to bring them together. Twice Caracalla tried to have Geta assassinated. The second time, he succeeded. At a meeting to work out their differences, mediated by their mother, Geta in good faith arrived without bodyguards. Caracalla's centurions slaughtered him on the spot. He died in his mother's arms.

Caracalla decreed that the Senate should damn Geta's memory and that all images of him should be destroyed. In every family portrait of the Severans in every city of the empire, one face was crudely erased. The effect was not to make people forget about Geta, but the opposite: to remember what happened to anyone who crossed Caracalla, even a younger brother.

Now, walking past the statue of Caracalla, it was Geta that both Gaius and Aulus thought of. "I remember him so clearly," said Aulus, "even though he's been dead for six years. I could sculpt him from memory."

"Don't even think such a thing!" whispered his father, for to possess even a coin with Geta's image could lead to arrest. Given Aulus's friendship with Geta, it was something of a miracle that the Pinarii had survived his assassination. Gaius credited their survival to two things: first and foremost, the fascinum, which glinted on Aulus's chest as father and son stripped off their togas in the changing room; and secondly, Domna and her continuing influence, despite everything, over her erratic and bad-tempered son. Gaius and Aulus were part of the empress's charmed circle of artists and writers, whom she shielded as best she could. In recent years, Gaius had seen little of her. Even now, Domna was off somewhere, accompanying Caracalla on campaign with the title Mother of the Camp, just as she had accompanied and advised Severus.

As father and son stepped into the cold plunge and then quickly stepped out, a slave attended each of them, drying them with linen cloths. Gaius never visited this place without being impressed. Whatever one thought of Caracalla, the baths that bore his name were enormous and extraordinarily beautiful and ornate, decorated with marble and sculptures everywhere one looked. Whatever else he might achieve, this establishment would be a true and lasting monument to the young emperor.

Among the decorations in this room was a statue Domna had ordered from the Pinarii some years ago, a serene bust of Apollonius of Tyana that offered a stark contrast to the scowling Caracalla in the vestibule.

"But look, here's Galen," said Aulus, who spotted the gray, stooped figure walking slowly toward them. The physician's energy and stamina had faded much in recent years, but his wits were still keen. "Are you ready for the cold plunge?" asked Aulus. "It's so exhilarating!"

"To a fellow your age, yes. You're not yet thirty. You young ones perpetually need cooling off! But not so, for an old man like myself. Moist, dry, hot, cold—the four primary characteristics of the living organism. To age is to gradually lose moisture and heat, to become ever drier, ever colder—until at last all heat and moisture leave the body and life ceases. That's why you see old men like me spending so much time in this place. We crave the moisture to slake our desiccation, and the hot plunge to replenish our dwindling heat. No, thank you—no cold plunge for me!"

In the room with the hot pool, Philostratus was waiting for them. He was back in Rome for only a short visit before returning east to join the imperial retinue as Caracalla and the Mother of the Camp made war on the Parthians.

When they were all comfortably settled up to their necks in the swirling, steaming water, Philostratus made an announcement. "It's finally finished. *The Life of Apollonius of Tyana*—it's done!"

"Congratulations!" said Gaius, slapping his palms against the water with genuine excitement.

Galen fussily avoided the resulting splashes. "Yes, congratulations," he said quietly.

"It's in Greek, of course, but the first copies are to be transcribed and released here in Rome. I'll oversee that process myself, making sure it's done accurately and expeditiously. Then I'll do the same in Athens, on my way east. Domna wants the book to be widely available in both cities as soon as possible, with Antioch and Alexandria and other cities to follow."

Aulus was impressed. "A new book, available everywhere at once, with the empress as publisher. Why, in a very short time, it might become the most widely read book in the whole empire."

"Perhaps. That's the idea. Domna's idea, I should say."

"Oh, I suspect there are works by Galen that will remain more widely read, at least for a while," said Gaius. "There are so many copies in circulation. What a remarkable pair you are, my learned Greek friends. Two men of different generations, one foremost of all those who seek to understand and alleviate the physical ailments of mortals, the other soon to be foremost of all who bring sacred knowledge by means of the book. Really, it's quite an honor that Aulus and I should know you both, and call you friends."

Philostratus smiled modestly, but Galen looked away. He felt both flattered and piqued that Gaius should equate him with Philostratus. He had always been a bit jealous of the younger man and the lavish praise, privileges, and advantages

Philostratus enjoyed thanks to Domna. Now that the biography of Apollonius of Tyana was finished, was it not time for someone to write the biography of Galen of Pergamum? In many ways Galen considered himself the equal of Apollonius, both as a teacher and as a wonder-worker. He, too, cured the lame and restored the sick to health, and not by supernatural means but by the application of reason and knowledge. No man alive understood the mysteries of the physical world better than Galen. Apollonius supposedly understood and had contact with some force beyond the world of the senses, transcending death, but Galen, too, as a physician and writer, had pondered the mystery of life and death. Apollonius was remembered and revered many decades after his death. Would Galen be remembered even a hundred years hence?

He was about to say something snappish to Philostratus, then stopped himself. Who wanted to hear the carping of an old man? With all his accomplishments, how could it be that Galen felt jealous of any man? Jealousy and pride were equally vain. How many mortals had envied Severus with all his glory and power, and yet, when Galen last saw the emperor, treating the man's gout before he set out for Britain, Severus said to him, "I have been everything—and gained nothing." *Everything* and *nothing*: the remark had stopped Galen cold. In the end, did the material world and the realm of the senses amount to nothing, then? In the end, could it be that *everything* and *nothing* were the same?

Galen cleared his throat and was about to say something— something important, he was quite sure, yet even as it formed in his mind and before it reached his lips the idea seemed to evaporate, like the vanishing mist on the water. The others stared at him, awaiting his utterance. They looked expectant, then suddenly alarmed. Was the look on his face so very strange? Curious to the end, Galen wished he could look in a mirror, so as to see what they saw, and thus understand their reaction. Then he felt a stabbing pain, so sharp it crowded out everything else. He clutched his chest and lost consciousness.

The others pulled him from the pool and tried to revive him. They called for help. Men came running. There were always plenty of physicians at the baths, dispensing advice and lecturing.

But there was nothing to be done. Galen was dead.

Philostratus was speechless. Gaius wept. Aulus comforted his father. Slaves arrived with a sheet to cover the body and a stretcher to bear it away. Death at the baths was not entirely uncommon.

The commotion had hardly subsided when another began. It started with cries from the vestibule and then moved through every room, carried on waves of murmurs and gasps. Even the death of Galen could not have caused such a reaction. It had to be something bigger.

One of Philostratus's slaves ran toward them.

"Dominus . . ." he began.

"Say it, man! Quickly!" They were already shaken, and now filled with dread.

"The emperor—they say he's dead."

"Caracalla? How?"

"Murdered by a common soldier over some petty slight. They were out riding, when the emperor dismounted, and walked behind some rocks . . . to relieve himself. While his guard was down, the killer struck."

"A disgusting story!" said Philostratus. "Too tawdry to be true."

"Too tawdry *not* to be true," said Aulus.

"But there's more news, Dominus. Bad news. The empress, when she received the news . . . she was already ill, suffering from a tumor in one breast. She ended her own life."

Philostratus closed his eyes and shook his head in disbelief.

"Poor Domna," said Aulus. "Her husband gone, then one son . . . then the other . . ."

With Geta murdered and the childless Caracalla assassinated, there was no line of succession. Domna, who might have masterminded a transition, was gone as well.

"Who will rule us now?" whispered Aulus, reaching up to touch the fascinum.

From the roof of their house Gaius and his son and seven-year-old grandson watched the awesome spectacle of Rome in flames. This time it was the Flavian Amphitheater that was on fire, as well as parts of the palace on the Palatine Hill. It was late August, the day of the Vulcanalia. The heat was sweltering. The sky was full of dark clouds. It was a lightning strike that started the fire, a thunderbolt so powerful it shook the walls of their house.

From their vantage point, the sight was shocking and bizarre. People thought of the amphitheater as made of solid stone, but there was abundant wood all through the structure. The amphitheater had become a gigantic bowl full of flames, spewing ash and plumes of cinders like a volcano. Standing next to the amphitheater and equally tall, the Colossus of Sol seemed to be watching the disaster with perverse enjoyment as the glow of the flames glittered across his golden, faintly smiling face.

"Why did we give him that insipid smile?" wondered Gaius aloud.

"We gave him the expression that Severus—or Domna, rather—desired," said Aulus.

"The Colossus originally looked like Nero. Some people will imagine they're seeing the face of Nero, watching the city burn once again."

"The city? But there's no reason to think the fire will spread," said Aulus uneasily. "There's a lot of open space around the structure to act as a firebreak, and plenty of water in all the aqueducts to douse the flames, and trained vigiles to direct the work. And these dark clouds might yet pour rain."

"Will the Colossus fall down?" asked a childish voice. Aulus's son, Titus, was standing between them.

"Of course it won't!" said Aulus. "Your grandfather and I rebuilt it to last for ages." But he shuddered at the thought. If the wooden supports inside the Colossus somehow caught fire, the whole statue might become a sort of oven, heating the metal sufficiently to bring down the entire structure—which might fall against the amphitheater. If that were to happen, the Colossus and the amphitheater might both be completely destroyed, and the heart of Rome turned into an inferno. A fire of such magnitude might quickly spread out of control.

Aulus touched the fascinum. His father saw, and reached over to do the same, as both whispered a prayer that the Colossus would be spared. Domna, their champion, was dead, and they had no ties to the new emperor. It would be an ill omen indeed if one of the Pinarii's finest and most visible achievements, the refurbished Colossus, should collapse.

"No matter what happens, the fire will be seen as a very bad portent," said Aulus. "It's the new emperor who'll be cast in a bad light. The Senate already hates him, if only because he's not one of them. The first man to be proclaimed emperor who's not from the ranks of the Senate—a Berber from Mauretania! The people hate him, too, because rumor has it he conspired to have Caracalla killed, after the emperor saw fit to make him Prefect of the Praetorian Guards. The people loved Caracalla, if only because he gave them such wonderful baths! Never mind that he bankrupted the state to pay for those baths, and also to raise the soldier's pay."

"Macrinus should come to Rome, and quickly," said Gaius. "It's all very well for an army at one end of the empire to call you emperor. The real test comes when a man appears in person before the Senate and the people of Rome. When he does arrive, we'll have to be on our guard. New emperors like to clean house."

"But Macrinus will need us, Father, if he wants to restore the amphitheater. Think of all those ruined statues!" In the arched niches that encircled the amphitheater stood scores of statues, of heroes, emperors, and gods, now stark silhouettes against the raging flames behind them. As the Pinarii watched, some of the statues fell from their crumbling pedestals, like desperate men jumping from the windows of a burning tenement.

"I wonder what Macrinus looks like? In his early fifties, they say, with short hair but a very full beard. We shall have to sculpt him, of course. And his little son, this ten-year-old he insists on calling his co-emperor."

"A little boy with a very big name—Diadumenianus," said Aulus.

"Dia—Dia—" Listening closely to his father, Titus tried to say the name, and failed.

"So now we're to be ruled by a man who's never set foot inside the Senate House, and a boy hardly older than Titus," said Gaius. "Let's hope they at least have interesting features, if sculpt them we must."

The idea of new imperial commissions gave Gaius a feeling of well-being starkly at odds with the horror of watching the amphitheater burn. There was no disaster so universal that it did not bring good fortune to someone. Was it hubris, to think such a thing? Wealth and success inevitably attracted the Evil Eye of the envious and the spiteful. The only way to stave off such malevolent ill will was the fascinum. Gaius reached toward it again. Aulus must have had similar thoughts, for the fingers of father and son met as they touched the amulet. Young Titus, watching them, somberly reached up to do likewise. All sensed the power of the ancient amulet as it joined the three of them, not just with each other but with all the ancestors in all the ages past.

A.D. 219

It was almost two years after the fire that Senator Gaius Pinarius joined his peers in the Senate House for a most unusual and very important event. On the wall behind the Altar of Victory and above her statue, a very unusual portrait was about to be unveiled. It was a painting of their new emperor, a young man very few people in Rome had ever seen.

Macrinus and his little son with the big name had ruled a little more than a year, without ever arriving in Rome. Unsettled affairs kept them in the East, and things went badly for them when another aspirant to the throne appeared, a fourteen-year-old claiming to be the son of the murdered Antoninus, or Caracalla as he was commonly known. This boy soon had the backing of the Third Legion. Macrinus sent a letter to the Senate in Rome denouncing his rival as "the False Antoninus" and claiming the young man was insane. The consuls and other high-ranking magistrates duly condemned the False Antoninus, and the Senate declared war on him.

Then, at a battle near Antioch, Macrinus was soundly defeated and his troops slaughtered. Those who survived defected to his rival.

Disguised as a courier, Macrinus made a headlong rush toward Rome. His little boy was sent in the opposite direction, to seek sanctuary with the king of Parthia. Both were quickly hunted down and assassinated.

The senators, receiving this news, were thrown into panic. They quickly reversed themselves, declaring that Macrinus had been the pretender and the young man calling himself Antoninus was in fact the legitimate emperor, and was also (though the evidence was thin) the son of Caracalla. In return, the fourteen-year-old emperor issued a blanket pardon to the Senate and began a slow journey westward, consolidating support along the way, heading for Rome.

Son of Caracalla or not, the new emperor was part of the imperial family. He was the son of one of the two teenage girls Gaius had seen in the palace years ago, squabbling with the brats Caracalla and Geta. That made him the grandson of Maesa and the grand-nephew of Severus and Domna. Now those girls were grown up and both widowed, but each had a teenaged son. It was the older of these boys, born and raised in Emesa, who was now emperor of Rome.

To Gaius, the assertion that the boy was the son of Caracalla seemed far-fetched, a ploy to legitimize his claim to power. His mother, Soaemias, was married (and not to Caracalla) at the time of his birth, so to claim that Caracalla was the father was to declare herself an unfaithful wife and her son a bastard. Gaius found it hard to imagine that the squabbling little boy and his angry teenaged cousin grew up to become lovers. Caracalla would have been fifteen at the time and his cousin Soaemias twenty-three. But stranger things had happened, and since both Soaemias and Caracalla had been in Rome at the time of the child's conception, it was not impossible that Caracalla was the father. At any rate, when the senators voted to ratify the boy's ascension, they legally affirmed Caracalla's paternity, so it was now a political fact, whether true or not.

The boy's name at birth had been Sextus Varius Avitus Bassianus. As emperor, his legal name was Marcus Aurelius Antoninus Augustus. Antoninus was now the most common name in the whole empire, thanks to Caracalla's extension of citizenship to every man who was not a slave. Thousands upon thousands of newly enfranchised citizens, many with no Latin name, took their patron's name and called themselves Antoninus. When Macrinus had called his rival the "False Antoninus," it had been something of a joke. Any man could call himself Antoninus, and a multitude of citizens did so.

As he waited for the unveiling of the portrait, Gaius overheard the conversation of two fellow senators who were standing close behind him in the crowd.

"How old is he?"

"Fourteen."

"Hardly old enough to rule an empire. Even Nero was older at the start."

"Domna's sister and her daughters are behind it. Some say the boy is merely a figurehead."

"But it was the boy, not his mother, who rode across the battlefield at Antioch to rally the Third Legion. They say the sight of such a fearless youth put fresh courage in the men. Macrinus turned tail and ran, and that was that."

"I wonder if he looks like Caracalla?"

"In the portrait, you mean? We'll soon see. But pictures can be deceiving. Soon enough we'll see him in the flesh, and judge the resemblance."

"The letter that accompanied the portrait used an odd turn of phrase. It said the painting was being sent ahead to Rome, 'so that the senators may accommodate themselves to his appearance.'"

"Because he looks so very young?"

"I don't know. Perhaps he has a disfigurement of some sort . . ."

The veil concealing the portrait was taller than a man, and equally wide, so the painting was presumably a full-length portrait. Its prominent placement in the vestibule meant that every senator would see it each time he entered or left the chamber.

"Enough idle talk," said one of the men behind Gaius, raising his voice. "Let's have a look, then!"

Others took up the cry, impatient for their first glimpse of the new emperor.

The imperial emissary in charge of the ceremony stepped forward. "Senators of Rome, so that you may see a likeness of our new Dominus before his arrival in the city, he sends you this painting. When you gaze up at Victory, gaze higher, upon our emperor, and remember his victory at Antioch. This is Caesar Marcus Aurelius Antoninus Augustus, grandson of Imperator Caesar Lucius Septimius Severus Eusebes Pertinax Augustus, son of Imperator Caesar Marcus Aurelius Antoninus Augustus who was called Caracalla by his loyal legions. He himself is imperator of all the legions and high priest of Elagabalus."

A cord was pulled. The veil fell away. There was a murmur as the painting was revealed, followed by absolute silence.

The picture was shocking, and not because the new emperor looked like a child, though in fact he did (and nothing at all like Caracalla, thought Gaius). It was the way he was dressed that left the senators speechless. Their new emperor was depicted not in a purple toga, nor in armor, nor heroically naked, but wearing the very ornate and exotic costume of a priest of Elagabalus. Next to him in the painting, and almost as tall, was a conical black stone.

The young man was in fact the high priest of Elagabalus at the god's temple in Emesa, a role he had inherited through his mother. But now that he was emperor he was also Pontifex Maximus, head of the Roman religion, and to appear as an Emesene priest was quite inappropriate.

The garment itself was very exotic to Roman eyes, and rather feminine. A long-sleeved undergarment covered him from head to foot, the bottom half appearing to be pantaloons of the sort that Parthians wore. The fabric was appropriately purple, but wildly ostentatious, with pleated sleeves and hems embroidered with gold thread and sewn with white pearls and colorful gems. On his feet were half-length boots with pointed toes, likewise decorated with jewels. A purple overgarment was draped like a mantle over his chest, then pulled over his shoulders onto his back, then pulled forward over his hips. A gold ring cinched the fabric below his waist, and the remaining fabric descended in folds beyond his knees.

On his head was a golden diadem. A single antenna-like object attached at the center pointed toward the viewer, rather like the cobra poised to strike atop certain Egyptian crowns.

"What is that thing?" Gaius whispered, wondering aloud, but in the silence everyone heard him.

"It's a dried bull's penis. That's what it is," said one of the older senators, with an authoritative tone. "I was in Emesa many years ago when the boy's grandfather was high priest of Elagabalus. I saw the fellow wearing this very outfit, with the same headgear. Don't ask me why, but that's a shriveled bull's penis mounted atop the diadem. And that object next to him is the sacred stone they worship. A baetyl, as the Greeks call such stones. They say he's lugging the thing with him all the way from Emesa, so that all of us can worship it, too."

There were scoffing noises, some nervous laughter, and then a loud hubbub as everyone spoke at once.

A.D. 221

It was a festive day in Rome. The new Temple of Elagabalus on the Palatine had just been finished, and on this day the sacred baetyl was to be paraded through the Forum and installed in the temple. Gaius, wearing his senatorial toga, was part of the procession. His son and grandson were in the crowd, as was his old friend Philostratus.

For better or worse, Gaius no longer enjoyed the privilege of being an insider at the palace. The Pinarii had almost no direct contact with the young emperor, who brought his own sculptors and artisans from Emesa to make portraits of the imperial court. The likenesses they sculpted looked oddly stiff and lifeless to Roman eyes.

Restoration of the burned Flavian Amphitheater had progressed slowly; the very rapid construction of the Temple of Elagabalus had been given priority. Nonetheless, the Pinarii stayed busy, salvaging charred statues or making new ones that would eventually decorate the many niches of the reconstructed amphitheater.

Since the emperor was only a teenager, no one expected him to have the judgment or sophistication of a man. It was widely assumed that his mother and grandmother were in charge. The Emesene women were no strangers to the palace, thanks to their kinship to the late Domna. They were just as ambitious as she had been, or more so. Domna had never presumed to set foot in the Senate House, but Soaemias appeared beside her son in the Senate, sharing the dais with him. (Agrippina, mother of Nero, had notoriously attended the Senate, but kept behind a curtain, out of sight.)

Was the new emperor a weakling, then? There were indications to the contrary. Young Antoninus was certainly headstrong when it came to promoting the worship of Elagabalus. Whenever any deity was invoked in a ceremony, Elagabalus had to be mentioned first, even ahead of Jupiter. The emperor was equally headstrong when it came to matters of state, promoting his loyal coterie of followers ahead of men from old Roman families. As magistrates, he appointed not only newcomers from Emesa, but also cooks, dancers, and athletes. A man once condemned to the galleys was now city prefect. As one disgruntled senator quipped, "This is the logical outcome of his so-called father's decision to make everyone in the empire a Roman citizen. Not only can any person call himself Antoninus, it seems that *anyone* can become *anything*!"

The emperor's unabashed femininity also raised eyebrows. It was one thing for a manly emperor to surround himself with manly gladiators and perhaps discreetly, to engage in manly sex with them; many assumed that Commodus had done so. It was something else for an emperor to relish the female role, and to blatantly advertise the fact. He had even introduced his favorite, a blond charioteer and ex-slave named Hierocles, as "my husband." Many of the low-born citizens and soldiers seemed to find such stories amusing, but senators were scandalized.

The Pinarii got most of their inside news about the palace from Philostratus, who was still part of the imperial court, though not as favored as he had been under Domna. He had met the new emperor only in passing. Young Antoninus cared nothing for philosophers or wise men, and did not read books.

"What does he care about, then?" asked Aulus. He was standing next to Philostratus on a viewing platform at the end of the parade route, close to the Temple of Elagabalus.

"Only two things, as far as I can tell. First, his god. Second, bedding men."

"You're being facetious," said Aulus.

"I am not. Nero wanted only to be an actor; Commodus, to be a gladiator; and young Antoninus . . . to be Venus!" Philostratus sighed and shook his head, affecting a dismay that Aulus found unconvincing. Philostratus was discreet about his personal life, but one had only to read some of his writings to see that he had a weakness for men, or at least an infatuation with dead Greek heroes.

"Some say the boy is as beautiful as Venus," said Aulus with a sly smile, for he sometimes enjoyed teasing the older man.

"I hadn't noticed, so I cannot comment," said Philostratus with a straight face, refusing to take the bait. "But look, here comes the procession. I think I see your father amid that sea of togas. Yes, there he is!"

The senators and magistrates came first, so that when they reached the temple they could assemble on the steps and watch the rest of the procession as it arrived. Their expressions were variously confused, pained, glum—anything but festive. That included Gaius Pinarius, who gave his son and friend a nod of recognition.

Behind the senators, in ornately carved and sumptuously upholstered litters, came the emperor's grandmother, mother, aunt, and younger cousin. The brawny slaves carrying them were nearly naked, in stark contrast to the female occupants, who were covered from head to foot, so that nothing could be seen but their faces and hands. Even these were largely covered, the hands by bracelets and rings, the faces by the sort of wig and makeup Domna had imported from Emesa and made fashionable in Rome. Their voluminous stolas were typically Roman, as was the suitably modest long-sleeved tunic worn by the thirteen-year-old Alexianus. The women looked straight ahead with serene expressions, ignoring the spectators, but the wide-eyed boy appeared overwhelmed at being the focus of so much attention, almost as if he might cry.

The boy's mother noticed, reached for his hand, and pulled it under a fold of her stola, so that she might hold it, out of sight. Alexianus appeared to gather strength from his mother's touch, and stiffened his jaw.

So far, there had been nothing exotic in the proceedings. Then came the priests of Elagabalus.

First, Aulus heard them. Their chanting was in a foreign tongue, accompanied by the shrill, clashing music of flutes, drums, and tambourines. Then the priests came into view, wearing outfits much like those of the emperor in the picture he had sent to the Senate—pleated sleeves and pants and an outer garment draped over the shoulders and gathered at the hips. These vestments were in many colors, and on their heads they wore high conical hats made of felt, with tasseled earflaps that stood straight from their heads as they whirled about, performing a hopping, leaping, spinning dance. The musicians were not as flamboyantly outfitted, but wore foreign costumes nonetheless and played decidedly foreign music. The tone was joyous, not somber, as befitted the introduction of the baetyl to the people of Rome and the stone's arrival at its new home.

Following the musicians, carried in wagons or by priests, came some of the most sacred objects in the city. These included the baetyl of Magna Mater, which had been imported to Rome in the desperate days of war against Carthage, and was believed to have tipped the scales in Rome's favor. There was also the fire of Vesta, and the sacred shields of Rome's dancing priests, the Salii, and the Palladium, the Trojan image of Athena brought to Rome by Aeneas. To see these things all in one place was marvelous, and the crowd reacted with cries of religious awe and wonderment. But Aulus felt a chill. If this were a triumph, these would be the captured subjects paraded before the people, ahead of the conqueror in his chariot. These revered objects had been removed from their ancient, rightful homes to be collected in a single place, where they would be subservient to the god of that temple, Elagabalus.

Then came an ornate chariot suitable for a triumphing commander and bearing a single occupant, not a man, but a man-sized stone—the baetyl that had been brought from the Temple of Elagabalus in Emesa. The thing was black and roughly conical in shape, but rounded at the top. It looked tremendously heavy; the chariot and its axles must have been reinforced to bear the weight. Reins were somehow attached to the baetyl, creating the bizarre illusion that the stone itself was driving the team of horses. The man who was in fact guiding the chariot, at a slow pace, was the emperor. In his purple and gold costume and golden diadem with its bull's penis, he held in his two hands leather leads attached to each horse, and pulled them onward while he himself walked backward, performing a sort of bowing and skipping dance as he did so. Never once did he turn his head or look over his shoulder; his eyes were fixed on the baetyl. His lips moved constantly, as if whispering a prayer just loud enough for the god in the chariot to hear. Priests sprinkled sand on the roadway ahead of him, so as to give his feet purchase, and other priests walked alongside him, prepared to steady him should he falter in his backward dance, which he never did. His bejeweled boots were constantly in motion, flashing in the sunlight and making a rhythmic, scraping sound against the sand.

Following the chariot of Elagabalus was a gilded wagon drawn by white oxen and festooned with flowers. In the wagon was another baetyl. This sacred stone had been brought to Rome from Carthage, where it had been worshipped for centuries as the heavenly goddess Urania, also called Astarte. Following the installation of the sacred objects inside the new temple, the two baetyls were to appear side by side on the porch of the temple for a divine wedding to unite Elagabalus and Urania, in a ceremony devised and performed by the emperor himself. Then the newly wedded baetyls would be taken inside the temple and installed in a place of honor.

The chariot arrived at the forecourt of the temple. The senators were already assembled on the steps to welcome the baetyls. Ramps, pulleys, and ropes were in place to raise the stones to the porch. Side by side the baetyls ascended. The teams of men pulling the ropes were entirely hidden behind curtains on the temple porch, so that the stones seemed to ascend under their own power. The effect was uncanny.

When the stones were in place, the wedding commenced. Both baetyls were strewn with flower petals, and the emperor, standing between them, made pronouncements in his boyish but quite strong voice. Very few people understood a word he said, since the ceremony was not in Latin.

There was no animal sacrifice. Instead, hundreds of white birds were released to signal that the marriage had been divinely consummated. While the heavenly husband and wife were dragged into the temple, the emperor strode down the steps and across the courtyard to a high tower that had been built as part of the temple complex, an architectural feature imported from Emesa and previously unknown in Rome.

From the top of the tower he looked down on the throng. "Elagabalus has come to Rome!" he cried. "Elagabalus has been wedded to a goddess worthy to rule over all other gods alongside him! Elagabalus and Urania are now at home in the temple I have built for them! All the blessings of Elagabalus will now be bestowed on the city of Rome, and on all Roman citizens everywhere across the world, wherever the light of the sun shines! Let feasting and celebration begin! Let tokens of the love of Elagabalus rain down upon the people, like golden rays of sunlight!"

He threw gold coins from the tower, which flashed and glittered as they rained upon the excited crowd. Then he threw small silver goblets and other prizes, and more coins.

This shower of gifts had been announced ahead of time, so that a huge, expectant multitude of citizens had gathered. The space was quite large, but constricted by the walls of the palace complex and the crowded viewing platform on which Aulus and Philostratus stood. People competed with each other to catch the falling prizes, laughing and shouting and making a game of it. Some fool had been spreading the absurd rumor that the emperor would throw live sheep and goats from the top of the tower. In fact, he threw wooden tokens that were redeemable for these prizes. There were no tokens for pigs, however. Like the Jews, the worshippers of Elagabalus did not eat pork, which they called "unclean."

Aulus and Philostratus, looking down on the surging crowd from the viewing platform, overheard a lively conversation between several men standing behind them.

". . . also like a Jew, he's circumcised. So I heard."

"No, he isn't cut *yet*, but he's going to be—and looking forward to it! It's to happen in the new temple. The priests will catch his blood and offer it to that stone."

"And then do what to the foreskin? Offer it to the lady stone? Imagine a grown man submitting to such a thing!"

"Takes courage, if you ask me. Christian men do it, to please the Jews in their cult. Isn't that so, Manlius? Don't you have a cousin who's a Christian?"

"To my shame. The idea of a man deliberately mutilating his penis is bad enough. I hear the emperor wants to cut it off—the whole thing! Then have the surgeons carve out a hole in its place."

"Surely that's not possible. Not even the great Galen could make a man into a woman! Just because he plays the woman in bed doesn't mean he wants to *be* a woman. What man could want that?"

"But he did marry a woman . . ."

"One of the Vestals. But the senators threw a fit. The marriage is over and the Vestal is still a virgin."

"I heard he wanted a wife so he could learn from her how to please a man—and the Vestal was useless for that, obviously!"

"Big ones. That's what he likes. Extremely large phalluses. Everyone says so. You've got a big one, Manlius. We've all seen you, showing that thing off in the latrina. *And* we know you have a taste for boys. The new Antoninus really is quite pretty. Maybe you should go to the palace—"

"No! Not if I have to stop eating pork, and cut off my—"

The chatter abruptly ceased as something like an earthquake rocked the viewing platform. There were screams from below, and more shaking, as panic erupted and spread through the crowd. What felt like an earthquake was actually the movement of thousands of bodies, some of them being shoved and crushed against the platform. The crowd was jubilant one moment, terrified the next. Even amid the chaos, some people were still trying to catch the prizes and tokens falling from the tower. Some dropped to their hands and knees, scrambling to pick up a coin or goblet. Some stole from others, for amid the screams there were cries of "Thief!" Some were throwing punches, and others ducking and trying to flee. There was blood on people's clothing and faces.

Still, prizes rained from the tower. The emperor was oblivious to the chaos down below.

Aulus looked at his father, who was still standing on the temple steps with the other senators. They were safely above the crowd, protected by Praetorian Guards. Aulus had never seen such a look on his father's face. Gaius looked horrified, furious, and grief-stricken all at once.

Philostratus grabbed his arm. Aulus turned around to see that the viewing platform was empty. Everyone else had scattered, heading away from the crowd. They were the only ones left. The platform was jolted again. It swayed unsteadily, like a ship's deck in a storm.

They fled for their lives.

That night, safe and sound again at home, Gaius and Aulus were both ready for bed when a summons arrived from the palace.

"At this ridiculous hour?" said Gaius, standing with his son in the vestibule where the imperial messenger stood waiting.

Aulus drew his father aside. "The hour is late, yes, but I

hear the emperor keeps odd hours. This could be the opening we've been hoping for, Father—an imperial commission."

"Very well, son. Go put on your toga, and I'll put on mine."

They crossed the city in an imperial litter, surrounded by slaves carrying torches. The streets were quiet, as was the vestibule of the palace, manned only by Praetorian Guards.

They were shown not to any of the usual audience chambers, but to a small room deep within the palace, where they found the young emperor surrounded not by philosophers or palace courtiers, but a coterie of young, handsome, athletic-looking men, some, to judge by their coarse manners, from the very lowest order of society. Strange music played in the background, presumably made by Emesene musicians. Strange perfumes wafted on the air. Even the fabrics and the furniture were foreign. Many of the men spoke neither Latin nor Greek, but some other language.

The young emperor was dressed in loose purple garments made entirely from silk. He wore numerous golden necklaces and bangles. He was indeed a beautiful boy, but it seemed he was not content with his natural beauty, for close up one could see that he wore cosmetics very skillfully applied. His eyes were lined with white lead and his cheeks lightly dusted with a reddish powder.

He seemed perpetually restless, always in motion, even when seated. His every movement, however small, seemed part of a sinuous, swaying dance. His arms were always in graceful motion, as were his hands, and even his fingers seemed to dance. His face, too, was always in motion—batting eyelashes, puckering lips, arching eyebrows. There was something lewd about all these movements, as if each gesture was a deliberately erotic provocation. He frequently made a sound the Pinarii took to be a laugh—a high, trilling ululation ending in a series of low, husky grunts.

"The Pinarii, father *and* son—how lovely to see you both. You were not already *in bed,* I take it?" He had a way of emphasizing some words more than others.

"We are always at the call of our Dominus," said Gaius.

"I'll remember *that*. So is this fellow—have you met my *husband,* Hierocles?" He gestured to the handsome blond youth who sat next to him. Hierocles was dressed as a charioteer of the Green faction, his arms and legs mostly bare. His green tunic fit tightly across his broad chest. The brown leather belt that cinched his narrow waist and the other leather straps of his outfit were not much darker than he was, for his skin was very tan.

"I see you staring at him. And who could *blame* you? What do you think?" The emperor sat forward abruptly and stared at the Pinarii, his lips pushed forward and his eyebrows arched.

"I . . . I was thinking how tan he is," blurted Gaius, for lack of anything more appropriate to say.

"Ah, yes. And do you know—but then, how *could* you?— that he is that same honey-gold color *everywhere*, not just on his arms and legs. The sun *loves* him, you see, as much as I do—it kisses him all over. Everywhere! I would be jealous, if I didn't have the same privilege. I insist that he spend an hour every day lying *nude* in the garden outside our bedchamber, so that Elagabalus may gaze down with delight upon such stunning perfection, and caress him all over with warm rays of sunshine."

The emperor paused and cocked his head, as if inviting a response, but neither of the Pinarii spoke.

"Do you know the story of how we met?" he continued. He clapped his hands, which caused the bangles to clatter and chime. "Oh, it's quite sweet, the sort of meeting some poet should immortalize in verse. It was in the Circus Maximus. Hierocles was racing a chariot for the Greens and took a *terrible* tumble, right in front of the imperial box—truly, Elagabalus intended us to meet in that *very* place and at that *very* moment. I looked down on the perfect youth lying there in the dust with his green tunic in tatters, his limbs scraped and bloody, his helmet thrown off. Oh, how that golden hair gleamed in the sunlight! It blinded me! For a moment I thought he was *dead,* and felt heartbroken. *Utterly* heartbroken! But then—he stirred. He raised himself on those brawny arms and looked up, straight at me. I melted. *Melted!* I sent attendants to fetch him and take him on a stretcher to the palace, and summoned all the best physicians to tend to his wounds."

He looked sidelong at Hierocles and sighed. "He still has a *most* interesting scar across one of his buttocks, which no one is allowed to see but myself, and of course Elagabalus. I forbid Hierocles to race now, for fear some jealous, lesser god might somehow contrive to *take* him from me, but I insist that he wear his racing uniform, though his tunic now is of green silk, not common linen. It shows off his physique so divinely! His only fault is that he comes from Caria, and the Carians are notorious for their hot tempers." He sat forward and lowered his voice. "Sometimes my husband beats me—but only when I've been *very* naughty and truly deserve it. But—enough chit-chat! I fetched you here for a *reason*."

"Yes, Dominus?" said Gaius.

"I possess many amulets, which I wear on different occasions, for different purposes. I'm wearing some of them now, as you may have observed." His dancing fingers played upon his necklaces and the talismans that dangled from them. "I have heard that you Pinarii also possess an amulet, an object of great power. Let me see it!"

Gaius felt the blood drain from his face. This was the last thing he had expected. Was the fascinum to be taken from them again?

Aulus looked at his father. He, too, had gone pale. He slowly removed the chain from his neck and stepped forward, offering the fascinum to the emperor, who reached for it eagerly.

Antoninus emitted a loud, ululating sound, then slapped one hand over his mouth, as if to stop himself from laughing. He held the fascinum dangling on its chain before his narrowed eyes, twisted his face into a sour expression, and made a clucking sound with his tongue.

"No, no, *no!*" he said, in a tone one might use with a particularly slow child. "This will never do. So very *small*. I was told it was a phallus. I had imagined—well, something more impressive than *this*. It's so tiny, and shapeless, and rather ugly—nothing like a penis at *all*! I can't imagine any use for such a thing."

Gaius was utterly taken aback. He had never heard a negative word about the fascinum, let alone such a crudely dismissive judgment. "It's very old, Dominus, and much worn by time—"

"Like your *own* organ, perhaps?" Antoninus laughed, as did Hierocles and several others in the room. "And is your own phallus so *bumpy*?"

"Bumpy, Dominus?"

"These two protrusions on either side of the shaft—"

"Wings, Dominus. Those were originally wings, but as I say, time has considerably worn—"

"*Wings?* Now *that* is the limit! They say we Emesenes have naughty minds, but you'll never see us putting *wings* on *penises*! Whatever would they be good for? I can only imagine they would get in the way."

"In the way, Dominus?"

"Think, man! *What* is a penis used for, and *how* is it used? Now imagine it with wings, and tell me how *that* would work. What nonsense! No, I have no use for this silly trinket, no use at all. Let it flutter its stumpy little wings and go flying *back* where it came from."

He made a show of shuddering and tossed the chain and talisman away from himself. Aulus bolted forward and barely managed to catch it.

"You may go," said Antoninus. "Go, I said. Go, go, *go*! Out of my sight!"

The Pinarii made a quick retreat.

A litter had brought them, but no such luxury was offered for their return home. They walked.

As they made their way down the dark streets, Gaius at last managed to speak. "Have you ever seen such a thing? Whatever else he may be, our new emperor is certainly . . . unique."

"Oh, I don't know about that, Father. The whole encounter was bizarre, but if you mean his flamboyant mannerisms and all that makeup, well, one sees such fellows at the baths, and hanging about on certain street corners—"

"You're talking about prostitutes!"

"Yes, but not only prostitutes. They say that every army barracks has a few such fellows among them. Sometimes they're quite popular."

Gaius considered this. "Yes, come to think of it, Uncle Kaeso had a close friend a bit like that, a big fellow appropriately named Magnus." He chuckled. "But everyone called him Rosa."

"Rosa?"

"As in 'sub rosa.' Rather a lot of ironic puns there, as Uncle Kaeso pointed out. The other soldiers were never 'under Rosa' because he preferred to be on the bottom, and all of this was done quite openly, not at all 'sub rosa'—in secret. No, you mustn't laugh, son. Poor Magnus died fighting the Germans. A hero's death, according to Uncle Kaeso, rescuing a wounded comrade and slaughtering barbarians to his last breath. Uncle Kaeso drank a toast to him every year on the birthday of Mars."

"So there, Father, you've made my point. Even a hero of the battlefield may flirt with men and play Venus. So, too, an emperor."

"But can this be the same dashing youth who rallied the troops at Antioch and won the day against Macrinus?"

"They say the Roman garrison at Emesa loved him long before the battle. When the rumor spread that he might be the son of Caracalla, they all wanted a closer look at him. His grandmother and mother brought him out for all to see. 'Little Dionysus,' the men called him, because he was such a beautiful boy. It didn't hurt that his grandmother was very generous to the troops with coins and wine. When the showdown with Macrinus came, no one expected Little Dionysus to appear on the battlefield, and when he did, who wouldn't be impressed by a boy with such nerve? He certainly has a penchant for the theatrical. Perhaps on the battlefield he imagined himself a fierce Amazon, instead of Venus. However he pulled it off, the soldiers have been loyal to him ever since."

"As long as he pays them, anyway." Gaius shook his head and looked over his shoulder. The dark street was deserted. "We shouldn't be talking this way about the emperor."

"I suppose not," said Aulus.

Gaius drew a deep breath and gritted his teeth. "As for those comments he made . . . the things he said about the fascinum—"

"Let us never speak of it." Aulus shuddered. Then he smiled. "Except perhaps to Philostratus. I can hardly wait to tell him about our visit!"

It was not until early in the month of June that the Pinarii saw the emperor again.

As before, a messenger arrived, though not at such a late hour, and a litter carried them to the palace. The emperor received them in the conventional setting of an audience room full of courtiers. They were formally announced, and the emperor showed no signs of ever having met them before.

"I am told that here in Rome, there are no sculptors more skilled than the two Pinarii, father and son, and the artisans you employ. Is that so?"

"I should like to think so, Dominus," said Gaius.

Antoninus looked at them shrewdly, then nodded. "Follow me. The rest of you, stay here. Except for you, scribe. I may need you to take notes."

The emperor conducted them down a short, dimly lit hallway and then into a smaller room that contained only one thing, a life-size marble statue upon a pedestal. It was the god Antinous, consort of Hadrian.

"We had a statue of him in Emesa, too, which I *adored*. I understand there are hundreds of statues of him, all over the empire."

"True, Dominus. Antinous is worshipped everywhere."

"But the *center* of his cult is here, just outside Rome, is it not?"

"Yes, Dominus, his foremost priest keeps the shrine at the villa of Hadrian. But many of the god's most ardent worshippers make a pilgrimage to the city founded by Hadrian called Antinopolis, on the Nile, in Egypt, where Antinous drowned."

"I see." The emperor dramatically extended his hand toward the scribe and wriggled his fingers. "Take a note! We must transfer *all* the most beautiful statues of the cult of Antinous, from all over the world, to the Temple of Elagabalus here in Rome, *at once*. The god will be delighted to have the company of so many beautiful consorts."

Gaius gritted his teeth, pained at the idea that the worship of Antinous should be subsumed by the worship of Elagabalus— the beautiful youth made the consort of a rock!

"Tell me," said the emperor, slowly circling the statue of Antinous and gazing up at it, pausing from time to time to appreciate a particular angle, "did there ever truly exist a mortal youth who possessed such physical perfection? I mean to say, was there *really* a living model for this statue, and all the other statues that bear his name? Or was this only someone's *idea* of a perfect youth?"

"I assure you, Dominus, there was indeed such a mortal. Antinous truly lived. He sacrificed himself in the Nile for the emperor Hadrian, so great was his love. But before that happened, my grandfather created the first statue of him, modeled from life. And it was my grandfather whom Hadrian ordered to make the first statues after Antinous died. So they are indeed true images. My grandfather was the first keeper of the cult of Antinous at Hadrian's villa—the Divine Youth, he called him, foreseen in his own dreams. Others now oversee the shrine at the villa, but Antinous is still the object of great devotion in our household, and we—"

"So *this* statue actually shows him *as he was*," said the emperor, still circling the statue, "unspeakably beautiful of face and form. The brow, the lips . . . the broad shoulder and deep chest . . . the muscular buttocks and thighs?"

"Yes, Dominus. All true to life."

"And is the statue *also* true in the way it depicts his sacred organ of generation? Was Antinous truly endowed with such a *tiny* phallus? Why, *mine* is considerably larger than that, and I have hardly any use for it!"

Aulus barely stifled a laugh, but Gaius, appalled, kept a straight face. "I believe the statue to be true to the original, Dominus."

"How sad for my predecessor, the Divine Hadrian. Face, form, phallus—in Antinous he had to be satisfied with only *two* counts of perfection out of *three*. But I do not, as you shall soon see!" He made a trilling laugh and clapped his hands. "So, old man, you yourself have made statues of Antinous, have you not?"

"That is correct, Dominus. I have sculpted many an image of Antinous, always staying true to the tradition established by my grandfather."

"I see. Because I require a sculptor of the very *greatest* talent to capture my *own* Antinous. Can you believe that a mortal of such outstanding physical perfection lives once again on earth? It's true. Not long after I arrived in Rome, I sent messengers to scour the empire. Their mission was to find the mortal who possesses the largest organ of generation of any man alive. I did this at the behest of Elagabalus, who instructed me to do so *in a dream.* My agents finally found the man they sought in the city of Smyrna, competing there as an athlete. I arranged that he should travel to Rome in a grand procession attended by dancers, musicians, and priests of Elagabalus. As he traveled the many hundreds of miles to come here, the excited crowds must have thought they beheld Apollo come down to earth, or perhaps the second coming of Alexander the Great. Imagine my *amazement,* when at long last I finally beheld this man, to discover that he not only surpasses all other men in the— what shall I call it?—the *grandeur* of his phallus, but he is also the most *beautiful* mortal to appear on earth since Antinous. Indeed, I declare that he is *more* beautiful. And so I have called you here today."

Gaius frowned. "Called us . . . for what, Dominus?"

The emperor threw back his head and laughed, and waved his hands so that the bangles clattered. "Think, man! To work your magic in stone. So that mortals can behold his perfection for generations to come, I wish this man to be sculpted, and by the same hand that first captured Antinous, or as close as I can get. And that would be *you,* would it not? Well? Are you ready to lay eyes upon him? Zoticus, come! *Behold!*"

Stepping past a curtain that covered a doorway, a young man entered the room.

The newcomer had bright blue eyes, a broad nose, and sensuous lips. His face was deeply tanned and his short, curly black hair glistened with oil. He was very tall and very broad, and dressed in a shimmering blue silk tunic tied at the waist with a golden rope. The emperor, who was much smaller, circled Zoticus as he had circled the statue, gazing up at him, and made a great fuss over him, trailing his fingertips over the youth's broad shoulders and down the silk-covered expanse of his chest, cooing with delight.

Zoticus was a figure of larger-than-life proportions, extraordinarily well-built and stunningly handsome. He seemed completely relaxed and at ease with the attention being paid to him. Like a fine horse or some other tame beast, he did not mind being exhibited.

"Disrobe, Zoticus," said the emperor. "The sculptors must see you *nude.*"

Zoticus smiled. He undid the golden rope and pulled the tunic over his head.

The emperor batted his eyes and swayed, as if he might faint. Gaius and Aulus both looked at the thing revealed, and then at each other. Zoticus's endowment was as impressive as the emperor had indicated. Indeed, it was almost freakish, like a thing not meant to be attached to a mortal man.

Then, as father and son stood dumbstruck, the emperor, without hesitation or inhibition, dropped to his knees, opened his mouth wide, and fellated Zoticus, who expanded his chest with a deep breath and stood with his arms at his sides. The towering youth narrowed his eyes and parted his lips with pleasure. He looked at the gaping Pinarii with a slight smirk on his face.

It was not long before the emperor drew back, rose to his feet, and stepped to one side. He gesticulated wildly with his hands.

"There! He must be sculpted like *that,* do you see? Just so, in all his stallion-like glory, with the full power of Elagabalus coursing through his phallus, which points like a spear to the sun! *This* is the awesome glory of Elagabalus made manifest to mortals! The very sight of it makes me *tremble* with exaltation."

For a long moment, Gaius was speechless. When he finally tried to speak, his mouth was dry and his tongue stiff, so that the words emerged only with great effort. "Dominus, there is a practical problem—that is to say, I feel certain that our art can do justice to the beauty of this man, but . . . to sculpt him . . . as you suggest . . . in *this* manner . . . would be . . . highly impractical."

"How so?"

"The . . . protrusion, Dominus. It would be . . . vulnerable to damage. Very vulnerable."

"Oh." The emperor tugged at his lower lip. "It might *be broken off,* you mean. Yes, I see. Oh, oh, *oh.* Perhaps the statue should be in bronze, then?" He frowned. "But marble is *so* much more beautiful, more glowing, more like actual flesh, more exciting to touch, more *worthy* of the subject, don't you think? And *who* would dare to break off such a magnificent thing? Well—my husband Hierocles just might, in a fit of anger. He's a Carian, you know, and very volatile, like a volcano, and *terribly* jealous of Zoticus, though he needn't be. The god Elagabalus can take as many spouses as he deems fit, so why should I, as his priest, not have as many as I wish?"

Gaius was speechless again. Seeing his father tongue-tied, Aulus cleared his throat and spoke up. "Dominus, no one damages a sacred statue on purpose. And yet, accidents happen."

"Yes, I see your point. But that's really *your* problem, not mine, isn't it? You're the sculptors. It's up to *you* to work out all the practical details. When can you begin?"

Gaius was silent. Aulus spoke up again. "For a commission directly from you, Dominus, we can start at once, of course. If Zoticus can come to our workshop tomorrow—"

"No, no, no, that is *too* soon. Over the next several days there are rites at the Temple of Elagabalus that require my participation, and Zoticus must attend, as well. Shall we say ten days from now?"

"Certainly, Dominus," said Aulus. "In the meantime, we'll search our inventory for the most suitable piece of marble."

Gaius, who had been staring into space, suddenly blinked and spoke again. "Dominus, there is another problem. We can hardly expect Zoticus to model for us in a state of excitation, and to maintain his—"

Antoninus laughed and interrupted him. "Oh, don't worry about *that,* old man! Zoticus can maintain himself in that state for *hours,* as upright and hard as the very baetyl of Elagabalus itself, so greatly has he been blessed by the greatest of all gods. Do you not see? There it is before you, showing no sign of faltering. So very . . . upright. Which makes me think that it's time for you Pinarii to go. And you, as well, scribe. *Shoo!* Off with the lot of you!" He extended his slender arms, gestured wildly with his hands, and screamed with laughter.

They took their leave. In the hallway outside, the scribe quickly disappeared, leaving them alone. Gaius saw a couch in a dimly lit corner and headed for it. He sat heavily, as if a great weight was upon him. Aulus sat beside him and put a hand on his shoulder.

"Father, do you see what this means?"

"Yes. The emperor is insane."

Aulus laughed. "Why do you say that?"

"You saw what he did. Right in front of us! And in front of that scribe, as well. He's lost his reason, if he ever had any. And this statue he wants us to make . . ."

"Yes, the statue! That's what matters. If the emperor finds it pleasing, this could mean endless commissions. He'll want statues of Zoticus everywhere. Think of the countless statues of Antinous that were commissioned by Hadrian."

"Antinous was a god. Zoticus is not."

"Are you sure, Father? He looked a bit godlike to me."

"Don't joke."

"I'm not."

"Son, we cannot possibly go along with this bizarre idea, to show this young man naked and in a state of arousal . . ."

"Why not?" Aulus touched the fascinum. "Do I not proudly and piously wear the image of a phallus, as did you, as did our forefathers, and as will my own son in a few years' time?"

"That's different. The fascinum is a sacred object."

"As will be our statue of Zoticus, and his 'sacred object.' The emperor seems to believe that Zoticus is some sort of incarnation of Elagabalus, or at least a sacred vessel through which the god manifests himself. We must take this commission every bit as seriously as if we had been asked to sculpt Mars or Mercury, or Jupiter himself."

"To do as the emperor asks flouts every convention of proportion and beauty handed down to us from the Greek sculptors—"

"We will innovate."

"We shall be laughing-stocks."

"To whom? Your staid friends in the Senate? The old goats who kneel before slaveboys and bend over for gladiators, but wag their fingers and find scandal in everything the emperor does?"

"I was thinking of other artists—or anyone with even a modicum of good taste."

"The emperor defines taste, Papa. He sets the standards. And we, the Pinarii, are to be the artists privileged to realize his visions in marble and bronze, and to—"

A voice interrupted him. "At the time, he seemed to us the better candidate."

It was a woman who spoke. They both gave a start, having thought they were alone. The woman had been standing there the whole time, motionless and hidden by shadows, listening to every word. As she stepped into the light, they realized it was the emperor's grandmother, Maesa. She was heavily made up, wearing an ill-fitting wig in the style made popular by her late sister.

The Pinarii both sprang to their feet. "Domina!" said Gaius, swallowing hard and bowing his head apologetically.

She held up a wizened hand to silence him. In the other hand she held a golden goblet studded with jewels. She stank of wine.

"As I was saying: at the time, he seemed to us the better candidate. His cousin was simply too young, still a child—and such a dull child at that. Oh, but we could do with a bit of dullness nowadays! Varius—as we called him then—Varius was not quite so young, and he had no fear. The boy's never been afraid of anyone or anything. He's absolutely fearless! The Roman soldiers in Emesa could see that. They adored him. 'Little Dionysus,' they used to call him, thinking to flatter him, but he never liked that. He has only ever loved and emulated one god, Elagabalus."

Maesa raised the goblet, then lowered it and smacked her lips. "Don't worry, Senator Pinarius. You will keep your precious integrity as an artist. You shall never have to stoop to sculpting that fellow's 'sacred object.'"

"No, Domina?" whispered Gaius.

"No! The inexhaustible and ever-ready Zoticus has severely upset the already delicate balance of this household. Something has to be done. Wheels are in motion. Steps are being taken. And so forth. All a great secret, of course!" She waved one hand dramatically. It appeared that the emperor had learned his mannerisms from his grandmother. Maesa laughed without mirth. "Oh, alright, I'll *tell* you. But you mustn't repeat a word. Do you swear? Swear by that amulet of yours, young Pinarius."

"Yes, Domina," said Aulus. He reached into his toga, grasped the fascinum, and held it tightly. "By the god Fascinus, we swear to be silent. Don't we, Father?"

"Yes," said Gaius, his mouth dry. "I swear by Fascinus, as well."

"I'm telling you two, because I understand that you both knew the famous physician Galen. Oh, don't look surprised. I know everything about *both* of you. I know *everything* about *everybody*!" She laughed, sounding uncannily like her grandson. "Anyway, it was in one of Galen's books that I found the *recipe*. Not one word! You swore! Yes? Well, then, I have concocted this recipe and tested it on more than one subject, and it seems to be foolproof. The first dose will be administered in his food this very night. And then . . . *poof*!"

Gaius was horrified. Had she just informed them of a poison plot against the emperor? "I . . . don't follow you, Domina."

"I think I do," said Aulus. "The recipe is for Zoticus. It will render him impotent."

"Exactly!" Maesa giggled. "The young man's legendary potency will wither away, until his donkey's member is as limp and useless as a donkey's tail."

"The divine favor of Elagabalus will be withdrawn from him," said Aulus.

"If you like. That is certainly how my grandson will see it. A night or two of that, and we shall soon see the end of Zoticus."

"The end?" said Gaius. "Do you think the emperor will—"

"No, no, no. I have no desire to see the young man dead. When my grandson's dissatisfaction comes to a head—after the tantrums and tears are spent—I will offer Zoticus a generous purse and send him scurrying back to Smyrna, where he can resume running races or throwing the discus or whatever it was he did before he came here. Or perhaps he can take up his father's profession and become a cook. Can you believe that? At this very moment, my grandson is probably down on his knees, worshipping the son of a cook! He thinks the fellow is a god!" She shook her head. "His religious mania we knew about, back in Emesa. He was always very pious, from earliest childhood. How he loves the worship of Elagabalus, every aspect of it—the chanting, the costumes, the ritual. And the god *has* returned the favor—how else did little Varius Avitus Bassianus from Emesa become Marcus Aurelius Antoninus Augustus, emperor of the whole world?"

Through the scheming of the Emesene women! Gaius longed to say it aloud, but was silent.

Maesa drank more wine. Her speech was now quite slurred. "Varius's piety paid off. And for his good fortune he is duly thankful to the god. His sole ambition is to return the favor, to make Elagabalus supreme among all the gods of Rome, greater than Jupiter. After a hard day of doing that, our Varius likes to play Venus with the manliest mortals he can find. Your staid, prudish senators don't like *either* of his passions. Well, it's *all* gotten out of hand." She shivered and her fingers performed a frantic dance in the air. "His priestly enthusiasm we anticipated. We thought we could channel it to our benefit. But the *other* thing we did *not* foresee. All this carrying-on, with one man after another, and making a public spectacle of himself—that all started when we got to Rome. His voice changed. He sprouted hair on his testicles. He showed the first hint of a beard. All the changes that signal a boy is becoming a man—but instead he seems to have become a woman, and a *whorish* woman at that! He didn't learn *that* kind of behavior from me, *or* my late sister, *or* from either of my daughters!"

It occurred to Gaius that the emperor's mother had in fact declared herself an unfaithful wife by claiming her cousin Caracalla was the boy's father. He kept his mouth shut.

"He simply will *not* be controlled, not by his mother and not by me. As I say, he *seemed* the better choice, at the time. But it was a mistake. Well, just as we have a plan for Zoticus, we have a plan to rectify *that* error, as well."

Gaius felt a thrill of alarm. He grabbed his son's arm, but too late to stop him from speaking.

"A plan, Domina?" asked Aulus.

Maesa snorted. "No, no, *no*! Oh, the look on your faces! Of course Varius will *not* be harmed. But he must be convinced to *share* his throne. Marcus and Verus ruled jointly, did they not? So there *is* a precedent. His cousin, dull as he is, is almost old enough now to be taken seriously, so why shouldn't Rome be blessed with not one but *two* young emperors—one to attend to the state religion, which is all Varius cares about, and the other to tend to wars and taxes and rebuilding the Flavian Amphitheater and all the rest of it? Varius shall be Augustus, his cousin shall be Caesar, and they shall rule jointly. My daughters and I are working out the details even now. First, we'll get this horrible Zoticus out of the way. Which means that *you*, Senator Pinarius, will never have to sculpt him. But don't worry—for your silence I shall see that you are rewarded. I know you did fine work for my dear sister, Domna—I mean to say, for my sister *and* her husband, of course." She threw back her head and cackled. "That *absurd* statue you made, of Septimius sitting on the dream-horse that raised him up! What a great deal of faith that man had in dreams and portents."

"Perhaps," said Aulus, his face suddenly bright, "we should make a statue of the young emperor on the horse he rode in Antioch, when he rallied the troops against Macrinus?"

"Oh, no! Absolutely *not*! I'm afraid my grandson Varius has no interest in being depicted in *any* warlike fashion. Quite the opposite. He hates the very idea of war. He believes that the marriage of Elagabalus and Urania will bring universal peace to all mankind. No, you can start by making busts of everyone in the imperial household, beginning with the oldest—myself. You must make me look very stern, so that all who see my statue will fear me."

That would not be too hard, thought Gaius.

"And you must make my *other* grandson look very mature and respectable and not nearly as dull as he is. Now that he's to become Caesar and rule with his cousin, Alexianus wants to be called Alexander—like the conqueror. That shows optimism, at least."

Or hubris, thought Gaius.

"But repeat not a word of what I've told you, do you understand? You swore—by *this*!" She suddenly reached for the fascinum and clutched it in a clawlike hand, pulling Aulus toward her and giving him a baleful stare. He was startled by her strength. The stench of wine on her breath made him dizzy.

Maesa released him. She gazed into her empty goblet. "I need more wine," she muttered, and then stepped back into the shadows, vanishing as abruptly as she had appeared.

It was only when they were well away from the palace that either dared to say a word. Aulus spoke first, sounding exhilarated. "She wouldn't shut up, would she?"

"That was the wine talking, my son."

"Maybe she has no one to talk to. And all that white lead on her face—she could learn a thing or two about makeup from her grandson. So, we won't have to sculpt Zoticus after all—but the thought of having that woman sit for a bust rather terrifies me. She has gorgon eyes!" He shivered. "And soon, Rome shall have two emperors—both of them teenagers!"

"While Maesa and her two daughters are actually in charge. What a curious place we've come to. What a long, long way we are from the days of the Divine Marcus!"

"Speaking of whom, can you believe she compared her grandsons to Marcus and Lucius? That's a bit of a stretch."

"A stretch? It's utterly absurd! But let's hope they're more like Marcus and Lucius than like . . . the other pair that comes to mind."

"Caracalla and Geta?"

"They were meant to rule jointly, too. Their father had such high hopes. We know how that turned out."

A.D. 222

Spring came early the next year. The Ides of March was still some days away, but the grass was green and along the roadsides wildflowers were in bloom.

Another monument had been added to the Pinarius family's plot outside the city, engraved with the letters GAIUS PINARIUS, followed by a eulogy of his accomplishments as a senator, builder, and sculptor.

Aulus stood before the monument. He poured a libation of wine, then lit a bit of incense. Philostratus was beside him. After a prayer to Fascinus, another to Antinous, a third to Apollonius of Tyana, and a fourth to the Divine Marcus, they returned to the litter that had brought them and headed back to the city.

"Your father's illness was brief," said Philostratus. "For that we can be thankful. He lived to sixty, which is longer than most mortals."

"But not as long as his own father, who lived to seventy-one. Tell me, Philostratus, do you subscribe to the school of philosophy that holds mankind is in a state of continual decline, beginning with the supermen of a long-ago Golden Age and descending to the present, so that each generation is a little less hardy, a little less touched with the original fire of creation than the last, so that we dwindle in vigor and lifespan from father to son? In that case, I shall be lucky to live as long as . . . as *you*."

"Aulus, I am barely in my fifties, and you are barely in your thirties. Neither of us is old! But you pose a serious question. The philosophers of whom you speak believe that the whole universe is in steady decline, not just mankind. They say the cosmos began in a blaze of glory that dims a bit each day, so that it shall end in frigid darkness. As evidence, they say that when they look up at night, the stars glimmer less brightly than when they were boys. But it's their own eyes that have grown weaker, not the starlight! However it happens, the world's heat is continually renewed, and so is the vigor of mankind. You shall live to be one hundred, Aulus! In which case, you are barely a third of the way through life."

"One hundred?" Aulus reflexively touched the fascinum. "That sounds more like a curse than a blessing. Can any mortal live that long? Would any mortal wish to?"

"It happens. Hadrian's friend Phlegon included in his *Book of Marvels* a list of mortals who reached one hundred."

"I wish only to be a man, not a marvel," said Aulus.

"Well put! An epigram worthy of the Divine Marcus— but not one likely to be quoted by his successor. You see the emperor regularly nowadays, do you not?"

"From time to time he submits to sitting still for a few moments, so that I can make progress on his bust."

"Tedious work?"

"Not really. He makes me laugh. Constantly flirting with me, even as he calls me 'old man'! It's just his way of conversing. 'I admit it,' he told me. 'I'm a born flirt—like the beautiful flower that nods to every passing bee.' He can be quite witty. Then out of nowhere he breaks into song—very *loud* song—in that ululating Phoenician dialect of the Emesenes. He's quite theatrical."

"A difficult subject for the sculptor?"

"Yes. Getting a likeness isn't the problem. It's capturing something of his essence, his particular vitality—the sparkle in his eyes just before he says something that makes me laugh."

"His witticisms are wasted on the senators. I never hear them laugh, only grumble."

"Let them! From what I can tell, affairs of state are proceeding as smoothly as they ever did under Severus and Caracalla. Or rather, Severus and Caracalla *and* Domna, I should say."

"How I miss her! She was the greatest patron of philosophy since the Divine Marcus."

"Now we have Maesa and her two daughters in charge. Amazing, isn't it? In fact if not in name, the Roman Empire is being run by women. Legitimacy runs through the female line—from the emperor's wife to her sister, thence to her daughters, and only then to the young emperor and his cousin. No woman has exercised such power since Cleopatra, and even she pales in comparison. Cleopatra had Egypt, and Asia for a while, but Maesa and her daughters rule every province of the Roman Empire."

"Like Cleopatra," observed Philostratus, "they reached such a pinnacle by using their connection to men: Cleopatra through Julius Caesar and Marc Antony, Domna through Severus, Maesa and her daughter through the two young cousins—one or both of them said to be the son of Caracalla. And now those boys rule jointly, since Antoninus adopted him and made him Caesar."

"And the day that happened, who was present in the Senate House to oversee the ceremony but all three Emesene women? What a scandal that caused! What would Father have made of it? I wish I'd been there to see it myself."

"Someday you, too, will be a senator, Aulus."

"Me? I'm neither a military man nor a politician. My only path to the Senate would be a direct appointment by the emperor."

"Antoninus certainly likes you. So may his cousin Alexander, when he gets to know you."

"Alexander—a Syrian boy with a Greek name, now Caesar and heir to the throne. I can hear my father say, 'We are a long way from the days of the Divine Marcus.'"

"Perhaps not so very far. His grandmother has asked me to instruct young Alexander in philosophy, particularly in the teachings of Apollonius of Tyana. We may yet have another philosopher-king on the throne."

Aulus looked skeptical. "I once heard Maesa herself say that the boy was very dull."

"He's quiet and withdrawn, I'll admit. But then, his cousin is extroverted enough for them both. Alexander may be a late bloomer. His mind is sharp enough, though I do despair of his Latin. The boy thinks in Phoenician and speaks in Greek. When he must use Latin, as when he addresses the Senate, you can see him translating in his head, and not always correctly. That halting delivery gives him the appearance of being less clever than he is. Also, he can't seem to shake his Syrian accent, and that makes him self-conscious. But then, Severus always sounded African, and they say Hadrian never lost his Spanish accent. Anyway, there's no point in judging him now. Alexander is still only a boy. How old is your Titus?"

"Twelve."

"Old enough to be trusted with a chisel and a priceless piece of marble, like a fully grown man?"

"Hardly! Not least because he shows so little interest in the craft. Titus always has a book in his hands."

"Alexander is not much older, just fourteen. Any regular Roman lad of fourteen is still many months away from donning his manly toga. Alexander still has plenty of growing to do, in body and mind. We can't expect him to be a man yet, but we shouldn't underestimate him, either. The fact that Maesa called on me to instruct him is a good sign."

"As Plato was to Alexander the Great, so you may be to Rome's own Alexander!" Aulus said the words half-teasingly, but also with a wish they might come true. "If war comes, can he lead the troops? Can his mother?"

"The Germans seem to be hibernating. The Parthians are busy with their own politics."

Aulus smiled. "The emperor says the heavenly marriage of Elagabalus and Urania brought peace to all mankind."

"I only wish that peace reigned in the imperial household!"

"Are the sisters at odds? Or is it the sons?"

Philostratus was quiet for a long moment. "It's become . . . quite unpleasant. And a little alarming. It's the loyalty of the Praetorian Guards they're fighting over. The last time Antoninus and Alexander appeared together before them, many of the Praetorians cheered for Alexander and ignored Antoninus. That made Antoninus furious."

"How fickle the Praetorians are. They loved Antoninus when he first arrived in Rome, despite his exotic clothes and his flamboyant personality. Now they love his staid cousin."

"I'm not sure the Praetorians really love either of them. It always comes down to money with that lot. The Praetorians literally sold the throne to the highest bidder after Commodus died. Now there's a bidding war between Soaemias and Mamaea, each putting her son forward. The cousins are supposed to be colleagues, not rivals, but all the courtiers feel pressed to take sides. The Praetorians take advantage of the situation. They play one side against the other, and demand more money."

"Unless one partner is the Divine Marcus, can any two mortals share so much power, in perfect balance? The slightest wobble, and the spinning coin skitters off the table." Aulus lowered his voice. "Are we seeing Caracalla and Geta, all over again?"

"No, no! The pot is simmering, not boiling over. The real problem for Antoninus is his attachment to that charioteer, Hierocles. What nerve that fellow has! He demands bribes for access to the emperor, and then gives nothing in return— 'selling smoke,' people call it. He even tried to give orders to the Praetorians, who all despise him. Maesa and the emperor's mother plead with him to at least send Hierocles away from Rome, but Antoninus refuses to be separated from him."

"Nero had a man he called his husband, and another he called his wife," said Aulus. "It's all there in Suetonius, as the emperor himself reminded me just the other day."

"You might remind him how Nero ended!" said Philostratus. "No, I don't mean that—touch your fascinum to avert an ill omen. But can't Antoninus find some other blond charioteer? Hierocles abuses him. It's a scandal! None of the Emesene women would take abuse from any man, but the emperor seems almost to boast of it. 'All Carians are wife-beaters,' he says, and laughs."

The litter came to a halt. Aulus peered out the curtains. They had arrived at their destination, the Flavian Amphitheater, where huge teams of laborers and artisans were at work on the final stages of reconstruction and repair.

Aulus and Philostratus stepped from the litter and slowly circled the vast structure, gazing up at the newly installed statues in their niches, the bronze ones gilded so that they shone in the sunlight, the marble ones painted to look remarkably life-like. The appearance was of a vast circular gallery on multiple levels displaying priceless images of gods and heroes and even a few philosophers, as Philostratus was happy to note.

On the facade of the structure and throughout the many stairways and landings within, all the damaged stonework and marble cladding and charred wood had been replaced. The workmen were busy now polishing stone and sanding wood, putting finishing touches on the enormous project. The fire that gutted the structure had been a portent of doom for Macrinus. The reopening, though still months away, would mark a major accomplishment for Antoninus, a portent of good times ahead.

The two men were inspecting the trappings of the luxuriously appointed imperial box when a figure came running toward them. It was young Titus, gasping for breath.

"What is it, son?" said Aulus.

"I was at the workshop, Papa, when one of the workmen told me. I don't know if it's true, but on my way here I heard other people saying the same thing—"

"Saying what, Titus?" asked Philostratus. He had never seen the boy so agitated.

"A rumor, a story—the emperor and his cousin—and their mothers—they're all in the compound of the Praetorian Guards, and something is happening. A riot, people say. The Praetorians—out of control, rioting!"

Even as Aulus and Philostratus wondered if the tale was true, a noise like the droning of bees filled the vast bowl of the amphitheater. Other messengers were arriving and spreading the news among the workmen. To Aulus the noise was uncannily like the hushed, tense murmur of the amphitheater crowd when two gladiators entered the arena, and everyone wondered which would die. The thought seemed ill-omened. Aulus touched the fascinum.

They left the amphitheater. At the foot of the Colossus, a huge crowd had gathered. There were merchants and sailors, priests and schoolboys, beggars and senators. All was confusion. It never ceased to amaze Aulus how such vast crowds could suddenly assemble in the city, seemingly in the blink of an eye. It was as if the city itself possessed a mind or spirit that alerted its occupants when some great calamity or cause for celebration was at hand.

They followed the crowd, which seemed to be moving not toward the Forum, where so many mass gatherings took place, but in the opposite direction, funneling into the streets that skirted the slope of the Palatine Hill. In the crush, the three of them were hard-pressed to stay together.

"Where are we all going?" Aulus shouted. Some in the crowd turned to look at him, but no one answered. At last Aulus saw a man he recognized, a nearly toothless beggar who frequented the Street of the Sandalmakers. "Where is everyone headed?"

"To the Circus Maximus!" shouted the man. Others overheard, and seemed to think it was an exhortation. They took up the cry. "To the Circus! To the Circus Maximus!" they shouted.

"But why?" asked Aulus.

"To see him dragged!" said the beggar, with a cackling laugh. Others took up that cry as well, shouting, "To see him dragged! We'll see him dragged!"

The crowd pressed into the Circus entrances, crushing some of the people against the walls. Aulus would have turned back, but they had no choice but to go along with the surge. Inside, while others rushed to the railing, getting as close to the track as they could, Aulus led Philostratus and Titus to a row of seats high in the stands, where they at last escaped the crush.

"What in the name of Jupiter is happening?" said Aulus.

"What in the name of *Elagabalus,* you mean!" shouted a man below them, looking over his shoulder with a leer. "Look, there's his priest!"

Below them, on the racetrack, in the midst of a mixed group of Praetorians and citizens, a body was held aloft. The naked flesh was bloodstained and mottled with dark bruises. It appeared to be the body of a young man. At first Aulus thought the wretch might still be alive, but the limpness of the figure as it was tossed about could only be that of a corpse. Aulus drew a sharp breath. The face was too distant to make out. Was it the emperor—or his cousin? The idea that it might be either was appalling.

"I hear they cut off his mother's head," said the leering man. "And they'll do the same to him! Like mother, like son!"

"Yes, cut off its head!" someone shouted, and the words became a chant, taken up by the mob. "Cut off its head! Cut off its head! Make sure it's dead! Cut off its head!"

The naked corpse vanished amid the crowd on the track, then an opening appeared, and a cheer went up as one of the Praetorians, with a bloody sword in one hand, held up a severed head in the other. For an instant, despite the great distance, Aulus saw the face clearly. His heart lurched in his chest. How well he knew that face, having spent hours trying to capture it in marble.

"The emperor!" he said.

Someone nearby overheard and shouted, "Not the emperor *anymore*, is he?" The wit was rewarded with peals of laughter.

On the track, the Praetorian with the bloody sword, grinning like a comic actor, brought the severed head closer and closer to his own face, and then gave the gaping mouth a sloppy kiss. The cheering crowd roared with laughter. The Praetorians then took turns tossing the head between them, each trying to outdo the others in a lewd pantomime of lust, sticking out their tongues and kissing the mouth of the dead Antoninus. One of the Praetorians clutched the head to his groins and gyrated his hips, as if forcing the dead emperor to fellate him.

Their antics amused the crowd for a while, but soon people took up another chant: "Drag it! Drag it! Drag it on the ground! All the way around!"

A team of horses arrived, pulling a riderless chariot. By its extravagant decoration, Aulus recognized the ceremonial chariot that had delivered the baetyl of Elagabalus to its temple, with the emperor guiding the horses as he walked backward.

A pair of laughing Praetorians mounted the chariot. The beheaded body was tied by the ankles to the back. One of the men cracked a whip. The other held the head of Antoninus aloft. The horses reared and set off at a gallop.

"Too bad his husband can't drive the chariot for him!" shouted someone.

A voice in the crowd answered, "Hierocles was the first one they killed. Chased him like a scared pig, then rammed a spear up his backside until it came out his belly! His bitch of a mother's been slaughtered, as well."

"You know who's lucky? Zoticus, the one who couldn't get it up! If he was still in town, the Praetorians would have cut off his penis and strangled him with it!"

"But they did hunt down the city prefect, and did away with him. And quite a few others from that rotten crowd in the palace . . ."

As the chariot raced around the track, waves of cheering erupted from the spectators who had gathered all around the course. More people were still pouring into the stands.

The chariot completed a full circuit. Praetorians stopped the horses and cut loose the body. The mangled corpse was a ghastly sight.

"Like the body of Hector, dragged by Achilles around the walls of Troy," muttered Philostratus. "To read such a thing in Homer is one thing. To actually see it . . . is another." He swallowed hard and pressed a fist to his mouth.

Aulus glanced at Philostratus, who looked pale and sick, and then at Titus. What was his wide-eyed son thinking and feeling at such a moment?

"Throw it in the sewer!" shouted someone.

"No!" shouted another. "Roman shit is too good for the Syrian! Throw it in the river, like they do with executed criminals. Throw it in the river!"

The words set off a new chant. "Throw it in the river! Throw it in the river!"

The Praetorians began to drag the body away, carrying the head on a spear, marching in the direction of the Tiber. The crowd, eager to miss nothing, moved to follow them.

"I've seen enough," said Aulus, turning away. Philostratus nodded, still pressing a fist to his mouth. But Titus stepped away from them, moving to follow the crowd.

"Come, Titus!" said Aulus.

"No, Father. I have to see what they do. I have to see it *all*."

Aulus opened his mouth to rebuke his son's disobedience, then stopped himself. Titus was as much a child of the city as he was. If he had the stomach for it, why shouldn't the boy witness with his own eyes the worst side of Rome?

"I'll go with you," he said.

Shaking his head, Philostratus stayed behind.

Through the Circus Maximus surged the crowd, and then through the valley where the Forum ended at the foot of the Capitoline Hill, and then past the Ara Maxima, the greatest and oldest of all altars in Rome, dedicated to Hercules and sanctified centuries ago by the ancestors of the Pinarii. Of all the horrors witnessed by all the ancestors over the ages, had any been as horrible as this?

Working their way through the crowd to the riverbank, downstream and at a considerable distance, Aulus and Titus saw the headless corpse carried onto the bridge across the Tiber. Then it was tossed, like so much rubbish, into the turbid brown waters below. At such a distance, the sound of the splash was more like a burp or a belch, as if the river Tiber itself had swallowed up all that remained of the eighteen-year-old Marcus Aurelius Antoninus Augustus, master of Rome and emperor of all her provinces, high priest of Elagabalus, born Varius Avitus Bassianus in the city of Emesa.

In the days that followed, there were many changes.

The black stone said to embody the god Elagabalus was removed from its temple, lashed to a wagon, and sent back to Emesa, along with all its attendant priests, musicians, and dancers. The various sacred items that had been moved to the Temple of Elagabalus were restored to their rightful places. The temple itself was reconsecrated to Jupiter, Most High.

Wherever the names of the late emperor were inscribed or written, the letters ANTONINUS were marked through or chiseled away. It was clear now that a mistake had been made in assuming that its bearer had been the child of Caracalla, since he had displayed no traits whatsoever in common with that legitimate ruler. It was revealed that it was actually his cousin, Alexander, son of Mamaea, who was the child of Caracalla, and thus rightful heir to the title of Augustus.

Alexander proclaimed that he was not to be addressed as Dominus by his fellow Romans. He preferred to be called Imperator.

He dismissed from the palace all those who had encouraged, abetted, or taken part in his cousin's depraved behaviors. He called back from exile some who had been banished by his cousin, including the renowned jurist, Ulpian. While the False Antoninus had considered the recruitment of men with large penises to be a proper imperial project, Alexander signaled that he would concern himself with serious, sober matters of state, such as the codification of Roman law.

He had no desire for the gaudy bangles, but wore plain white tunics and ordinary cloaks and togas. The jewels of his predecessor he sold, putting the proceeds in the public treasury. Jewels were for women, he said. A man had no need of them.

Because of his youth, a council of senators was appointed, experts who could advise him regarding imperial management, statecraft, and war. Alexander never appointed a man to the Senate without first conferring with the senators.

In emulation of Marcus Aurelius, he installed in his private quarters a sanctuary of guiding spirits—Lares, as they were called in Latin, though he preferred to call them demons, which came from a Greek word. Here he kept statues of the best of the deified emperors, like Marcus, and also of certain holy men, preeminent among them Apollonius of Tyana, so beloved by his grandmother Maesa and her late sister, Domna. Some said he also kept an image of Orpheus, the subject of many sacred texts, and of the Jewish holy men Abraham and Jesus. There was also a portrait of Alexander the Great, his chosen namesake, whom he ranked as a demon even more powerful than Achilles.

The Syrian chants and wild music and orgiastic dancing that had corrupted the religion of the Roman state were banished. In their place was set a far more somber and pious religious tone, as exemplified by the heady, almost incantatory proclamation of the Senate on the occasion of the new emperor's first visit to the Senate House. This proclamation was posted all over the Forum and was read aloud by criers in every part of the city:

"Augustus, free from all guilt, may the gods keep you! Alexander, our Emperor, may the gods keep you! The gods have given you to us, may the gods preserve you! The gods have rescued you from the hands of the foul man, may the gods preserve you forever! You too have endured the foul tyrant, you too had reason to grieve that the filthy and foul one lived. The gods cast him forth root and branch, but you they saved. The infamous emperor has been duly condemned. Happy shall we be in your rule; happy too shall be the state. The infamous emperor has been dragged with the hook. Justly punished was the voluptuous emperor, punished justly he who defiled the sacred relics. Thus are the judgments of the gods revealed. May the gods grant long life to Alexander! In you is our salvation, in you our life. That we may have joy in living, long life to Alexander of the house of the Antonines!"

Inside the Senator House, Alexander stood alone before the senators to receive these accolades, with no mother or grandmother present to guide him. His first reform had been to ban any woman from entering the Senate House under any circumstances. Neither Mamaea nor Maesa complained of their exclusion.

"Indeed, the ban was their idea," Aulus said to his friend Philostratus one day as they stood in the Forum, reading the posted proclamation and talking about all the changes afoot.

"So I had assumed," said Philostratus. "It seems likely."

"Oh, no, it's a fact. Maesa herself confided it to me."

"Really?"

"It was in the first days of Alexander's reign. Maesa summoned me to the palace. I was in a sweat, thinking it would be bad news—we were all in a bit of a panic, weren't we? I was shown to a small, private room. There was only the new emperor's grandmother and myself, and a slave who stood by, holding a pitcher.

"And there on a table was my unfinished bust of . . . what *do* we call him now? The False Antoninus? Anyway, Maesa had some idea that it could perhaps be turned into a portrait of Alexander. Sometimes that kind of alteration can work, with a bit of chiseling here and there, but in this case I told her I didn't think it would be possible. Do you know what she did? She picked up the marble bust—a heavy lift for such a frail-looking old woman—carried it to a balcony, and dropped it three stories to the pavement below.

"I heard the crash and ran to look over the parapet. She barely missed killing a couple of courtiers! They stood there, staring up—the look on their faces! The marble was smashed to bits. All that work, destroyed in an instant! When she turned to face me, I thought I saw something like tears in her eyes. She launched into a long, drunken tirade.

"'So it must be,' she said, 'with everything and anything to do with my grandson Varius. Alexander must now become in every way the opposite of his cousin. He will champion Roman religion. He will defend the Senate, and allow no woman to enter the Senate House. He will respect Roman law and Roman jurists. He will speak Latin, not Greek and *never* Phoenician—and he will speak it like a Roman, by Jupiter, or else I will strangle that miserable wretch Philostratus!'"

"She didn't say that!"

Aulus chuckled. "No, she didn't. I think her exact words were 'the miserable army of tutors I've employed to instruct him.' And then, thinking that Maesa would be too drunk to even remember our conversation, I dared to ask her, 'How does Alexander feel about all the things demanded of him?'"

"Yes? What did Maesa say?"

"She said, 'Alexander's *feelings*'—she said the word with great derision—'his *feelings* are irrelevant! He will do as his mother and I tell him. We have only to remind him of the fate of his cousin and aunt to keep him on the proper course. Alexander knows what's at stake. He will do what he must do—what Mamaea and I tell him to do.'"

"And then?"

"I thought she would dismiss me. I was certainly ready to go! But she drank a bit more wine, and insisted that I do so, too—wine flavored with roses. 'The only thing we still have around the palace that reminds me of Varius,' she said. And then she said something that really shocked me. It's hard to imagine she actually said such a thing aloud . . ."

"Yes?"

"'The real nightmare,' she said, 'would have been if Varius and his mother had been the winners—if they had succeeded in bribing the Praetorians to kill Alexander and Mamaea, instead of the other way around. Then I would have been stuck with Varius and Soaemias digging us deeper and deeper into a pit. We would all have perished in the end, leaving chaos behind us. How disappointed with us my beloved sister Domna would have been, how ashamed of our failure! But with Alexander, there's hope. No, more than hope—he *must* succeed, and he will. He may be the youngest boy ever to be emperor, but he will become the man we need him to be. He has no other choice now, and neither do I.'"

"Nor do *we*," said Philostratus quietly.

A.D. 223

The emperor and his mother were taking a tour of the Flavian Amphitheater, its restoration finally complete. Maesa was not with them, being too ill to leave the palace. As far as Aulus could tell, her daughter was a near copy of her, a generation younger and considerably more sober. Mamaea wore strictly Roman dress. Her plain stola was so old-fashioned it might have been worn by Augustus's wife, Livia.

Alexander said little, but Mamaea lavishly praised Aulus for his exemplary work. "How is it that a man as competent and valuable as you is not in the Senate? Alexander, perhaps you should add Aulus Pinarius to the list of men you wish to appoint to the Senate."

The young man nodded vaguely, more interested in a nearby statue of Hercules—or more precisely, as Aulus observed, in a bird that sat atop the statue's head. But a scribe quickly made a note of Mamaea's comment, and Aulus's heart skipped a beat. To become a senator! If only his father were still alive to see it.

After the tour of inspection, Aulus and a number of other men involved in the restoration accompanied the imperial party to the palace, where there was to be a celebratory banquet.

Once inside the palace, Alexander became more animated. "Mother, can I show Aulus Pinarius my birds?"

"Whatever for?" Mamaea made a sour face.

"He might sculpt them."

"Make sculptures . . . of *birds*? What a silly idea," said Mamaea. "Well, do as you wish. We have a bit of time before the banquet. I'm going to look in on your grandmother."

Alexander conducted Aulus into a private area of the palace. In a large, enclosed garden, an aviary had been constructed. There were hundreds of birds, of all sorts—pea-fowl, pheasants, hens, ducks, and partridges, and a great many doves.

"It's the doves I love most of all," Alexander said, holding forth some seeds on the palm of his hand and letting a pair of doves peck at it. "They're so beautiful. The sounds they make are very soothing. They coo at me, and I coo back at them." He proceeded to demonstrate. The young man showed far greater enthusiasm for the birds than he had had for anything to do with the amphitheater.

Another boy-emperor who dreams of being something else, thought Aulus. *But not an actor, or a gladiator, or Venus—this one wants to be a bird-keeper!*

"My grandmother didn't want me to have the aviary," confided Alexander. "Frivolous, she called it. She even quoted Marcus Aurelius—some nonsense about quails."

"I believe Marcus wrote about training quails to fight. He disapproved."

"As do I! I would never hurt my birds, or make them hurt each other. But anyway, grandmother is too ill now to say much of anything. My mother allowed me to build the aviary, and in return I allowed her to spend a small fortune building her own wing of apartments."

Aulus nodded. The tremendous expense and extravagant luxury of the palace addition had become the subject of gossip. Courtiers called it the Mamaea wing, but rude wags in the Forum had another name for it: *The mammary wing—where baby Alexander goes to suckle Mama's teats!*

"You've sculpted a lot of people, haven't you?" asked Alexander. "You've seen all sorts of people. Do I look Syrian to you?"

Aulus was taken aback and made no reply.

"I know I *sound* Syrian, but do I *look* Syrian?" The boy's earnest solicitation of his opinion was oddly touching. The correct answer was obvious.

"Not at all, Imperator."

"You have a son, don't you? How old is he?"

"Titus is a bit younger than you. Thirteen."

"Does he wrestle? Perhaps he and I could wrestle sometime. My mother says it's the only exercise worthy of a young Roman. Marcus Aurelius wrestled, did you know that?"

"Yes. As a matter of fact, my grandfather wrestled him."

"Truly?"

"But I fear that Titus is not much for wrestling. He loves books, especially history. He's like the Divine Marcus in that way, at least."

"My trainers are all bigger and better than me, so anytime I win I know it's only because they let me. And I know hardly any boys my own age. Varius was older, of course . . ."

Aulus was a bit surprised to hear the young man mention his cousin.

Alexander saw the look on his face. "People think I hated him, but I didn't. Not really. It was wrong that he tried to have me killed, but I think that was mostly his mother's doing. I tried to wrestle Varius once, a long time ago, back in Emesa. But when we grappled, I realized he had . . . something else in mind . . ." He frowned and shuddered. "Well, we're not supposed to talk about him. I'd like to be like Marcus Aurelius. Not just wrestling, I mean. And like Alexander the Great, too. That's why I took his name, though some of the senators seem to think it was wrong of me to take a Greek name. Mother thinks I should add Severus to my name—Severus Alexander—to include my grandfather, and why not? He was also a mighty warrior. I admire them all. Septimius Severus humbled the Parthians. Marcus saved the Roman Empire. And Alexander conquered the whole world!"

The boy might have Marcus's mild disposition, Aulus thought, but would he ever have the intellect and political savvy? And was there any reason, other than his name, to think he might have the military genius of Alexander, or Severus for that matter? If his reign lasted any time at all, there was sure to be warfare on one border or another, if not both.

"Mother said it would be silly to ask you to sculpt my birds. But there's another project I have in mind for you, now that the amphitheater is done. A rather grand project. There's an area in the Forum of Nerva that has room for some statues— colossal statues, I should like them to be, of the very best of the emperors, and columns of bronze engraved with their exploits and achievements. Would you be able to do something like that?"

"Why, yes, Imperator. Yes, indeed." In his imagination, Aulus heard the delightful, reassuring sound of cascading coins. Not only might he soon become a senator, but here, from the emperor himself, was the promise of more imperial patronage on the way, to keep his workshop busy and the Pinarii prosperous. If only young Titus would put down his books and show a greater interest in the family business . . .

On the way out, Alexander showed Aulus something else that few people had seen, his private sanctuary of guiding spirits. In the quiet, dimly lit alcove, Aulus saw a bust of Marcus Aurelius, a statue of Apollonius of Tyana, and—

Alexander suddenly seemed to realize that the doors of a certain cabinet were open, and he quickly moved to shut them, but not before Aulus glimpsed the object within. It was a small replica of the baetyl worshipped as Elagabalus. Alexander closed the doors of the cabinet and looked flustered.

The boy still venerated the stone, but he preferred that no one should know—and who could blame him?

The banquet was elegant but restrained, conducted in a manner opposite to that of the False Antoninus. The guests, Aulus noticed, included not just men involved with the amphitheater, but also a number of high-ranking palace officials.

After a number of courses there was an interval, and everyone was invited to a long gallery that overlooked a sandy, rectangular arena. Aulus had heard of this space but had never seen it. Here, generations of emperors and their guests had looked down on private gladiator contests, animal exhibits, and other amusements.

Alexander himself introduced the entertainment. He seemed to be reciting a text from memory, like a schoolboy. Aulus could not help but notice his Syrian accent.

"Under me and in my name, there will be no toleration of bribery, false accusations, or any other chicanery by any member or servant of the imperial household. That includes Verconius Turninus, who until recently was a trusted courtier. He has now been exposed as a greedy and totally unscrupulous 'seller of smoke'—as the saying goes. Bring forth Verconius Turninus!"

In the arena below, doors opened. The miscreant was led onto the sandy ground and tied to a post. Bales of hay were bought in, and flaming torches. At first, with a gasp, Aulus thought he was about to witness a man burned alive, a punishment not seen since the days of Nero, when it was inflicted on the Christians who burned Rome—including, according to family legend, a Christian Pinarius.

Alexander spoke again. "Let the seller of smoke be punished by smoke."

The bales of hay were set aflame. Water was sprinkled on them, to produce smoke. Using large pieces of canvas, the men below wafted the smoke at Turninus. The bound man coughed and choked, gasped and wheezed. He was swallowed up by the smoke, made invisible, but still his suffering could be heard. There was so much smoke that many in the gallery coughed, as well. This went on for quite some time, until the flames were extinguished and the last of the smoke dispersed, and the seller of smoke was seen to be slumped against the pole, dead from smoke inhalation.

Many of the onlookers were aghast. The execution was

clearly intended to set a stark example and to put all those present on notice. Uneasily, a few of them applauded, and one ventured to cry out, "Well done, Imperator! Well done!"

Alexander smiled and looked pleased with himself. Mamaea also looked pleased. She was the last in the line of the Emesene women, thought Aulus, and of them all, the most powerful. What a long and fretful road Rome has traversed, from the rule of the Divine Marcus to the triumph of Mamaea.

PART III

MILLENNIUM
(A.D. 248–260)

A.D. 248

On the first day of the year, Titus Pinarius, thirty-eight years old, was living in one of the grandest, oldest, and most famous houses in Rome: the so-called House of the Beaks once owned by Pompey the Great, Marc Antony, and various later luminaries.

Some said the name of the house derived from Pompey's decoration of the large vestibule with the bronze "beaks" of pirate ships he had captured in battle—fearsome objects, often fanciful in shape, intended for the deadly purpose of ramming and crippling other ships. If so, three hundred years after Pompey, no sign of any such beaks remained in the vestibule.

With Titus that New Year's Day was Philostratus, who was still healthy and robust despite having reached his seventies. He had been away from Rome, in retirement at Athens, but had come back to assist Titus with a very special commission from the new emperor.

"A thousand-year history of Rome—what a splendid idea!" said Philostratus. "Long after the grand games and processions of the millennial celebration are forgotten, such a book may yet live on—perhaps for the next thousand years."

"You do understand that the finished work will not be entirely, or even mostly, mine," said Titus. "I'll be researching and writing only the concluding section, which begins in my own lifetime, with the reign of Severus Alexander. The emperor originally commissioned a scholar named Gaius Asinius Quadratus, who wrote the great bulk of it, in Greek, before he died. Perhaps the strain of writing about the False Antoninus finished him off."

"At least you'll be spared from having to write *that* chapter," said Philostratus.

"The task before me is to complete the work, writing in the same brisk style as Quadratus, recounting the last twenty-five years as succinctly as possible. I'll also review and edit Quadratus's work—the first nine hundred seventy-five years—and produce a Latin translation, so that simultaneous editions can appear in the Greek-speaking and Latin-speaking parts of the empire. I've been working steadily for months, but now the deadline looms: *The Millennium* must be finished well before April, when the Millennial Games will take place. I have an excellent library and a competent staff of scribes and secretaries to help me, but even so, the task was beginning to seem impossible—until now. With your help, Philostratus, and the assistance of the scribes who arrived in your entourage, I think I may just be able to meet the deadline—and avoid the emperor's wrath."

"And is the emperor particularly wrathful? I haven't met him, and there's not been much gossip about him in Athens."

"Frankly, I don't know what to make of him. Despite his Greek name he really *is* the son of an Arab chieftain—but his father was *not* a brigand, as some say. His family are Arabs—he speaks Latin with a heavy accent—but also Roman citizens. He was born and raised not too far from Damascus, in a tiny village with an unpronounceable name—it sounds rather like the cough of a man with a chest cold."

"Chahba?"

"Easy for you to say! He's renamed it, after himself, of course—Philippopolis—and lavished the place with a theater and baths and even a triumphal arch, all honoring himself. One imagines that such a place in the midst of a desert must appear rather dreamlike—or perhaps nightmarish, being built of the local black basalt."

"He sounds quite typically Roman, in his own way," said Philostratus with a wry smile.

"Monomaniacal, you mean. Yes. Also monotheistic, which is decidedly *not* Roman."

"Monotheistic?" Philostratus made a face. "What an ugly word. Did you coin it? Whatever can it mean? That a man can *see* only one god? How sad for him. Or that he worships one god only, and ignores all the others? That would be foolhardy. Or does it mean that a person believes, literally, that there is and ever was only one god?"

"Perhaps it's a trait passed in the blood," said Titus. "All this 'one god' business seems to originate from people at the eastern end of the empire—the False Antoninus from Emesa with his Elagabalus, the Jews with their Yahweh, the Christians with their Jesus. Did you know that Philip consorts with Christians? I've seen them in the palace."

"But Philip must honor all the gods, surely. He's Pontifex Maximus. The whole state religion depends on him."

"Of course. We have the example of the False Antoninus to demonstrate what happens if an emperor rejects that duty." Titus shuddered, reliving for an instant the horrific scene he had witnessed in the Circus Maximus when he was a boy. In his nightmares he sometimes still heard the chant: *Cut off its head! Cut off its head! Make sure it's dead!* "Yes, I'm glad that particular chapter of the history was already written."

"Mamaea gave an ear to Christians, too," said Philostratus. "When she went east with Alexander to make war on the Persians, she agreed to meet with a Christian named Origen, in Antioch. She wrote me a long letter about it. She was not impressed. 'Their pallid Jesus will never supplant our beloved Apollonius of Tyana,' she said."

"Apollonius's biography is certainly better written," said Titus, and Philostratus smiled at the compliment. "I mean that seriously. Have you ever tried to read any of the so-called biographies of Jesus? Wretchedly written. But then, few authors could hope to match your Greek. And *The Life of Apollonius* is your masterpiece."

"And I'm sure *The Millennium* will be yours."

"Don't be absurd! Quadratus's Greek will appall you, but you must resist the urge to rewrite the whole thing. We simply haven't time. We must forge ahead."

"We certainly have the tools to do the research," said Philostratus, as they strolled into the first of many rooms in the House of the Beaks devoted to a vast and sumptuously appointed library.

"Yes, the library is the reason Philip is allowing me to live here, so that I have easy access to all these books. Before the Roman state took possession of the house, the last private owners were the Gordians, of course. The old man was one of the richest citizens in the empire, and his son amassed an astonishing library—over sixty thousand volumes, or so the head librarian tells me. He and his staff come attached to the library. I could never hope to locate anything without them. It is said to be the most comprehensive collection anywhere of books on the history of Rome. Everything from Herodotus to Herodian, and all the memoirs, from Sulla to Septimius Severus."

"No one since Severus has reigned long enough to write a memoir," said Philostratus thoughtfully. "Severus Alexander ruled for several years, as did the third Gordian. But they both died so very young . . ."

"Yes, well, I shall have to deal with all that—the ugly end of Alexander and his mother, and then the giant barbarian, Maximinus Thrax, and then the first two Gordians, father and son, and then poor Pupienus and Balbinus, gone in the blink of an eye, and then the third Gordian, the boy-emperor, who reigned for six years . . . which brings us up to Philip—and the Millennium of Rome."

"I suppose," says Philostratus carefully, "dealing as you are with events within living memory, you will necessarily need to adopt a certain . . . point of view."

"I'll need to tailor the narrative to suit the emperor, you mean."

"Put bluntly."

"Yes, some events are problematical. But I have no intention of writing falsehoods. When a controversy or embarrassment arises, I simply write around it. What did Berossus say? 'When in doubt, leave it out.'"

"He was talking about florid or obscure words, I believe, not inconvenient facts."

"Even so, I hope *The Millennium* will be, if not a masterpiece, at least something I can be proud of—that *you* can be proud of, as well. At any rate, I have this marvelous house to live in and a marvelous friend to help me. And this marvelous library at my disposal, at least until the book is finished. If Philip likes the book, perhaps I can stay here."

"You might become his court historian, and Philip your imperial patron—as Domna was my patron?"

"Why not?"

Provided that Philip lasts for much longer, thought Philostratus. No emperor since Severus Alexander had reigned for long—young Gordian was the longest, at six years. The empire was like an unsteady ship, pitching and shuddering in a storm. Along with the incessant threats from barbarians along the borders, within the empire insurrections and civil wars had become commonplace. There were plenty of ambitious generals and provincial governors ready and eager to dethrone Philip and to take his place. The only positive thing about the situation was that in such a turbulent world people of all stations increasingly turned to the wisdom and comfort of Apollonius of Tyana.

"This is a beautiful house, and a magnificent library," said Philostratus. "What a tragedy that your family compound on the Esquiline was destroyed in the great fire."

"Yes. Can you believe it was ten years ago? All our property in Rome, burned to ashes. The house, the workshop—with quite a few of the artists and craftsmen trapped inside. As well as . . ." *My father,* he meant to say, but his breath ran short and his voice trailed off. The memory was too painful. "Life hasn't been easy since then. Of course, the fire will have to be in the book, and the chaos that came before it and caused it—the fighting in the streets, the looting, the arson. Terrible days. You were lucky not to be here."

"I've seen many reminders of the fire, since I arrived—buildings still in ruins, empty plots overgrown with weeds. But there also seems to be a great deal of recent construction."

"Rebuilding houses and baths and aqueducts kept the young Gordian busy. That's why he built nothing in the way of monuments. And Philip has done what he can to scrub the temples and patch the potholes and repaint the statues, to have the city looking its best for its one thousandth birthday. His grandest project was to restore Augustus's giant boating lake on the far side of the Tiber, so big it has an island in the middle. The Millennial celebrations will include gladiators staging famous naval combats—Pompey against the pirates, Augustus against Antony and Cleopatra at Actium, and so on."

"I suppose some of the participants will actually die in those mock battles," said Philostratus.

"Of course. You're not in Athens now, my friend. This is Rome."

That night, as he did often, Titus dreamed about the fire. There was no narrative to the dream and no specific location. All was confusion, suffocating smoke, searing flames.

He woke in a cold sweat. He walked through the dark house to a balcony that looked toward the Flavian Amphitheater and the Colossus with its radiant crown. The city looked strangely unreal beneath the full moon, drained of color and eerily quiet on this chilly winter night, the silence broken only by the barking of a dog that echoed from somewhere in the Subura.

Titus thought of the task before him, to tell the story of a time and place he knew from personal experience, though there must be no hint of himself in the story, or of his father, by far the most important person in his own life. History was an odd thing, he thought, because of all the things it leaves out. It was like a stage play with only a handful of actors, when the tale to be told involved teeming multitudes.

The fire would certainly figure in his history, and the devastation it caused—but the huge scar it left across his own existence, the death of his father, would not be mentioned.

He went back in his mind to the point where his story must begin, the reign of the young Severus Alexander and his mother, Mamaea. (How to include her role in the story would be a special challenge, since women hardly ever appeared in history.) Under their rule, things went quite smoothly for several years, and then came the challenge from the East—an aggressive new dynasty of Persians in charge of the Parthian Empire, now more properly called the Persian Empire. Young Alexander in his vanity thought he had become a reasonable facsimile of the Divine Marcus—was not the steadiness of the state ample evidence?—and with the Persian menace he had the chance to imitate his two namesakes, Alexander the Great and Septimius Severus. As Severus had taken Domna on campaign, calling her Mother of the Camp, so Alexander took his mother. Some made jokes about the emperor who still suckled his mama's teats, but success on the battlefield would silence any snickering.

But the outcome was mixed—a three-pronged attack into the enemy's empire saw one Roman army annihilated, a second returning in tatters, and the third (with the emperor himself in charge) failing to strike when the opportunity arose. Still, a peace accord was reached, and Alexander hastened back to Rome to stage a triumph.

Then trouble arose from the Divine Marcus's old nemesis, the Germans. Soldiers who had fought the Persians returned to find their own homes along the northern border burned and looted and their women raped. Alexander and his mother hurried north, but when Alexander chose to give payments to the Germans instead of fighting them, resentment in the ranks boiled over, and the troops declared a new emperor.

Maximinus Thrax could not have been more the opposite of Alexander. He was huge—some say abnormally large, as if his body simply never stopped growing—ugly to look at, easy to anger, and of very low birth. Some even called him a barbarian, but he was a merely a Thracian provincial with uncouth manners and little education outside the army, where as a soldier he excelled.

Hundreds of miles from Rome, at the northernmost outpost of the empire in a town called Mogontiacum (named for a barbarian god), the rebellious troops came for Alexander. The twenty-eight-year-old emperor and his mother and the few officers and guards who remained loyal to them were pursued into their tent and slaughtered. Severus Alexander had reigned for thirteen years.

Once again it was soldiers, not senators, who chose Rome's ruler. Presented with a fait accompli, the Senate had no choice but to declare him emperor.

Maximinus Thrax aggressively pursued war with the Germans and did not even bother to visit Rome. The little support he had in the Senate vanished when he began giving orders to kill senators (he called them traitors) and seize their property.

A plot against Thrax was inevitable. A secret faction developed in support of the two Gordians, father and son, both men of impeccable senatorial pedigree and service to the state, immensely rich, highly educated, and popular with the Roman citizenry, thanks to the many gladiator shows and other festivals they had staged in the city. Both Gordians were away from Rome, across the sea in Carthage (where they were equally popular), ruling the province of Africa, with the eighty-year-old Gordian acting as governor and his son as his legate. In Rome, the Gordians owned the House of the Beaks, the very house in which Titus was now living. It was their library that surrounded him every day.

In Rome, the Senate negated the imperium of Maximinus Thrax and declared Gordian and his son co-emperors, with equal powers, and eagerly awaited their arrival with troops from Africa to protect the city against the inevitable assault from Maximinus Thrax.

Unexpectedly, the troops in Africa turned out to be loyal to Maximinus Thrax instead of the Gordians. The people of Carthage rallied in support of the Gordians and took up whatever arms they could improvise, but they were no match for the soldiers. The Gordians were besieged in Carthage. The son died fighting. The father committed suicide. They had reigned as emperors for only twenty-two days.

In Rome, panic ensued. The Gordians were dead even before they could arrive, and Maximinus Thrax, the dreaded barbarian-emperor, was marching toward Rome. A bloodbath loomed.

Since they had already cast the die, on the Ides of March (an unlucky day, some said) the senators voted to issue a declaration of war against Maximinus Thrax. They chose two men from their own ranks to reign, like the Gordians, as joint emperors. So equal would be their powers that both would serve as Pontifex Maximus, a sharing of sacred status that had never occurred before. Like the Gordians, the men chosen were of impeccable pedigree, one of greater military experience and the other with greater experience at civil administration. Their names were Balbinus and Pupienus.

Titus remembered the excitement his father had shown when the selection of Pupienus was announced. The man was a distant cousin, and had been raised just outside Rome by some of Titus's kinsmen, the Pinarii clan of Tibur, one of whom became Pupienus's first appointment, as city prefect. "This is a great day for the Pinarii," Aulus told his son. "We will always have a friend in the palace as long as cousin Pupienus is emperor, especially with a Pinarius running the city."

Pupienus and Balbinus, provided they could fend off Thrax and remain allies, promised a return to what many thought of as a golden age, the reign of the Divine Marcus. Both emperors were great admirers and emulators of Marcus and his predecessor, Antoninus Pius, without question the wisest and gentlest men ever to rule Rome. And, like Pius, they were already reaching old age (Balbinus in his sixties, Pupienus in his seventies) and might be expected, when the time came, to pass the throne to men of merit rather than blood kin. Even the Divine Marcus had erred when he arranged for his son to succeed him.

Pupienus was sent north with an army to stop Thrax before he could enter Italy. The city held its breath, awaiting news of the outcome, torn between hope and dread.

Then a new problem arose.

Partly spurred by a senatorial faction that had favored the Gordians, partly by the perverse sentimentality of the populace, and partly by the Praetorian Guards (jealous that the Senate had taken back the prerogative of choosing emperors), a mass movement sprang up asserting that only someone of Gordian blood could legitimately succeed the dead emperors in Africa. The elderly Gordian's grandson lived in Rome and was put forward. Though the boy's name was not Gordian, his supporters called him that. He was only thirteen—Rome's youngest emperor yet.

Young Gordian's supporters carried him on their shoulders and loudly demonstrated in the Forum, even as a rattled Senate debated what to do inside the Senate House. Aulus Pinarius was in attendance. Titus, then twenty-eight and not yet a senator, was allowed inside to watch, a technical breach of protocol that was overlooked in the uproar. Also overlooked was the law that no senator could bear arms in the chamber. The state of the city was so precarious that many senators were openly carrying daggers for their personal protection.

After an acrimonious debate, it was decided that Balbinus and Pupienus would both remain Pontifex Maximus and retain the title of Augustus, or senior emperor, while young Gordian would be named Caesar, or junior emperor and heir apparent. Surrounded by his supporters in the Senate, Gordian was admitted into the chamber. Seeing him, Titus thought how young and overwhelmed the boy looked.

Then a group of unarmed Praetorians, suspicious of the senators and fearing the boy would be hurt, forced their way into the Senate House. Two senators, already highly agitated by the debate, were outraged at seeing Praetorians in the chamber, rushed toward them and attacked them with knives, stabbing two of them in the heart. The two soldiers fell dead at the foot of the Altar of Victory. Young Gordian was standing nearby and looked horrified. Titus also witnessed the murders, and felt a cold dread, a presentiment that something truly disastrous had just occurred, a horror that would reach far beyond the death of two reckless soldiers at the hands of two reckless senators. He remembered quite clearly how he had clutched the fascinum, which had been given to him by his father when he put on his manly toga.

Now, ten years later, Titus clutched the amulet as he looked out at the moonlit city and remembered the disaster that followed the murders in the Senate House.

The rest of the unarmed Praetorians fled from the chamber. On the steps of the Senate House, the senators held up their bloody daggers and harangued the crowd, proclaiming that two enemies of the Roman state had just been killed. They accused the Praetorians of a plot to take over the city and massacre the citizens on behalf of the dreaded Maximinus Thrax. The volatile mob was swayed by the speeches, and headed in a fury for the Praetorian camp. The only substantial stores of available weapons were in gladiator barracks. While looting these arms, the mob also set free the gladiators, who joined the siege of the fortified Praetorian camp. When their water supply was cut off, the Praetorians finally emerged, well armed and desperate. There was a horrendous slaughter of citizens.

What followed was complete chaos—days of street fighting between the people of Rome and the vastly outnumbered but highly trained Praetorians. Criminals took advantage of the disorder to loot, rape, and murder with impunity. The emperor Balbinus was helpless. There was still no news of Pupienus's attempt to fend off Thrax.

It seemed the fortunes of the city could reach no lower ebb, until the fire broke out.

Whether set accidentally, or deliberately (as some claimed) by soldiers, the fires spread rapidly out of control. A huge swath of the city was consumed, concentrated in the poorer residential areas where large wooden buildings were packed close together.

The fire consumed the home of the Pinarii, as well as their workshop, killing many of the slaves and artisans. Also killed in the fire were Titus's father and mother. Spared were his wife and two small children, his son, named Gnaeus, and his daughter, Pinaria.

From where he stood on the balcony of the House of the Beaks, overlooking the pale moonlit city, large areas of destruction could still be seen as deep shadows, like gaping wounds in the cityscape. Titus felt a sudden despair. How could he possibly write of those horrible days? They were the worst of his life. They haunted his nightmares.

Given the brevity of each chapter within the thousand-year history, a few words would have to suffice, and the fewer the better. But was such deliberate brevity not an insult to the dead? Was their humanity and their suffering not dishonored by a superficial gloss that spoke of such immense catastrophe only in passing, leaving their names unrecorded, their fates unexamined, their individual destines forgotten?

Titus realized that he was unconsciously touching the fascinum at his breast. He had not been wearing it on the day the fire consumed their house. He had run inside to get it. It lay nestled with its chain amid other precious items at the shrine to Apollonius of Tyana. As flames and falling debris surrounded him, Titus managed to grab only the fascinum, leaving all the other sacred objects behind. The family shrines to Apollonius and Antinous, as well as the wax masks of the ancestors—all were lost in the fire, and so much more.

The disaster marked a cleavage not only in his own life—a demarcation of all things *before* and *after* the fire—but also in the history of the Pinarii. Gone were his father and mother, gone every family heirloom and sentimental treasure (except the fascinum), and gone too were almost all of their property and wealth, including the human wealth that resided in the highly trained artisans of the workshop. Gone with those slaves and their ability to create sculpture and art was the means of creating new wealth. All that remained was Titus himself and the ancient talisman that linked him to the ancestors . . .

"You still have me," said a quiet voice. The slender arms of his wife embraced him from behind. "And your children."

It was uncanny, the way Clodia was able to read his moods and even his thoughts. Yes, he still had his immediate family— precious but few, all that remained of the Pinarii of Rome *after* the fire. And to be sure, he still owned a few small country properties outside Rome with cattle and vineyards that provided income. In the city itself, since the fire, they had been living for ten years as renters. Houses had become outrageously expensive after so many were destroyed in the fire. There had been times when Titus had struggled to make ends meet.

But for the time being, all was well. At the emperor's invitation, Titus and his family resided in the House of the Beaks. If only they could stay there permanently! Its beauty and opulence—the sculptures in the gardens, the dazzling mosaic floors, the paintings on the walls—were daily reminders of all the wealth and property the Pinarii no longer possessed.

"I saw Pompey's ghost tonight," said Clodia.

"Did you?" Titus had never encountered a ghost, but his wife did so regularly.

"He was in the small garden off our bedroom, conversing with Marc Antony and Fulvia, Antony's wife. I recognized them from their statues." In one of the larger courtyards of the house there were marble statues and busts of almost all the previous owners, from Pompey and Antony all the way to the young Gordian, who inherited it from his grandfather. The statues had been meticulously maintained and repainted as needed, so that in daylight they often looked as if they were alive and breathing. By night they were even more uncannily lifelike, so much so that Titus found the effect unnerving and avoided looking at them.

Clodia had encountered the ghosts of almost all the past owners.

"Do they speak, when you see them—the ghosts?"

"Not to me. They seemed unable to see me. They speak to each other, but I can never make out the words. I hear only a vague murmur."

"The ghosts of those who lived in this house seem particularly restless."

Clodia nodded thoughtfully. "Many of them died by violence, or by suicide—Pompey and Antony, and the Gordians in Africa, and so many in between. My mother always said that a violent death is more likely to leave behind a restless spirit to wander the earth. It makes sense that they would linger in this house, where they must have spent many happy hours. It's such a beautiful house."

"We mustn't grow attached to it, my love. Once I've completed the history for the emperor, my reason for living here will be at an end."

"Unless the emperor is so pleased with your work that he commissions more books from you. Surely there are more histories to write. Perhaps a history of Philip's own family?"

"Not that! There's nothing in the library here about them, I assure you. I would have to go to Philippopolis to do the research. I don't think you would like living in a dry gulch with Damascus for the nearest city."

"It sounds terribly dusty."

"Let's not find out. But you're right. After *The Millennium*, if he likes it, perhaps I can interest Philip in some other project that would justify my continued residence here. But first I have to finish *this* book."

"Is it difficult?"

Titus gazed at the bone-white city under moonlight and sighed. "To write about long-dead people is one thing. To write about one's own lifetime is different. And of course I must take care to avoid writing anything that gives offense to the emperor. Yes, I'm finding it difficult. But never fear, I *shall* finish it, and Philip *will* be impressed."

He left unspoken his dearest wish—that Philip, as a reward for his service, would see fit to admit him into the Senate, as Alexander had elevated his father. He came from ancient patrician stock, with many senators among his ancestors, but his relative poverty would count against him. Of course, Philip could reward him financially as well, granting him both greater wealth and senatorial status at a single stroke. This was all only a dream, and Titus felt he must not get his hopes up. But how pleased his late father would be, to see Titus regain some of the family's wealth and become a senator!

"Tell me, wife, do you ever see the ghost . . . of my father?"

Clodia was quiet for a long moment, then slowly nodded. "I see him now. He's standing right there." She pointed to a nearby spot on the terrace. Titus followed her gaze, but saw only empty air. Even so, he felt a shiver, and choked back a sudden sob in his throat.

Much of the terrace was filled with long shadows—the month was February—but the day was not too chilly and Titus had found a sunny spot where he could sit with a scribe on either side, one to take his dictation and the other to scroll through various books and documents and read aloud passages pertinent to Titus's research. A low brazier nearby offered a bit of heat. More scribes waited at the doorway into the house, ready to shuttle back and forth to the library to fetch or return scrolls. They were all idle at the moment. A document Titus wished to consult seemed not to be in its pigeonhole, and the head librarian himself was searching for it. If it had been misplaced among so many scrolls and scraps of parchment, Titus feared it might never be found.

He gazed across the way at the top of the Flavian Amphitheater, where a vast team of workers was installing new canvas awnings to provide shade for the audience that would fill the seats for Philip's Millennial Games. Other workers were tending to the huge statues that occupied the multitude of arched openings all around the structure, cleaning them and retouching the vivid paint that made their features discernable even at this distance. Titus recalled his father's pride in creating and installing many of those statues, after the fire in the reign of Macrinus and the reconstruction of the amphitheater by the two young cousins from Emesa, or more precisely, by their mothers and grandmother.

As the Millennium approached, the whole city had become a beehive of activity. Not only the amphitheater, but also the Circus Maximus, the Forum, and various other public areas of the city were being refurbished. The games and chariot races and plays and feasts must all be as splendid as possible. The Millennium was the Arab's chance to make an unforgettable impression on the people of Rome.

It was also Titus's chance to make an impression on Philip, to win the favor of the emperor with his history. Philostratus had been of great assistance. His experience as a writer navigating court politics had helped Titus shape his narrative in various ways that would both enlighten his readers and please Philip. Philostratus had told him, "You must think of this not as history but as an exercise in rhetoric, my boy. You need not tell falsehoods to flatter Philip, only find facts that flatter him, bring those facts to the fore, and state them with eloquence."

Today Titus was reflecting on the aftermath of the great fire. His own memory of the period was confused and hazy;

the death of his parents and the loss of his home had left him dazed. Tens of thousands of people in Rome must have felt the same way. Once the fires were finally extinguished and the immediate threat receded, people only gradually came to their senses. What had all the rioting and bloodshed been about? No one seemed quite able to remember, and a sort of numb paralysis seized the city, an uneasy calm to follow the firestorm.

And then, at a stroke, the mood of the city changed. The head of Maximinus Thrax arrived, carried into the city on the end of a spear by a horseman in advance of the returning Pupienus. The barbarian was dead. The threat from the north was over. The city burst into celebration. Mourning was replaced by jubilation.

The whole Senate, the Vestal virgins, and a huge crowd of citizens went out to greet the arrival of Pupienus and his troops. They were hailed as heroes and saviors of the city—never mind that not one of them had shot an arrow or raised a sword against Thrax, as it turned out. His destruction had been accomplished even before Pupienus arrived at the frontier. Crossing the Alps, Thrax had paused to lay siege to the city of Aquileia, but without success. As the stalemate wore on, Thrax's troops ran out of winter provisions. The people of Aquileia taunted them by feasting on the ramparts. Facing starvation, the soldiers turned on Thrax and murdered him.

When Pupienus arrived at Aquileia shortly thereafter, he declared amnesty for everyone, and welcomed the troops of Thrax into his ranks. The Roman state and the Roman legions were reunited.

In Rome, too, a general amnesty was declared. Neither the people nor the Praetorians (nor the Senate, for that matter) would be held accountable for the rioting and destruction. This was to be a time of reconciliation and celebration. The barbarian was dead and the two best men in Rome now presided over the empire, with the young Gordian as their heir. The joint reign of Pupienus and Balbinus could commence in earnest. Rome could at last return to the reason and prudence of the days when the Divine Marcus reigned, with the best senators running the state, and the army in its rightful role, fighting barbarians at the borders instead of choosing emperors.

How did that dream come to such an abrupt halt? Why did the two venerable emperors suffer a fate such as only the most depraved criminal could deserve? Titus had never fully understood what happened at the time. He had been too distant from the palace, too distraught over his personal tragedies, too overwhelmed by his family's daily struggle for survival in the aftermath of the fire. So it was with some chagrin that he discovered through his research that, to some extent, his kinsman Pupienus had brought about his own destruction and that of Balbinus—or more precisely, the distrust between the two men had done so.

Popular opinion held that the joint emperors were in perfect harmony, but in fact, with the threat of Thrax gone and the furor in the city spent, the emperors began to eye each other a bit warily, and behind the public show of concord there was private discord and petty sniping. Balbinus asked: What great military feat had Pupienus accomplished, marching against Thrax and sending back his head, but without engaging in even a skirmish? Pupienus asked: What sort of civic leader was Balbinus, who had allowed the whole city to descend into chaos? The mood of the populace began to sour, as well. Despite the celebrations, much of the city lay in smoldering ruins.

Did each emperor actively plot against the other? Certainly, each came to suspect the other of doing so.

Pupienus had brought back from the frontier a troop of German soldiers to act as his personal bodyguard. This especially alerted the suspicion of Balbinus.

One day in June, while the whole city was in the midst of festivities for the Capitoline Games, a group of drunken Praetorians—still seething with anger and resentment despite the amnesty—broke into the palace. The emperors were conferring at the time. When a courtier ran in, warning them about the Praetorians, Pupienus at once dispatched a messenger to bring his German bodyguard. But Balbinus became suspicious, thinking it was an ambush, that no Praetorians were on the way and Pupienus was manufacturing an excuse to summon his German guards to murder his rival. Balbinus called back the messenger. The poor courtier stood there as the two emperors argued, one shouting at him to fetch the German guards at once, the other shouting at him to do no such thing, both threatening him with dire punishments. While they squabbled, the drunken Praetorians arrived, slaughtered the few courtiers who dared to resist them, and laid hold of both emperors.

What followed was a nauseating orgy of violence, as the two old men were stripped and beaten, then driven naked out of the palace. Using spears, the soldiers goaded the two men through the streets. A mob gathered and followed along. Men who had previously sung the praises of Pupienus and Balbinus were suddenly quite joyful at seeing the two naked emperors abused. The humiliation of powerful men delighted the mob.

In the Praetorian camp, the soldiers split into two groups and competed at torturing the two emperors—jabbing them with spears, slashing at them with swords, pulling out their beards, chopping off their fingers, slicing away their lips and noses, delighting in the screams and pleas for mercy and prolonging the agony as long as possible. Eventually, whether from loss of blood or because their hearts burst from terror, the two men died.

Pupienus and Balbinus, who many hoped would bring about a new golden age, had reigned for only ninety-nine days . . .

With a shiver—for he was deep in thought—Titus realized that Philostratus had joined him on the terrace.

"Thus does the mob delight in the humiliation of powerful men," Titus whispered. The scribe cocked his head, not quite catching the words. "Yes, write that down," said Titus. He repeated the phrase, thinking it rather good.

"Well, I think I can guess where your thoughts have taken you," said Philostratus. "Pupienus and Balbinus."

Titus nodded.

"A grim business. But I come to you on a more immediate matter. Is *this* the document you've been looking for?" He held forth a small scroll tied with a purple ribbon. "I'm afraid I took it from its pigeon-hole myself, without informing anyone. The poor scribes have been scuttling all over the house in a panic, while all along I sat on the balcony off my room, reading it at my leisure. But why so downcast? Are you depressed at remembering the downfall of your kinsman Pupienus?"

Titus sighed. "Do you think there's any truth to the idea that the same faction that championed the Gordians put the Praetorians up to it? With Balbinus and Pupienus out of the way, the only legitimate successor was young Gordian. They were determined to have a Gordian, and they got one."

Philostratus pursed his lips thoughtfully. "Do I believe that a group of senators, frustrated that the two elder Gordians had died in Africa, conspired to have Praetorians break into the palace and murder two emperors, all so that a thirteen-year-old boy could take their place? It seems a terrible gamble, don't you think? So much could go wrong. But, to be sure, once that terrible year was over, it *was* a Gordian on the throne, and the Gordian faction was ascendant in the Senate. But I think one might . . . with a bit of imagination . . . perceive in all this not a conspiracy of mortals, but a pattern woven by the Fates."

"How so?"

"The last emperor who could claim a successful reign, however badly it ended, was Severus Alexander—who had started as a youth. So it was with his eventual successor, the young Gordian, who was even younger upon his accession. The empire was twice given by the Fates to very young men who ruled with a great deal of help and guidance from the Senate."

Titus nodded. "And both of those young emperors might have reigned for many more years—for a full lifetime—had they not died far from Rome, brought down by . . ."

"By angry soldiers, in the case of Alexander," said Philostratus, lowering his voice slightly. "The case of young Gordian, dying on the Persian frontier, was quite another matter, of course." He narrowed his eyes. "Perhaps you might ask these scribes to leave us for a while. They deserve a brief rest, after all the bother I've caused by taking this scroll without telling anyone."

Titus nodded and dismissed the slaves.

Philostratus touched his fingertips together. "You reach the part of your history where you must tread most cautiously. The thousand years must end, indeed, must culminate with the accession of Philip. Everything that comes before is prelude, especially the reign of his immediate predecessor."

"But Philip himself saw to it that the ashes of Gordian were brought back to Rome, and that he was deified. Gordian wasn't even twenty."

"And so you may say good things about Gordian. But not *too* good. There must be no possible inference that the reign of Gordian was *better* than that of Philip, that Philip's reign is, in any way, a step down."

"Of course not. I understand that."

"Indeed, Gordian was so young that his reign was largely conducted by his father-in-law, Timesitheus, yes? You should stress that."

"Until both his father-in-law, and then Gordian, after six years as emperor, died during the Persian campaign, and then it was Philip—"

"*How* they both died must be handled with the utmost finesse."

"Timesitheus died of dysentery. So say all the accounts. Some say the doctors did more harm than good, giving him a potion that made his symptoms even worse . . ."

"That is an extraneous detail that need not be included. It's mere speculation, for one thing. And for another, it might encourage some reader to imagine that the doctors were compelled to give Timesitheus a remedy that was actually a poison. That would be deliberate murder. And then one would have to ask: Who was the murderer? Do you see the problem?"

Titus nodded. "Timesitheus died of natural causes, then, as happens to many a soldier in the camps."

"Exactly."

"And his successor, as Praetorian Prefect, was Philip."

"So the Fates saw fit to weave the strands of his life. Philip may have been born the son of an Arab chieftain, but he was a Roman military officer of proven ability."

"And as Gordian had looked upon Timesitheus as a father, so he began to look upon Philip. And Philip looked upon Gordian as a son."

"Yes. That is a lovely way to put it; almost poetic. You should use that in your account."

"But then there comes a detail that puzzles me. Timesitheus was known for setting up excellent supply lines and storing caches of food, so that the army never went hungry. But after his death, there was a sudden food shortage, so severe that there was serious grumbling in the ranks, and harsh words against Gordian. Soldiers said he was still too young to rule on his own—only nineteen—and that his youthful incompetence was starving them to death. How did such a state of affairs develop, if Timesitheus had done such a good job of management?"

"Yes, it *is* a mystery. One might almost think there was deliberate treachery at work. But no responsible historian would make such a charge without conclusive evidence."

"At any rate, there was a demand from the troops that Gordian should take Philip on as his co-emperor, and that Philip, being older, should be the senior of the partners."

"So it came about."

"And with Philip in charge, the food shortage was quickly alleviated."

"Proof of his able management, and the wisdom of the ranks."

Titus stood and paced the terrace, making sure they were alone. "Or could it be that the man who engineered the shortage was the man able to relieve it?"

"Titus! You cannot even *hint* at such a possibility in your work."

"The closer my history comes to the present, the more circumspect it must be?"

"Exactly."

"It will be challenging then to deal with the end of Gordian. There are the official reports, to which I have access. And certain other documents—letters written by a centurion to his father—were made available to me. And even some conversations I had with soldiers who were there . . ."

The witnesses, guaranteed confidentiality, had told him stories of the growing hostility between the high-born young Gordian and the older, low-born Philip, and the vote of no confidence given to Gordian by the troops. Had Gordian been murdered by Philip—even, as some said, raped—or had he died of disease, or in battle? No single truth had emerged from Titus's research.

Ultimately, Titus would need to shape his account of recent history so as to give no offense to the emperor. It would be better not to suggest that conspiracies were at work in the elevation of the Gordians, or the fall of Pupienus and Balbinus, or the death of Timesitheus and the end of Gordian; better to suggest that these events had somehow been decided by the Fates or by the gods.

"Is this how history is written?" Titus asked. "This can't be how Thucydides went about it."

"He was not writing for an emperor."

"Or Suetonius."

"He wrote for an emperor, but about men long dead."

"This can't be how *you* would do it!"

"Perhaps not. But I am a man at the end of a long life, while you are young and have much to lose—and much to gain."

"But surely, to ascribe certain events, clearly the outcome of deliberate human acts, to the Fates or the gods does the immortals a disservice as well—indeed, it approaches impiety. It is certainly not 'truth' in any meaningful sense. I might as well simply make it *all* up, as if I were writing a novel about imaginary people, set in some invented land!"

Philostratus raised an eyebrow. "Then you will not be needing *this*." He held up the scroll that had been missing from the library.

Titus took a deep breath. "I glanced at it once, but only very briefly before I put it back. Is it what I think it is?

"I suspect it is. An official dispatch written by Philip himself, just after the death of Gordian, and sent to Philip's brother, who was also a prefect at the front. The document is not unusual—a simple announcement of Gordian's death, with no real explanation, certainly no startling revelation. But at the very bottom of the document there is a bit of writing that appears to be a private note intended for the eyes of the emperor's brother only. Almost certainly it was meant to be torn off and destroyed after being read, but for some reason that did not happen. The note is written in code, but the cypher is not complex enough to puzzle an old scholar like myself. I was engaged in working it out in my head while sitting on the balcony off my room, before I came here."

"And? What does it say?

"It tells the true story of how Gordian died."

"Then hand it to me!

"Are you sure? My old hands are weak. They tend to shake. How easily I might, by a whim of Fate or the will of some immortal, or simply from my own ineptitude, drop it . . . right here . . . into the flames of this brazier . . ."

They looked at each other for a long moment, and then, having read the look in Titus's eyes, Philostratus dropped the parchment into the flames, where it quickly caught fire and emitted a burst of light and heat, warming them both for a brief moment before turning to ash.

Philostratus put his hand on Titus's shoulder. "And now, my boy, you really must get back to work, and finish your history. The emperor is waiting for it, and so are a great many readers eager to discover how, over the course of a thousand years, the Republic of Brutus became the empire of Philip the Arab."

Titus paced nervously in the vestibule outside the imperial audience chamber. His history was finished. Some days ago it had been delivered to the emperor. Now Titus awaited the judgment of Philip. He realized he was biting his fingernails— a terrible habit, for which Clodia would chide him later.

A door opened. A small party, the emperor's previous guests, emerged from the audience chamber, conversing quietly. Overhearing a few words, Titus realized they were the heads of the Christian sect in Rome. As Titus knew from his research, Maximinus Thrax had been hostile to the sect, and had exiled the leaders in Rome to the Sardinian mines. Gordian had allowed their return. Philip, it seemed, welcomed them into the palace.

A chamberlain called his name. Titus was admitted.

Sitting on the dais next to Philip was his ten-year-old son, to whom, retaining the title of Augustus for himself, Philip had given the title of Caesar. With their swarthy features they both looked rather exotic to Titus. Whether Philip came from a more reputable, less "barbaric" family than Maximinus Thrax remained a question. Titus himself had been spared from having to delve too deeply into the matter, since he had been instructed to end his history with the tragic and untimely death of young Gordian, and the moment of Philip's elevation. Titus was rather proud of the very carefully worded sentence he had concocted, which strongly suggested that the teenaged emperor died in combat fighting the Persians, without literally saying so, whereupon Philip, as the obvious and most legitimate successor, had humbly assumed the throne.

In such turbulent, uncertain times, who could say what an emperor should look like, or where he should come from? If Philip could maintain his hold on the throne, and if his son succeeded him, this dynasty might rule Rome for the rest of Titus's lifetime.

"Titus Pinarius! What a happy coincidence," said Philip. "I was just talking about *The Millennium*—the book—with my previous petitioners."

"The Christians, Dominus?"

"Yes. They very earnestly proposed that I ban all prostitution in the city ahead of the upcoming celebrations. With all the visitors in town, and the inevitable inebriation, they fear that Rome will become nothing but a huge open-air brothel. They described their fears in quite lurid detail. What vivid imaginations these Christians have, especially when describing the so-called sins of others! Well, even if I wanted to grant their request, enforcing such a ban would be impossible. But I did agree to one new law, something I'd decided anyway, which is to put a stop to the prostitution of young boys." He sighed and shook his head. "Just a few days ago, I was out and about in the city, inspecting progress on venues for the upcoming celebration, and I happened to duck into the latrina at the old Theater of Pompey. A lad no older than my own son approached me and offered to do—well, as he put it, 'anything Dominus can imagine.' The child had no idea who I was, he simply addressed me as a slave addresses a master. He looked clean and well fed, and reasonably dressed, not at all like a beggar. I asked him a few questions, and his story is just what you'd imagine: orphaned young, thrown onto the streets to fend for himself, until a pimp scooped him up, cleaned him up, and put him to work as a whore. I decided then and there to issue a law banning the prostitution of boys his age. The Christians thought I gave them a crumb, but they were glad to get it."

"But Dominus, how will that boy feed himself? And what of other boys in the same situation?"

"You're right, there should be an increase in funds to the orphans' charity established by Hadrian. If only I had the money for it! But more to the point, the Christians have another request. Word has spread about the thousand-year history you've been working on."

"And these Christians have a suggestion, I presume?" Titus tried not to make a face.

"Yes. Several suggestions, but one in particular. They have some idea that the famous Rain Miracle that took place under the Divine Marcus was brought about by the prayers of Christian soldiers. They want to see the episode presented that way in the history."

Titus grimaced. "As you must know, Dominus, any such version of the story is not in accordance with the facts. I myself had a great-uncle who was present at the Rain Miracle, and so I have some privileged knowledge in this regard. And in any case—"

"You need not lecture me, Pinarius."

"Dominus, I mean no disrespect—"

"Anyway, as you and I both know, that particular episode does not even appear in *The Millennium*. It would have occurred in the part of the book written by the late Quadratus. I suppose he didn't think the Rain Miracle important enough to include it."

Titus nodded. "To be sure, the reign of the Divine Marcus is filled with so many important events—"

"Yes, yes, I understand. Brevity was Quadratus's assignment, as it is yours. So we will *not* mention the Rain Miracle. And the Christians may continue to tell the story however they wish, to whomever will listen."

"But, Dominus, that hardly seems right. Is it not impious of these Christians to discredit the role of Harnouphis the Egyptian, and more importantly the god Mercury, whom we know to have been the bringer of the rain?"

"Do we actually *know* that, Pinarius? For a certainty?"

Already nervous, Titus became flustered. He had always been more comfortable writing than speaking. "As I said, my own great-uncle—"

"Did you hear the story from his lips?"

"No, he died before I was born. But when I was small, I was told by my grandfather—"

The emperor silenced him with a wave of his hand. "A slippery thing, is it not, this history business? Very slippery indeed." His sardonic gaze was unnerving. Titus's heart sank. Did the emperor hate his book? "Even more slippery than history is religion. Might it not be, Pinarius, that in some way, at the furthest limit of human understanding, all the many gods whom we address by many names are truly but one god, each being a manifestation of the same substance, that which we call the Divine?"

Titus fumbled for words. "Indeed, Apollonius of Tyana spoke of a great singularity . . . a power . . . a sort of divine . . ."

"We are not here to talk about religion. But rather, this satchel full of scrolls you've delivered to me, this book of many words, *The Millennium*—vast enough to terrify the bravest schoolboy and give pause to the most ambitious tutor."

"Too many words, Dominus?" said Titus, his mouth dry.

"No. Just the right number required to tell the story, as Quadratus set out to tell it. Your revisions of Quadratus, and your Latin translations of his Greek, are quite good. And your own account of more recent events is . . . quite scrupulous. Judicious, I would say."

Titus was immediately relieved, but also a bit disappointed. The emperor's praise struck him as faint, perhaps even backhanded.

Philip saw his disappointment. "You writers! One would think you lived off praise rather than gold and silver like the rest of us. Never fear, your work is more than merely scrupulous or judicious—as important as those qualities may be—and in some places quite excellent, even occasionally poetic. I was inspired to mark some of the better passages." He called to a scribe to hand him a particular scroll, searched a bit, and then handed it to the scribe to pass along to Titus. "Here, since you wrote it, I'll let you read it aloud. The passage I've marked as 'good' in the margin."

"'Good,' Dominus? I don't see . . ."

"The Greek letters *chi* and *rho,* short for the word *chrestos,* or good. The *P* has a longish tail with the *X* atop it. Is this abbreviation not familiar to you?"

Titus stared at the symbol in the margin:

"Ah, yes," said Titus. "I do recall seeing this symbol from time to time. But only in books that are themselves in Greek."

"And this text is Latin. I see. Force of habit. My tutor when I was a boy had a satchel full of Greek scrolls in which that abbreviation was often written in the margin to denote some important or well-written passage. And if I wrote a particularly good composition myself, he would mark the *chi-rho* with his stylus upon the wax tablet, and I would feel very proud."

Titus nodded. "I remember now. Philostratus once told me, when I was a schoolboy myself, that the abbreviation was first coined—so to speak—by King Ptolemy Euergetes of Egypt, who used it on his coins as an assurance that the purity and weight could be relied upon."

Philip grunted. "Would that my own coinage could be worthy of such a stamp." Titus feared he had raised a touchy subject—the debasement of the coinage that had been going on for years—but Philip smiled. "Even so, I think the commemorative coins we are issuing to celebrate the Millennium are handsome enough as they are, and have no need of Greek letters to guarantee their value. But go ahead, read the passage aloud."

As he did so, Titus recalled that this was a passage that had been heavily rewritten by Philostratus. As he finished reading, he scrolled ahead and saw that all the passages with a *chi-rho* beside them had been written or rewritten by Philostratus. He sighed. Could he legitimately claim authorship of a work that had been so heavily rewritten by the greatest of living writers?

As it turned out, he had no need to worry on this score.

"I am thinking that authorship should be credited to Quadratus alone," said Philip. "Otherwise, the reader will be confused, don't you think? A work of such stature should be seen to issue from a single author, no matter how many researchers or scribes or writers worked on it. Single authorship gives the reader confidence in the book's integrity—rather like a *chi-rho* symbol. In the same way, the emperor must often take credit for the work of those under him, so that the citizens, and our enemies for that matter, will see the work of empire proceeding from a single source, a fountainhead if you will—just as the fount of all creation must originate from some single divine source, however multiplicitous it may seem to us mortals. We may even presume that the emperor, in his unique capacity, is himself the agent of that divine singularity, its manifestation on earth . . ."

Titus was not listening. He was profoundly disappointed, but dared not show it. He was to be invisible to the readers of the book. He had hoped to see his name on every copy, not the name of a dead man. *The Millennium* was to have made him a famous author, a notable historian; but it was not to be. Philostratus had happily helped him with no expectation of credit, but Philostratus was celebrated all over the world and had no need for more fame. Titus had toiled in the expectation that the book would be the making of him.

Then Philip mentioned the upcoming Millennial Celebration, and casually, as if in passing, asked if Titus would enjoy viewing the games in the Flavian Amphitheater from the senators' section. It took a moment for the words to sink in. As a reward for his work—and his discretion—the emperor was going to grant Titus's fondest wish.

Titus Pinarius was to become a senator.

The date was the twenty-first of April. Rome was one thousand years old.

Wearing the senatorial toga that had once been worn by his father, Titus looked down on the grand celebrations in the arena of the Flavian Amphitheater. Beside him sat his son. Gnaeus, now a man, was wearing his first toga, handed down to him from Titus.

When they arrived, a few of the other senators had given them sidelong glances. The more conservative members were dismayed that any man could join their ranks merely for having written a book, especially a history book. History was something to be written *after* a man became a senator, perhaps in his retirement. Titus had overheard one of them say, "His father, you know, was also a senator—and a mere *sculptor.* Still, the Pinarii do come from patrician stock . . ."

Titus was unfazed by such comments, delighted to be sitting where his father once sat, with his own son beside him. Gnaeus's sixteenth birthday had been only a few days ago, marked by the family ritual of passing the fascinum from father to son. Hanging from a necklace around the young man's neck, proudly worn outside his toga for this occasion, the golden amulet glimmered in the spring sunshine, brighter than the young man's golden hair.

Gnaeus's mother and sister were elsewhere, in seats reserved for the wives and daughters of senators. Thinking of Pinaria, Titus frowned. The girl was fourteen already, and not yet married or even betrothed. Her mother had found several suitable matches for her—the girl was pretty, and the Pinarius name still carried a patrician gloss—but Pinaria had rejected all suitors. *My fault,* Titus thought, *for allowing the girl to have any say whatsoever.* Why was she so choosy? But perhaps it was for the best. Now that he was a senator, they might hope for a better match.

Philip had not only elevated him to the Senate; for services rendered, Titus had been rewarded with the House of the Beaks and all its contents, including the library and its staff, and all the household slaves, thereby raising Titus's personal wealth to the level required of a senator without having to pay him in coin. "Because, dear boy, he cannot afford to pay you," Philostratus had told him, just before leaving for Athens. "With all his lavish expenditures on the games, there's not a coin left in the treasury. And now the House of the Beaks will be one less expense in his ledgers, since you, not the state, must see to the upkeep."

To make it a true home, in the vestibule Titus had set up new shrines to Antinous and to Apollonius, finding venerable old statues of both.

To feed the slaves and give his wife a household budget, Titus had sold his country properties. After all was said and done, he was not nearly as wealthy as his father had been before the catastrophe of the great fire, but he had made a start at restoring the family's fortunes.

All looked bright for the Pinarii, but their good fortune was tinged by sadness. Only days ago, a message had arrived from Athens: Philostratus was dead.

As soon as Philip approved *The Millennium*, Philostratus had sailed for Athens with the Greek version of the book, charged by the emperor to employ his own scribes to make copies for distribution throughout the Greek-speaking provinces of the empire.

"But you'll miss the Millennial Games!" young Gnaeus had protested.

Philostratus had answered, "My dear boy, I have neither need nor desire to witness yet more of the endless self-congratulations of Romans."

"You will miss Rome, surely," Gnaeus had insisted.

"Miss Rome? I think not. I look forward to the quiet and calm of Athens—and to the auditory delight of hearing Greek spoken everywhere, by everyone, from philosophers to fishermen. But I *will* miss you, dear boy, and your father, too."

Philostratus had written to them regularly, but in his last letter had complained of a sudden illness. That message had been followed by another, written by the scholar's chief secretary, delivering the news that Philostratus was dead.

Titus would never forget the help that Philostratus had given him, and the extraordinary friendship the great man had shared with four generations of Pinarii. As a man of letters, Titus would do all he could to keep the great man's books alive, though a masterpiece like the biography of Apollonius of Tyana hardly needed his assistance. It would undoubtedly outlast *The Millennium*, he thought, and perhaps even the empire itself, and would be read not one but two thousands of years hence—if mortals in such a distant future still had need of wisdom, and still read books . . .

Titus was drawn from his reverie by a blaring of trumpets, and he returned his attention to the pageant taking place in the arena. A troupe of dancers from the farthest reaches of the Nile, wearing bracelets and necklaces of bones and not much else, had formed a circle around a trained elephant, which blew its trunk like a trumpet and then appeared to sway the long appendage in time with the music. The crowd was greatly amused.

The spectacle was magnificent, at least to living Romans. Would it have impressed their ancestors who lived under Domitian, or Trajan, or Hadrian? Or would it have struck them as a bit threadbare and makeshift?

Philip had done his best, using every asset at his disposal. The one thousand gladiators and one thousand exotic animals from all corners of the empire—hippopotami, leopards, lions, giraffes, several types of apes, and a lone rhinoceros—had originally been collected and sent to Rome by the great organizer Timesitheus in anticipation of young Gordian's triumph over the Persians. That spectacle was to have reintroduced Gordian to the citizens of Rome as the emperor who left for the Persian frontier a boy but came back a conqueror. Instead, only Gordian's ashes had returned, and Philip had made use of the gladiators and animals for his own celebration.

As a historian, Titus saw a sad and bitter irony in such a twist of fortune, and he looked on the games themselves as yet another example of the futility of human affairs, the endless cycle of violence and larceny attended by empty promises, half-truths, and outright lies. The crowd, on the other hand, including his fellow senators, seemed merely to see the grand spectacle as it occurred in the moment. Had they not loved Gordian? Did they not miss him, and wonder about his fate? They seemed to have forgotten all about him, and now they loved Philip, as long as he entertained them with spectacles, stuffed them with feasts, and kept the barbarians far from Rome.

Following the elephant dance, which left the spectators in high spirits, Philip made a speech from the imperial box. He announced that his little son, who stood beside him, was to be elevated from Caesar to Augustus, to rule as co-emperor along with him. The games were not just about the glorious past, he said, but a celebration of Rome's bright future as well.

The announcement came as a surprise to everyone. The crowd was delighted by such a grandiose display of paternal largesse. They cheered for Philip the Elder and Philip the Younger.

But some of the senators were more cynical. "Our youngest emperor yet!" quipped a bald, gray-bearded senator in the row in front of Titus. "Are we eventually to be ruled by babes in the cradle?"

A colleague answered, "We've *already* had a baby emperor —the one who still suckled his mother's teats!"—a crude reference to the ill-fated Alexander and Mamaea.

Another said, "At least the little Arab's accent is somewhat less atrocious than his father's. The child has a decent Latin tutor."

The bald senator shook his head. "If Philip the Younger has any sense, he'll never set foot outside Rome. Young emperors who head for the frontier never come back—except as ashes."

The banter was grim, but so was the news from the frontiers. Both the Germans and the Persians appeared poised to attack, and ambitious Roman generals were plotting insurrection and civil war. The premature elevation of Philip's son to Augustus was not a sign of strength, thought Titus, but of weakness. Making the boy Caesar, second-in-command and heir, had not been enough. If Philip had decided to push forward the succession and make his son Augustus and co-emperor, it was because he feared for his own safety. If Philip should die, his son would already be in power.

The splendors of Philip's games spoke of greatness, security, and continuity with all that had come before, but Philip's announcement indicated that he was very uncertain of the future.

In that uncertainty, Philip was not alone. During their research for *The Millennium*, Philostratus had pointed out to Titus the general unease among men and women from all walks of life and all religions, an anxiety that seemed to stem from the one thousandth anniversary of Rome—a fear of the Millennium itself. The number 1,000 exerted a mystical claim on men's imaginations. Some predicted that with the Millennium Rome would reach its climax, and quickly come to an end. Some thought the earth itself was exhausted, and the end of all things was fast approaching. People looked for signs and portents of doom, and had no trouble finding them.

Such eschatological thinking had been encouraged by cryptic oracles that circulated in secret. These strange verses claimed to be divinely inspired prophecies from long ago. Philostratus had shown some to Titus, scoffing at them, but Titus was not sure what to make of them. If indeed this world should end, what would come next? Would there be punishment for the wicked and rewards for the just? Would there be only a vast nothingness? Or would the world restart at its beginning, like the serpent that eats its own tail? Some, like the Christians, delighted in speculating about the end of the world, but most, like Titus, pondered the possibility with dread.

The cheering for the emperor's announcement finally died down, and the grand pageant in the arena recommenced.

Later that day, when the spectacles were over and the public feasting began, Titus took his son to the Senate House, just as his own father used to do when Titus himself was a boy. Before the Altar of Victory, like his father before him, he uttered prayers to the goddess and to Jupiter to watch over the emperor—or rather, emperors—and to keep them safe. "Let Philip reign for a long lifetime! Let his son have a long reign as well! Let there be peace within and without the empire, an end to this age of unceasing bloodshed and civil strife and the birth of a new and better millennium."

Reflexively he reached to touch the fascinum at his breast, but it was not there. Gnaeus was wearing it, of course, which was as it should be. Titus felt an urge to reach over and touch it where it hung from the necklace around his son's neck, but he resisted. The protective power of the fascinum belonged now to Gnaeus, so that he might survive to pass it on when he had a son, and so on.

His uneasiness subsided before a surge of pride. The republic and the empire of Rome were a thousand years old— but the history of the Pinarii was older still, centuries older, reaching back to the days when demigods and demons like Hercules openly walked the earth.

The fascinum had protected his ancestors for over a thousand years. "May it protect my descendants for a thousand more!" he whispered.

A.D. 260

A dozen years after the Millennium, the world had turned upside-down. Rome, the thousand-year empire, was at its lowest ebb.

At fifty, Titus Pinarius had become one of those gray-haired senators he had once admired and envied; he had become, in many ways, his father. Gnaeus reminded him of the eager, ambitious young man he himself had been at the age of twenty-eight. The two of them, accompanied by a small entourage of bodyguards and secretaries, hurried toward the Senate House, summoned there for an emergency session.

Around them, as they traversed the city, all was panic and confusion. Women wept. Men shouted. Crowds flocked to the temples to beg the gods to save the city.

Philip the Arab was dust now, along with his son, both killed away from Rome by the usurper Decius. Decius and his young son were murdered in their turn. Since then, the usurpers and pretenders had been so numerous, Titus could not keep them straight.

How long ago the Millennium seemed! Those who predicted catastrophes and disasters had been prescient after all.

A new plague was raging throughout the empire, having spread from Alexandria to Syria, then to Greece, and then to Africa and Rome. In many places, the newly dead outnumbered the living. Whole towns had been wiped out. Some thought the plague of Marcus had returned, but some of the symptoms were different, and this pestilence seemed to be even more contagious—so contagious it could be passed from one person to another not just by touch, but by sight. A man could die simply from looking at a sick person, or from being looked at!

The plague first reached Rome at the end of Decius's short reign, ten years ago, killing tens of thousands. In recent years it had abated somewhat, and appeared to follow a seasonal cycle, spiking in autumn and waning at high summer. But the dying never stopped.

Barbarians, taking advantage of the weakened empire, had invaded from both north and east. The German tribes, so long held at bay, had come back in numbers greater than ever before. The Persians were now led by a vindictive and utterly ruthless ruler, Shapur.

Shapur was the cause of the worst catastrophe of all, a humiliation that had never occurred in the whole history of the empire. The aged emperor Valerian, at the head of a plague-decimated Roman army, was defeated and taken captive by the Persians. It was assumed that he would be returned in due course, in exchange for some dreadful accommodation by the Romans. But no ransom message arrived. Diplomatic entreaties were sent. Shapur replied with a series of insulting letters, boasting that he had made the great Roman emperor into the very lowest of his slaves, stripping the old man of his imperial garments and dressing him in ass skins, then using him as a footstool to mount his horse. There were rumors that Shapur had ordered Valerian to be castrated—a Roman emperor made into a eunuch!

Valerian's son and co-emperor, Gallienus, had been ruling the western half of the empire when the disaster occurred. Now Gallienus was sole emperor, facing would-be usurpers on every side. In the east, the Roman vassal Odenathus of Palmyra had proven a bulwark against the Persians, but looked poised to become a king himself. In the west, every senator in command of a legion seemed to think himself destined to be Rome's next ruler. There was a constant state of civil war.

Now the truly unthinkable had happened, throwing the city into a mad panic.

Titus and his entourage came to an abrupt halt as their way was blocked by an angry mob. Listening to the shouts and looking beyond the furious crowd, he realized the cause of their outrage. Some poor wretches had been rounded up and accused of being Christians.

Many people had come to believe that the Christians were at the root of all the city's ills. When Philip's short-lived successor, Decius, already full of superstitious dread of the Millennium, received the first terrifying reports of the plague that had broken out in Alexandria, he had issued an emergency edict: all citizens throughout the empire were to publicly beseech the gods for their blessing with a ritual burning of incense. It was a matter of religious and civic duty, for the safety and perhaps the very survival of the empire. Anyone who refused, for whatever reason, would be committing a crime and be duly punished. Christians all over the empire had refused, igniting a firestorm of hatred against them. This hatred grew fiercer as Rome was beset not just by pestilence but by one military humiliation after another.

When he rose to power, Valerian went a step further. He decided to target Christians not for any failure to act or for wrong action, but explicitly for *being* Christians—the first emperor to do so since Nero blamed them for the great fire and put as many as he could find to the torch. The penalties imposed by Valerian had been harsh: Christians could no longer hold meetings or enter their cemeteries, where they customarily gathered for worship. At the whim of local magistrates, they were subject to confiscation of their property and summary execution.

Now it appeared that a mob was about to do their worst to some of the wretched fools. Mob violence was never a good thing. As a senator, Titus felt an obligation to rein in their fury.

He ascended the steps of a nearby temple and shouted until he had their attention. There were at least some people in the crowd who respected the sight of a senatorial toga.

"Citizens!" he shouted. "You must stop this disorderly behavior at once! We are Romans. Do we murder fellow citizens right here in the Forum, without a trial? Let their cases be heard by a proper magistrate, and proper penalties carried out—by the state, not by a mob. Instead of perpetrating violence, get yourselves to the temples of the gods and beg them for their help in our moment of greatest need!"

Amid a great deal of muttering, most in the mob seemed to be swayed by his words, until one of the Christians spoke up. "We are not to blame for Rome's miseries! Those who are *not* Christians are responsible, because the gods you worship are not gods at all, but evil spirits, nothing more than demons."

Someone spoke back—and with a groan, Titus realized that it was his own son. "How dare you?" shouted Gnaeus. "Jupiter, Apollo, Venus—evil spirits? What foul blasphemers you Christians are! Can you never keep your mouths shut? No wonder the gods punish us! I lost my wife and my seven-year-old son to the plague. My sister lost her husband and children. Our generation is destroyed. And who is to blame? You!"

"No, *you* are to blame!" answered another of the Christians, with a smirk on his face. While most of the trapped Christians looked terrified, this man seemed completely unfrightened. Indeed, he seemed to be enjoying himself. "And the proof that you follow false gods? The fate of your wicked emperor, Valerian! For persecuting us Christians, he was punished by the wrath of the one true god, who brought him low, humbled him, stripped him of all his earthly pride, and reduced the emperor of Rome to a cowering slave. Now the same fate has come to the sinful city of Rome! Using the barbarians as his tool, the one god will have his vengeance! You will all be killed horribly, or else raped and carried off as slaves—"

He was silenced by the infuriated mob, which now threw off all restraint. The people set about murdering the Christians, using clubs or knives or their bare hands. A small corner of the Forum looked like a butcher's shop, with blood and gore everywhere.

With a shudder, Titus grabbed Gnaeus by the arm and headed away from the chaos as quickly as he could, hurrying toward the Senate House.

Like any pious Roman, he sympathized with the mob's anger and his son's bitterness, but he also felt a cold chill, because there was a member of his own household who was a Christian, or at least claimed to be. Titus could hardly bear to think of it: *his own wife* called herself a Christian! Gnaeus had lost his wife to the plague, but Titus felt that he had lost Clodia as well, not to plague but to the pestilence called Christianity. Of all the tragedies that had beset him and his family in recent years, he sometimes thought this was the worst, and certainly the most shameful. He had so far managed to shield Clodia from the judgment of the law, but it had not been easy.

At last they reached the Senate House. While Titus entered, Gnaeus and the slaves stayed outside on the steps, along with the retinues of the other senators already inside.

Before the Altar of Victory, Titus paused to say a quick prayer. Then he braced himself to join the raucous session already in progress.

The emergency could not have been direr. An army of barbarians had suddenly appeared north of the city—some said they were Scythians, others said they were Juthungi—*and Rome had no army to defend itself.* Nor did it even have defensive walls. Many lifetimes ago the city had spread beyond its ancient walls, and even those had fallen into disrepair. Who would ever have imagined that Rome, at the very heart of the empire, would need walls?

Messengers had been sent to the emperor Gallienus, but he was hundreds of miles away, beyond the Alps, fighting yet more barbarians along the German frontier. Somehow this band, reported to be particularly bloodthirsty, had slipped past all the legions. Some rumors claimed they had arrived in Italy by boat. Hurrying past other cities they might have plundered, they headed for Rome, like a dagger thrusting toward the heart of the civilized world.

Barbarians had managed to penetrate to Italy a handful of times since the days of the Divine Marcus, each time giving the people of Rome a scare, but none had ever actually managed to reach the city. Totally unprepared for such a threat, the Roman populace was in a panic. So were the senators.

Disorder reigned in the chamber as many senators demanded to be heard. As he had with the mob in the Forum, Titus felt obliged to impose order. Since his elevation to the Senate he had become an excellent and effective orator; both Valerian and Gallienus had called on him to write and deliver speeches. Titus was not a military man, and had not risen to high magistracies like the consulship, but he had spent his life studying the great men of the past, frequently inventing speeches for them; thinking up appropriate words to put in the mouths of dead generals and kings was part of the historian's craft. Titus had simply to imagine himself in their place, and the right words came easily to him.

He also had a very loud voice. Shouting repeatedly for silence, he at last gained the attention of the chamber.

"Senators! We can expect no help from the emperor. He and all his troops are too far away. We must rely upon ourselves, and ourselves alone."

There was renewed shouting, but once again Titus managed to quiet the chamber.

"Senators! Let me remind you of the last time barbarians attacked Rome, when Gauls sacked the city—hundreds of years ago, in the early days of the Republic. On that legendary occasion a handful of Romans retreated to the top of the Capitoline Hill and never surrendered. One night, the barbarians scaled the cliff and would have killed them all in a surprise attack, but the honking of Juno's sacred geese alerted the Romans. Among the recorded names of those brave Romans atop the Capitoline was a Vestal called Pinaria—a distant cousin of myself, I have no doubt—"

"Or maybe your *direct* ancestor? Perhaps this Vestal Pinaria experienced a virgin birth—like the mother of the Christians' man-god!"

Titus saw who made the quip and was not surprised. Senator Titus Messius Extricatus had long been his political adversary. And who but Extricatus would make a joke in such poor taste—not just picturing a pregnant Vestal, but equating her to a Christian in the same breath! Nevertheless, Extricatus got some laughs from the assembly, though these were drowned by a chorus of boos.

Titus ignored the distraction. "Senators! Are we worthy of our ancestors? Are we worthy to become the stuff of legend?"

"But how?" demanded Extricatus. "There is not a single capable general among us—every competent commander is either fighting at the frontiers, or off in the hinterlands stamping out insurrections. There are not even any Praetorian Guards in the city anymore, thanks to some emperor or other who disbanded them. We have no one to lead us. No one! And there is no one to be led. *We have no army.*"

"Then we must lead ourselves!" cried Titus. "We must arm ourselves with whatever weapons we can find, and round up every able-bodied citizen, beginning with the war veterans among us, but also the old and the young, and even gladiators and slaves—"

"Why not women, while you're at it?" said Extricatus.

"Why not, if they're willing to fight?"

"Or perhaps those suffering from the plague?" Extricatus jeered. "The dying in the city outnumber the living. They would at least fill the ranks!"

"You scoff and mock, Senator Extricatus, as is your habit, even at this dreadful moment, but I say that anyone who can pick up a weapon should join us! We must immediately arm the best force we can muster, and then march out to meet this loathsome horde of barbarians, and either kill them all, to the last man, or be killed ourselves. And before we go about this honorable task, we must ask the blessing of our ancestors, and of all the gods, foremost among them Jupiter Highest and Best, and we must all say a prayer before the Altar of Victory. She has never abandoned us, nor has Father Jupiter. The Senate of Rome has existed for more than a thousand years, and I for one believe it will exist for a thousand more. But if that is to happen, we must stand by the gods, and pray that they will stand by us."

The assembly gave him a loud, prolonged ovation. When the noise died down, Titus called on the senators he knew best and set about organizing them.

That night, from the roof of a tall building, Titus and Gnaeus peered at the campfires of the barbarians on the far side of the Tiber, in the open fields just across the Milvian Bridge.

The horde had evidently come marching down the broad and well-kept Flaminian Way. The roads of Rome were one of the empire's greatest achievements. For centuries, Roman roads had been used not just for commerce, but by countless Roman armies marching forth to conquest. Now an enemy had arrived using one of the oldest and most legendary of all Roman roads, using a tool of conquest against the city itself.

That the barbarians had not already crossed the Milvian Bridge was something of a puzzle. Had they done so immediately upon arriving, they easily could have rampaged through the city, unopposed, ransacking as they pleased. Perhaps they were weary from their journey and needed rest, or perhaps, unused to cities, they were awed by the sheer size of Rome. Perhaps they suspected that an ambush awaited them once they crossed the bridge, imagining, as any reasonable mortal would, that Rome must surely have soldiers to defend it.

From the number of campfires spread across the wide plain, the horde appeared to be enormous. Titus could hear the banging of drums and snatches of a barbaric war chant.

"What are we going to do, Father?" asked Gnaeus. "There

are so many of them! Do you really think we have a chance of
holding them off?"

"Hold them off? We must do more than that, son. We must
kill them all, or at least enough of them so that the others will
make a quick retreat."

Gnaeus frowned. "If they take the city, what will they do?
Will they burn it? Will they murder us all? Enslave us? I never
thought I should be grateful that my wife and my son are
already dead . . ."

"Don't talk like that, son! What if someone overheard you?
We must keep our spirits up. Think of the ancestors who wore
the fascinum before you."

Gnaeus touched the talisman he had been privileged to
wear for the last ten years. He knew the family lore. Marcus
Aurelius himself considered it a powerful amulet and sure
protection against plague. It might have protected Gnaeus, but
it had not saved his wife, Camilla, or Aulus, the son they had
named after his grandfather. Gnaeus had no heir to pass it on
to. "Think of the ancestors? They're all dead, as dead as my
wife and son. If only the dead could save us!"

Titus raised an eyebrow. "Perhaps they can."

"What do you mean, Father?"

"If not the dead, then the dying. I was struck by something
Messius Extricatus said—probably the only useful thing that
braying ass has ever uttered in the Senate House. I do have a
plan . . ."

"And what is that?"

Titus shook his head. "It will probably come to naught. But
until then, we must wait and hope, and pray to all the gods—
even the god of the Christians."

Gnaeus was puzzled by a statement so out of character for
his father. "Christians? What are you up to, Father?"

"Call it a secret mission."

"I'll join you, then!"

"No, for this mission, you would not be suitable."

"Father, I insist—"

"No, son, stay here with the others on the front line and keep watch. I'll rejoin you at first light. Now I'm off to see your mother. I'll give her your love."

"Wife, I need your help."

"Truly?" The look on Clodia's face reminded him of Gnaeus's puzzled expression. Mother and son looked much alike. Titus himself suddenly felt confused, torn between his enduring love for his wife and his disdain, even disgust, for the perverse nonsense she called a religion.

They were alone in their bedroom in the House of the Beaks. Usually this would have been a quiet hour, but from outside came noises of constant bustle and movement in the streets. No one in Rome slept. Almost every house was lit with lamps. Some citizens were barricading their homes. Others were loading up carts and fleeing south on the Appian Way.

Titus, so proud of his eloquence, did not know how to begin; the subject was so distasteful. "Clodia, you know I can't understand the choice you've made, or claim to have made—this business of a bloody Jew on a cross—no, that is not what I want to say. The gods work in mysterious ways—even your crucified god, perhaps . . ."

Clodia was unfazed. "What is it you're trying to say, husband? Yes, I'm a Christian. You know that. We've had this conversation many times."

Their daughter Pinaria suddenly barged into the room. At twenty-six, two years younger than Gnaeus, she already wore widow's black, thanks to the plague. There was a manic glint in her eyes.

"Mother, you are *not* a Christian!"

"No?"

"You can't be."

"Why not?"

"Because people like *us* are *not* Christians."

"What do you mean? People of senatorial family, of ancient pedigree?"

"Exactly."

"Oh, I think you might be surprised, my dear. The names I could name! But in this time of persecution it is not right for any Christian to name another. We do not make martyrs of one another. Nor do we choose martyrdom for ourselves. That would be selfish and presumptuous. The happy fate of martyrdom comes to the blessed only when the holy spirit decides the time is right. It would be vanity to choose martyrdom. Martyrdom chooses the martyr, so to speak. If only I may someday be so blessed—"

"Mother, stop babbling!" Pinaria looked ready to scream.

Titus also found it hard to listen to such crazy talk. The scene playing out was nothing new. The family had been around this gatepost countless times, repeating the same arguments. Could Clodia not see how damaging her atheism was to the whole family? Or at least what was left of the family. Not long ago the house had rung with the cries of his grandchildren. The children of Gnaeus and Pinaria, and their spouses, were all gone now, every one of them, carried off by the horrible plague . . .

He was reminded of his purpose. He tried to calm Pinaria. Clodia needed no calming. His wife never lost her composure. She perpetually wore the placid, slightly dazed look one so often saw on the faces of Christians.

"Wife, do you remember how you became a Christian?"

"Of course. I've told you the story many times."

"It was because of the plague. Or rather, the way the Christians reacted to it, as opposed to so many others."

"Exactly. Suddenly, everyone was taking sick and dying all around us. What dark days those were, before I found the one true god and our savior, Jesus Christ! I, too, feared the plague, more than anything else. When my own grandchildren were dying, I shunned them—I made the slaves look after them. I was too afraid even to enter the room, even when I heard them weeping." She had tears in her eyes, though she still smiled. "And then the slaves tending the children grew sick, and what did we do to those slaves? We threw them into the street, where the rabble pelted them with stones and drove them out of the city. Some of the sick were forced to wear blindfolds, or sacks over their heads, because people were afraid they'd catch the plague if a dying slave dared to look them in the eye. Imagine the horror and misery of such a death, to be terribly sick and then to be driven blindfolded through the streets, out of the city, to die amid gutters and weeds and heaps of trash. And all the time, I locked myself away, not wanting to see, heedless of the suffering of strangers—heedless even of my own grandchildren's final gasping breaths."

Pinaria began to sob. "Make her stop, Papa! Make her shut up!"

Titus raised a hand to quiet his daughter, for he wanted to hear what came next.

Clodia continued, with a beatific smile and eyes that glittered with tears. She loved to tell this story. "But then, one day when I dared to venture out with the slaves—we had to find sustenance somehow—I passed a neighbor's house and heard singing inside. Not sorrowful singing, but a happy song, a song of pure joy! I was drawn inside, and what should I see but many beds crowded together in every room of the house, and in those beds men and women and children who were desperately ill, some of them on the very point of dying. I was horrified, and frightened, but also full of wonder, for the people in that house were tending to the ill, caring for them, giving them sips of water to comfort them and wiping their brows, not afraid to touch them, even kissing them on the forehead. What sort of place was this? What sort of people were these?"

"Christians," said Pinaria through gritted teeth. The word dripped with loathing.

"Yes, Christians! They were not afraid to tend the ill and the dying. Indeed, they saw it as a duty, a duty to each other and to their savior, Jesus Christ. 'But what if you catch the plague yourself?' I asked. 'Why, then we too will be taken home to Him, to a better life after this one, a life of eternal bliss, free of the burdens of our mortal bodies.'"

" 'But do you not see how they suffer?' I asked, for everywhere I looked was horror. Until you've seen it with your own eyes, you can't imagine just how horrible are the final stages of the illness. After the bowels turn to water and fever scalds the body from the inside out, then comes the deafness, and the blindness, and then the rotted hands and feet and whole limbs turned to putrefaction—"

"Mother, please!"

"I know, you can barely stand to hear me speak of these things aloud. Can you imagine seeing such horror all around you, at every hour of the day? So I asked the people in that house, 'Do you not see? Are you not afraid?'

"And they answered, 'We see all this, of course—and we envy the dying, for they are blessed to go ahead of us.'

" 'You *envy* them?' I said, not trusting my ears.

" 'Yes. Envy is a sin, to be sure, and for this sin we pray to be forgiven. No mortal should rush to martyrdom, but if martyrdom comes, we must recognize it for what it is, not the horror the world deems it, but a blessing from our eternal and loving father, who would have us know the full frailty of our mortal frames before we shake them off, for how can we truly appreciate the ceasing of pain unless we have experienced pain, the more agonizing the better?'

"And then they invited me to join them—I think they saw how desperately I wanted to—and so I did, caring for the sick, and listening to the carers tell stories of Jesus and his followers, and little by little my heart was opened—"

"Like a flower to the sun!" cried Pinaria. "Yes, Mother, we have heard it all before!"

"If only you would hear and *understand*," said Clodia, reaching out. Her eyes showed her dismay, but she never stopped smiling. Pinaria snatched her arm away.

"I think *I* might understand," said Titus quietly. "I think . . . I may see a way . . ."

"Yes, husband?" Clodia's face grew bright.

"You must take me to one of these houses, where the sick are cared for by your fellow Christians."

Pinaria was aghast. "*Now,* Papa? In the middle of the night? With barbarians about to murder us all? This is what you want? To follow Mother into a madhouse?"

"Yes. The quicker the better."

The next morning, the makeshift army of Romans that had gathered along the Flaminian Way made ready to march toward the Milvian Bridge, to meet the barbarians if they dared to cross.

"The muster went on all night," Gnaeus told his father, whom he had just found amid the crowd. "We rousted every available able-bodied man—and a good number from taverns! We separated the novices from army veterans, collected and issued arms. What a haphazard, ramshackle mess! What must the gods think, looking down at us? They test us at every turn. The gods strike discord in every corner of the empire, they send Germans and Persians across our frontiers, they even allow our emperor to be captured and made a slave—and now this. A horde of barbarians is massed outside the city, and this is the best we can do? Surely when Gallienus returns, if he ever does, he'll find Rome a mass of smoking rubble. Or worse, the barbarians will still be here, living as conquerors, taking their time as they go about beheading senators and raping our women—"

"Son! Stop this talk!" Titus grabbed him by the shoulders. "There is still hope. The muster has produced a great number of armed men, many more than I expected."

In truth, looking at all the rusty swords and ill-fitting armor, the wide-eyed boys and gray-haired men, Titus was reminded of a famous episode from history—the annihilation by Cicero of the pitiful insurgent army of Catilina, which was armed with fence posts and helmeted with gourds. This army, if one dared call it that, was not quite as pitiful as that, but it was pitiful nonetheless.

The makeshift army marched up the Flaminian Way and then spread out along the bank of the Tiber, hoping to make their numbers look as great as possible. A thick mist hovered above the river, obscuring the opposite bank. Perhaps that was a good thing, thought Titus. The untrained Romans might break ranks and run at the sight of a terrifying opponent. But sounds, muffled by the fog, came from the opposite riverbank—shouting in some barbaric tongue, horns blowing, horses neighing. Was this the noise of the barbarian army preparing to cross the bridge? Might they be floating across the water on rafts? The heavy mist seemed to make anything possible. Many of the Romans began to quail from fright.

But as the sun rose and the mist very slowly dispersed, Titus saw an astonishing sight. The barbarian horde was in the very last stages of retreating. They must have broken camp and begun their departure before first light. Only a few stragglers still remained. Some looked over their shoulders and made obscene gestures, and shouted what Titus took to be insults across the water. Then they were gone.

"Ha! What a bunch of sniveling cowards!" shouted someone nearby. Titus recognized the irritating voice. He turned to see Messius Extricatus, who was practically dancing with elation. "Do you all see what's happened? Do you understand? The very sight of us made them turn tail and scamper off! Just as it should be, whenever a worthless barbarian sees a Roman!"

"Nonsense," said a man nearby, another senator. "Look around you! We're hardly a fearsome sight. Besides, the mist was too thick for them to see us. It was not us but the gods who did this. The gods heard our prayers, and they filled the enemy's hearts with fear. Praise the gods!"

"Is that what happened? Was it a miracle, Father?" asked Gnaeus. "Maybe the gods confounded them somehow, made them see an illusion across the water, a real Roman army ready to meet them. One hears of such things happening—like the Rain Miracle that saved the army of Marcus Aurelius, when the gigantic rain god peered down from the sky and terrified the barbarians, then blew them down with his mighty breath and drowned them with a flood."

Titus smiled. "If only mighty Jupiter would do just that— appear from the sky like a god at the end of a play and annihilate those barbarians. And perhaps . . . in some future version of today's events . . . that is just what will occur. Historians of the future will have to come up with some explanation, since no one will know . . . the real story."

"Papa, what are you talking about? Does this have to do with your 'secret mission' last night?"

"If you're brave enough to cross the Milvian Bridge with me, I'll show you."

"How much bravery does it take to enter an empty camp? But why are you so grim, Papa? We should be rejoicing."

"Not yet. Not quite yet . . ."

A few scouts on horseback, all gray-haired veterans, crossed to the other bank to make sure the barbarians had really left. On foot, Titus and Gnaeus followed them across the Milvian Bridge.

They saw around them the detritus of a vast camp hastily abandoned. A few slaves and Roman captives had been left behind, but there was not a warrior to be seen. The mounted scouts rode off to track the army's retreat. Titus and Gnaeus remained amid the rubbish and the smoldering campfires.

Titus seemed to be looking for something or someone. He suddenly let out a gasp. Gnaeus followed him and saw a group of corpses, twenty or more, men and women dressed in humble tunics and all of them pierced with arrows. Some lay on the ground while others lay on hand carts of the sort a single man could push down the road. As they drew closer to the bodies, Titus became increasingly agitated, trembling and wringing his hands. Gaius approached the nearest cart and looked at the arrow-pierced corpse upon it, then jumped back and let out a cry.

"Plague! Papa, these are plague victims. All of them!"

"Only the poor wretches in the carts, son. Someone had to push these carts across the bridge, long before sunrise. That task required a healthy man. Or woman. A very brave man or woman, I should add. Brave enough to tend to such sick people, and brave enough to confront the barbarians face to face. Dead, every one of them! I feared it would end like this, but still I hoped . . ."

"That *I* would live?" Clodia emerged from beneath one of the carts.

Gnaeus was astonished to see his mother.

Titus wept with relief and ran to embrace her. "You brave woman! You very foolish, very brave, wonderful woman!"

"Not brave enough," she said, also weeping. "I intended to die with the others—to become a martyr alongside them. But at the last moment, when the archers appeared, I lost my courage. I hid myself! I heard the screams when the arrows struck, and moans of suffering as they died. But not me. I stayed where I was, trembling like a leaf. I was a coward—"

"No, wife! Not one woman in a thousand, in a hundred thousand, would have dared to do what you did. You and your friends have saved the city!"

Another figure emerged from hiding, an old man who looked slightly dazed and wore a crooked grin. "I did exactly as you instructed, Senator. And like your wife, I managed to escape the arrows. I only hope that I haven't caught the plague."

Gnaeus looked at his mother and father and shook his head. "I don't understand."

"This man is Quintus Horatius," says Titus. "The bravest man in Rome, I daresay! And our savior on this blessed day. He's not a Christian, like all these others, but a retired military courier with many years of experience. He speaks several barbarian languages, including that of the Scythians."

The old man beamed. "I must say, Senator Pinarius, today I outdid myself. Over the years I've met with many barbarians in many dangerous situations, and I've learned to show a brave face no matter what, but today I put on the best performance of my life! Just as you said to do, I told them that Rome was full of plague, and for proof we brought with us a few of the sick and dying. This band of Scythians came from so far away, and traveled here so quickly, they had only heard rumors of the plague and had not yet seen it. When they saw what it does, and when I told them how easily it spreads—by sight alone—their leaders held a hasty meeting. They issued orders to retreat." His smile faded. "I thought—I hoped—that would be the end of it. But the barbarian wanted to make sure that none of the sick would follow. I heard them call for archers. I cried out in Latin to the Christians, telling them to flee. But they stood where they were, beside the carts. I realized that running would only draw attention to myself, so I hid, as best I could."

"We saw the archers coming," said Clodia, fighting back tears. "We knew what was about to happen. Instead of running, we joined hands and prayed, and then sang, as the brave Christians did when Nero slaughtered them. But I . . . I lost my courage . . . I pulled my hands free . . . I slipped behind the others, and then I ducked beneath a cart . . ."

"Now I understand, Papa," said Gnaeus. "You used the plague to drive them off. No amount of talking about it would have frightened them. They had to see for themselves what it does to people. And who but the Christians would be suicidal enough to take on such a mission?" He frowned. "But what did you mean, last night, about getting the idea from Messius Extricatus?"

"Yesterday in the Senate he mocked my call to arms by suggesting I enlist plague victims to fight for the city. A thought struck me: Who better to frighten the barbarians? But how could the invaders be made to see the sick with their own eyes? Even if the sick volunteered for such a task, they were unable to walk. Healthy volunteers would have to lift them onto carts and wheel them across the bridge and into the barbarian camp. And who would willingly perform such a dangerous task? Only Christians! Only people like your mother could be so foolhardy, or so brave. They fear neither plague nor barbarians. Death holds no fear for them. As for Horatius here, he is certainly no Christian, but he did as I asked, thanks to his great patriotism—and only partly, I'm sure, for the very large reward I promised him. And now the plague victims and the Christians have saved the city!"

"That fool Extricatus thought it was the sight of our ragtag army that did it," said Gnaeus, laughing scornfully.

"In that he's not *entirely* wrong," said Horatius. "While I hid, the barbarians carried out their retreat, until only a few remained. The fog must have lifted just enough to offer a hazy view of the Romans across the river. I heard one of the barbarians say, 'If they're all so sick from this plague, how can they muster so many men to face us?' My heart sank. If they suspected a ruse, they might halt the retreat. But then another said, 'But look at them! Have you ever seen a sorrier lot! If that's the best army the greatest city on earth can scrape together, if the plague is *that* terrible, we can't leave quickly enough. There must be other cities in Italy, not as big or as rich, but maybe free from the plague. Leave quickly, and don't look back!'"

Clodia pulled free of her husband's embrace. "The city is saved. The sick died quickly and no longer suffer. And my friends—they're in paradise right now, jubilant martyrs one and all. You call me brave, husband, but I failed to die a martyr this day, as I thought I would. Was it because I deliberately sought martyrdom? I was not worthy. I'm too vain, too cowardly. Perhaps another day . . ."

Gnaeus looked at his father. "When you sent Mother on this mission with the others, did you think she would die?"

"I did everything I could to protect her. I prayed at the Altar of Victory that the plan would work—and it did, for this *is* a victory, even if there was no battle. I burned incense to Antinous and to Apollonius of Tyana, asking them to watch over your mother. I trained my thoughts upon the fascinum that hangs from your neck, son, which has looked over the fortunes of this family for so many generations. I knew in my heart that your mother would survive."

Clodia shook her head. "Your false gods had nothing to do with it, husband. I still live for only one reason: because it does not yet please Jesus Christ to take me."

"We both invoke religion, wife, yet we disagree. Well, you know the old Etruscan saying: gods move in mysterious ways. That adage certainly applies to *your* god. How peculiar he is, how jealous of the other gods, that he permits you to worship no others, only him. But I begin to think he might possess considerable power. Without all these dead Christians— martyrs, as you call them—many more Romans would have died today. The whole city might have been destroyed. When I give thanks to the gods at the Altar of Victory, I shall include your crucified man-god, whether he likes being named among the other gods or not. And when the emperor returns to Rome, I'll tell him what happened here today and I'll try to persuade him to rescind his father's decrees against the Christians. He may actually welcome the idea. Gallienus has never been as hostile to the Christians as was Valerian. His disposition is milder, more like that of Philip."

Instead of being cheered by this promise, Clodia pushed out her chin and looked thoroughly vexed. "But if Gallienus ends the persecution—how am I *ever* to become a martyr?"

Titus and Gnaeus looked at each other for a long moment, then roared with laughter. All the tensions of the preceding two days were released in gales of tearful mirth. Gnaeus embraced Clodia and lifted her off the ground. "Oh, Mother, what a strange creature you are! And how glad I am, that you are still among the living!"

PART IV

THE WALLED CITY
(A.D. 274)

A.D. 274

"When I was a little girl," said Zenobia, "long ago and far away, in Palmyra, my tutors taught me that the city of Rome had no walls. I could not imagine that. Why then did Palmyra have walls? They told me: sitting at the intersection of so many trade routes, and possessing so much wealth, how else could the city of Palmyra be safe? But Rome was so vast, they told me, that no wall could encircle it, and so powerful, so terrifying to the entire world, it needed no walls. No one would ever dare to attack it. No one would even think of such a thing. But all these years later, now that I am here, in Rome, I see there *are* walls, encircling the whole city. New walls, very tall and very thick."

Zenobia stood on the roof terrace atop the House of the Beaks. She leaned on the parapet and gazed at the skyline of the vast city around her. She was of a dark complexion. Her eyes were almost black, yet they seemed to glitter more brightly than the eyes of other mortals. So white was her smile that some said she had pearls in place of teeth.

Here in the privacy of her home, she wore not a Roman matron's stola, but her colorful native dress. Her neck and her bare arms were adorned with shimmering gold and sparkling jewels. So striking was she, so naturally regal, that a crown or diadem would not look at all out of place on her head, thought Gnaeus. But Zenobia was no longer queen of Palmyra. She was lucky to be alive; lucky that she had been allowed to keep any of her jewelry; luckier still not to be a conquered slave, but the wife of a Roman senator, and not a doddering old gray-beard but a man in the prime of life.

Gnaeus Pinarius smiled as he often did at his wife's exotic accent. He couldn't help thinking that she sounded just a bit dim when she spoke Latin. But dim-witted Zenobia most certainly was not. Her Greek was impeccable and quite elevated, far better than his. But she wished to perfect her Latin, so that was the language in which husband and wife conversed.

She was trying to trace the course of the wall with her eyes, but lost sight of it in the midst of so many hills and rooftops. "Is that the wall I see over there?" She pointed.

"No," said Gnaeus, "that's a bit of the ancient Servian Walls. Those were built hundreds of years ago, after Brennus the Gaul sacked the city, to keep the Gauls from ever doing it again. But no Gaul ever even tried, and nor did any other barbarian, not for hundreds of years. Even Hannibal quailed at the prospect. The only commanders who ever took Rome by force were Roman generals waging civil war. After Julius Caesar conquered Gaul, and put an end to that threat for good, he marched on Rome, but the Servian Walls meant nothing, since all the opposition fled. Meanwhile, the city grew far beyond the old Servian Walls. Some stretches of the walls were incorporated into buildings. Other parts were neglected and left to crumble. Weeds sprouted all over them. In some places the Servian Walls look like a huge, overgrown flower bed. And people thought nothing of it. As you say, the idea that anyone would ever dare to attack Rome was simply . . . unthinkable. Those days are gone."

Gnaeus let out a long sigh, partly from sadness at the faded invincibility of his beloved city, and partly because, if Zenobia were any other woman, he would now be walking up and embracing her from behind. She *was* his wife, after all. But there were strict limits to their intimacy, dictated by Zenobia. He'd agreed to them before they married, and he was a man of his word.

"No, the new walls built by Aurelian are much farther out," he said. "In that direction, I don't think you can see them from here at all. You'd have to go up on the Capitoline Hill, or climb to the top tiers of the Flavian Amphitheater to see them in all directions." He drew close to her, as if to share in the view, but really so that he could feel the warmth of her naked shoulders, smell her scent, hear her breathing.

"It was fourteen years ago that the Scythians dared to set up camp outside the city. I was here at the time. So was my father. But the emperor—Gallienus, at the time—was far away, and so were all the legions. The Senate mustered the best army it could, calling up old veterans and gladiators and slaves who had served as bodyguards . . ."

"And the Scythians saw the brave defenders, took fright, and ran!" said Zenobia. "That was the story we heard in Palmyra."

"And a fine story it is."

She arched an eyebrow. "Is it not a *true* story?"

"True, as far as it goes. But sometimes, behind one truth, there is another truth."

"You sound like Longinus," she said. She never missed a chance to remind him that the world's leading philosopher had graced her court in Palmyra.

"The *late* Longinus," he noted. Serving as advisor to the queen of Palmyra ultimately proved fatal for the famous thinker, after Aurelian took the city.

She ignored this jab. "But you were here, when it happened," she said. "So you know this *other* truth."

"Perhaps . . ." Should he tell her? He thought not. Better to hold on to any little scrap that piqued her curiosity or elicited her desire for knowledge. His marriage was a daily transaction. She needed or wanted certain things from him. He desired other things from her. Information was one form of currency.

"Remind me, wife, to tell you the story some day." She glared at him and said something in her native language.

"What did you say, wife?"

"I said you are a beast. A big, mean, Roman beast." Her

accent was so funny he almost laughed. How desirable she looked at that moment, with her eyes narrowed and her lips taut. He was aching to take her in his arms.

Seeing the spark in his eyes, sensing his desire, she smiled faintly and turned her gaze back to the skyline. "And after the Scythians left?"

"Oh, they marauded all up and down Italy, sacking one city after another—those cities, too, had no walls—looting and burning and enslaving a great many Roman citizens who were never heard from again. All those cities have walls now. And a good thing, because after the Scythians there came yet more barbarians, all eager to have a go at taking Rome. They were all repelled—some of them, just barely. Aurelian himself, not long after he became emperor, suffered a huge loss at Placentia, so devastating that many thought the barbarians would push straight to Rome. The Sibylline Books were consulted—something the Senate does only in direst emergency. The verses dictated that certain sacrifices should be performed at various river crossings and mountain passes, so as to keep out the barbarians."

"Did these magical spells work?" she asked.

"Not magic, my dearest. Appeals for divine protection."

"What is the difference?"

Gnaeus snorted. Had it come to this, that he must argue theology with a woman? He sidestepped. "However one puts it, the efficacy of those rituals was never actually tested. Aurelian regrouped and routed the barbarians. His success on the battlefield was astonishing. Nonetheless, he decided not to try his luck twice, and announced that the time had come to build a new wall around Rome, long enough and thick enough and tall enough to keep out the most determined barbarian horde. With Rome secure, he was free to set about on an even bigger task, clawing back the breakaway kingdoms in the west . . . and in the east." Here he meant Palmyra, so he spoke carefully. "For a few years it seemed that the empire was coming apart at the seams, splitting into warring kingdoms, until Aurelian took matters in hand—and just in time. 'Restorer of the World,' it says on his coins, and so he is. Savior of the Roman world, at least. The greatest man of his generation, and one of the greatest of all Roman emperors."

Zenobia sighed. In a way, he had flattered her. If one must be conquered, let it be by a great commander, not by accident or because of one's own failings.

"He restored my own family's fortunes, as well. Or at least his wall did." Gnaeus had never before discussed with her the source of his wealth. Had she been a Roman matron he wished to court and marry, the families would have discussed money matters openly; but Zenobia was in no way a typical bride.

"The wall?"

"Much of the building was carried out by soldiers, but such a huge project demanded the best designers and artisans in the city. That is how the Pinarii made their fortune in past generations, as builders and artists. Then my grandfather died in the great fire, and my father lost virtually everything. Then, the patronage of the emperor Philip gave us this house. After that, my father struggled to reestablish the family business, but there was not much call for art and embellishment under Valerian and Gallienus, no grand projects here in the city. There was no money for such things, especially when people were dying right and left from plague. Gallienus mostly built fortifications and walls for cities menaced by the barbarians, like Athens. There was no such building project here in Rome—until Aurelian decided the time had come. I happened to be in the right place at the right time, able to put together a workshop of men with all the right skills. Building that wall made me a very rich man." *Rich enough to marry a queen*, he thought. "Twelve miles of wall more than ten feet thick and twenty-five feet high, built of concrete and faced with brick, with a square tower every hundred feet, and nineteen gates. Along with all the construction, there was also a great deal of demolition, getting rid of obstacles in the way.

"The wall marked a change, of course. For many old-timers, including my father, the very sight of it is hard to take." Gnaeus mimicked the slightly pompous voice his father used when reading aloud from his histories: "'A Rome with walls is no longer *my* Rome! Nor is it the Rome of Augustus, or of Marcus Aurelius!' Never mind that building that wall filled the family coffers! I tell the old fellow, 'This is the Rome of Aurelian. Walls keep out barbarians, Papa. And usurpers.'"

"The same walls that keep some out, keep others in," said Zenobia quietly.

"Do you feel like a prisoner, wife?"

"How can it be otherwise?" Though nothing about her expression seemed to change, she suddenly looked tragic. Her shoulders stiffened as she drew a deep breath. Gnaeus could not resist embracing her. But she remained stiff inside his arms. After a brief, awkward moment, he stepped back.

Her tragic posture reminded him of the first moment he saw her, which was the moment he fell in love with her. It was the day of Aurelian's triumph . . .

In only three years as emperor, Aurelian seemed to have crammed a whole lifetime of accomplishment.

The empire had reached its lowest ebb when he became emperor. Gallienus had managed to hold power for fifteen years, a remarkable achievement considering the endless disasters of his reign. Invasions from without and insurrections within had split the empire into three parts, with Gaul a breakaway state to the west and Palmyra in the east behaving more like an independent kingdom than a client state. Gallienus's father, Valerian, had been captured by the resurgent Persians and was never seen again. His two young sons had been cruelly murdered by would-be usurpers. Year after year the plague wore on, a pestilence even worse than that of Marcus Aurelius's days. And to make matters yet worse, in the year Gallienus ventured to celebrate ten years of rule by staging Decennalia festivities, earthquakes devastated cities all around the Mediterranean.

One of the greatest disasters of his reign was man-made—the massacre of the entire population of the city of Byzantium by Roman soldiers on a rampage. Gallienus with an army traveled to Byzantium, convinced the miscreant soldiers to open the gates to him, and summarily put them all to death. Byzantium, one of the jewels of the empire, became a ghost city, populated by vultures and wolves.

As Titus had once noted, "No wonder people like your mother turn to bizarre cults like Christianity. A reasonable man might well conclude that the gods have turned irrevocably against mankind, or have simply abandoned the world—or perhaps never existed at all."

Gallienus was remarkably resilient and brave, but eventually went the way of his predecessors, murdered in murky circumstances while on military campaign. His successor had been a military man of humble origins, Claudius, who seemed a competent general but who died of plague in Sirmium, far from Rome, after a reign of only fifteen months.

From the ensuing scramble for power emerged Aurelian, another military man of humble origin in his mid-fifties. Thus far his reign had been like a comet blazing across the night sky. As a dedicated worshipper of Sol, Aurelian preferred comparison to the sun breaking through clouds.

In short order Aurelian defeated the latest of the barbarian threats from the north, the Goths, and largely through diplomacy reclaimed the breakaway province of Gaul. When Zenobia, after the death of her husband, attempted to make Palmyra a kingdom independent of Rome, with its own imperial ambitions—she claimed Egypt as well—Aurelian trounced her armies and successfully laid siege to Palmyra. He executed most of the queen's court—including the unfortunate philosopher Longinus—but he spared the queen, wanting her to adorn his triumph back in Rome.

And what a triumph it had been! Who would ever forget the sight of Aurelian's chariot pulled by four elephants, their flesh dyed white and their tusks brightly gilded? They were followed by twenty more elephants, part of the booty from Zenobia's palace in Palmyra that had been transported by sea to Rome.

Gnaeus and his father, both senators, had taken part in the procession, walking near the end, just ahead of Aurelian. Gnaeus had not worn the fascinum, though his father practically begged him to. Having lost his wife and son to plague, and never having remarried, of what use to him was a family heirloom? A few years previously, on the date when his son, had the boy lived, would have turned sixteen and been given the fascinum, Gnaeus put the talisman away. He had not looked at it since.

While waiting in the staging area for the triumph, Gnaeus had been able to see the contingents ahead of him as they moved into place on the Sacred Way. That was when he caught his first glimpse of Zenobia.

By including her in the procession, Aurelian wanted both to show the people what a prize he had captured, and to completely humiliate his captive. The sight of Zenobia was at once titillating and pathetic. She was adorned with so much gold and silver and gems that she labored under the weight of her ornaments. She managed to keep her head stiffly upright, but staggered from time to time, not only from the load of her jewelry, but because her feet had been bound with shackles of gold and her hands with golden fetters. Around her neck was a golden collar attached to a leather leash more suitable for a dog, which was carried before her by a dwarf dressed in the motley costume of a Persian buffoon, with long pointed shoes and a false nose in the shape of an erect phallus. The dwarf mocked her whenever she paused, and encouraged the gaping, jeering crowd to do likewise.

Gnaeus had been stunned at the sight of her. How could anyone jeer or mock such an extraordinary creature? That was how he thought of her, as a nearly supernatural being, more beautiful and majestic than any mortal woman possibly could be. He had turned to look up at the emperor, who watched from a high, screened platform above the staging area where he could observe the crowd without being seen. Aurelian looked pleased by his captive's sensational effect on the crowd.

Night after night, following the triumph, Gnaeus could not sleep. He tossed and turned. He summoned the prettiest of his slave girls to his bed, but could find no interest in them. What was wrong with him? For years, ever since he was widowed, he had been quite satisfied with slaves and courtesans. He never thought of remarrying. The loss of his wife had been too devastating. When guests came to the House of the Beaks, his widowed younger sister, Pinaria, served as his hostess. She, too, showed no interest in remarrying.

But from the moment he saw Zenobia in chains, a mad desire possessed him. Gnaeus had to have her. He knew such a desire was out of bounds, irrational, but still it hounded him, every waking hour of the day and then in his dreams. At his household shrine, he prayed to Antinous that his impossible love might find a way, but he avoided the shrine of Apollonius. The only proper prayer to the wise man of Tyana would be to rid himself of such an earthly desire altogether, and Gnaeus could not bear to give up his obsession.

Finally, Gnaeus sent a letter to the emperor begging for an audience. The audience was granted.

Seated on a golden throne on a high dais, Aurelian was literally dazzling. His purple robes were embroidered with golden threads and countless jewels of every color. On his head he wore a golden diadem with radiant spikes, so that pointed beams of golden sunlight appeared to radiate from his brow. His courtiers observed protocols inspired by the royal courts of the East, so that there were a great many steps of formal ceremony before Gnaeus finally came face to face with his Dominus.

Early in his reign, some had said the new emperor was just another boorish soldier from peasant stock. This was Aurelian's way of proving just how wrong they were. But it seemed to Gnaeus that it was precisely Aurelian's humble origins that accounted for the man's taste for gaudy display and his demand that everyone bow before him. Erudite, high-born men like the Divine Marcus had never needed such trappings to bolster their confidence or to exert their authority.

Although Gnaeus had requested a private audience, they were by no means alone. Secretaries and courtiers stood all around. The two men already had a professional relationship, because of Gnaeus's work on the wall. Aurelian began the conversation by saying he was a great admirer of the history written by Gnaeus's father. Whatever his upbringing, the emperor was old-fashioned enough to start by complimenting his visitor's family—and canny enough to know that Roman aristocrats were easily disarmed by courtesies that cost nothing.

"How old *is* your father?" Aurelian asked.

"Sixty-four, Dominus."

"Ah, then, not much older than I. Perhaps he'll be around long enough to write an account of *my* reign. If I live long enough to have a reign worth recounting."

"Dominus, in a very short time, you have already achieved the work of many lifetimes," said Gnaeus. He knew the words sounded fawning, but he meant them sincerely. "You reunified the empire, you built the magnificent new walls, you led Rome to victories over the Vandals, the Juthungi, and the Sarmatians. Even the lowliest inhabitants of Rome sing your praises, grateful for your increase of the dole." This was certainly true. The bread dole was now daily rather than monthly, and regularly included wine, pork, salt, and olive oil.

Aurelian seemed pleased. "You are very cognizant of my accomplishments, Senator Pinarius. Perhaps *you,* not your father, should become my court historian." Gnaeus was taken aback by the suggestion—he had not inherited his father's way with words—but Aurelian did not wait for a response. "I'm glad that you mention the dole. All the rest is obvious, of course, but not only did I drive back the barbarians and secure Rome with a wall, I saved her people from starvation. It was an outrage, that Romans were literally starving in their homes, and virtually every farm and vineyard in Italy lay fallow because the barbarians had wreaked such havoc. I've put the farmers and the vintners back to work. I feed the people. And I give them all a bit of wine so that they can enjoy the spectacles I put on. Because that is what emperors *do*. But you, Senator Pinarius, look quite well fed, so I do not think you are here to thank me for the dole. Why *are* you here?"

Gnaeus took a deep breath. "What will become of the queen of Palmyra?"

Aurelian frowned. "First of all, Zenobia is not a queen. Nor was she ever one. Palmyra never left the possession of Rome. She and her husband raised troops to hold the Persian threat in check, but they did so on behalf of Rome. After her husband died, Zenobia seems to have misunderstood the relationship. She put her young son on a throne. She started wearing a diadem herself—that is, when she was not wearing a helmet and waging war on horseback."

"Those stories are true? About Zenobia leading men into battle?"

Aurelian nodded. "I thought about dressing her in her warrior's armor for the triumph—let the people of Rome see a *real* Amazon for once, not the make-believe sort who fight as gladiators—but I decided against it. That would make her appear a beaten rival rather than a trophy, and what Roman could be proud of besting a woman on the battlefield? An upstart would-be queen weighed down by golden chains— that's another matter. Augustus never got to show off Cleopatra in his triumph. The Egyptian queen killed herself rather than be captured. Not so Zenobia, though she claims to come from Cleopatra's bloodline. When we took the city, she fled from Palmyra, hoping to find sanctuary with the Persians, but I tracked her down—and caught her!" He leered at the memory. "The men in the crowd certainly enjoyed the sight of her in the procession. So did the women. They all loved seeing a haughty beauty brought low."

"But . . . what will become of her?" asked Gnaeus, his mouth dry.

"I haven't yet decided. Her son is dead. I'd have paraded him in chains, as well, but he managed to escape his irons on the ship crossing the Bosphorus and jumped overboard. My men found his body washed up on the shore. Did he think to escape, or did he deliberately drown himself? When I gave his mother the news, not the faintest glimmer of emotion crossed her face. She's either very strong, or quite coldhearted."

Gnaeus remembered the death of his own son. He had wept like a child. He had lost a beloved son, and so had Zenobia, and they both had lost a spouse. He felt a pang of sympathy for her. Might she not feel a similar sympathy for him?

Aurelian ticked off his fingers. "She now has no husband, no son, no kingdom. To execute Zenobia at this point might seem churlish, or an admission that she poses a threat, or at least once did. But she can hardly be set free to plot mischief, and she is more than capable of doing that. I blame her for the second siege of Palmyra. I decided to be merciful and to spare the city when I took it the first time. But then, on my way back to Rome, the city rebelled, and so did the Egyptians, saying they were still loyal to Zenobia and her brat. How she managed to plot rebellion while held captive I don't know, but she's crafty enough. So I turned back. I had to stage one bloodbath in Egypt and another in Palmyra. A nasty business! So what now? I suppose I should keep her under constant guard in some appropriately remote location, perhaps a small island somewhere . . ."

"I want to marry her!" Gnaeus blurted out.

Aurelian stared at him for a long moment, then laughed. "If by *marry* her you mean *copulate* with her, every man who's seen her has felt the same itch." He looked knowingly at some of the surrounding courtiers, who snickered and laughed.

"I'm serious, Dominus."

"Yes, I see you are. How old are you, Senator Pinarius?"

"Forty-two, Dominus."

"And a widower, as I recall." Like all good generals, Aurelian had a memory for the personal details of underlings.

"My wife died from the plague, many years ago. As did my son."

"A widowed, childless Roman senator wants to marry Zenobia of Palmyra—and then what, beget little Palmyrene upstarts to raise trouble for me when I'm old and gray?"

"I . . . hadn't thought that far ahead."

"You should, if you ever want to copulate with the bitch. Do you not know the stipulation she imposed on her husband? Before they married, she told Odenathus she would submit to having intercourse with him for one purpose only, to beget children, and if she was not at the time of the month to do so, she would not allow him in her bedchamber. Poor Odenathus actually went along with her demands. Well, you can hardly call such a man a man—or such a woman a woman!"

The courtiers laughed. Gnaeus felt his face grow hot. "Even so, Dominus . . ."

Aurelian nodded thoughtfully. "Keeping her here in Rome might actually be preferable to exiling her to some island. Easier to keep an eye on her. I would expect her husband to do just that—keep a close watch. There can be no plotting or scheming, no contact whatsoever with any of her old friends and relations from Palmyra."

"As you wish, Dominus."

"And—man to man, Senator—I think you should understand that she comes to you . . . not untouched."

"If you mean . . . ?"

"You know exactly what I mean. If she tells you she's never submitted to any man except to make a baby, well, ask some of my higher-ranking officers about that."

"Do you mean to say that they . . . ?"

Aurelian grinned. "Only after I took *my* turn. Several turns, I should say. What do you think happened after I chased her down and caught her in the desert? A chase like that heats a man's blood. A woman's, too." His courtiers smirked. Aurelian shrugged. "What's the point of conquering a woman in battle if you don't enjoy the spoils? She's lucky I didn't do the same to her brat—he was pretty enough. Afterward, I could have crucified them both." He sighed. "But when I prayed on the matter, Apollonius told me to be merciful."

"Apollonius?"

"The sage of Tyana. Oh yes, I remember now, your family has a personal connection to him. And to Philostratus, the man who wrote the biography. He also helped your father write *The Millennium*."

"That's right. But you were saying, about Apollonius . . . ?"

"I saw the old fellow with my own eyes. As clearly as I see you now. And he spoke to me."

"When was this, Dominus?"

"In Tyana, of course!" Aurelian smiled. He clearly did not mind telling the story. "Before Palmyra, we came to Tyana, which was also loyal to Zenobia. The men were hungry for booty, so I promised them that when we took Tyana we would—my exact words—'leave not a dog alive!' The siege commenced, and went well, but then one night, in my tent, Apollonius appeared to me. He told me that I must spare the people of his hometown, and before I could question him— he vanished! I don't mind admitting that I broke into a cold sweat. Demons can have that effect, even on the bravest mortal. Well, I had to do as he asked, but that meant going back on my promise to the soldiers. Or did it? Do you know how I solved the problem?"

"No, Dominus."

"I told the men to spare the people of Tyana . . . not to harm a hair on anyone's head . . . but to kill all the dogs!" He laughed. "Do you see? I stayed true to my word—I left no dog alive—but I also did as Apollonius commanded."

The emperor sat back in his throne, relishing the memory. "Before Tyana, I had another vision, when we were laying siege to Emesa. I looked up and saw a black stone floating in midair. It passed directly in front of the sun, so that it was circled by a fiery halo. I wasn't the only one who saw the thing. Many of my soldiers saw it, too. And I heard it speak. 'You will be victorious,' the stone said, 'but you must honor me!' After I took Emesa, the first thing I did was to visit the Temple of Elagabalus. I went into the sanctum—and there I saw the divine form again! It was the baetyl they worship, the stone that fell from the sky long ago, a shard of the Sun's divine being.

"And right there in the temple, I saw the stone rise up in the air, and again it spoke to me, promising me that I would conquer Palmyra, and saying that when I returned to Rome I must straightaway build a new temple to Sol Invictus, the Unconquerable Sun. 'Make it the greatest temple Rome has ever seen and dedicate it to me, but make it a home for all the gods, where every god may be worshipped under a single roof. As the sun is singular and indivisible and brings life to all the world, so the sun manifests in itself all things divine.'"

"The False Antoninus wanted to do something like that," muttered Gnaeus.

"What's that? Ah yes, him! That poor boy hauled the baetyl all the way from Emesa to Rome, then ended up headless and dragged through the streets with his mother. Well, his heart was in the right place. Ahead of his time, when it came to religion. A generation from now, we shall all worship Sol, in whose light all gods reside. And for daily wisdom, all men shall look to Apollonius, the wisest man who ever lived. Ha! The look on your face, Senator Pinarius! Yes, I have a philosophical side to me, low-born soldier that I am. The campaign to take Palmyra also became a journey of religious awakening. Now, Sol Invictus and the sage of Tyana guide all that I do, inform every decision I make."

He was quiet for a moment, then grunted. "But we were talking of something much more mundane—the fate of Zenobia. Well . . . if you want her, you can have her. A senator's wife—what better way to stash her out of sight? Gallienus did a wise thing, when he decreed that you senators could no longer command legions. Now all generals must rise from the ranks, as I did. And because no man will ever rule this empire without commanding legions first, that means no senator will ever sit on the throne again. So let Zenobia be a senator's wife and live in a senator's house, where she can quietly fade into obscurity."

So it came about that Gnaeus had been granted his wish. Aurelian stipulated that the nuptials be conducted without fanfare or festivity, which suited Gnaeus. The marriage was known to few. Most Romans had no idea of what had become of Zenobia. If they thought of her at all, they might assume she was strangled at the end of the triumph, which was the traditional fate of a conquered enemy. Zenobia herself was content to seldom leave the house. She had no desire to be recognized and gawked at. Gnaeus alone had the privilege of gazing upon her at leisure, as he was doing at that very moment on the roof terrace of the House of the Beaks, desiring her.

But, as she had done with Odenathus, Zenobia had refused to marry Gnaeus unless he agreed that they would copulate only on occasions when it was likely and desirable to create a child. Since their marriage, they had done so only a handful of times, and he had been disappointed by her lack of enthusiasm. Vain male that he was, Gnaeus had assumed that his lovemaking would seduce her, or that she would at least feign enjoyment out of gratitude for saving her from exile. Her obstinacy only piqued his desire for her. He sometimes entertained a fantasy of forcing her against her will. Then he would remember that she claimed descent from Cleopatra. It was said that Cleopatra wrote a whole book about poisons and how to use them. Zenobia was not a wife to be trifled with.

Rebuffed and frustrated once more, he turned away and without another word left her alone on the terrace, gazing at the moonlit city.

In the house, he encountered his sister. "Have you seen Zenobia?" Pinaria asked.

Gnaeus pointed toward the roof terrace. Pinaria passed

him, and a few moments later, from the terrace, he heard the two of them laughing. Why did Zenobia never laugh that way with him? Was she so frightened of him? Or did she hold him in contempt? If so, she hid her feelings well. She was always respectful to him, and sometimes even seemed to be a bit fond of him. Zenobia neither loved nor loathed him. Her response was steadfastly lukewarm—which maddened him.

He heard the women laugh again, and then engage in animated conversation, though he couldn't make out the words. What did the two of them find to talk about? Feminine matters, he supposed, not sure what that meant. Curious, he stepped to the doorway, drawing close enough to eavesdrop.

They were talking about religion.

Pinaria made her perennial complaint, frustration with her mother's unremitting Christianity, which was no longer illegal but was still shameful. Zenobia, too, expressed disdain for the Christians, but fondly recalled a meeting with the prophet Mani, who had once visited Palmyra and healed Zenobia's desperately ill sister. Gnaeus didn't know much about Mani, except that he had gained a large following among the Persians.

The wise man whom Zenobia most revered was the philosopher Longinus, who had been a towering figure in the court at Palmyra. Longinus had advised her to resist Aurelian, saying that Rome was the past and Palmyra the future. For that bad counsel he had been beheaded by Aurelian, despite Zenobia's pleas for clemency. In the House of the Beaks she had set up a shrine to Longinus alongside those of Antinous and Apollonius of Tyana.

"But Longinus is *here*. He followed you to Rome," said Pinaria. "I'm almost certain it was his ghost I saw last night. He didn't speak, but I recognized him from that painting of him, in your shrine."

Pinaria, like her mother, regularly saw the ghosts of those who had lived in the house—Pompey the Great, Antony and Fulvia, the emperor Tiberius, and the ill-fated Gordians. Their Christian mother had decided that these spirits of once-living

Romans were now demons unworthy of paradise, doomed to haunt their earthly abode as punishment for their sins.

For better or worse, Gnaeus had never seen a ghost. Nor had Zenobia. "Not even my husband Odenathus," he heard her tell Pinaria, "though I would gladly have welcomed his counsel when Aurelian laid siege to Palmyra! If you see Longinus again, tell him to visit me. I miss him so!"

A thought occurred to Gnaeus. Might he win over Zenobia by appealing to her intellect?

The dinner was a formal affair and very old-fashioned, with couches to recline on and only six diners: Titus Pinarius presiding as paterfamilias, Clodia, Gnaeus, Pinaria, Zenobia, and their guest, the philosopher Porphyry, who had promised to give a recitation.

Porphyry was only forty or so, but, according to everyone Gnaeus asked, he was the most respected intellectual in the city. He was a champion of the late philosopher Plotinus, but in younger days had lived in the East and at that time was equally close to Longinus. When he learned that Zenobia would be present, getting him to come to dinner took some doing. Porphyry was not eager to meet the same fate as Longinus. But in the end he could not pass up a chance to meet the legendary queen.

For her part, Zenobia was magnificently arrayed in the few pieces of jewelry Aurelian had allowed her to keep. Golden serpents with ruby eyes were wrapped around her bare arms. Rings flashed and bracelets made delicate music at her slightest gesture. Her necklace, said to have been worn by Cleopatra, displayed a single, very large, flawless pearl with golden wings to either side, a depiction of the Egyptian sun god, Ra. It reminded Gnaeus of the fascinum, which depicted a phallus with wings. He touched the place on his chest where it would have rested had he not put it aside after the death of his wife and son.

Gnaeus worried that one or the other might be disappointed, but the two of them hit it off at once. Porphyry dared to ask about the last days of Longinus, and praised his memory. Zenobia was curious about Porphyry's studies under Plotinus, whom she had never met, though she had read all his works. Titus, who was a student of philosophy as well as history, joined in their lively discussion of Neo-Platonism, but the topic went completely over Gnaeus's head. From the bits he could follow, the conversation reminded him of what Aurelian had said about folding the worship of all gods into worship of a single deity, the sun.

At a pause in the discussion, he shared the emperor's comments.

"If I understood Aurelian correctly," said Gnaeus, "whether one calls it Sol Invictus or Elagabalus or Helios or Apollo—or Ra, as the Egyptians do—the sun is always the sun, everywhere, the one and only, the manifest source of all life and enabler of all human activity. It occurs to me, Zenobia, that there is a certain similarity between the image of Ra that you wear tonight, and the image of Fascinus that has been passed down in my family for many centuries. Both are winged, and both are givers of life. It all comes back to the sun—or so Aurelian would have it. Well, such a streamlined religion would certainly simplify things. There are far too many deities and cults and shrines for any one man to keep track of them all."

"Well then, son," said Clodia, who until then had stayed aloof from the discussion, "you might as well acknowledge the one true god of the Jews and Christians."

Porphyry winced. "With all due apologies to my hostess, I felt obliged some while ago to write a treatise opposing the Christians. Let me point out just one example of their contradictory thinking. Christians forbid killing, yes? They glorify meekness, and they boast of their refusal to acknowledge any god but their own. And yet, one sees Christians who seem determined to serve in the army, where they must be bold, not meek, must slaughter the enemies of Rome, and must swear allegiance to both the emperor and to the gods of Rome. They preach one thing, but do the opposite."

Clodia shrugged. "I'm no philosopher, as my husband and children will be happy to tell you. But there is a long and fabled tradition of Christians serving in the legions, going back at least to the legendary Twelfth Legion, which was composed entirely of Christians. Under Marcus Aurelius, when the Romans were hemmed in by the enemy and dying of thirst, the Christians of the Twelfth prayed to the One True God, who in return deluged the battlefield with rain, drowning the barbarians even as the joyful Romans quenched their thirst by drinking from their shields— shields which thereafter they decorated with thunderbolts to mark their deliverance by the One True God's thunderstorm. Thus our god's existence was proved to the emperor Marcus Aurelius, who wrote a letter to the Senate praising the Christian soldiers, and proclaiming that from that day forward the Twelfth should be known as the Thundering Legion. And he ordered that upon his column, decorated by the Pinarii, the scene of the legendary Rain Miracle should depict our god above the battlefield, shown as a wise old man with a long beard."

Titus groaned and wearily shook his head. "Wife, wife, wife! Where should I begin? Your version of history is a tissue of half-truths, false assumptions, and outright nonsense. I personally reviewed every scrap of evidence about the Rain Miracle when I was researching *The Millennium*, so I know what I'm talking about!

"First of all, while there may have been a few Christians scattered here and there among the legions back in days of the Divine Marcus—the plague of his day made it necessary to lower standards and take just about anyone willing to serve, even criminals and atheists—there was certainly never an entire legion made up of Christians. The idea is simply absurd. If the legions have since then been infiltrated by Christians, I don't know, but I rather doubt it, given the severe scouring of the ranks done by Decius, who demanded strict observance of proper Roman religion by the troops.

"Second, the Rain Miracle occurred after the Egyptian Harnouphis summoned Mercury, so Mercury was the god who brought the rain. The storm is personified as a long-bearded river god on the Column of Marcus. That is *not* an image of the god of the Jews.

"Third, the shields of the Twelfth Legion were already decorated with thunderbolts—symbol of Jupiter—and had been so for at least a century, going back to the days of Augustus. They did *not* acquire their name from the Rain Miracle. And since words and their precise meaning do matter, I must point out that they are called 'Twelfth Legion Thunderbolt,' *not* 'Thundering Legion,' as you would have it."

Clodia was unperturbed. "I have read the *true* version of history, husband, in the works of the Christian writers Apollinaris and Tertullian."

Porphyry wrinkled his nose. Clearly he did not think much of these authors.

Titus sighed. "For the proliferation of such nonsense, I feel a bit responsible. I could have forestalled it when I wrote *The Millennium,* by including all of the pertinent details of the Rain Miracle. But Philip kept demanding that I cut, cut, cut, and the Rain Miracle disappeared from the book."

"Then he saved you from making an embarrassing mistake, husband. There always was something about Philip I liked. Anyway, the version of events told by Apollinaris and Tertullian is proved by the letter Marcus Aurelius himself wrote to the Senate, praising the Christian soldiers of the Thundering Legion—"

"No, no, no! Not that old nonsense about the letter, yet again! In the archives of the Senate, with my own eyes, wife, I have read the letter in question, and in discussing the battle, Marcus made no mention, none whatsoever, of your fictitious Christian legion, which I must insist be called the Twelfth Legion Thunderbolt. And furthermore—"

"Perhaps, if I could see this letter with my own eyes, I could judge for myself. I *am* capable of reading—"

"The letter is not permitted to be taken from the archive, and no woman is allowed inside, so you know that would be impossible."

As the old couple's argument increased in volume, Porphyry and Zenobia exchanged looks of mock alarm, and could barely contain their laughter. How bemused the two of them must be, thought Gnaeus, his face turning hot, to find themselves surrounded by a family of such intellectual lightweights. He looked at his sister to see her reaction. Pinaria was gazing at Zenobia with almost worshipful admiration.

Irritated by his parents' verbal sparring, Gnaeus reached for his sister's hand, reflexively, to calm himself. Pinaria took her eyes from Zenobia and gave him a warm smile. After the deaths of their spouses and children, each had become the helpmate and comforter of the other. Now Gnaeus had remarried, but what of Pinaria?

Looking sidelong at his parents, who continued to argue, he said to Pinaria in a low voice, "Not the best advertisement for marriage, are they?"

"They love each other madly," she whispered back. "They must!"

"And what about you, sister? Has the time come to think again of marriage? You're still very attractive, and young enough to have children. Do you not want your own household? Keeping you here, I feel I'm robbing you of a woman's greatest pleasure and purpose, to bear children and to be mistress of her own household."

The question seemed almost to embarrass her. "Oh, Gnaeus, don't be silly! I'm perfectly happy here. I have all I need. And if I did leave the House of the Beaks, who would take care of our dear parents?"

"Perhaps your hypothetical husband would agree to take them under his own roof," said Gnaeus.

Their mother overheard these last words, and clucked her tongue. "Trying to get rid of us, are you, son? You should remember the primeval debt that every Roman owes to his mother—going all the way back to Romulus and Remus and that she-wolf who suckled them!"

"Trying to replace me as paterfamilias?" said Titus, matching his wife's pretense of dismay. "Want the House of the Beaks all to yourself, do you? Are the old folks getting in the way of your new marriage?"

"Father, Mother, you know I have no desire to . . ." Gnaeus became tongue-tied, chagrinned at being teased by his parents in front of his new wife and the city's leading intellectual. His befuddlement caused his parents to tease him even more, with Pinaria joining in. Zenobia and Porphyry looked at each other and chuckled.

Gnaeus was not amused. Everyone else was having a fine time, at his expense. The evening had not gone as he hoped.

Later, after Porphyry had departed and the others went to their bedrooms, Gnaeus ascended the stairs to the roof terrace and paced under bright moonlight. The streets of the city were pits of darkness, but from various directions came distant sounds—bursts of laughter, a shouted name, snatches of a drinking song.

In his fantasy, he had thought that Zenobia would be so pleased by his efforts to bring her a kindred soul, Porphyry, to comfort and amuse her, that she would be properly grateful, and amenable to his advances. But when he had moved to embrace her in the hallway leading to their adjoining bedrooms, she had insisted that the evening's full moon was not propitious for the production of offspring. She withdrew to her own chamber and closed the door behind her.

Going over the events of the evening and brooding on his bitter disappointment, Gnaeus became increasingly agitated. It was absurd that he, a Roman husband—a senator!—should be rebuffed under his own roof, by his own wife. It was more than absurd, it was *wrong*—morally, legally, and in every other way wrong.

He found himself back in the hallway, loitering outside Zenobia's door. This, too, was absurd, and wrong, that he should have to skulk, that in his own home there should be any door he could not freely open, any room he could not immediately enter.

He finally raised his hand to rap on the door, then heard a noise from the room beyond. It was a moan of some sort. It had to be Zenobia, but he did not recognize her voice at all. Was she having a nightmare, or was she in physical pain? Had she hurt herself? His pulse began to race. His greatest fear since he married Zenobia was that she might follow the example of her ancestress Cleopatra and kill herself. He had tried to make her happy. He had done everything he could think of. Was she that miserable in her captivity?

He tried the handle, but the door was latched. In a sudden panic, he forced the door open with his shoulder and stumbled into the room.

On Zenobia's bed he saw not one person, but two. They were naked, and their naked bodies were entwined in a most suggestive configuration. At first, Gnaeus thought it must be one of the household slaves with his wife, and he felt a sharp sting of outrage. This was truly the stuff of Roman comedy, that an upright senator should find himself cuckolded by a lowly slave! He would throttle the wretched fellow with his bare hands, and make Zenobia watch.

But . . . the body entwined with that of his wife was not a man, he realized. It was a woman, with sumptuous hips and quite large breasts. And it was not one of the slaves, either.

It was his own sister who abruptly turned her head and stared back at him.

For a long, strange moment, he saw what he saw, and yet did not see it. It was so confounding that his mind could not make sense of it. It was like seeing a person walk upside-down on the ceiling. The eyes beheld, but the eyes were surely at fault, for no such possibility existed.

Zenobia and Pinaria were making love. Passionate, sweaty, moan-inducing love.

Gnaeus stood speechless and frozen on the spot, at a complete loss as to what he should do or say. Or think, for that matter—though the one thing he most certainly felt was jealousy, that his wife should refuse to be intimate with him and then, minutes later, engage in such activity with his own sister!

Pinaria made a stifled, mouse-like squeak and averted her eyes. She snatched up her sleeping gown and fled, brushing past him as she ran out the door.

Zenobia, on the other hand, seemed not at all embarrassed or ashamed, merely annoyed that he had interrupted them. "Husband, did you have to barge in? And just when I was very near to reaching the climax—a pleasure that you, husband, have never been able to provide me, in case you hadn't noticed during all your huffing and puffing on top of me."

Gnaeus wrinkled his brow. "Huffing . . . and . . . puffing?"

"What would you call it?"

"I would call it trying to make a son!"

She snorted. "Why not a daughter, to follow in her mother's footsteps?"

"Into defeat and captivity, do you mean?"

Now he had angered her. Zenobia stepped from the bed, naked but for her jewelry with her dark hair all astray and her black eyes flashing. The sight of her stunned him. It was as if he had never actually seen her before. He felt a sudden, aching heat in his loins. At the same time, he felt almost afraid of her. He staggered back, then turned and left the room.

His heart was pounding. He could not seem to catch a breath.

In the vestibule, the slave on night watch was leaning against the wall, just nodding off. Gnaeus rapped his knuckles against the man's forehead. The brute gave a start, rubbing his eyes.

"Come with me," said Gnaeus as he unlatched the door. He was not such a fool that he would walk the dark streets without a bodyguard. "Stay behind me. Keep your distance. Don't talk to me."

Where the light of the full moon fell, all was bright and bone-white, but where there was shadow all was pitch-dark. Striding quickly through dim streets lit only by occasional lamps or faint lights from houses and taverns, he remembered a line from Juvenal, or rather, remembered roughly what it said: no woman performs cunnilingus on another woman, whereas countless men fellate and take it up the backside with other men.

"Well," he said aloud, "apparently Juvenal didn't know everything!" He glanced over his shoulder. His bodyguard probably thought his master had lost his wits.

His pulse racing, his head on fire, he aimlessly walked the streets—or perhaps not so aimlessly after all, for eventually he found himself approaching the great Temple of Sol Invictus built by Aurelian. Even at this late hour, braziers flickered at either side of the open doors, and the soft glow of lamps shone from within. The bodyguard stayed on the porch as Gnaeus stepped inside the sumptuous space of marble and gold, newly finished and wonderfully pristine, unlike so many of the ancient temples that had become shabby and neglected. The temple was adorned with armaments captured from the generals of the many nations who had served Zenobia, and booty from Palmyra—not only jewels and paintings and sculptures, but fantastic garments from the East encrusted with gems and dyed with a purple previously unknown to Rome.

Among these glittering wonders he found himself standing before a shrine that had been dedicated by Aurelian himself to Apollonius of Tyana, adorned with images and relics of the holy man. Gnaeus purchased a bit of incense from a priest and lit it. He whispered a prayer to Apollonius to give him wisdom and fortitude, and to relieve him of his burning, painful, unrequited passion. But no miracle was immediately forthcoming, and Gnaeus felt like a fool—like a love-smitten lad in some ridiculous Greek novel, pining for a girl he could never have. But Gnaeus was not a callow youth, and Zenobia was not an inaccessible princess. She was his wife!

He left the Temple of Sol Invictus and began walking again. Eventually he found himself approaching a portion of the great wall that had been built by Aurelian—it seemed the hand of the emperor loomed wherever he went. Gnaeus suddenly found his way blocked by a huge pile of debris, the remains of one of the many buildings that had been demolished to make room for the wall.

He tried to remember what building used to stand there, but the wall had so altered the area that he couldn't recall. Much of the pile was shapeless rubble, but there were also bits and pieces of architectural details, some of them quite substantial—beautifully carved marble decorations and column drums and pedestals.

He drew a sharp breath when he saw among the rubble a group of tondi, large round medallions of marble carved with life-size images in high relief. Once these massive sculptures had been brightly painted, to make them stand out on the demolished building they had decorated, but the paint had long ago faded and the images appeared in stark white and black under the full moon. Why were these tondi here, lying in the open? They were surely too precious to destroy, but perhaps too difficult to move until a proper place could be found for them. The things one saw in Rome—artwork that would dazzle even a Persian emperor, lying abandoned amid rubble!

Looking closer, he recognized the nearest tondo, and then recalled the building it had adorned. There were eight tondi, all depicting the emperor Hadrian. One image showed the famous incident, immortalized in verse—Gnaeus knew the poem by heart—when Hadrian and Antinous were hunting, and the emperor used his spear to save his young lover from a stampeding boar. The starkness of the moonlight gave the image a dreamlike quality, so beautiful it took his breath away.

The moment was uncanny. Gnaeus reached out and touched the face of Hadrian, and then the face of Antinous, and felt a warm, tingling sensation that began in his fingertips and then swept through his entire body.

His seemingly aimless steps had led him to the family's two most venerated demons—beings who were mortals once, but were now immortal. Would Antinous be of more help to him than Apollonius? The Divine Youth was no stranger to passion. There had always been people who considered Hadrian's obsession with the boy to be frivolous, not understanding that Antinous had drowned in the Nile so that Hadrian might continue to live. Antinous represented not only youthful perfection but also the power of undying love and loyalty. What would Antinous have thought, had he come upon Zenobia and Pinaria that night? Would he have run from the house in jealousy and confusion? Or would he have felt some innate understanding of what was happening under Gnaeus's roof, indeed, under his very nose?

Gnaeus experienced an odd epiphany—an experience he would never be able to put into words. It was more a feeling than a thought, but it was very powerful, very comforting— exactly the thing he had been seeking on his nocturnal quest.

From the corner of his eye, he saw that his bodyguard was kneeling before another of the tondi. As his master had done, the slave reached out to touch the face of Antinous, and whispered a prayer. Master and slave both felt compelled to worship. The power of the demon Antinous was very strong that night, in that quiet, unforeseen moment in an unexpected, neglected place.

Gnaeus slept that night in his own room. In the morning, as early as he dared, he ventured to knock on Zenobia's door, which stood slightly open, its latch broken. He spoke her name. After a long silence, Zenobia called for him to enter.

She was sitting up in bed, wearing a modest gown and no jewelry. This was quite a contrast to his last sight of her, naked and imperious, but if anything she looked even more formidable, and braced for an argument.

But an argument was not what he had come for. Quite the contrary.

He stood at the foot of her bed. "Do you love my sister?" he asked quietly.

She took a long moment to answer. "Perhaps. I'm not used to being asked such an intimate question, by anyone."

"I understand. But is it your intention to continue . . . carrying on with her in the fashion . . . in which I saw the two of you last night?"

She lifted her chin. "I don't see why not."

He bristled a bit—was she deliberately provoking him?—but took a deep breath and steadied himself. "Very well. As you wish."

Zenobia sensed that a bargain was being proposed, and awaited the catch.

"But in return for my acquiescence—cooperation—turning a blind eye—whatever you wish to call it," said Gnaeus, "you will sleep with me on every night when your cycle makes it likely that you might conceive. I expect at least five such nights a month."

"Consecutive nights?"

"Yes."

She sighed. "Very well."

"Even after you become pregnant, I will expect you to accommodate my desires on a similar schedule—as often, but no more often, than before. Until, of course, your pregnancy precludes such activity."

"You seem very certain that we will conceive a child."

"I *am* certain. Because last night I prayed on the matter, and received wisdom from the Divine Youth. I heard him speak, as clearly as I hear you now. We will have a son, and when he comes of age, he will wear *this*." He pulled off his tunic, baring his chest, and showed her, for the very first time, the fascinum, worn on its necklace. "I put this aside for a long time, but Antinous told me to start wearing it again, because . . . because I will have a son to give it to."

"Step closer," said Zenobia. She reached out to touch the fascinum and studied it. "A phallus with wings?"

"The features are much worn by time."

"Even so . . . I feel its power."

Gnaeus drew a deep breath. Her fingertips, holding the amulet, gently touched his chest. "And also . . ." he said.

"Yes?" She lowered her voice and stiffened her jaw, bracing for some unreasonable demand.

"When we make love, Zenobia, you will show me . . . that is, instruct me . . . in whatever practice or technique it is that induces your greatest pleasure. I mean to say, if my wife is to experience what last night you called 'the climax,' I intend for her to experience it . . . *with me.*"

Zenobia smiled. "Very well, husband. If you insist."

PART V

THE SCEPTER OF MAXENTIUS
(A.D. 312–326)

A.D. 312

It was the twenty-seventh day of the month of October. Like a multitude of birds flocking to a single tree, from all directions came the citizens of Rome to gather in the Flavian Amphitheater—or simply the Amphitheater, as most Romans called it even in formal speech, since hardly anyone in the city, except the most educated, could have named a Flavian emperor or said when the amphitheater was built. It was not *an* amphitheater, but *the* Amphitheater, and it had been there forever, the living, throbbing heart of the empire—or so it seemed to the people of Rome.

These were the days of not one but of four emperors, ever since Diocletian had divided the imperial power between himself and three others. The Roman Empire had become too big and unwieldy, some of its institutions too decrepit, and the menace on every border too great, for any single man, or even two men, to rule the whole of it.

This day was a celebration of one of those four emperors, Maxentius, the only one who actually resided in Rome. This was the eve of the anniversary of his reign. He had been emperor in Rome, ruling over Italy and Africa, for six years.

But the mood of the city was not entirely celebratory. There was something manic about the gaiety, an air of festivity and giddiness but also of unease and even panic—because there happened to be an invading army, just to the north of Rome, poised to lay siege to the city, the most formidable force to do so since Julius Caesar crossed the Rubicon and sent Pompey running.

Before going to the Amphitheater, Marcus Pinarius Zenobius, who had grown up in the House of the Beaks and had lived in Rome for all of his thirty-seven years on earth, put on his senatorial toga and prepared to take his fifteen-year-old son, Kaeso, on a tour of the city. At this critical moment, with the future of the Pinarii and that of Rome itself hanging in the balance, he wanted to remind his son of all the buildings and monuments the Pinarii had helped to construct and to decorate over many generations. After a low point in their fortunes, his own father, Gnaeus, had reestablished the family business by building the walls of Aurelian—fortifications that might be about to receive their first substantial test.

Zenobius could not show his son the whole length of that enormous wall, of course, but he could show him the Colossus originally built by Nero, the huge quadriga atop Hadrian's Mausoleum, the towering columns erected in honor of Trajan and of Marcus Aurelius, and many more landmarks, which displayed the artistry of the Pinarii and their engineering skills. In recent years, Zenobius himself had contributed substantially to the family legacy, with his many projects for the emperor Maxentius. It seemed to Zenobius that this was the precise moment to reflect upon and to celebrate all these accomplishments, for in the days to come—perhaps as soon as tomorrow—anything could happen, even the unthinkable: the complete destruction of Rome, especially if the attackers resorted to fire in their determination to conquer and subdue the city.

In the vestibule of the House of the Beaks, his father checked that Zenobius's toga was properly draped and then gave young Kaeso a kiss on the forehead. Kaeso was not quite a man yet, and still wore a boy's simple, long-sleeve tunic.

"Will you not come with us, Father?" asked Zenobius.

"No, I think not." At eighty, Gnaeus Pinarius still had his wits, but his voice quavered. His back was stooped and his legs frail. "To go any distance from this house I would have to take a litter, and on a day like this, with so many people out, I don't care to deal with large crowds, nor to be seen by the common folk resorting to the luxury of a litter. Call me old-fashioned, but I still think that such vehicles are for the effete and the lazy—and for women, of course. Your late mother always used a litter, with the curtains shut, on those rare occasions when she left this house." He sighed. Zenobia—melancholy, philosophical, imperious, beautiful Zenobia—was now many years dead, making Gnaeus twice a widower. Gone, too, was his sister, Pinaria. So close to each other in life, the two women had died within a month of each other.

"Besides, I'm retired. The family legacy is yours now, Zenobius, to show off to your own boy." Gnaeus had always addressed his son not by his first name but by his last, the cognomen that proclaimed his distinguished pedigree. Saying it aloud reminded Gnaeus of Zenobia, and did her honor.

"You *are* wearing the fascinum?" he asked.

"Of course." Zenobius touched the place where it lay hidden on its chain, beneath his toga.

"Good. The occasion demands it, eh? Maxentius's anniversary—six years of sound rule, with plenty of imperial commissions for the Pinarii." He reached out and touched his fingers to his son's chest, above the place where the talisman lay hidden. "Keep it close about you, son. Especially . . . in days to come." He did not have to elaborate. The threat posed by the invader hung over them all.

The family's prosperity and influence were at the highest they had been in many decades. For the last six years, Zenobius and his artisans and engineers had been kept very busy by the new emperor. Like Zenobius, Maxentius was in his thirties, and he had directed his considerable energy toward the most ambitious building program in Rome since the era of Septimius Severus and the Emesene women, which now seemed a far-off golden age. Once again, the Pinarii had been in the right place at the right time, under the right emperor, to see a grand flourishing of their fortunes.

This followed upon a period of hardship and uncertainty endured by the generation that came of age with Zenobius in Rome. Aurelian had reunited the empire, but ruled only five years before being murdered. Once again, a military coup had determined Rome's future. After a series of short-lived rulers, the emperor who emerged victorious was Diocletian, a military man from Dalmatian peasant stock. His origins were as far from those of Rome's senatorial ruling class as could be imagined, but he possessed a keen intellect and a powerful personality. Like the unfortunate emperors before him, Diocletian might have been overwhelmed by the job of administering the state and fighting wars on multiple borders. His innovation, which seemed an act of genius at the time, was to split the empire into four parts, to be ruled by two senior partners (each with the title Augustus) and their junior partners (each with the title Caesar). The co-rulers he had chosen were not Roman in the strict sense. They did not even come from Italy, but from a clique of military men south of the Danube frontier. One of them, Galerius, pointedly and proudly called himself a Dacian rather than a Roman—and even called his quadrant the Dacian Empire. Nonetheless, this system of Tetrarchy, as it was called, was productive and stable.

Diocletian was in power for over twenty years. His reign (with his fellow Augustus, Maximian) had seen plenty of building projects in Rome, some involving the Pinarii, but except for a triumphal arch and a new baths complex, these were mostly repairs and reconstructions, including the Senate House (which had been destroyed by fire) and a large section of stands and boxes in the Circus Maximus, after a huge collapse that killed thirteen thousand spectators, the most lethal disaster in the city's history.

Diocletian himself had no interest in ruling from Rome, and little interest even in visiting. The idea of a single capital city seemed outmoded. There were four capitals now, and these were located wherever each of the four emperors needed to be at a given moment, a circumstance usually determined by threats at the frontiers. The imperial courts followed the rulers. Lip service was duly paid to the religious and state institutions of Rome, but months and even years had passed without any of the emperors setting foot in the city.

Diocletian did visit Rome to celebrate his Vicennalia, marking twenty years in power. The occasion was a grand show of unity with his fellow Augustus, the short, blustering Maximian. That was the only time young Kaeso Pinarius ever had a chance to see the great Diocletian. The boy had been seven at the time, and all he could remember clearly were the thirteen elephants that appeared in the grand procession.

A couple of years later, Diocletian innovated again, doing something no emperor had done before: he resigned his office, and retired to the land of his childhood, Dalmatia. Begrudgingly, Maximian also retired, to a villa in Campania. Their two Caesars moved up in rank to became Augusti, and two new Caesars were appointed.

Diocletian had hoped that his Tetrarchy would provide a second generation of harmony, but without his firm leadership, the arrangement quickly descended into bickering, backstabbing, and civil war. As Zenobius had explained the situation to Kaeso, the empire was like an unseaworthy boat on a stormy sea, with not one but four captains, each plotting to throw the others overboard.

To put an end to the conflicts, many senators begged Diocletian to come out of retirement. He issued a curt refusal, saying he preferred—"as would any sane man!"—to grow cabbages at his gigantic new palace on the Dalmatian coast across from Italy.

Now the great man was dead, and so was his partner, Maximian, who attempted a return to power but failed miserably, and was driven to suicide—by the very man who was now poised to attack Rome.

Amid the turmoil there had been one very positive development. Rome now had an emperor who not only resided in the city, but seemed intent on making it once again the true capital of the empire, or at least his portion of it: Maxentius, the son of Diocletian's now-dead partner, Maximian.

Early in Maxentius's reign there was an incident that might have ended it. A fire broke out in the Temple of Venus and Roma. When a frustrated soldier fighting the flames let slip some blasphemous slur against Venus, a mob of outraged citizens tore him to pieces. Leaving the fire unchecked, the soldiers turned on the mob. A wholesale riot ensued. More soldiers were killed, and a great many citizens. It was a test of Maxentius's authority to put an end to the violence, which he did, first gaining control of the soldiers, ordering them to retreat, and then dispersing the mob. Meanwhile, the fire burned itself out, sparing most of the temple. Maxentius proclaimed this to be a merciful omen from Venus. Afterward, the Temple of Venus and Roma was splendidly refurbished, making it once again what Hadrian had intended, one of the most lavish temples in Rome—a project that brought much work to the Pinarii.

Maxentius emerged from the crisis as a pacifier and unifier of the many quarrelsome factions in the city. "We are one people, one Rome," as he put it. Diocletian had renewed long-dormant laws against Christians, which barred them from government service, deprived them of legal rights, and punished them with imprisonment and execution if they refused to comply with religious rites. Maxentius magnanimously put an end to all such persecution in Rome and throughout the provinces he ruled. "Such edicts only serve to divide us," he said. To be sure, there were far fewer Christians in Rome and the western provinces than in the East, where the cult had originated, and where most of the friction between Christians and their neighbors occurred. In Rome, the small sect was so riven by squabbles over arcane doctrines that for a while they did not even have a bishop, as they called their leaders. Christians were simply not a big problem in Rome. Maxentius saw no reason to draw attention to them by creating more martyrs.

Maxentius also gained popularity by putting an end to a scheme by Diocletian's successor, Galerius, to directly tax the citizens of Rome. The idea was unprecedented. Romans taxed others; they themselves were never taxed. Yet tax-gatherers from distant parts of the empire had been sent by Galerius to Rome, to compile lists of citizens, take inventories, and assess property values in advance of taxation—as if Rome were a conquered province! The indignity of it had outraged every Roman. Maxentius canceled the scheme. He alone of the multiple emperors seemed to understand the primacy of the capital city and the special status of those who lived there.

Somewhat controversially, Maxentius had decided not to live on the Palatine. ("Too old and musty," he said. "One can hardly breathe for the mold!") While the decrepit Palatine complex was being extensively refurbished, Maxentius built a new palace for himself on the Appian Way, calling upon the Pinarii to oversee the overall design and decoration. This included a private stadium and racetrack, where the emperor and his young sons could enjoy riding horseback and racing chariots.

Maxentius commissioned a great many new sculptures to decorate every part of the city. Many of these were statues of himself, but the most striking new sculpture was a bronze statue of the she-wolf that suckled Romulus and Remus, her udders hanging heavy with milk. Zenobius himself had designed it, and, despite its modest size, it was one of his proudest accomplishments. The she-wolf was dedicated, on the birthday of Rome, "to unconquered Mars and to the founders of our eternal city, by Our Lord Imperator Maxentius Pius Felix, Unconquered Augustus." The words "eternal" and "unconquered" were not casually chosen; nor was the dedication to Mars. As the ferocious she-wolf had protected the

Twins from all danger, so Mars—through the instrument of his pious servant, the emperor Maxentius—would defend the city, now and forever.

Then tragedy struck: the death of the older of the emperor's two sons, who was then only fourteen, about the same age as Kaeso. The whole city was plunged into mourning. The Senate, at Maxentius's behest, deified the boy. Valerius Romulus was his name. Next to the new palace, Maxentius erected a temple to Romulus the Founder to house a mausoleum for his son. It was Zenobius who suggested it be round, to recall the ancient temples of Hercules and of Vesta. The lavishly decorated interior made it seem a small version of the Pantheon.

The Colossus, overdue for a major refurbishment, was reconsecrated as a statue of the Deified Romulus—meaning the late son of Maxentius, not the founder. The Pinarii had overseen every previous makeover of the Colossus, from Nero to Severus. All the relevant plans and records had been lost in the fire that destroyed their house and workshop on the Esquiline, but Maxentius, ever the traditionalist, never considered anyone but the Pinarii for such an important and prestigious project.

Directly to the west of the restored Temple of Venus and Roma, overlooking and dominating the ancient Forum, was the grandest of all Maxentius's projects, the New Basilica, a building where elaborate court ceremonials could be staged in a vast hall with a raised apse at the far end from the entrance. It was the biggest building by far in the Forum. When fully finished and decorated inside, it would be as lavish as any temple or palace that had ever existed on earth. Zenobius had been allowed to bring all his creativity to bear on the project.

Zenobius's tour of the city with his son at last brought them to the center of the city, the ancient Forum, which Maxentius had made once more the center of the world. They strolled through the unfinished New Basilica, then ventured inside both halves of the gleaming Temple of Venus and Roma, and then arrived at the Amphitheater, where the teeming multitude was dwarfed by the towering Colossus of the Deified Romulus.

"Rather tall for a fourteen-year-old," quipped Kaeso. "And so muscular! I remember wrestling with the real Valerius Romulus at the gymnasium. A rather skinny boy, as I recall."

Zenobius smiled. The boy had his grandfather's dry sense of humor. Altering the statue's face, so high in the air, had presented a huge challenge. Changing the physique had never been an option, so the face of a teenager now looked out from the magnificently proportioned body that had previously been that of Sol Invictus.

Zenobius and Kaeso made their way through the privileged gate reserved for senators and their families. They took their seats, close to those of the Vestal virgins. As Zenobius looked around the vast circle of the Amphitheater, he noted the great number of soldiers in the crowd. In response to the threat now approaching Rome, Maxentius had assembled a large army. There were his own soldiers and those he had taken over from his late father; there were troops who had defected to him from two fellow emperors, Severus and Galerius, who had each disputed his right to rule, tried to invade Italy, and miserably failed; there were even legions brought from across the sea, from grain-rich Africa and Mauritania.

Many of those troops were now camped north of the city, on both sides of the Tiber, preparing to do battle with the approaching enemy. More troops were garrisoned all over the city. Despite inevitable friction between soldiers and civilians, the crowd was united in giving Maxentius a thunderous ovation when he appeared in the imperial box along with his wife and young son.

The opening ceremony began with a pious invocation to the gods, with special attention to the Deified Romulus, founder of the city. A huge replica of Zenobius's she-wolf statue was wheeled into the arena, made of terra-cotta and painted to look like bronze. The Pinarii's workshop had created this elaborate prop, and Zenobius was gratified to see its effect on the crowd, which set to howling. The sound echoed all around the circular space, rising to such a din that even the invaders north of the city must have heard the baleful wolf-calls.

"May the sound fill them with dread!" Zenobius whispered.

His thoughts wandered, from the she-wolf to her whelps, the original Romulus and his twin, Remus—the brother murdered by Romulus when the city was founded. The man set to attack Rome was a sort of brother to Maxentius, his brother-in-law, married to Maxentius's sister. Marriage alliances were meant to bring peace. This one had failed. The conflict could be seen as a sort of sibling rivalry, like that between Romulus and Remus, which would end only when one was dead. Zenobius touched the fascinum under his toga and whispered a prayer that Maxentius, rightful and beloved ruler of Rome, would be victorious.

As the howling continued, Maxentius rose from his throne. He stepped to the front of the imperial box. He raised his hands in the air and waved them flamboyantly, like the conductor of a chorus, encouraging the howls and seeming to bask in the noise. Then he threw back his head, cupped his hands around his mouth, and howled.

Zenobius was acquainted with the program for the day's events, and knew that the howling was not planned, but completely spontaneous. Maxentius had seized the moment, and by joining in had done exactly the thing that would delight his audience most. People elbowed each other and laughed with joy, releasing their tension and forgetting their fears. Gradually the howling died down, turned into cheers, and then dropped to a murmur as the emperor raised his hands for silence.

He held forth his right arm. His young son stepped forward and placed in his father's hand a scepter, a staff that culminated in a metal flower, its petals holding a blue-green glass globe, a symbol of the earth, that glittered in the sunlight.

Maxentius spoke of that which was uppermost on the mind of everyone present: the usurper who had swept down from

Gaul, just like the Gauls of old who attacked Rome, and with the same intention—to sack the city, to enslave its people, to destroy the temples and the shrines of the ancestors, to put an end to the long and glorious status of Rome as capital of empire and center of the world. The invader was a canny military commander, to be sure, which made him a very serious threat—indeed, the greatest threat to Rome in all her long and fabled existence.

The enemy of Rome was also the emperor's personal enemy. "First he took my sister as his wife," said Maxentius, "thinking to insinuate himself into a family far more ancient and accomplished than his own—for is he not the son of a common whore? The marriage is illegal and bigamous, because he was already married to a peasant woman."

Zenobius smiled wryly at this assertion, for in fact Maxentius and his family were hardly "Roman" in the strictest sense, not the way the Pinarii were Roman, with roots going back centuries. Maxentius's father came from Pannonian stock, and his mother was Syrian. But what did it mean, anyway, to call one family more ancient than another? Were not all families equally ancient? Zenobius himself came from mixed stock, though his mother had been no ordinary barbarian but a queen, of course, descended from Cleopatra. It amused him that Maxentius was always seeking to portray himself as more Roman than the most native Roman.

Maxentius continued his invective against the invader. "After taking my sister unlawfully in marriage, this half barbarian as good as murdered my father, who ruled so wisely for so many years alongside the Deified Diocletian. He ceaselessly threatened and hounded the old man— supposedly his own father-in-law—until he drove him to suicide. Now this man looks to depose *me*—but *not* to take my place. He has no desire to become ruler of Rome, your champion and defender, because he has no love for this city. He despises Rome! The man is more a Gaul or a Briton than a Roman, and as savage and bloodthirsty as any barbarian.

After he slaughtered the Franks and the Alemanni and captured their kings, he held games and exposed his captives to wild beasts, smiling as he saw them torn to shreds, laughing when they screamed, smacking his lips as the wretches were eaten alive! What will such a man do to the people of Rome? If he should take the city, he will tear down your temples, enslave your children, make a mockery of all that sets Rome apart as the greatest and noblest of all the cities on earth. He is your enemy and mine. He calls himself . . . Constantine."

At the utterance of this despicable name, many in the crowd jeered and booed. Others cried out their love for Maxentius, especially women. The handsome young emperor's grandiose mourning for his dead son Romulus had won him the sympathy of every mother in Rome.

Zenobius observed the emperor closely. Never had he seen such an exalted look on any man's face. Maxentius was transfigured. The adoration of the crowd seemed to vindicate all he had done over the last six years, lavishing attention on Rome in a way the city had not enjoyed in a very long time. Now Maxentius had assumed the role of savior of the city. He had tied his fate irrevocably to the fate of Rome. In return, he was asking the people to tie their fate to his. No stage for such an event could be more appropriate than the Amphitheater, where all of Rome could gather in one place and gaze upon itself. In that moment, city and people and emperor were one.

When Maxentius raised his hands and began to speak again, an unearthly silence fell on the crowd. Every face was turned in his direction. Every eye was upon him. "People of Rome, we have a choice to make. Constantine will lay siege to the city, perhaps as soon as tomorrow. Rome can withstand such a siege, I have no doubt. Since I became your emperor, we have strengthened the city gates and made the walls of Aurelian even stronger and taller. In recent days, our loyal soldiers have been fitting catapults and ballistae on the walls and stockpiling projectiles to hurl destruction on the enemy from a distance. Rome will not be taken!

"But is that the proper course? Should we stay here within our walls, and await whatever is to come? Or . . . should we go on the offensive? Should I, as your emperor, your champion, march out of the city at the head of our legions, meet the threat head-on, and put an end to it?"

Looking at Maxentius's face, Zenobius realized that the emperor genuinely had not yet decided which course to take. Other emperors might have sought guidance from generals or philosophers, from omens or oracles, but Maxentius was looking to the city itself—to the genius of the city as incarnated in its people—to make up his mind.

"Which should it be?" cried Maxentius. "Siege, or battle? Battle or siege? Raise your voices! Shout your answer!"

At first, only scattered voices answered, some saying one thing, some the other. Then more and more people began to shout. Like the howling that had preceded it, this noise rose in volume until it was almost deafening. Both words were being shouted over and over, until each resolved into a steady chant.

Battle, battle, battle!

Siege, siege, siege!

Only very slowly, very gradually, did one word win over the other, and as it gained ascendance, those on the opposite side were won over. An unseen force seemed to steer the people toward a choice that was unanimous, inevitable, irrevocable. One word was settled upon, and every voice in the Amphitheater began to chant it in unison, with a slight pause before each utterance, so that the word rang out as clearly and distinctly as if shouted by a single, thundering voice.

"Battle!—Battle!—Battle!—Battle!"

If Constantine and his army had heard the howls before, they were surely hearing this battle cry, which was even louder and more sustained. The city of Rome would not passively wait for the would-be conqueror to make his move. The city was ready and eager to take the battle to the enemy. The decision was the right one, Zenobius had no doubt. Rome was always the conqueror, never the conquered. So the gods had ordained. Read a thousand years of history, roll the dice a thousand times—the outcome was always the same. Constantine was mad to think he could cast the dice and get a different result.

On the emperor's face, Zenobius saw a look of calm resolution. The decision had been made. Maxentius was at peace. He raised his hands. The chanting ceased.

"It is what *you* want," he said. "It is what the *gods* want. It is what *I* want. Rome will not cower behind her walls. Tomorrow, Rome goes to war!"

The emperor's anniversary games were as splendid as anyone could have wished. The blood of many gladiators was spilled, each death a sacred offering to the gods. But after the spontaneous howling and the emperor's rousing speech, all that followed was anticlimactic.

As soon as the games were concluded, the Roman Senate convened in emergency session. In his role as Pontifex Maximus, the emperor brought forth the Sibylline Books. The priests consulted calendars and indices. An oracle was found to show that on the very next day, "The wretched enemy of Rome shall die a wretched death."

The emperor burned incense and prayed before the Altar of Victory. After him, Zenobius and all the other senators solemnly did the same. They followed him to the unfinished New Basilica, with its great room many times larger than the Senate chamber. Maxentius ceremonially took off his purple and gold toga and put on the gilded armor and purple cape in which he would do battle the next day. Young and handsome, smiling serenely, he inspired confidence in every man present.

Zenobius had no doubt. Maxentius would prevail.

* * *

"I don't believe it. I can't believe it."

"But Father, it's true! Everyone says so! The battle is over. The enemy has won. Maxentius . . . is dead."

As the news spread, the sound of wailing echoed through the city. Many people were already in temples, having arrived that morning to pray continuously for the emperor's victory in battle. Now their prayers turned to lamentation.

Like a hot wind, a thrill of panic swept through the city. Where would any man or woman be safe? More people streamed into the temples, desperate to find sanctuary.

But amid the wails and shrieks, there were scattered noises of celebration from those who had secretly hoped for Constantine's success. Who even knew that such people existed? They had been silent the previous day, in the Amphitheater. Now they shouted from windows and rooftops, and some even dared to dance in the streets. Outraged Romans loyal to Maxentius jeered at the celebrants, but no one dared to attack them. If the unthinkable was true, and the emperor was dead, then these people were the winners. Very soon they would have the upper hand in the city.

Zenobius had been in the House of the Beaks with his aged father, waiting for news, when Kaeso arrived, out of breath from running.

"The battle took place on the far side of the Tiber—across from the Milvian Bridge," he gasped.

His grandfather spoke up, stirred by a vivid memory of long ago. "Why, that was the very place where the barbarians made camp and threatened to invade when I was a young man, and we used the threat of plague to scare them off!"

But this time the enemy did not retreat, and neither stratagem nor force of arms had been able to save the city.

In the middle of the night, to prevent Constantine from easily crossing the Tiber, Maxentius had preemptively destroyed the center of the Milvian Bridge. Watching as his engineers located the weakest points of the stone bridge and went to work with staves and rams, Maxentius was overheard to say: "'Horatius dared to bring down the bridge!'" How like him that was, to quote Virgil and evoke the memory of one of Rome's earliest heroes.

So that his own troops could cross to the far side, pontoon bridges were put in place. These were easily and quickly assembled by the engineers, and steady enough, as long as men crossed in regular order. Many thousands of Maxentius's troops were already stationed north of the river, forming a bulwark against the invader. When Maxentius rode out of the Flaminian Gate the next morning and crossed the pontoon bridges at the head of his cavalry, both sides assumed battle formations and the combat commenced.

For Maxentius, the day was an unmitigated disaster. Constantine's men were battle-hardened after years of fighting in Gaul. Their morale was high from their string of victories on the long march to Rome. Maxentius's men, gathered from many provinces, were greater in number, but strangers to each other. They were no match for the enemy. They broke ranks and fled. Many died under a hail of arrows that struck them in the back. The bravest, who fled last, tripped over the bodies of those who fled first.

On horseback with his sword drawn, Maxentius repeatedly tried to rally his men, but the advance of Constantine's soldiers pushed him back to the Tiber. As his horse cantered onto one of the pontoon bridges, a rush of men and horses came stampeding behind him.

The pontoon bridge broke into pieces and instantly collapsed under the weight of so many horses and men. Wearing heavy armor, Maxentius sank beneath the churning water and vanished.

Witnesses from both sides spread the news. The remnants of Maxentius's troops were utterly demoralized. Many were slaughtered. Many fled. Some were allowed to surrender. The battle was over. Constantine's victory was complete.

Like so many when they heard the news, Zenobius was in a state of shock. He had allowed himself to believe, along with the emperor, that the gods were entirely on the side of Maxentius—on the side of Rome! How could it be otherwise? And yet . . . Constantine's reputation as a general was formidable. Some said he had never lost a battle. Maxentius, on the other hand, had never really proved himself in the field. His successes in Africa had been won by surrogates. When Severus and Galerius each invaded Italy and were turned back, it had been the sheer number of Maxentius's troops, the disloyalty of their own men, and their intimidation at seeing the walls of Rome that sent them into retreat. It had seemed at the time that these bloodless victories had been god-sent. In retrospect, it might have been better if Maxentius and his troops had been tested in battle before taking on the likes of Constantine.

"Did I let religion blind me?" muttered Zenobius. "Did Maxentius do the same? Did we fool ourselves into thinking he was invincible because the gods wanted it so, when the superiority of Constantine as a general should have been obvious all along? Or . . . is *this* the will of the gods? Did the gods turn against Maxentius? Do they now love Constantine? But how can that be? I still can't believe it. I won't—not until we know . . . for certain . . . that Maxentius is dead."

"But, Father," said Kaeso, "there can be no doubt—"

Gnaeus spoke up, his voice quavering. "Did you see him drown, my boy, with your own eyes? Did anyone?"

"They say the river was so filled with corpses, a man could walk from one bank to the other."

"Amid so much carnage," said Zenobius, "how could the body of one man be found? As long as there is no absolute *proof*—"

They heard a sudden noise from the direction of the Forum—a tumult of screaming, wailing, and cheering. Loudest of all was the blaring of the horns traditionally used to clear the streets for a procession.

Gnaeus looked alarmed. The old man blinked his rheumy eyes and shivered.

"Father, stay here," said Zenobius, heading toward the door.

"I'm coming with you!" said Kaeso.

"If you must."

The mass of people heading toward the Forum displayed every possible emotion, from dismay and horror to giddy delight. Zenobius spotted a number of senators wearing their togas, as he was, and moved to join them. Then he saw that they seemed to be celebrating and congratulating one another— men who only the day before had prayed with Maxentius at the Altar of Victory. Zenobius angrily forced his way toward one of the senators, the latest of his line to bear the name Titus Messius Extricatus. There had been hostility between the two families since the days of Zenobius's grandfather.

"What does this mean, Senator Extricatus? What are you smiling about?"

"Why, it's Senator Pinarius *Zenobius*!" Extricatus twisted the cognomen on his tongue, as if there were something unsavory or scandalous about it. "Ignorant of the facts, as usual. There has long been a faction in the Roman Senate sympathetic to Constantine—secret partisans, if you will, covertly working on his behalf."

"Spying, you mean?"

"If you like. There is no sin in being a spy for the emperor chosen by the gods."

"You impious wretch! Only yesterday you stood by while Maxentius consulted the Sibylline Books. I saw you nod and cry, 'Thank Jupiter!' when he read the text."

"Of course I did. What did the text say? What were the *exact* words?"

"It said, 'The wretched enemy of Rome . . . shall die . . . a wretched death.'" Saying the words aloud, Zenobius felt a chill.

"And that is *precisely* what happened! Maxentius was the enemy of Rome, you idiot, not Constantine! And now he's dead, just as the oracle foretold—a truly wretched death, with river moss up his nose and minnows in his lungs."

"You don't know that! Maxentius may still be alive, and if he is—"

"Open your eyes, you fool!" Extricatus pointed to a cordon of soldiers who were clearing the way for a procession. Horns blared. Zenobius was filled with dread.

Atop a long spear, held aloft so that all could see, was a disembodied head. Gore oozed and spilled from the severed neck. The jaw was broken, and the sharp end of the spear projected from the gaping mouth. The wide-open eyes stared upward as if in shock, reproaching the heavens. Despite its twisted features, the head was undeniably that of Maxentius. The defender of the eternal city, the champion of Mars, the Unconquered Augustus had reentered Rome with his head on a spike.

Zenobius staggered and would have fallen had Kaeso not been there to steady him.

"Fool! Idiot!" Extricatus wrinkled his nose. "But what can one expect from the son of a Palmyrene whore?"

Above a roaring in his ears, Zenobius heard the insult, but was too stunned to react. Extricatus and the other senators turned away, laughing and cheering as they followed the emperor's head up the Sacred Way.

"Are you Senator Pinarius?" The gruff whisper came from a hooded figure who suddenly stood before him. The man's face was in shadow.

Zenobius nodded. "What do you want?"

The man stepped closer. Two more hooded men stood behind him. He carried something. He raised both arms.

Zenobius flinched and braced for a blow. Had it come to this, that a senator loyal to Maxentius was to be assassinated here in the Forum, in broad daylight, in front of his son?

But the thing the man held forth was not a weapon. It was a long bundle of some sort, wrapped in coarse wool and tied with thin rope. "I bring this to you from the emperor himself," the man said, speaking barely above a whisper. "He told me that I was to give this to you, Senator Pinarius—to you and *only* you."

"What is it?"

"Take it. Unwrap it in private, and see for yourself. The emperor said you would know what to do with it, that you would make sure it doesn't fall . . . into the hands . . . of the usurper." The words ended in a sob. A spot of sunlight piercing the shadow of his hood shone on gaunt cheeks wet with tears.

Zenobius took the bundle. He opened the woolen wrapping a bit. He caught a glimpse of silk and the glint of colored glass. He was puzzled for a moment, then knew what the man had given him. He knew at once what he must do. He took a deep breath, steadied himself, and stood upright, no longer needing Kaeso to steady him.

"There is more," said the man. The two hooded figures stepped from behind him. They also carried bundles.

"The three of you, follow me," said Zenobius. His dizziness was gone. His voice was calm. His gait was steady as he led the way.

He had been given a final mission by his emperor.

Zenobius led Kaeso and the hooded men toward the Temple of Venus and Roma. The crowd was thick at first, but people reflexively made way at the sight of a senator's toga. The crowd thinned as they left the crush along the Sacred Way. They ascended the steps of the temple and entered the sanctuary.

There were people inside the temple, but they were too busy weeping and praying to notice as Zenobius stepped into a shadowy alcove off the vestibule.

"Leave your burdens here, with me," he said to the hooded men.

They looked to their leader, who seemed to hesitate.

"Leave them here, I said. By my authority. By the authority given to me by the emperor."

The leader nodded. They put down the bundles and slipped away.

By a mechanism known only to Maxentius and a handful of others, Zenobius opened a hidden door. He and Kaeso descended into an underground chamber, carrying the bundles.

The secret room had been commissioned by Maxentius when the temple was rebuilt after the fire early in his reign. In the event of extreme catastrophe or utmost crisis, this was to be a safe hiding place for items of great value, which could then be retrieved later.

The opened door from above provided the only light. By its faint illumination, Zenobius and Kaeso undid the bundles and took inventory of the treasures. Wrapped in pennants of linen and silk were three lances and four javelins, and a base in which these battle standards could be set upright. Along with these insignia were three large spheres made of glass and chalcedony. Most precious of all was the imperial scepter. The staff culminated in a metal flower, its petals holding a blue-green globe. Zenobius remembered how brightly that globe had glinted in the sunlight when the emperor held it aloft the previous day at the Amphitheater. Maxentius had carried it again in the Senate House, and then in the New Basilica when he put on his armor, full of hope and certain of victory.

Zenobius's final act of loyalty to the emperor was to see that these treasures were safely hidden. Would the son of Maxentius retrieve them some day, and wield his father's scepter? It seemed very unlikely. Young sons of fallen emperors did not live long.

They did not linger, but hurried back up into the light. Zenobius closed the hidden door behind him. "And that," he said quietly to Kaeso, "is all that is left of the Unconquered Augustus and his dazzling court."

The summons from Constantine came a few days later.

Putting on his toga, Zenobius felt a tremor of fear, but also curiosity. He had refused to attend Constantine's triumphal entry into the city, quite a vulgar affair from all he had heard, so this would be his first look at the man.

The new emperor was holding court at the New Basilica.

The vast space teemed with aides and courtiers all looking quite busy and very important. The murmur of voices and the patter of footsteps echoed off the marble walls. Zenobius felt calm at stepping inside the familiar surroundings, a place where he had spent many hours as a planner and builder, conferring with Maxentius. He was determined to maintain that composure.

Constantine sat on a throne on a high dais in the apse opposite the main entrance, from which he could see and be seen by everyone in the room. Zenobius had expected to see Constantine in armor, but the emperor had put on a purple and gold toga. Perhaps it was the same toga worn by Maxentius, for it fit him rather tightly. Constantine was considerably broader than his predecessor, not just across the shoulders but across the middle as well. On his head the emperor wore a fillet of golden laurel leaves.

As Zenobius took the long walk across the chamber, he got a closer look at the man. Maxentius had had a dimple in his chin, but Constantine's broad, clean-shaven jaw had a deep cleft, and his nose was very large. So were his eyes, which seemed to flash as he turned his gaze to look down on Zenobius.

Zenobius was formally announced. Then Constantine spoke. "Senator Pinarius, I am looking to recover an item of the imperial court that seems to have gone missing: the scepter."

Zenobius tried to swallow, but could not. He loudly cleared his throat. "A scepter, Dominus?" he managed to say.

"Not *a* scepter, *the* scepter. The scepter my late brother-in-law wielded. Surely you know what I'm talking about, Senator."

"I do, Dominus. Yes. The scepter, yes . . . I do . . ."

"I've asked everyone else, so I might as well ask you. No one seems to know what's become of it. My agents managed to trace it to—and I quote—'a fellow who was seen lurking about the Forum, carrying a long bundle and wearing a hood.' The fellow has since been apprehended and is even now being questioned under torture. Of course, no one need be tortured, if someone could produce this scepter for me." He smiled.

Constantine had a pleasant voice, measured and calm and deep, like the steady purring of a cat.

Zenobius finally managed to swallow. The lump felt hard in his chest. "Is it so important that this item be found? Surely it's of little value, compared to many other imperial treasures."

"The metal and glass are mere trinkets, true. But certain objects are sometimes invested with a special kind of power."

"True. A loyal citizen bows to the imperial scepter—"

"I mean something more than that. A power invisible, but not intangible."

"If Dominus is speaking of . . . magic . . . I can assure you that Maxentius never resorted—"

"Magic? Yes, perhaps magic—in which case the scepter is best destroyed. I'll have no sorcery around me. Or perhaps the scepter possesses a power that is the *opposite* of magic—a power not corrupt, as is all magic, but truly divine."

Nervously, Zenobius touched the fascinum hidden under his toga.

"I thought perhaps *you,* Senator, as one of his chief architects, would know of any secret chamber . . . or hidden treasure room . . . ?" Constantine raised his large eyebrows.

Zenobius managed to keep his face a blank. He shook his head.

"Well, perhaps this missing scepter is of no importance. Perhaps it's just a stick, and nothing more. It certainly did Maxentius little good. Never mind. I called you here on more important business."

Zenobius thought about the man who had given him the scepter, who even now was being tortured. Would the man die before speaking? Would he betray Zenobius?

But Constantine was talking. He tried to listen. "First, you will make out for me a list of all statues, monuments, and buildings that Maxentius constructed or refurbished."

"There are official lists—"

"Yes, but it will take time for my secretaries to locate and scroll through all those lists, and they may overlook something.

You will make a list for me yourself, and it will be *complete*. Understood?"

"Yes, Dominus."

"Some things will have to be pulled down, of course— his statues, for a start. All of them. We mustn't miss any. And something must be done *immediately* to correct the outrage he committed against the Colossus. Replacing the face of Sol! What was Maxentius thinking, to mock the sun god? If that was his idea of piety, no wonder I routed him so easily. Piety is very important. Do you understand?"

"I do, Dominus."

"Do you, really?" Constantine pressed his fingertips together. "A few years ago, I was in the south of Gaul—this was right after my victory over Maxentius's father, when the old man rounded up some troops and made his ill-advised bid to regain power. I came upon a small temple of Apollo by the roadside, and I felt compelled to stop and have a look inside. My men stayed back. I entered alone. The place was very dimly lit, but in the shadows I saw a rather lovely statue of Apollo. Our heads were at the same level, so that the god and I stood face to face. The longer I looked at the statue, the brighter it became, as if it glowed with light. The face that looked back at me seemed to be . . . my own face. It was uncanny, as if I looked in a polished mirror. And then I became aware of another presence in the sanctuary, a thing with wings, for I heard them rustle—Victory, it must have been, since she had just favored me on the battlefield. And the two of them, Apollo and Victory, spoke to me, saying the battle I won that day was only the first of many to come."

Constantine was quiet for a long moment. The entire basilica had gone quiet. One by one, the bustling courtiers had stopped to listen to the emperor's story.

"What I saw and heard there, in that temple of Apollo, seemed to be not of this world, yet not unreal—quite the opposite, it was *more* real than the ordinary things one sees and touches every day. Something like that happened again, the day before I met Maxentius on the battlefield. In the sky I saw a strange bending of the light. Others saw it, as well . . ." His voice trailed off. When he resumed he sounded no longer dreamy but very matter-of-fact. "They say it's Sol who lights the sky, and isn't Sol the same as Apollo, only with a different name and a different priesthood? And are not Apollo and Sol the same as Elagabalus, the sun as it is worshipped by the Syrians? There is only one sun, after all. And could there be any power greater than the sun?" He looked at Zenobius intently.

"I'm not a priest or a scholar of religion, Dominus."

"Have you ever received a direct communication from a god? Seen a vision? Heard a voice?"

"Like everyone, from time to time, especially when in doubt, I look for signs and omens, and sometimes I perceive them—"

"No, I mean a *voice*—as clear as my voice right now. Or a *vision,* something manifestly—without any doubt—of divine origin."

Zenobius thought for a long moment before answering. "No, Dominus. I have not had that experience."

"Ah. But you knew Maxentius. You spoke with him often. You were perhaps his confidant. Did *he* ever hear or see such things?"

"Not to my knowledge, Dominus. But he was a pious man—"

"Yes, well, some of us hear voices and see visions—and others do not. And those who see and hear, like myself—are the winners! Earthly success is proof of the favor of Divine Will. That Will also manifests itself in dreams. The day before the battle with Maxentius, I not only saw a sign in the sky. That night I had a dream. I saw a curious emblem—rather like an X with a perpendicular line through its center, and the top of the line curved round. In my dream I was told that if my soldiers painted this device on their shields I would be victorious. Rome would be mine."

Zenobius nodded. "I've seen the shields your soldiers carry, bearing the mark you speak of, Dominus. I've seen that mark before."

"Have you?"

Zenobius took a deep breath. "Yes. It's a combination of two Greek letters, *chi* and *rho*—the first letters of the Greek word *chrestos,* meaning *good.* It's a bit of antiquated shorthand one sees in the margins of very old scrolls, to denote a passage of special importance. My grandfather taught it to me when I was very small, and I never forgot. I still use it myself sometimes, as a mark on architectural plans. Perhaps, when you were preparing for the battle, you saw the *chi-rho* somewhere—on an old plan or map of Rome—and remembered it in your dream."

Constantine looked thoughtful. "Possibly. I *had* been looking at maps and other documents, diagrams of catapults and such, in case there was a siege. Yes, well, it was a *good* thing that I defeated Maxentius—quite *chrestos* indeed, eh? The Divine Will is a mysterious thing. Whence comes it, and by what name should we call it? Mortals worship so many gods, and each god has so many different names and attributes. Or could it be that there is only one?"

"One . . . god?" What was the point of this long digression? At least Constantine was no longer talking about the scepter. "The great Apollonius spoke of a divine singularity—"

"Apollonius, the wonder-worker of Tyana, you mean? So you *are* a religious scholar."

"Not at all, Dominus. But I do know a bit about Apollonius, from family lore. An ancestor of the Pinarii knew him and was a devout follower. And my grandfather knew Philostratus, who wrote the biography of Apollonius."

"Ah, yes, a very famous book. Rather full of nonsense."

Zenobius frowned.

Constantine saw his reaction. "Well, I haven't read the book myself, but it was read aloud to me by my wife. I like to have books read to me, while I fall asleep. My wife has a lovely voice."

Was Constantine illiterate? Maxentius had said so.

"Philostratus does have a way with words," Constantine continued, "and he does keep the plot moving. But who could

take seriously that bit about swans surrounding the mother of
Apollonius and assisting her to give birth?"

"A very beautiful and poetical scene in the book—"

"Laughable, I would say. Can you imagine a flock of swans
flapping their wings and squawking encouragement to a
woman in labor? I think Philostratus never witnessed a birth,
to invent such a silly detail. Or spent any time around swans.
Nasty creatures! The whole book is about Apollonius traveling
hither and yon and practicing magic in one way or another,
even though the author repeatedly insists the man was not a
wizard. No one brings the dead back to life without practicing
magic! As for the wise man's so-called philosophy, it's all down
to the Fates. According to Apollonius, if a man is destined to
be a carpenter, he will be one, even if you cut his arms off at
birth. If destined to win the race at Olympia, so he will, even
if you break both his legs the night before. And if meant to
be a great painter, so he will be, even if you blind him. Ha!
I should like to see any one of those examples tested in the
real world. I can tell you how it would turn out. Oh, I know
the counter-argument: if you do blind some poor fellow, that
means he was *not* destined by the Fates to paint. So it's just a
circular argument, of no practical use to anyone. Fate is what
happens. What happens is Fate. Put aside silly books, I say,
and get along with the business of living. Show me the god
who rewards a loyal follower, and tell me how to please him."

Zenobius could not suppress a sigh. The emperor took no
notice.

"But I didn't call you here to talk religion. I am told that
Maxentius trusted you with a great many large-scale projects,
not least among them this magnificent building around us."

"Yes, Dominus."

"I'm also told that you are competent, honest, and punctual."

"If others say so—"

"They do. As for your skill and good taste, your projects
speak for themselves. How soon can you build me a triumphal
arch?"

Zenobius was startled, then felt such a rush of relief that he could not speak. Only now, when his fear was alleviated, did he realize just how frightened he had been, ever since receiving the emperor's summons. Many of the senators closest to Maxentius had vanished in recent days.

"I don't mean a small arch, or a plain one," said Constantine. "I want a triumphal arch every bit as big and impressive as the one the emperor Titus built after he conquered the Jews. I want it beautifully inscribed, covered with sculptures depicting my liberation of Rome, all exquisitely painted."

Zenobius pictured the Arch of Titus in his mind. He nodded slowly. "The sculptures would present the largest challenge. To produce so many, I mean, and on such a large scale."

"Why is that?"

"To be frank, Dominus, there is a scarcity in Rome of sculptors of the very highest skill. It has been so all my life. Plague, war, the death of so many old masters, the lapse in training—the extraordinary level of quality such as one sees in the Arch of Titus was made possible only by maintaining certain high standards from generation to generation, without interruption."

"Are you saying there are no sculptors of adequate skill to decorate my arch?"

"A scarcity, I would say, not a complete absence. That is to say, if you wish to create large-scale works that can be compared to those on the Arch of Titus, there are only so many sculptors with that level or artistry, and they can work only so many hours a day—"

"It must be done quickly. As soon as possible."

Zenobius remembered how straightforward and easy his working relationship with Maxentius had been. That Constantine wanted to retain him at all was wonderful, but working for him might be difficult, perhaps very difficult. His heart sank further when Constantine made a helpful suggestion.

"Can't you simply reuse bits and pieces of old sculpture? I've seen an awful lot of top-notch stuff, all over this city. Rome really is an amazing place, at least when it comes to architecture and statues. If today's artists can't match the standard of yesterday's artists, then I say, use the work of yesterday's artists *today*!"

Zenobius winced. "Is Dominus suggesting that sculptures should be removed from existing monuments? That might pose some problems. To do so could inflict damage to the existing monument, indeed, might even require its demolition. If the monument in question has been religiously sanctified, as almost all of them have been, then priests would need to be consulted, and proper rituals observed—"

"Then leave those monuments alone, and use the bric-a-brac that's lying all about the city."

"Bric-a-brac, Dominus?"

"It's all over the place, wherever buildings were torn down to make way for Aurelian's wall, or demolished for some other reason. Statues and medallions and tondi, whole stacks of them. You must know what I mean."

Zenobius nodded slowly. "Yes, there is a certain supply of cast-off items. Does Dominus suggest that such pieces could somehow be used on the new arch?"

"I don't see why not. Just be sure to work my image into them."

"Your image, Dominus?"

"My face, you silly man! If the statue is of some other emperor—say, Hadrian—re-carve it so that it looks like me. Chisel away the beard, give the face my nose, my mouth, and so on. How hard can that be? To satisfy a whim of Maxentius you made the Colossus of Sol look like a teenage boy! Make an inventory of available artwork and figure out how those pieces can be used on the arch. Some new sculptures will be required, as there are certain very specific scenes that must be on the arch—Maxentius and his men toppling into the Tiber, for instance. What a spectacle that was!" He laughed harshly, savoring the memory. "People must never forget the complete humiliation of his defeat. One of my secretaries will give you a list of tableaux to be depicted. I shall expect some plans and drawings from you as soon as possible. Very soon! I have no desire to dawdle here in Rome any longer than I have to."

Zenobius nodded mutely.

"What else? Ah, yes, there's a very large house—a palace, really, a sprawling place with baths and terraces and wings— where my wife wishes to have some private apartments."

What sort of person was Fausta, Zenobius wondered. She was the wife of Constantine—but also the daughter of the Diocletian's co-emperor Maximian, and sister of Maxentius, both of whom had been destroyed by her husband. She was said to be quite young, not much older than Crispus, Constantine's son by his first wife. Maxentius had never talked to Zenobius about his sister. Even if Fausta was entirely devoted to Constantine, surely she had felt a twinge of sadness when her father hanged himself and her brother drowned in the Tiber.

"Perhaps you know the place?" Constantine went on, talking about his wife's choice of residence. "It's on the Caelian Hill. I remember, it's called the House of the Laterani, though I have no idea who these Laterani were, or are."

"I know the building, Dominus. No one named Lateranus has owned it for quite some time. Nero confiscated it from them. Severus gave it back. Aurelian got his hands on it somehow."

"How you Romans like to hold on to the old names of things! I suppose we can call her wing of the place the House of Fausta. You'll help her find decorators, yes? Honest ones, I mean. She's young and a bit naive."

"Certainly, Dominus."

"But the place is much too big for Fausta alone. I'm thinking another wing would make suitable living quarters for the bishop of Rome."

Zenobius frowned, not sure he heard correctly. "Bishop?"

"Yes."

"Do the Christians in Rome even have a bishop?"

"Indeed they do. His personal needs may be simple—the Christians make a great fuss about their austerity—but his residence will need some large rooms, to serve as meeting chambers for the Christians. We may have to take down some interior walls."

Zenobius swallowed hard. "Meeting chambers . . . for Christians, Dominus?"

"Yes. The current bishop of Rome is named Miltiades. He'll let you know what he wants. He plans to hold some large conferences, so that he and his fellow Christians can work out their differences. Some believe one thing, some believe another, all sides claim to be the one true version of the faith—it all gives me a headache. Just tell me what to believe to get into paradise, and let's get on with it! Lock them in a room, I say, and make them come to agreement—and give them no dinner until they do!" He laughed, not quite as harshly as he had when recalling the end of Maxentius.

Zenobius was baffled by Constantine's jocular manner. Did he take the Christians seriously, or not? Zenobius had met some Christians when he was young, friends of his late grandmother, who had been a Christian herself, and they were mostly a dour lot. What would they think of Constantine making light of the conflicting doctrines that they took so seriously?

"Also, the bishop wants a place where his flock can worship, as openly as other people do when they go to the Temple of Jupiter or Hercules. When he was here in this building the other day, he greatly admired it. Well, he's not getting the New Basilica! But we could build something similar in layout, if rather smaller. He can decorate it as he sees fit. It will be interesting to see just what sort of temple the Christians come up with when they're free to do as they please, and given a reasonable budget from the state. There'll be plenty of room to build the bishop's new Christian basilica after we demolish the largest wing of the House of the Laterani, the part where Maxentius housed his horse guards. How my late brother-in-law doted on his cavalry. They were loyal to the end. Most of them followed Maxentius into the Tiber and never came out."

Zenobius was quite confused. The emperor of Rome, Pontifex Maximus of the state religion, was talking about granting an official residence to the bishop of the Christians, with conference rooms where they could gather and debate— and planning to build them a temple as well! Were the Christians and their crucified god now to be part of the state religion? Would their priesthood be funded from the state coffers, like the priests of Jupiter and the rest? Would their holidays be entered into the Roman calendar and publicly celebrated like the rites of the Lupercal and all the other ancient festivals? How could the Christian priests interact with everyone else in the hierarchy, when they denied the very existence of the gods?

Constantine was still talking about the end of Maxentius and his horse guards. "Rome has no need for garrisons or barracks—or Praetorian Guards. I'm told that more than one previous emperor saw fit to disband the Praetorian Guards, and yet they kept reappearing, like weeds in a garden. I shall put an end to them once and for all. Rome has no need of a resident armed force. I think I might ban weapons altogether from Rome. Perhaps military uniforms, as well."

Again Zenobius was taken aback. "Would Dominus leave the city . . . defenseless?" As soon as he said the words, Zenobius realized that this was exactly what the emperor intended to do. Rome would never resist him again.

Constantine arched one of his prominent eyebrows. "This city will be lucky if I let her keep her walls!"

"But Dominus, to demolish the walls of Aurelian— Hercules himself would balk at such a labor."

"Then perhaps I should consult the Jews. I believe one of their heroes was able to bring down a city's walls simply by blowing a horn."

Was Constantine making a joke? If so, his sense of humor eluded Zenobius. He recalled something Constantine had said earlier, and a thought struck him. "Don't the Christians claim that Jesus brought a dead man back to life? Did he practice magic, then?"

Constantine stroked his clefted chin. "I believe you're right. I shall have to ask the bishop to explain that part to me." He narrowed his big eyes. "For a fellow who claims he's no religious expert, you're a subtle one, Pinarius. Subtlety is not always a virtue." He continued to stare at Zenobius for a while, stroking his chin, then rolled up his eyes to gaze at their surroundings. "What a marvelous building! Nothing subtle about this place, eh? Such a grand space, so light and airy. Not entirely finished out yet, but you'll see to that. If I have a complaint, it's that the place has no focal point, no dominating feature. When you enter a temple, no matter how dazzling the marble or the columns or the paintings, one thing always dominates—the statue of the god. Think of Jupiter on his throne in the temple at Olympia—so gigantic, if he stood he'd burst through the roof!"

"But this building is not a temple, Dominus."

"No? It's a temple of sorts, a shrine to the power of the state. What if we placed a statue right here where I'm sitting, a statue seated on a throne, just as I am, but as big as Jupiter's statue at Olympus, so that throne and statue filled the whole apse?"

"A statue of whom?"

"Of myself, silly man! A colossal statue of the emperor enthroned, presiding over every conversation and transaction conducted here in the emperor's official place of business, even when the emperor himself is far away. But the gaze shouldn't look down, but up, heavenward, to the source of the emperor's power. The face must nonetheless be quite stern, as if to say: I speak not, I do not deign to look at you, yet I hear every whisper and the clinking of every coin that changes hands. A statue like that should keep the courtiers honest!"

Intentionally or not, Constantine peered upward and made just such a face as he had described. With his sculptor's trained eye, Zenobius instantly visualized the statue exactly as it should appear. To properly fill the apse it would have to be enormous, indeed. Gilded bronze would cost a fortune. Marble would be even less practical . . . or would it? His imagination was fired, anticipating the huge challenges of such an undertaking and trying to think of solutions.

Zenobius sighed. In spite of his dismay at the end of Maxentius, and his deep distrust of Constantine, he now found himself not only relieved but looking forward to serving the new emperor. He was to be given work, even if the work was not entirely to his taste. The projects would be very large, and hopefully very remunerative. The Pinarii—so long as they did not run afoul of the emperor—would continue to flourish. His thumb and forefinger found the outline of the fascinum beneath the wool of his toga and he gently squeezed it, relieved that he and his family had survived amid so much death and upheaval, grateful for the continuing favor of the gods.

"They must be somewhere close by. I'm almost certain this is where I saw them. Of course, it was so many years ago . . ."

With a stooped back and wobbly legs, Gnaeus Pinarius poked his walking stick into a drift of leaves. A stretch of the Aurelian Walls loomed nearby. Zenobius and Kaeso were with him, both fearful that the old man would trip and fall as he picked his way through the rubble.

There was a deep knocking sound as his stick struck stone. "Ah-ha! This is it."

Gnaeus stepped back as slaves moved forward to clear away leaves and weeds and rubbish and at last uncovered the artifact the Pinarii had come searching for: one of the large marble tondi that had been salvaged from a demolished building, set aside while the wall was built, and then forgotten. The once-bright paint was almost entirely faded, and the marble was spotted with lichen and streaked with filth, but the faces of Hadrian and Antinous were instantly recognizable.

"There should be four of them, as I recall," whispered Gnaeus, awed at seeing once again the face of the Divine Youth. It was Antinous on that night so long ago who had given him the comfort and guidance that saved his marriage to Zenobia and led to the birth of their son, who now had produced his own son.

One by one, the four circular tondi were uncovered.

"How could these ever have been abandoned, much less forgotten?" asked Zenobius. "They're magnificent. Surely, when the building was demolished, these were catalogued somewhere."

"Yes, and I'm sure the catalogue was then rolled up tight, tucked away on a high shelf, and forgotten," said his father. "Rome is like a doddering old woman with so many jewels and baubles she can't remember where she put them all. But I never forgot *these*. Yet whenever I thought of them, instead of telling others, I realized I wanted them to stay right where they were, unseen and undisturbed—like a secret between Antinous and me . . . and Zenobia . . ."

"My mother knew about these?"

"Yes. And only Zenobia! I never told anyone else how I came upon them one night when I despaired of ever having another son, and I prayed to the demon of Antinous. Yes, to *this very image* I prayed." He reached out and touched the Divine Youth's marble cheek.

"What exactly did you pray for?" asked Kaeso.

"That, my boy, is none of your business! Suffice to say, without that answered prayer, *you* would never have been born."

His grandson grinned. "Is this a riddle?"

"Never mind! I remembered these tondi, I knew exactly where I'd seen them, and I led you straight here. So much for my old mind getting rusty! Here they are, ready to be dug out and dusted off, crated, winched, carted, cleaned, polished, painted, and put to use again. Imagine, there may be no living person other than myself who's ever seen these, or even knew they existed!"

"They're truly extraordinary, Grandfather."

"But can they possibly be altered so as to depict Constantine?" Zenobius muttered.

"What did you say?" Gnaeus cupped a hand behind one ear.

"Nothing. Talking to myself." Zenobius had told his father that Constantine was looking for discarded works to restore and reuse, but he had not mentioned the emperor's impious idea to re-carve the face of the Deified Hadrian and replace it with his own. Why upset the old fellow?

"It's a marvelous rediscovery, Papa. Now the whole world will see and appreciate them once again. Well, no dawdling, my fellow Pinarii." He put his arms around the shoulders of his stooped father on one side and his gangly son on the other and drew them close. "We have a lot of work to do!"

A.D. 315

Appropriately, in the month named for that other Roman conqueror of Rome, Julius Caesar, Constantine made his return to the city. After the defeat of Maxentius, his first stay in Rome had been brief. He had been away for more than two years.

The visit was to mark a celebration of his tenth year in power, first as a Caesar and then as undisputed Augustus of the West. His Decennalia festivities were to be magnificent. Among the events would be the official dedication of some of the great building projects that had been completed in his absence.

The imperial retinue entered the city in a grand procession. The crowds of people along the Sacred Way and the senators on the steps of the Senate House gazed not only on their emperor, driving a chariot, but also on his considerably younger wife, Fausta, seated atop a gilded carriage. Her beauty was evident even at a distance. She looked, thought Zenobius, a great deal like her late brother, Maxentius.

Also in the procession, riding a magnificent white steed, was the emperor's eldest son, Crispus, who had been born to Constantine's previous wife. He was still a teenager, a little younger than Zenobius's own son, Kaeso, but much larger, a broad-shouldered young man with the same rugged features of his father, though not yet worn and weathered by time.

Riding alongside Crispus, wearing dark, somber robes, was the elderly scholar Lactantius, a Christian. Officially, he was Crispus's Latin tutor, but clearly, given his prominent place in the retinue, he was much more than that. Some said he held the strong-minded Constantine in a sort of spell. Zenobius doubted that, but whether as court philosopher or honored wise man, Lactantius did appear to have an intellectual hold on Constantine, and had exercised it to the advantage of the Christians. Lactantius was said to be behind the Edict of Milan. This was a joint accord signed by both Constantine and his sole surviving co-emperor, Licinius, Augustus of the East, that extended "to Christians and to everyone else the free power to follow whatever religion each person prefers." This remarkable edict went far beyond a simple stop to persecutions. Ostensibly, it removed all the prerogatives of religion from the hands of priests or the state and left it up to each individual in the empire to decide how and when and to whom to render worship.

How such an arrangement would work in practice was anyone's guess. Who would decide what holidays to observe, or which oracles to consult, or what god to pray to before a battle? The situation worried Zenobius, but he was not as anxious as some of his fellow senators, who in darker moments suspected the Christians of plotting a takeover of the state religion. To Zenobius that seemed highly unlikely, if not impossible, for how could a small minority of disbelievers and gods-haters impose their ridiculous pseudo-religion on the vast majority of pious worshippers? That would mean the triumph of the lonely, jealous god worshipped by the Jews over all the gods of Olympus, as well as their countless divine and semi-divine offspring.

More credible were rumors that Constantine himself had become a Christian, or was considering becoming one. But in practice, what could that possibly mean? Would an emperor of the Roman Empire no longer honor Jupiter and Apollo and Sol and all the other gods?

* * *

The rise of the Christians in imperial favor had of late been the subject of much discussion in the House of the Beaks. Gnaeus, Zenobius, and Kaeso had taken turns reading aloud to each other a short list of books that everyone seemed to be talking about. Sossianus Hierocles's *Truth-Loving Words to the Christians* exalted Apollonius of Tyana and, by way of comparison, ridiculed and denigrated Jesus; the author had been active in Diocletian's court and had encouraged him to persecute the Christians. A mocking rejoinder to Hierocles had been written by a Christian, Eusebius, with the cumbersome title *Against* The Life of Apollonius of Tyana *written by Philostratus, Occasioned by the Parallel Drawn by Hierocles Between Him and Christ.*

A much older Christian manifesto was also making the rounds. *Address to the Greeks* had been written long ago by Tatian, a follower of Justin Martyr during the reign of the Divine Marcus. Tatian made the wild claim that there had only ever been a single god, the one worshipped by the Jews, and that all other beings called gods were not gods at all, but mere demons, and wicked ones at that, as could be observed by their lewd and cruel behavior in so many of the stories about them—Jupiter making himself into animals so as to seduce unsuspecting women and trick them into bestiality, Bacchus causing a mother to cannibalize her own son, Apollo flaying poor Marsyas alive, and all the horror stories of Ovid's *Metamorphoses* in which the gods (or demons, using magic) turned hapless mortals into animals or stones or trees.

Tatian had essentially turned "demon" into a dirty word, a practice carried on by later Christians. He said that men of previous centuries had worshipped these demons only because the demons were cleverer and more powerful than men and had managed to distract even the smartest mortals from the existence of the one true god.

That night, after the grand procession of the emperor's arrival, on a balcony of the House of the Beaks, the Pinarii continued reading a brand-new work by Constantine's advisor

Lactantius, called *Deaths of the Persecutors*, in which the author openly gloated over the untimely ends of various emperors who had taken action against Christians, claiming that the Christian god had brought about their destruction. Though he didn't call Maxentius a persecutor—that would have been an outright lie—Lactantius did include the death of Maxentius in his book, taking the opportunity to unfavorably compare him to Constantine, whom Lactantius praised at every turn. The implication was clear that the Christian god had chosen Constantine over Maxentius, making Constantine's rise to power a divine act.

Lactantius's book was a racy read, full of salacious revelations. He told the heretofore "unknown true story" about the end of Maximian, erstwhile partner of Diocletian and father of Maxentius and Fausta, whom Lactantius condemned as a reprobate and rapist. Everyone knew that the former emperor had attempted an armed insurrection against Constantine, had failed, was captured, and was then driven to suicide. But Lactantius gave the juicy details:

Now a captive and stripped of all pretensions to power, Maximian formed a new plot against Constantine. He entreated his daughter, Fausta, flattering her, cajoling her, and begging her to betray Constantine. Maximian asked her to arrange that the door of the emperor's bedchamber would be left unlocked and only slightly guarded. Fausta agreed to do as her father asked, then instantly revealed the plot to her husband. A plan was laid for detecting Maximian in the very execution of his crime. In the emperor's bed, in place of Constantine, they put a worthless eunuch, to be murdered instead of the emperor.

In the dead of night Maximian arose and hid a dagger in his nightclothes. Venturing out, he perceived that all things appeared to be favorable for his insidious purpose. There were few soldiers on guard, and these at some distance from the bedchamber. However, rather than skulk and risk attracting suspicion, Maximian openly approached one guard, feigning alarm and saying he had just been visited by a prophetic dream that he must share immediately with his son-in-law.

The guard escorted him to the door. Maximian was allowed to enter. Running to the bed, he drew his dagger and stabbed the eunuch to death. He then threw his arms up in joy, exulting in his crime and loudly proclaiming himself the killer of Constantine.

At that very moment, Constantine stepped into the chamber by another door, followed by a band of soldiers. The covers were drawn back and the bloody corpse revealed. The murderer, realizing that he had been tricked, stood aghast, as silent and still "as if made of flint or Marpesian stone," while Constantine castigated him for his wickedness and sin.

In the end, Maximian was allowed to choose the manner of his death, and he hanged himself.

After reading this passage aloud to his father and grandfather, Kaeso put down the book and quipped: "Pity the 'worthless' eunuch!"

"Yes, you'd think they could have used the old pillow trick, instead," said Zenobius.

Kaeso laughed. "Like something in a comedy by Plautus!"

"No, pillows do not bleed," observed Gnaeus. "It was necessary that Maximian be caught literally red-handed, next to a dead body. Pity the eunuch, yes, but also Fausta, having to chose which one must die, father or husband!"

"How did they make the eunuch lie still, and not cry out?" asked Kaeso. "Do you think they tied him up and gagged him?"

"More likely they drugged him, so that he was unconscious," suggested Gnaeus. "Not a pretty detail, however it was done— arranging for another human being to be stabbed to death in one's stead."

"And yet," said Zenobius, "this must be the version of events approved by Constantine himself—the official version—since it comes from Lactantius."

"How did such a radical Christian ever insinuate himself into the emperor's household? The charlatan dares to quote Virgil!" Gnaeus shook his head. In his old age, the rapid changes of recent years had left him increasingly baffled. He had become strenuously anti-Christian, and was especially offended by any criticism or mockery of Apollonius of Tyana, as happened in Eusebius's book.

Gnaeus found it alarming that his grandson, who was now eighteen and the wearer of the fascinum, did not seem at all anti-Christian. Instead, Kaeso was open to dangerous new ideas, including the notion that Christianity might have some real value, and that Jesus had been a wonder-worker greater than Apollonius.

Zenobius had largely stayed aloof from arguments between his father and his son. His mandate to please the emperor, whom he would soon see face to face, put him in a delicate position.

Gnaeus was inveighing, and not for the first time, against the Edict of Milan: "If it is now up to any given individual to decide which gods do or do not exist, does that mean *no* gods exist, except in the imagination of each individual? Or is it that *all* gods exist, but any mortal can freely choose which are important or not important? So, if I say Jupiter is king of the gods, and you say Jupiter does not even exist, or at best is a mere demon, surely we cannot *both* be right. One of us is right and the other wrong. And surely the right opinion should dictate *all* religious observance and ritual, and the wrong opinion should be discarded, and those who hold that opinion made to see the error of their ways. The result of this edict must inevitably be chaos—and the gods will not be amused!"

"But Grandfather, for the sake of argument," said Kaeso, "what if the Christians *are* right, and there is only one god, their own, and all other so-called gods are mere pretenders? As you say, it cannot be that both sides are right, and, as you say, surely the right opinion should dictate all religious observance. In that case, if the Christians gain the upper hand, would they be justified in persecuting adherents of the old religion, since impiety by one invites divine retribution on all?"

"'If the Christians gain the upper hand'?" Gnaeus shuddered. "Kaeso, Kaeso, Kaeso! I know you say such things only to bait me, which is unkind of you. I am a very old man, and you should not exasperate me." He drew a deep breath. "We—I mean the Pinarii, but also all Romans—are faithful and we should remain faithful, no matter what happens, to that which Christians now disparage as 'the old religion' precisely because it *is* old, because it is received wisdom, ancient wisdom, the wisdom handed down to us by our ancestors, those who created this city and this empire. Indeed, the religion of our ancestors is the most precious inheritance we have.

"The same principle applies to all fields of knowledge. Consider Galen and his practice of medicine. The list of known cures handed down to him carried authority precisely because that list predated him. Many generations were required to build up such a vast body of knowledge. Should physicians simply throw out the formulary of cures and start anew with each generation? Of course not! Yet that is what Christians would have us do—throw out all the gods and rituals that made Rome great, and have kept us great, century after century, while other cities and empires have come and gone. By reflex, we as Romans reject the novel and the exotic—and what could be more foreign to Roman ways of thinking than this bizarre mandate of the Jews and Christians, to worship one god only?"

Kaeso nodded slowly, weighing his grandfather's argument. "But monotheism is not an exotic notion to many people in the eastern parts of the empire. Their religions are also ancient, with rituals and observances going back countless generations. Are those in the East not just as much citizens of Rome as those in the West, and do their notions have no validity?"

Gnaeus grunted. "We have Caracalla to blame for extending citizenship to every farmer and fishmonger in the empire. At least the Jews keep to themselves—except when staging bloody rebellions. But Christians are another matter. They would make a world in which *no* god may be worshipped *except* their own. And then, worshipped only in this way, not that. You see how they squabble among themselves, quite viciously, so that whichever faction is currently most powerful takes retribution on the others, casting them out, persecuting them, even stoning them. The idea that such people might someday rule over the rest of us is appalling!"

"But don't you see, Grandfather, that is why Constantine's edict protects everyone. It allows freedom of worship to each citizen—"

"For now it does. For *now*," said Gaius. "But if things proceed down the path you postulate—if, gods forbid, we should someday be forced to endure a Christian emperor—well, I can't even imagine such a thing, it's so patently absurd, like those preposterous situations one encounters in the satires of Lucian, where people travel to the moon or set themselves on fire to prove a point."

Zenobius felt obliged to interject. "Actually, Father, I believe Peregrinus really did set himself on fire. Lucian witnessed him do so."

"But traveling to the moon, you will agree, is a preposterous idea—yet no more preposterous than this inexplicable drift toward Christianity. *Our* religion and *our* gods *work*. Theirs do not. Otherwise, Jerusalem would be the capital of an empire and Rome would be a backwater, a subject city. We would have been the slaves, and they our masters. Our religion has brought us thus far—it has created the greatest empire in history. Can the Jews and the Christians make any similar claim? Quite the opposite. The Jews' religion has brought them nothing but misery and bondage. The Christians' religion has brought them nothing but the scorn of decent people, and made them outcasts, not just from true religion but from common society. They produce no philosophers—quite the opposite. They produce no art or literature except of the poorest and most childish quality. This rubbish by Eusebius, mocking Apollonius, is a case in point."

His grandfather had become so emotional that Kaeso refrained from making a rebuttal. Zenobius took advantage of the pause to change the subject.

"Any day now a messenger will arrive at our door, and I shall be called to deliver an accounting of all the work we've accomplished while the emperor was away. Hopefully, Constantine will have more work for us, in conjunction with his Decennalia celebration. Let there be no dissention or arguments in the House of the Beaks. The Pinarii must all pull together!"

The summons arrived the next day.

While Gnaeus stayed home, Zenobius and Kaeso accompanied the emperor and his eldest son on a tour of the city's new and reconstructed works. Crispus was near Kaeso in age, and Zenobius had hoped the two of them might hit it off, but Crispus projected a haughty demeanor, much like that of his father. It was abundantly clear that the Pinarii were considered not collaborators but mere servants.

At one point, Zenobius overheard Crispus ask Kaeso, "Is it true that your grandmother was Zenobia of Palmyra?" Kaeso answered with a simple nod of his head, after which Crispus remarked, "That's the way of the world, isn't it? Some rise. Some fall." He laughed then, a harsh laugh identical to that of his father.

The face of the Colossus was once again that of Sol. The makeover had posed many technical challenges, and Zenobius was proud of the final result, but a part of him remained sentimental about Maxentius and all he had done for the city. Zenobius had even dared to disobey Constantine in a quietly subversive way. Constantine had explicitly demanded that the stone at the base of the Colossus, inscribed with Maxentius's dedication to young Romulus, was to be destroyed. Instead, Zenobius had preserved the stone and had reused it in the top of the new Arch of Constantine. The stone was placed backward, so that the intact inscription was hidden from sight, and would remain that way for as long as the arch stood.

That arch, aligned so that its central passageway framed the Colossus of Sol in the distance, was a stupendous achievement, with not just one archway but three, the largest in the center. It was clad on every surface with marble relief sculptures, all brightly painted.

Zenobius remained uneasy about the juxtaposition of exquisite older pieces of sculpture alongside new reliefs that were clearly inferior. These new panels nonetheless seemed to please Constantine, who had dictated their content, including the destruction of Maxentius at the Milvian Bridge. That Constantine seemed unable to tell the difference in sculptural quality was a relief to Zenobius, but also a disappointment. He could not help but imagine the scathing critique Maxentius would have given the arch. But Maxentius would have been amused by another bit of subversion Zenobius had wrought on the arch. The tondo depicting Hadrian and Antinous had been duly re-carved so that it now depicted Constantine, happily hunting alongside Hadrian's young lover, for the face of Antinous was unchanged. Kaeso had laughingly called it "Constantine and Antinous, together again, for the very first time." This unlikely pairing struck Zenobius, depending on his mood, as comical, tragic, or blasphemous. Art connoisseurs and worshippers of Antinous would be in on the joke. Constantine did not fall into either category.

There was another problem with the reuse of the old tondi. After being re-carved, Constantine's head was too small for his body. The body could not be similarly reduced in size without making the emperor smaller than the other figures, which would only create more problems. In some cases these disparities in scale were painfully obvious, at least to Zenobius. Certain tricks employed in painting the images had helped to disguise the incongruity.

Constantine seemed not to notice the smallness of his head, or to recognize Antinous. The emperor was quite pleased. "I do love to hunt," he said, gazing up at the tondo. "And that young man with me—that would be Crispus, I suppose? Though it rather flatters you, son."

Crispus snorted, and looked bored. He was not an art lover.

"Which emperors were originally depicted in these scenes?" asked Constantine.

Zenobius identified the figures, now made into Constantine, which were variously engaged in making war, hunting, or offering sacrifices.

"And to think," said Constantine, "now these images depict not Trajan, not Hadrian, not Marcus—but *me*. I love it!" He threw back his head and laughed.

"It's like a palimpsest," said Kaeso with a smile. It was an observation he had once shared during family dinner at the House of the Beaks, whereupon both Gnaeus and Zenobius had praised his cleverness. That was probably why Kaeso repeated it now, though Zenobius would have advised against doing so. It was always better to let the emperor make his own clever observations.

"Like a *what*?" asked Crispus.

"A palimpsest," answered Kaeso. "You know, a piece of parchment on which the letters have grown so faded that you write over them, reusing the parchment—though sometimes you can still make out bits and pieces of the original text. Or a schoolboy's wax tablet, where you rub out the letters and make new ones with your stylus. These sculptures, too, are a kind of palimpsest, don't you think?"

Crispus narrowed his eyes suspiciously and made no reply. Zenobius had the impression that the young man did not spend a lot of time around books, notwithstanding the efforts of his famous Latin teacher.

Zenobius cast a fretful glance at Constantine, worried that he, too, might take offense, but the emperor was thoughtfully rubbing the cleft in his chin. "History itself is a sort of palimpsest," said Constantine. "One can almost always detect faint traces of the people who once existed and the things they once did in a particular place. But by the very act of living we erase the past and write over it."

Kaeso nodded. "And those who come after us, in their turn, will rub the tablet smooth, and write their own story," he said. Such old-fashioned Stoic logic took the metaphor a step too far. Now it was Constantine who narrowed his eyes. Kaeso turned a bit pale.

"We must see to it," said the emperor, "that the story we write is *never* written over. It must be permanent. Indelible. Impossible to erase."

As the party moved on, and left the arch behind, a jarring thought occurred to Zenobius. Did Constantine think of religion as a palimpsest? Did he think the gods of Olympus could somehow be erased, and a Christian god put in their place? Would faded scrolls of Homer and Virgil be written over with the works of Lactantius? Zenobius felt a tremor of guilt at even thinking such impious thoughts, but also a sinking horror, almost a physical sensation, as if a trapdoor had suddenly opened under his feet.

The party next took a tour at the site of the old House of the Laterani. The empress Fausta's quarters had been finished, quite luxuriously, and she was reportedly very pleased. Finished too were the more austere living quarters and the council chambers of the Christian bishop.

The basilica where the Christians would worship was still under construction. The bishop met them. He and the emperor discussed what sort of decorations might be appropriate. Zenobius gathered that it was desirable to have paintings and statues of Jesus and the martyrs, but no images of the Christian god. The appearance and attributes, and even the gender of this deity were still unclear to Zenobius, and to the god's worshippers, too, it seemed.

Constantine had allowed a very lavish budget for the project. To Zenobius it was still very strange that the emperor was funding and actively engaged in the construction of a Christian temple in the very heart of Rome—but work was work, he told himself, quashing his misgivings. Kaeso, on the other hand, seemed to take each new development in stride, as if everything were perfectly normal. What a generational difference there was between the easygoing Kaeso and his rabidly anti-Christian grandfather, with Zenobius muddling along somewhere in the middle.

Their last stop was back in the Forum, at the New Basilica, which was finally finished and decorated inside, a riot of polished marble and some truly magnificent mosaics. Though Maxentius had not lived to see it, his vision had at last been fully realized.

But Maxentius could never have foreseen the object that dominated the space, despite the vastness of the room— the truly gigantic, seven-times-larger-than-life statue of Constantine enthroned in the apse. In the end, after much wrangling and experimentation, Zenobius had decided to make the statue not from bronze but from marble. More precisely, the head and exposed parts of the arms and legs were of marble. The clothed parts of the statue were merely a framework made of bricks, wood, and plaster covered with drapery. Like the Arch of Constantine, the thing was a hodgepodge, a jumble of diverse parts assembled piecemeal, but presented as a singular, fully finished work of art.

The marble flesh was tinted to look lifelike. One hand held a scepter, and here again Zenobius had added his own secret, subversive flourish, for this giant replica was modeled on the actual scepter of Maxentius, which remained hidden at the nearby Temple of Venus and Roma, safe in the crypt where

Zenobius had placed it, to which he and Kaeso alone knew the means of access. As long as the seven-times-larger-than-life scepter was held aloft, to Zenobius it would represent his private, secret memorial to Maxentius. As the party drew near the statue, a shaft of sunlight from a high window struck the huge glass orb of the scepter. Multicolored lozenges of light were cast across the wall and ceiling.

Zenobius found the huge statue itself rather grotesque, but Constantine, seeing it for the first time, seemed awed by his own image. He turned to Crispus. "Do you think it looks like your father?" He turned around and stood so that his son could observe his face and that of the statue, which by a trick of distance and perspective appeared to be the same size. Crispus frowned. "It's a bit frightening, how much it looks like you."

"No, no! Not frightening at all," said a dark-robed figure walking quickly toward them, his soft-soled shoes padding gently on the gleaming marble. "The statue is very wise looking, I think. And very pious, not gazing down at the viewer, but upward—at some divine symbol in the sky, perhaps."

What sort of man, Zenobius wondered, could simply walk up and join a conversation with the emperor? The elderly fellow was well dressed in robes of some costly fabric, but he clearly was neither a senator nor a military man. When he exchanged a familiar nod with Crispus, Zenobius remembered seeing the man's face at a distance in the imperial procession when it entered the city. This was Lactantius, the Christian scholar, Latin tutor to Crispus, and author of *Deaths of the Persecutors.*

Constantine took the man's hand and clasped his shoulder. His face became quite animated, assuming a liveliness Zenobius had not seen before. "Lactantius! Your appearance is propitious. I've been wanting to introduce you to Zenobius here, because it was Zenobius, when we first met, who suggested to me that my dream of the *chi-rho* symbol before the battle at the Milvian Bridge might have been prompted by a memory of seeing it on some document or map, used as shorthand for *chrestos*." Constantine turned to Zenobius. "But Lactantius here, hearing the same story from my lips, suggested quite a different explanation, which to me makes much more sense: *chi* and *rho* are the first two letters of *Christ*. So there I was, prompted by my dream, having all my men make that sign on their shields—a symbol of Jesus Christ, though I had no way of knowing that at the time. And yet, by writing the sign of Christ on their shields, my soldiers triumphed!"

He seemed to expect a response. Zenobius was flummoxed for a moment, then managed to say, "Yes, I read that passage in *Deaths of the Persecutors*, about the *chi-rho* symbol." Lactantius smiled, pleased, like all authors, by a knowledgeable reference to his work. He and the emperor both looked at Zenobius, as if expecting more. "I know only a little about Jesus, I must admit," said Zenobius, speaking slowly, "but I thought his doctrine was one of peace and brotherly love—hardly warlike. Does he not admonish his followers to turn the other cheek when struck by an enemy?"

Constantine gave Lactantius a penetrating look. "By that reasoning, no emperor could ever become a Christian. The emperor can never ignore threats or insults to himself, or to his empire. He must be free to practice violence whenever necessary. What do you say, Lactantius? Would a Christian emperor need to be a pacifist to follow Christ? No doubt you've addressed the question in one of your long—very long—treatises, but you know my 'barracks Latin' is inadequate to follow the more abstruse passages."

"The answer is not abstruse at all, Dominus," said Lactantius. "The emperor, just like every other mortal, has a role to play in God's creation. As do the emperor's soldiers. Even the persecutors, in their own way, were instruments of the Divine Will, for they produced martyrs to serve as examples of courage and righteousness to the rest of us."

"Still, an emblem of Jesus on a shield taken into a bloody battle does seem rather out of place, does it not?" asked Kaeso. He sounded genuinely curious.

"Not at all," said Lactantius. "Christians make excellent soldiers. They make even better soldiers when they carry into battle the emblem of their Savior. This is nothing new. It has been so for generations. Think of the legion made entirely of Christians who fought under Marcus Aurelius. Cornered by the barbarians, worn down by heat, desperate with thirst, they prayed to God to save them. God answered their prayers with the famous Rain Miracle. A gentle shower cooled and quenched the thirst of the Romans, but when it rained upon the enemy it became a downpour that drowned them and swept them away, like Pharaoh's soldiers when they dared to pursue Moses. With that mighty rain came thunder, which was the voice of God. In remembrance, the Christians took the name 'Thundering Legion.'"

Zenobius bit his tongue, but Kaeso unabashedly spoke up. "I'm pretty sure it was Augustus, long before the Rain Miracle, who created the legion with a thunderbolt on their shields— Twelfth Legion Thunderbolt. I could be wrong about that. But we Pinarii *do* know a bit about the Rain Miracle, because one of our ancestors witnessed it with his own eyes, and described it to another Pinarius who conceived the images you see on the Column of Marcus. It was Harnouphis the Egyptian who called upon Mercury, and Mercury who brought about the miracle. So I'm pretty sure the Rain Miracle had nothing to do with Christians, and Christians had nothing to do with the Rain Miracle."

"Wrong again!" said Constantine, not in the least offended. He was glad, in fact, for the opportunity to reveal an exciting discovery. "Here in Rome, Lactantius has located a very remarkable document that offers proof of his version of events—a letter about the Rain Miracle submitted by Marcus Aurelius himself to the Senate."

Lactantius nodded. "Its existence has been known for a long time, but the document simply could not be found. It was presumed to have been destroyed by insects or fire, like so many documents from olden days. Upon our arrival in Rome, our Dominus gave me full access to the senatorial archives—a rare privilege for a mere scholar such as myself—and after much searching, at long last I located it. It is on my person right now—or rather, a copy of it, made by my own hand. The original scroll is too brittle and fragile to leave the archives."

He pulled a slender scroll from a leather sleeve elaborately decorated with gems, pearls, and gold filigree. "Here, young man, you can read it for yourself."

"Yes, read it aloud," said Constantine.

Kaeso took the scroll. With his father peering over his shoulder, he read the text aloud.

"From the Emperor Caesar Marcus Aurelius Antoninus, Germanicus, Parthicus, Sarmaticus, to the Senate and to the People of Rome, greetings. Previously I have explained to you my grand design, and by what means I gained ground on the Germans, with much labor and suffering, with the consequence that I found myself surrounded by the enemy in great numbers, the scouts of our general Pompeianus calculating them to number 977,000 men.

"Having examined my own position with respect to this army of barbarians, which vastly outnumbered us, I betook myself to pray to the gods of my country. But being disregarded by them, I summoned those among us who go by the name of Christians. For having previously made inquiry, I had discovered a great number of these men among us, and previously I had railed against them, which was a grave error—for I was soon to learn of their power.

"As I watched, the Christians made preparation for the battle, but not by honing their weapons nor blowing horns. Instead they cast themselves on the ground, and prayed not only for me, but also for the whole army, that we might be delivered from thirst and famine. For five days we had been without fresh water, for we were in the heart of Germany, a barren land with few rivers and little rain. But after the Christians cast themselves on the ground and prayed to their god (a god of whom I was ignorant), water poured from heaven.

Upon us it was a gentle and refreshingly cool rain, but upon the enemies of Rome it became a hail of fire.

"Immediately I recognized the presence of something divine at work. Clearly, those whom we supposed to be atheists have on their side a god unconquerable and indestructible. Therefore, let us pardon all the Christians among us, lest they pray for and obtain such a weapon against ourselves. And if anyone be accused as a Christian, and acknowledges that he is one, let the governor of the province neither force him to retract his faith nor put him in prison, but release him. And let the man who accuses him be burned alive. And I desire that these things be confirmed by a decree of the Senate. And I command that this my edict be published in the Forum of Trajan, in order that it may be read by all. The prefect Vitrasius Pollio will see that it is transmitted to all the provinces round about, and that no one be hindered from obtaining a copy of the document I now publish."

Kaeso finished reading and lowered the scroll. He wrinkled his brow and looked at his father.

Zenobius grimaced. He would gladly have bit through his tongue rather than speak, but the look on his son's face demanded that he say something. Either the lore passed down by generations of Pinarii was completely mistaken, or the letter was a fraud. "But, Dominus," he said, clearing his throat, "you realize this can't possibly be . . . there's simply no way that the Divine Marcus would have used this kind of . . . or that he would ever have ordered men burned alive . . . I mean to say, it has to be . . . it must be a . . ."

"A revelation?" said Constantine. "Is that what you're trying to say, Senator? Because that's precisely what it is—a wondrous revelation! Who knows what other remarkable documents Lactantius may yet discover, looking through those moldering, musty archives? Evidence for all the wrong-headed persecutions of Christians over the years and the wickedness of the persecutors, evidence of miracles performed by Christian martyrs, and who knows what else?"

"Who . . . indeed?" said Zenobius quietly.

Lactantius took back the scroll, rolled it up, and slipped it back into the exquisitely decorated sleeve. "But to address your question regarding the fitness of Christian soldiers: we Christians are as loyal to the emperor and the empire as anyone else. We accept our responsibility to protect the empire against the adversaries sent by the Devil."

"The Devil?" asked Kaeso.

"He is the infernal king of wickedness, the great liar, the enemy of mankind's salvation. It is he who sends barbarians against us, and it was the Devil who empowered the wicked emperors who persecuted us."

"But . . . why did your god permit this Devil to do so?" asked Kaeso. "If he is so powerful, why does he not vanquish this enemy once and for all, and be done with him?"

"God himself provided this adversary for us."

"Your god created his own enemy?"

"How else are we mortals to gain moral strength, unless we are tried and tested? When the Devil sends enemies against us, whether barbarians from without or insurrectionists from within, Christians must submit to military service, indeed, must be willing to shed the last drop of blood. What does their physical suffering on this earth matter, when they shall be rewarded with eternal bliss in Heaven? We follow the orders of the emperor, but God is our ultimate commander. Amazing as it might seem, the emperors and the empire of Rome have been instruments of his will all along. With the final demise of the persecutors, and with power in the hands of divinely inspired men like Constantine and Licinius, the Roman Empire is now ready to assume a new role in the history of mankind."

Constantine put a hand on Zenobius's shoulder, drew him aside, and spoke in his ear. "Don't you see? When Lactantius puts it all together like that, everything makes sense. There really is only one Divine Power, whatever name mortals give it. All my many victories on the battlefield did not come about by accident. The visions I've seen, the voices I've heard, all come from the same source."

"But . . . it was a vision of Apollo you saw in Gaul—or so you once told me."

"Did I? There *was* a statue of Apollo in that temple, to be sure. But the light worked upon it in a wondrous way, transforming it. I begin to think it must have been Jesus I saw that day. And the winged figure that joined us, which I took to be Victory— that might very well have been an angel, such as the Christians speak of. And before the battle for Rome, when I dreamed of the *chi-rho* emblem—well, what does it matter *how* it came into my head? Perhaps I did see it on a map, because I was *meant* to see it, and then dream of it. You say *chi-rho* stands for *chrestos*. Lactantius says it stands for *Christ*. But aren't those two words interchangeable, both expressions of the *goodness* of the Divine Will? And did I not conquer by using that emblem? That's what matters, Senator Pinarius. Results! I know it all sounds very spiritual, but this new paradigm is also very, very practical."

"Practical, Dominus?"

"Perhaps the Christians don't have everything exactly right— they do seem always to be squabbling among themselves—but I think they can be made to reach a consensus. And once that happens, the basic idea is sound. Do you see? One empire, one people, one god. Everyone pulling together toward a single purpose, decided by their emperor, who shall be inspired by the Christian god. Everyone sharing the same morals and following the same rules, decided by the same rule book, which the Christians shall put together—likewise inspired by their god, of course. Everyone *believing* the same thing—again, we shall put it in writing. The simpler the rules, the morals, and the beliefs, the better, so that even a cowherd can understand. Everything will be so much easier for everyone—not least the emperor! Once it's all settled, people will wonder how we ever got along before."

"You seem to speak of a single emperor, Dominus. Are you forgetting your colleague, Licinius?"

"Oh no, I assure you, I am *not* forgetting my dear brother-in-law." Two years had passed since Licinius married

Constantine's half sister. It occurred to Zenobius that an in-law of Constantine was a dangerous thing to be.

Constantine gave him a sharp look. "What are you thinking now, Senator? You seem always to be thinking. You're very astute. So is that son of yours. You do excellent work. But you really must leave religion to those who know what they're talking about, men like Lactantius. As I say: one god, one empire, one emperor. You stick to re-carving the statues. Leave it to others to remake the world."

A.D. 326

Ten years had passed since the Decennalia. Constantine was returning once more to Rome, this time to mark the celebration of his Vicennalia, twenty years as emperor.

He was no longer one emperor among four, or even two, having defeated his brother-in-law Licinius, Augustus of the East, in a series of titanic battles. The two of them had mustered the military might of the entire Roman world, marshaling the largest armies to be seen in two hundred years, the likes of which would not be seen again for a thousand years to come.

Licinius had finally been captured and eventually put to death by hanging, meeting the same wretched fate as Maximian. For the first time in forty years, the entire Roman world was ruled by a single man.

Returning to Rome as part of the imperial retinue was Senator Marcus Pinarius Zenobius, who a few years previously had been summoned, along with a great many other architects, builders, and artists from across the empire, to join Constantine in the East, there to begin work on a project of unprecedented ambition—the creation of a new city virtually from scratch, grand enough to rival Rome.

The site chosen by Constantine was the ancient town of Byzantium. Half a century had passed since renegade soldiers during the reign of Gallienus massacred the entire population.

Despite its strategic location, the town had remained largely abandoned. At a critical point in the war, Licinius took refuge there. Laying siege to the crumbling walls of Byzantium, Constantine had seen firsthand just how strategic was its location.

The site had been razed. All that remained of Byzantium vanished from the earth—leaving an ideal spot for Constantine to create a completely new city, to be laid out, decorated, fortified, populated, and renamed exactly to his liking.

The work had only just begun. First, the site had to be carefully measured and mapped. Then meticulously detailed plans were drawn. Streets were still being laid out and paved, harbors dredged, piers and moorings built. The first buildings were under construction. Because the Pinarii's projects in Rome had pleased the emperor, Zenobius had been summoned to the new city to do his part. As long as his work continued to please Constantine, he would have secure employment for years to come. His fortunes were secure, but his duties at Byzantium were likely to keep him away from Rome for years to come.

Already profoundly homesick, missing his wife and son and elderly father, he had convinced the emperor to include him in the imperial retinue headed for Rome to celebrate the Vicennalia.

Rumors concerning the new city swept back and forth across the empire. It was said that the city was to have its own senate, equal in stature to the Roman Senate, with members handpicked by the emperor and consisting entirely of Christians; that the city would have no temples honoring the gods, but instead would be full of Christian churches; that Constantine was carrying out a systematic confiscation of temple treasuries all over the East, carting off statues and obelisks and paintings to decorate his new city or to sell, and melting down priceless artworks of gold and silver to mint coins to pay for all the new construction. Thus far, none of Rome's treasures had been touched.

Some said Constantine would call the city New Rome, or Second Rome, but it seemed most likely that he intended to name it after himself: Constantinople. The frenzy of activity focused on the new city caused considerable anxiety in Rome. What would become of old Rome when "New Rome" was built?

Since Constantine had last been to Rome, there had been changes all over the empire, many of them due to the influence of his Christian advisers, like the late Lactantius and the emperor's favorite historian, Eusebius. Few people had realized just how much the traditional religion relied on the state's funding and support; for countless generations, the situation had been taken completely for granted by all concerned. Nor had anyone foreseen just how quickly and radically the status quo could change when the state shifted its financial support entirely to the Christians.

In a startling turnabout, the Edict of Milan with its policy of toleration had now come to protect followers of the old religion. They were free to believe whatever they wanted, and they were allowed, if they could afford it, to assume ownership and maintenance of shrines and temples no longer supported by the state. Since many of the richest citizens had abruptly converted to Christianity, and hardly anyone else could afford such expenses, in short order the new owners of the temples were forced to sell off treasures accumulated over centuries, or even to shut their temples altogether.

The Edict of Milan forbade the use of violence to compel anyone to convert to Christianity, but numerous religious activities were nonetheless restricted or banned outright. New edicts forbade the erection of new cult statues, the consultation of oracles ("summoning demons," as the Christians called it), or divination of any sort, which was now considered black magic. Even animal sacrifice to the gods, the central event of so many ceremonies and festivals, was forbidden. Penalties were severe. The ancient practice of Etruscan haruspicy—reading entrails—long a part of marriage and other family ceremonies, now carried a penalty of death by fire. Priests were stripped of longstanding, often hereditary, privileges and publicly humiliated. It was ordered that the doors of temples must be left open at all times, so that Christians could monitor the activities within, to make sure no magic or other outlawed activity was taking place. Some ancient rituals were deemed intrinsically obscene, which led to crackdowns on behavior considered licentious in temples of "the demon Venus" and elsewhere.

Constantine, who had once declared that kidnappers should be thrown to wild beasts in the arena or sent to gladiator schools to be cut down by practiced fighters, had now pronounced a ban on gladiator games. In cities all over the empire, Constantine's magistrates and governors were pressuring local elites to shift their traditional support from arena spectacles to chariot races. Plans for the emperor's new city included no amphitheater, but did set land aside for a gigantic hippodrome, the Greek equivalent of what in Rome was called the Circus Maximus.

To be sure, all these changes had been more uniformly enforced in the East than in the West. Rome, where the influence of the Senate was still strong and the traditions of Roman religion were most entrenched, had been the place most resistant to change. But what would happen once Christians were put in charge, even in Rome? Constantine had not long ago appointed the first Christian consul, Acilius Severus, who was now the first Christian urban prefect, charged with readying the city for the emperor's Vicennalia visit. The city's legal jurisdiction, which had once extended over much of Italy, had been severely cut back, to a mere one-hundred-mile radius. The emperor seemed increasingly indifferent or even hostile to the unique status of Rome.

Other changes were more innocuous. The use of a seven-day week dated back to Augustus, with names of the days linked to the sun, moon, and five planets; Constantine had now prohibited any official business or manufacturing on Sol's day, which he called the Lord's Day. Making the day named for the sun into the day of the Christians' god was yet another step in the long linkage of that deity with Apollo and Sol and Elagabalus.

Locally in Rome, two of the most important annual holidays were now October 28, Expulsion of the Tyrant (meaning Maxentius), and October 29, Arrival of the Divine (meaning Constantine).

Constantine's open hostility to the old religion was matched by his growing interest (some said interference) in Christianity. He had taken an active role in trying to bring uniformity to the faith's patchwork of conflicting theologies. "How am I to build a city of churches," he had said, "until I know precisely what is to be worshipped in those churches?"

At the Council of Nicaea, not far from Byzantium, Constantine had called the bishops together, overseen their debates, and relentlessly pressed them for a result. Zenobius, at that time shuttling back and forth between Byzantium and Nicaea to consult with both the emperor and with city planners, had seen and overheard much that was going on at the Council. He had written about what he called "religious sausage-making" to his father, though he hesitated to infuriate a man as old and frail as Gnaeus, who was now in his nineties:

Their talk is all about divine "substances" and especially pedigree—whether Jesus was younger than God, having been made by him, and thus subordinate, as anyone would presume was the case with a father and son, or whether Jesus was in fact the same age as God, having existed just as long, that is to say since before time began, and thus not God's junior but his equal, and so on and on. Then there is a third something called the Holy Spirit, which is either the same stuff as God and Jesus, or different stuff, in which case, where did it come from, how long has it existed, and is it superior or inferior or exactly equal to God and Jesus? Since this is all (as you call it, Father) "made-up nonsense," no one can possibly either "prove" or "disprove" any of it, so the debaters resort to esoteric terminology and obscure references, impossible for any outsider to understand. It is hard to imagine that the emperor with his "barracks Greek" (his term, not mine) can follow their arguments. I suspect he hasn't the least idea what is going on at Nicaea. All he wants is a unanimous vote. Share this letter with Kaeso and then burn it.

Pausing in Aquileia on his way to Rome on the first day of April, Constantine announced a number of new laws to address a perceived crisis of licentious behaviors. These included rape, sex outside marriage, the keeping of concubines, and adultery.

Some of the penalties were horrific. Rapists—a category including any man who had intercourse with a consenting girl without marrying her first—were to be burned alive. Any girl who willingly consented to "abduction" and ravishment—in other words, a girl who eloped without her father's consent and had intercourse with her "abductor"—was to be burned alive as well. Any nursemaid who assisted her charge in such an elopement was to have molten lead poured down her throat.

A married man was not to keep any concubines. Any man who did so committed adultery, and adulterers were to be exiled. Charges of adultery could only be brought by a close family member. This was to protect innocent men from spurious charges contrived by political enemies or business rivals.

From Aquileia, Zenobius wrote ahead to Kaeso:

As you know, high on the emperor's agenda will be his first visit to the newly constructed Christian basilica next to the House of the Laterani. I cannot stress enough how important it is that everything about this structure, inside and out, lives up to the emperor's expectations. (It *is* entirely finished and decorated, yes?) The emperor's mother has kept him abreast of progress, sending regular letters along with plans and drawings and even samples of marble. From your letters, I gather that Helena personally oversaw much of the project herself. I can imagine the lady has not made your life easy! I gather that even the Bishop of Rome is cowed by her.

I am told that Bishop Sylvester, after consultation with Helena, will dedicate the structure to "Our Savior," so that is what the worshippers will call this basilica. Since this is the very first public Christian church in Rome, it will be closely scrutinized by everyone. If it pleases the emperor (and his mother), it may serve as a model for the many churches he intends to be built in his new city.

To more mundane matters: her apartments in the House of the Laterani (or Lateran Palace as some now call it) must be made ready for the empress Fausta and her retinue, including her two daughters and three sons and all those charged with tutoring, feeding, and looking after them. I attach a list. Her older stepson, Crispus, also needs lodgings in the palace. These rooms should have a separate entrance from the others, since young men, including military officers, will likely be coming and going and Fausta and her daughters must not be exposed to any coarse language or unseemly behavior.

I trust that the emperor's mother and the Bishop of Rome are still pleased with their lodgings at the Lateran Palace. But I do fear that Fausta's long-vacant chambers are likely to be full of spider webs and dust, or, worse, that some parts may have been commandeered as storage rooms for Helena and the bishop. I trust you to find a diplomatic way to clear up any such problems before we arrive.

Another matter: when you greet the emperor's entourage upon our arrival—how I look forward to seeing you again after so many months!—I ask that you do *not* wear the family fascinum. It pains me to ask this, but the emperor frowns on what he calls "magic amulets and demonic talismans." I realize that it would be under your toga anyway, and out of sight, but nonetheless I think it better that you leave it at home. Why tempt the Fates? But

do not tell your grandfather about this request. No need to
upset him. Burn this letter.

Constantine's entry into Rome commenced with a ceremonial
crossing of the Milvian Bridge, with Constantine leading the
way on horseback and carrying his battle standard, called
the labarum. This was a gilded spear with a cross-bar toward
the top. Its resemblance to a crucifix was not accidental.
Surmounting this cross was a much-bejeweled golden wreath,
and inside the wreath was a *chi-rho* symbol. The labarum
had been carried into every battle between Constantine and
Licinius. No soldier charged with carrying it had ever been
struck by an arrow.

At the highest point of the Milvian Bridge—the newest
part, rebuilt after Maxentius had destroyed it—Constantine
stopped and held the labarum aloft so that it could be seen by
everyone in the party behind him as well as by the spectators
gathered along the river and on the city wall.

"The day before the battle, in the sky above Rome I saw
the cross of Christ, and a divine voice spoke in my ear and
said, 'In this sign, conquer!' And the night before the battle,
I dreamed of the emblem of Christ, the *chi-rho,* and a divine
messenger instructed me to have my men paint it on their
shields. I did so. The next day, at this very spot, as Maxentius
made a cowardly retreat, the bridge collapsed beneath him and
the tyrant drowned in the Tiber!"

From his place in the imperial retinue some distance
behind Constantine, Zenobius heard the emperor clearly, and
released a sigh of exasperation. Some of the details as related
by Constantine were not as Zenobius remembered. For one
thing, Maxentius had not fallen from the Milvian Bridge;
he himself had ordered the demolition of the central part,
before the battle. But many subsequent accounts of the battle
left out the complicated detail of the pontoon bridges, and it
had become an accepted historical fact that the stone bridge
had miraculously collapsed beneath Maxentius. If Constantine

himself remembered it that way, who was Zenobius to contradict him?

Also, Zenobius had been present at a dinner in Nicaea when Constantine, drinking wine and telling war stories to the bishops, suddenly seemed to realize, for the first time, that the strange bending of the light he saw in the sky before the battle must have been a cross, and at the same time he revealed that a voice had said to him, "In this sign, conquer." Zenobius himself had been told by Constantine, shortly after the battle, about the odd phenomenon in the sky, but at that time Constantine had not described it as a cross. Nor had he mentioned hearing a voice; Zenobius was quite sure of that. But who was Zenobius to assert that his memory was sharper than that of the emperor, especially when Constantine now remembered the incident so vividly? The bishops had been much impressed, and since that night, the story had become one of the emperor's standard anecdotes.

The procession entered the city and paraded down the Flaminian Way, the longest stretch of straight road in the city. Cheering crowds greeted the emperor. The excitement was genuine. Above all else, Constantine was a winner, the warmaker who brought peace, the man who put an end to decades of civil strife. The spectacular plans for his Vicennalia—no gladiator games, but plenty of horse races, animal hunts in the arena, and lavish banquets—demonstrated that he cared about and respected the ancient city after all, despite his long absence and his plans for the new city.

Many in the crowd were giddy with excitement when they caught glimpses of the imperial family—the emperor and his empress, who was still surprisingly youthful and beautiful, and also his two daughters and his four sons, who ranged in age from a toddler to the oldest, Crispus, the dashing war hero who had conducted himself so brilliantly in the war against Licinius. Women swooned at the sight of Crispus. More fearsome than handsome were the emperor's half brothers, two very stern square-jawed war veterans.

Constantine's first stop was the Church of Our Savior. His mother and Bishop Sylvester greeted him on the steps. Helena bestowed kisses on her daughter-in-law and on all her grandchildren, much to the delight of the crowd.

Feeling a bit nervous, Zenobius followed the imperial party inside. He was struck anew by the curious fact that the Christians had chosen for their first state-built temple a structure in the shape of a basilica, essentially a regal throne room and audience chamber. All seemed finished. The materials were of the very highest quality, as was the workmanship. He was most apprehensive about two silver statues of Jesus that had been ordered by the bishop. Any art lover could judge the quality of a Hercules or Apollo or Antinous, but what did a first-rate Jesus look like? This deity, with his long hair and beard and his flowing robes, looked to Zenobius more like a Jewish magician than a god. But the work done by the silversmiths was excellent, and Zenobius was relieved to see the pride with which Helena showed them off. Constantine was pleased.

Fausta and her children remained with Helena, to settle in at their apartments at the House of the Laterani. Then Constantine, his religious duty done, was eager to see the New Basilica—or more precisely, to see a change to his colossal statue there. Following the emperor, his half brothers, and Crispus, Zenobius was again a bit nervous, for like the emperor he would be seeing for the first time the alteration to the statue carried out by Kaeso at the emperor's behest.

They were met at the entrance of the New Basilica by the Christian city prefect, Acilius Severus, and by Kaeso, whom Zenobius eagerly embraced.

"The fascinum?" Zenobius whispered in his son's ear.

"Safe at home, Father, as you requested."

Zenobius nodded, but felt a sentimental twinge of regret. Here he was, back in Rome at last, reunited with his son. What would have been the harm, after all, if Kaeso had worn the family heirloom, as would only be right and proper? But Kaeso had done as he requested. If Zenobius had been over-cautious, he had only himself to blame.

The imperial party entered the basilica. Like a seated giant, the statue loomed at the far end of the building. Zenobius had forgotten just how big it was. Reflecting the beams of sunlight from high windows and, lower down, the flickering light of lamps and torches, the flesh-colored marble seemed to glow, as if it would be warm to the touch. The illusion of a living, breathing, sentient colossus present in the chamber was so uncanny it was almost unnerving. To Zenobius, this place felt more like a temple of worship than did the Christian church, housing as it did such a huge statue, even if the statue was that of a living mortal.

Zenobius held his breath as they crossed the enormous space, then relaxed as he saw Constantine's delighted reaction. Replacing the giant scepter with a glass orb in the statue's hand was a replica of the labarum, seven times larger than life. Great expense had been lavished to make the giant battle standard as magnificent as the original, gilding it and covering it with countless jewels. Now the colossal Constantine presided over the space holding a giant cross displaying the *chi-rho* symbol of Christ. The new religion was triumphant even here, in the secular heart of the Forum.

Zenobius felt a stab of nostalgia. His subversive tribute to the dead emperor—putting a giant replica of Maxentius's still-hidden scepter in the Constantine statue's hand—had been superseded. The last, covert traces of Maxentius, who so loved and doted on the city of Rome, had vanished for good.

With his two half brothers, as well as Crispus, the city prefect, and a troop of bodyguards, Constantine left the New Basilica and took a stroll through the Forum. The Pinarii followed along. The open spaces and temple steps were crowded with citizens enjoying the holiday. People cheered with delight at seeing the emperor along with his son and heir apparent, the two of them at last returned to the heart of Rome's empire.

But this was also the heart of the old religion, with age-old temples all around—their doors all conspicuously open, as the law now required. If Constantine no longer believed in the gods inside those temples, the vast majority of the city's population did. They seemed to interpret the emperor's presence as homage paid to the primacy of the city of Rome and the primal values and traditions the city embodied.

Constantine reached the Senate House. Rebuilt by Diocletian and Maximian after a fire, it still looked quite new amid so many old buildings, its freshly scrubbed steps white and gleaming. At the top of those steps, among the senators waiting to greet the emperor, Zenobius was surprised to see his father. At ninety-four, Gnaeus Pinarius was probably the oldest senator alive. He was certainly the oldest one present. Knowing how deeply his father detested Constantine's religious policies, Zenobius could only assume that the old man's respect for decorum had trumped his personal distaste: when a Roman emperor visited Rome, a Roman senator must show up to greet him.

Zenobius's heart swelled with pride at the sight of his father, until he saw that the old man was wearing the fascinum—not tucked out of sight, but outside his toga, plainly visible, the gold glinting brightly in the sunlight.

Constantine slowly ascended the steps, seeming to relish the moment. To either side, senators bowed their heads as he passed. When Constantine reached the porch he noticed Gnaeus Pinarius. He gave the old senator a deferential nod, acknowledging his great age.

Then Constantine saw the fascinum. He frowned. "Do I know you, Senator?"

"I am Gnaeus Pinarius, Dominus."

"Ah, yes, patriarch of the Pinarii. Your son and grandson have served me well. You can be very proud of them."

"I am, Dominus. I am proud of all the Pinarii, living and dead. Our ancestors go back to the founding of Rome, and before." Gnaeus reached up to touch the fascinum, as if deliberately to draw attention to it.

"That thing you wear . . ." Constantine leaned closer and peered at it. "Is it a cross?"

"No, Dominus. I suppose it does look a bit like a cross, which I understand to be a symbol of those who worship the crucified god. No, this amulet is very old. Even older than myself," he said with a smile, "and I am old enough to remember when the emperor Philip celebrated the Millennium of Rome. This amulet long predates the birth of Jesus. It predates even the founding of Rome. Time has worn away its original form: a phallus with wings, an image of the great god Fascinus."

Constantine drew back, wrinkling his nose.

"Fascinus was the first god ever to appear to the first mortals who lived among the Seven Hills," continued Gnaeus. "The Vestal virgins keep an image of the god in the House of the Vestals, which they bring out only when a triumph is staged at Rome. They place it under the triumphal chariot, out of sight, where it wards off the Evil Eye. It was there beneath *your* feet, Dominus, protecting you, when you celebrated your triumph over the man you call 'the Tyrant,' the late emperor Maxentius."

Constantine's frown grew more pronounced.

"But of course, as Pontifex Maximus, you know that already."

"Of course," said Constantine. "The Vestals were allowed to practice their ancient tradition. An old custom. Very old, very quaint. Very 'pagan,' as we say nowadays."

Now it was Gnaeus who frowned. "'Pagan'?" he asked. The word came from old Latin. It had originally referred to a peasant or anyone living in the countryside, as opposed to a sophisticated city-dweller. Over time it had become an insult. A pagan was a hayseed, a country bumpkin, a clod. "I don't understand your use of that word, Dominus."

Constantine smiled. He slapped Gnaeus on the shoulder, hard enough to make him wince. "Really, old man, you must keep up with the times! 'Pagan' is what we call believers in the old religions, the kind of people who wear magic amulets and worship genitalia with wings." Constantine's brothers and his son Crispus laughed, as did the city prefect. "One is either a Christian . . . or a pagan. And you, Senator Pinarius—are you . . . a *pagan*?" He said the word with contempt.

Gnaeus made no reply. He was furious at being insulted—at seeing religion itself insulted!—but he also felt like a foolish old man. What had he been thinking, to verbally spar with the emperor, the man whose slightest whim could decide the fortunes of his son and grandson and all the Pinarii yet to be born? His face turned hot, but he felt a cold pain in his chest. He felt lightheaded and took a step back. He clutched the fascinum.

Constantine interpreted this retreat as an acknowledgment of defeat, and shook his head at the old pagan's faith in a foolish amulet. He would have liked to rip it from the old man's neck, but to do so would be unworthy of his dignity.

Another senator, the youngest of the Messius Extricatus line, pushed Gnaeus aside. "We bid you welcome, Dominus, to the home of the Roman Senate. Please enter. We have arranged a small welcoming ceremony before the Altar of Victory."

Constantine nodded. "Ah, winged Victory. I thought I saw her once, at a shrine in Gaul. But I was mistaken. It was an angel who visited me that day. No, I shall not enter. I thank the Roman Senate for the invitation, but I have no business in the Senate House today."

The senators were dumbstruck. Even Messius Extricatus could produce only a sputter of disbelief.

Constantine turned to the city prefect. "What is next on the agenda, Severus?"

Taking this as a cue to deliver a speech he had carefully rehearsed, Acilius Severus stepped to the front of the porch and raised his hands to silence the crowd below. After making a long and very formal welcome to the emperor and his family, Severus announced what he called "the capstone of the day's events—an open-air festival atop the Capitoline Hill, where all the senators and citizens of Rome and the spirits of all our ancestors will celebrate the emperor's return to his capital. There shall be much joy and feasting!"

The crowd cheered. People begin to move toward the Capitoline Hill, smiling and laughing.

Looking very pleased with himself, Severus turned back to Constantine, who gave him a sour look. "When I asked what was next, Prefect, I expected a word in my ear, not a public announcement!"

Severus turned pale.

"The Capitoline, I know, is thought by most Romans to be the most sacred precinct in the whole city," said Constantine, "being the site of the Temple of Jupiter, whom pagans worship as the highest and most powerful of all their gods. Can you promise me, Severus, that at this festival there will be *no* invocation to the demon Jupiter?"

Severus looked blank for a moment, then nodded. "I understand, Dominus. I am a Christian myself. I promise you, there will be no mention whatsoever of Jupiter." His tone was slightly tenuous, as if he were unsure of the facts, but determined to make everything work in the end.

As Constantine descended the steps of the Senate House, his entourage following, Zenobius whispered to Kaeso, "You stay here, son, with your grandfather. I don't like the way he looks." The old man's confrontation with Constantine had been unexpected, and might prove disastrous, but Zenobius nonetheless felt rather proud of his father for standing up to the emperor.

While Kaeso stayed behind, Zenobius followed the imperial entourage as it moved toward the Capitoline. Constantine's bodyguards cleared a way through the crowd. They made swift progress for a while, but then the way narrowed as it began to ascend, and the crowd grew thicker.

Constantine scowled. He came to a stop and raised his hand. "No. I will *not* attend this festival. It has been a long day. I shall withdraw to my private chambers and spend what remains of the day with my family."

Severus was flummoxed. "But, Dominus . . . the people expect you. What of the ancestors?"

"I shall commune with my own ancestors."

As the imperial party turned back, word of Constantine's decision quickly spread. There was an abrupt and dramatic shift in the mood of the crowd. Those who had cheered began to grumble. Some dared to jeer. Protected by the anonymity of the crowd, more and more people begin to hiss and boo. Some even shouted ridicule at the emperor's appearance, targeting his prominent nose.

"Bigger than what's between his legs, I'll bet!" cried someone.

"I hear his giant statue in the New Basilica doesn't even *have* a penis!" cried another.

"No—just a very long nose!"

Constantine turned ashen. Zenobius was close enough to overhear when his half brother Hannibalianus growled in the emperor's ear, "Set the bodyguards on them! Teach them a lesson!" The big man clutched the handle of his sword. "I'll lop off a few heads myself!"

Zenobius felt a thrill of panic, imagining the bloodbath about to take place.

Constantine's other half brother, Julius, spoke in his other ear. "Take no notice of them, Dominus! These lowly pagans are dust beneath your feet. Pretend they don't exist. In all the ways that matter, they don't."

After a long, tense moment, Constantine raised a hand to silence Hannibalianus. He gripped Julius's shoulder. "You speak wisely, brother. From time to time, all rulers must put up with a bit of . . . skittishness . . . from the people."

They walked some distance, with the sullen crowd parting before them. There was a loud, clanging noise ahead.

"But *this*! This *cannot* be allowed!" cried Julius. Ahead of them stood a row of statues on pillars, including a life-size bronze of Constantine. Boys were pelting it with stones.

As the imperial retinue and its bodyguards drew closer, the crowd gathered at the statues scattered with screams of panic. The boys ran off, giggling and making rude noises.

"Those little demon-lovers should be rounded up and burned alive!" said Julius.

"Brother!" Constantine shook his head and clucked his tongue. "So peaceable when words were hurled, but now so bellicose when a few rocks are thrown against metal."

"But Dominus," Julius protested, "this is injury, not insult. Look at the face! The dent in the nose! That ugly scratch across the cheek!"

With a quizzical expression, Constantine touched his own forehead, nose, and chin. "I am quite unable to perceive any wound inflicted on my face. Nor has my diadem been knocked the slightest bit askew."

"But Dominus—"

"The statue cannot turn the other cheek, as Our Savior prescribes—but I can. No, brothers, it will not do to slaughter Roman citizens in the Forum. Not today. We will show mercy. And a sense of humor! The emperor must allow the people to have a joke or two at his expense. Why, look at these other fellows here, on their pedestals." He gestured to the statues to either side of his own. "What good company I keep. Here we have a selection of the greatest emperors of all time, don't you agree? And yet . . . consider that fellow there, Augustus. Not one of his statues ever looked a day over thirty—even though the man lived to seventy-five! I call him 'Fortune's Chess Piece'—a king who was never more than a pawn of history."

Zenobius thought this was a stupid comment, but everyone else in the entourage laughed.

"And that one there, Hadrian—a third-rate artist, but a great emperor. Or . . . was it the other way around? One imagines him as a human paintbrush—fuzzy-headed and rather stiff."

Constantine's wit evoked more laughter. Zenobius tried to crack a smile.

"And here we see Trajan. He chiseled his own name on so many monuments—taking credit for the work of other men— that I call him 'Creeping Ivy.'

"And that fellow there, looking so dour. You may call him Marcus Aurelius. I call him . . . a buffoon."

Crispus was laughing so hard that he could barely speak. "Oh, no, Father! Not a buffoon!"

Constantine kept a straight face. Only the barest hint of a smile showed that he had regained his good humor.

Not so Zenobius, whose forced smile went flat. "The Divine Marcus," he whispered to himself, "a *buffoon*? Thank all the gods my father isn't hearing this!"

Constantine was not finished. "Marcus was a meditating mess. An ass. A laughingstock."

"Because he was a cuckold!" said Crispus, joining in. "While Marcus was thinking deep thoughts, his shallow wife . . . was taking it deep . . . from thrusting gladiators! Another reason to ban them, eh? Wasn't her name Fausta . . . too?" His grin vanished and his voice trailed off as he realized what he said. Amid such ribald talk, to link his stepmother to Marcus's wife went too far.

Constantine frowned. "Marcus's wife was named Faustina, not Fausta. If Commodus *was* the child of a gladiator, and Marcus a cuckold, what should he have done about it?" He stared at Crispus as if awaiting an answer, but no one spoke. There was no more laughter.

Constantine turned and scanned the entourage. "You, Senator Pinarius! See to it this statue is repaired. Immediately!"

"Yes, Dominus."

Zenobius was glad to stay behind as the retinue moved on. The long day of putting on a proper face had exhausted him. The practical challenge of fixing the statue was much more to his liking. He gazed up at it, pondering how best to repair the scratched cheek and the dented nose.

"Dominus!"

He turned to see one of his slaves approaching, a young messenger. The boy's arrival seemed a godsend. Zenobius could use him to summon artisans and scaffold-builders.

Then Zenobius saw the look on the boy's face. He felt a lump in his throat.

"Is this about my father?"

The boy nodded and burst into tears.

"I'll never forget the moment he died, right in front of me, there on the porch of the Senate House," said Kaeso. "To make a last stand, no place would have pleased him more. He died speaking up for what he believed in. When I think of how it happened . . ." He shook his head. "Taunting him like that, the emperor as good as killed him!"

Kaeso was dressed all in black, as was everyone in the House of the Beaks that day, after holding the funeral and placing the ashes of Gnaeus Pinarius alongside those of his ancestors in the family monument outside the city. From within the house could be heard the sound of weeping.

He and his father were alone on one of the balconies, where no outsider could possibly overhear them, but Zenobius reflexively waved his hand, cautioning his son not to speak such a thought out loud.

Kaeso was quiet for a moment, then spoke again. "If we were Christians, we'd be praying right now for Grandfather's arrival in the everlasting hereafter."

"What in Hades put that thought in your mind?"

"Hades, indeed. Roman religion tells us exactly how to bury the dead, how to mourn them, how to remember them. But it doesn't have much to say about what exactly *happens* to the dead."

Zenobius nodded. "Down in Egypt, people have always believed in an afterlife—but there's a catch. What happens to you in the next world is closely linked to the ongoing condition of your body back in this world. People who can afford a perfectly preserved mummy, and can pay for its perpetual upkeep, do rather well in the afterlife, but the poor who can afford only to be soaked in a vat of natron must continue as they did on earth, in want and misery."

"Pity Alexander the Great!" Kaeso smiled. "You know the old story: Augustus was so amazed at the preservation of Alexander's mummy that he felt compelled to touch it—and snapped off the nose. Do the Egyptians think Alexander is now noseless in the afterlife?"

Zenobius laughed softly. "It seems to me that mandatory upkeep of the mummy is just a scheme to enrich the industry that prepares and stores the mummies. Since the mummies are regularly brought out of storage, to join the family on holidays, the remains *do* need to look presentable. But we Romans—we definitely have no use for the corpse. We burn it. For what happens next, the educated Roman nowadays looks not to priests for answers, but to the followers of Plato. Philosophers ponder such questions all day long."

"Yes, Father, and the various philosophers have come up with all sort of schemes, and they all claim to make perfect sense, but what man of ordinary intellect can follow their arguments? All those long Greek words, and long-winded suppositions. They can't seem to explain in any intelligible way what existence is—much less nonexistence. The Christians, on the other hand, claim to have it all figured out. In life you behave a certain way, and in death you receive your reward—or punishment. Heaven for the good. And for the bad, Hell—a place far worse than the Hades described by Homer."

"Yes and these so-called wicked who will be perpetually punished invariably include those of us who don't agree with the Christians," observed Zenobius. "As I understand it, even other Christians, unless they believe in precisely the 'correct' dogma, are doomed to be punished forever. To be sure, among Romans there has long been a school of thought that the spirits of the dead end up in this place or that. The greatest of the great, demi-gods like Hercules and the best of the emperors, are deified and get to live with the gods in Olympus. Heroes and others who were great on earth—even athletes, if you believe the Greeks—end up in a leafy, sun-dappled place called Elysium, which they leave on occasion to help us mortals back here on earth. But most of us end up in Hades, which according to the poets is rather chilly and dimly lit, and very, very boring. Thus the dead remember their days on earth with nostalgia, and envy the living."

Kaeso was not really listening. He was still thinking about the Christians. "One's admission to the Christian Heaven is not entirely contingent on belief. There's at least one prerequisite, called baptism. A priest administers magical water, and it washes away all the grubby sins accrued from day-to-day living. As I understand it, this cleansing is absolutely mandatory. No matter how good you might have been, you can't get into Heaven without first being baptized here on earth. Nor can anyone truly be called a Christian until he or she has received this baptism. That's why some wishful thinkers cling to the hope that Constantine isn't really a Christian, because he's never yet submitted to baptism."

"But he has a perfectly logical reason for waiting," said Zenobius. "I overheard Constantine himself explain it to a bishop in Nicaea—Eusebius, I think—when a group of us were going over some plans for the new city at Byzantium. Baptism washes away sin and gives one a fresh start. Morally, one becomes an infant again, a blank slate, sinless. But there is always the possibility of relapse! Commit enough fresh sin and you're right back where you started. And I don't think you can be baptized a second time. Constantine said, 'I am an emperor and a warrior, not a bishop or a martyr. A ruler by necessity must continue to sin until the very last day of his life.' Eusebius tried to object, but Constantine silenced him. He said, 'I have much to do in this life before I am ready to put sinning behind me.'"

Kaeso nodded. "So any reasonable man would want to postpone baptism as long as possible—but not *too* long. If you arranged to be baptized on your deathbed, but the magical water arrived a moment too late, then you'd be headed straight for Hell—on a technicality. You'd never stop kicking yourself."

"And that would be your everlasting punishment!" Zenobius chuckled. It was good to be cheered up, however slightly, on such a sad day. "But it's all a bunch of made-up nonsense anyway."

Kaeso looked thoughtful, but made no reply.

The Circus Maximus was filled to capacity, with children piled on laps and latecomers jamming the aisles. All of Rome, and visitors from every corner of the empire, were present for a special day of races to celebrate the Vicennalia.

The teams and their most avid supporters wore one of four colors: blue, green, red, or white. Partisans waved colored pennants, and each team had its own chants, usually built around the name of a favorite charioteer. The pennants rippled and waved on the warm breeze, and the cheering and chants echoed constantly around the Circus Maximus.

Constantine and Fausta, all in purple and gold, sat in the imperial box, along with their five children and Constantine's half brothers. Missing was the emperor's mother. Helena was not feeling well.

Also absent was Crispus. Rumor had it that he had left Rome hurriedly, rushing off to deal with some urgent military matter on the other side of the Adriatic Sea. Crispus had proved himself a reliable general in the war with Licinius, and an able strategist on land or at sea. People said it was a fine thing ("a blessing," as the Christians put it) that the emperor had a grown son of such talent upon whom he could rely with complete confidence.

In the section reserved for senators and their families, Zenobius rose to his feet, as did thousands of other spectators, as one of the races came to a thrilling end, with all four chariots in a virtual tie. He hardly noticed when Kaeso returned from a visit to the latrina. Then he caught a glimpse of the very odd expression on his son's face.

"Kaeso, is something wrong?"

Kaeso leaned close and spoke in a low voice. "I just heard the strangest bit of gossip from an old acquaintance I happened to see outside the latrina. Others were talking about it, too. They say Crispus is dead."

"What? But how?" Crispus was so robust and full of life, Zenobius could only imagine him felled by some terrible accident.

"That's the oddest part. They say he was *strangled* to death. This was in Pola, on the Dalmatian coast."

"Murdered?" The idea was outrageous. "By some assassin?"

"Not exactly. He wasn't murdered—that's not the right word. He was executed. Put to death, so the man told me, on his father's orders. Crispus wasn't in Pola because Constantine sent him there. He was running away from Rome, and that's as far as he got."

Zenobius was stunned. He looked toward the nearby imperial box. The children looked happy and excited by all the noise and colorful activity of the races, but Constantine and Fausta were as stiff as statues. Hannibalianus and Julius also sat very still and stared straight ahead without expression.

Then, beginning with a glimpse from the corner of his eye, Zenobius perceived a subtle motion that seemed to take place everywhere in the crowd at once, something quite different from the constant, chaotic movements of waving arms and pennants. He was not the only one who had turned to look at the imperial family. Thousands and thousands of others, from one end of the circus to the other, were doing the same thing—they suddenly stopped their frantic waving and turned to stare at the emperor. There was a change in the constant roar of the crowd, as the cheering was replaced by an undertone of many gasps and exclamations of surprise, and even a sort of menacing sound, like a growl of disapproval. The rumor of Crispus's death had spread like wildfire through every part of the Circus Maximus.

When Zenobius looked toward the imperial box again, he saw the emperor's young sons and daughters and their attendants, but Constantine and his wife and half brothers had vanished.

The next race was announced and the competing chariots appeared at the starting gate. Some semblance of normality returned to the crowd as chants were shouted and pennants were waved. The murmur of confusion grew quieter, but persisted nonetheless. Many of the spectators looked anxious or alarmed.

"Death by strangulation?" whispered Zenobius. Fausta's father, Maximian, and the last of Constantine's rivals, his brother-in-law Licinius, had both died with ropes around their necks. And now Crispus, who to all appearances had been the apple of his father's eye. Striking closer and closer, the cold hand of death had now reached into the very heart of Constantine's family.

"I wonder if they allowed him to be baptized first?" said Kaeso quietly, staring thoughtfully into the distance.

Summoned by the emperor, Zenobius arrived at the Lateran Palace with great trepidation. To his surprise, he was not shown to a reception room but conducted into the family quarters, and then to the private baths used by only the imperial family.

Several days had passed since news arrived in Rome of the death of Crispus. The Vicennalia celebrations were winding down. Everything had gone smoothly—there were no more unpleasant incidents like the stoning of the emperor's statue— but the mood of the city had become subdued, almost sullen. One sensed that Rome had had enough of Constantine, and that Constantine had had enough of Rome.

Crispus, handsome and in the prime of manhood, had been presented to the people of Rome as a sort of ideal warrior-prince, not just heroic and brave but also charming and lovable. Perhaps too charming, perhaps too lovable, if one believed the wild rumors that had circulated since his death. Rumors were all one had to go on, since no official explanation had yet been given for his apparent execution. The mystery generated endless gossip, some of it so dangerous it could be shared only in nervous whispers.

Zenobius had tried to ignore all these rumors, deciding there was no use in holding an opinion until the truth of the matter was revealed, if indeed that ever happened.

Waiting alone in the antechamber of one of the private baths— the summons had specified that he should bring not even a scribe with him—Zenobius cast a critical eye on his surroundings. He was quite familiar with these baths, having overseen their construction and decoration as part of the transformation of the House of the Laterani. Testing with his fingertips, he detected a loose tile or two, but all in all the mosaics underfoot and the beautifully painted ceilings were holding up very well.

He sighed at the repetitious simplicity of the images, which were not at all of the sort to be found in the older bathing establishment in Rome. Here there were no depictions of erotic stories or images of what Constantine called "pagan" deities and demons—no gods and goddesses seducing hapless mortals, no satyrs and nymphs cavorting, no Bacchus celebrating the joys of wine, none of the often wonderful, sometimes tragic stories passed down through countless generations, now superseded, in Constantine's view, by tales of Moses and martyrs. Here the images were all of gardens and woods and seascapes, of birds and beasts and sea creatures—nice enough, but a considerable step down from the highest attainments of Roman art.

Not for the first time, Zenobius pondered a large and looming question: If Constantine prevailed, what was to become of all the great art that did not fit with the worldview of the Christians? The citizens of Rome would never stand for desecration of their age-old treasures, but what about other cities around the empire where the Christians were now in ascendance, their fortunes buoyed by the emperor's largesse? What about the new city Constantine was building? To decorate such a vast expanse, the emperor spoke of "importing" treasures from other cities. Did he mean to loot only marble columns, floral and fish motifs, and portrait statues, or were "pagan" images of gods and heroes also to adorn Constantine's new hippodrome and his imperial palace? What would the hand-picked senate of the new city, presumably made entirely of Christians, make of that?

Such were Zenobius's thoughts when he abruptly realized that the emperor was present in the room. Not a single courtier attended him, which was very odd. Zenobius had never actually been alone with Constantine. Suddenly coming face to face with the emperor, with no ceremony or ritual whatsoever, was disconcerting. So were Constantine's first words.

"You are not a Christian, are you, Senator Pinarius?"

Zenobius felt a knot in the pit of his stomach. What was the point of this question? Did the emperor intend to strip Zenobius of his ongoing projects in the new city, purely on account of his religion? Or was Constantine about to insist that Zenobius become a Christian?

"No, Dominus, I am not a Christian."

"Good. You will advise me on a delicate matter. You will be completely honest, and completely discreet. You will repeat not one word of what we say here, to anyone. Do you understand?"

Constantine's gaze was so intense, so grim, that Zenobius felt slightly terrified.

"I understand, Dominus."

"I believe you have a thorough knowledge of these particular baths and how they are made to operate."

"That is correct, Dominus. Are they in need of repair?"

"No. I want to know how a person might be made to die in one of the heated rooms. Not from water, you understand, but from the heated air itself. Such a thing is possible, yes?"

Zenobius blinked once, twice, and then rapidly several times. He managed to take a deep breath. He was reminded of something his father had taught him, that there is seldom any point in trying to anticipate what a rich and powerful client will request. What such men will ask is likely to be something you cannot possibly anticipate. That was certainly the case here.

He could see that Constantine was deadly serious. No wonder they were meeting with no other mortal present— Zenobius was being asked to take part in a murder! He felt suddenly lightheaded, and wanted to shout: *Can the victim not be strangled?* That appeared to be Constantine's usual mode of execution. Why was Zenobius to be made complicit?

He swallowed his consternation and proceeded to answer as dispassionately and as factually as he could. He did in fact know of instances where a person had died in an overheated room, though in those cases the victim had been either elderly or in poor health. But it seemed likely that any person could be made to die if a room was made sufficiently hot, and if, of course, the person was unable to leave the room.

Constantine wanted him to look at a specific room in the baths, to see if it might be suitable for such an event to occur, given the source of its heat and other particulars. They walked down a narrow hallway. Constantine opened a thick wooden door, and they stepped into a circular, modestly proportioned room tiled on all sides, with a tiled bench in the center to sit on. A soft, glowing light came from an elaborate polycandelion overhead.

This was the room. To achieve the desired result, what problems might be anticipated, and how could they be solved? Constantine's manner was completely unemotional, as if he were asking perfectly normal questions of the sort any client might ask any builder.

"I must stress," he said, "that the operation must be absolutely foolproof."

The small room was a good choice for the task. Not only the floor but the bench and the lower portions of the walls were all heated by means of a hypocaust, with hot air piped directly from the nearby furnace room. If one deliberately wished to do so, those surfaces could be made quite hot—so hot that a person could not bear to touch them.

"Do I understand you to say," asked Constantine, "that the floor would be so hot that a person could not stand on it? That the bench would so hot that a person could not sit on it?"

"That seems entirely possible, Dominus. We've all been in baths where patrons complained that the floor was too hot, which is never the operator's intention. The solution is simply to mix cool air with the hot air in circulation, so as to regulate the heat. But if one shut off the cool air . . . if making a floor unbearably hot was the actual *goal* . . . yes, I believe that could be done."

"And death would occur . . . ?"

"I'm not a physician, but I suspect the victim would suffocate, or the blood would thicken, causing a stoppage of the heart. The four humors would be thrown completely out of balance."

"Good. There is a man in the furnace room you will speak to. He expects you. You will explain to him in technical terms precisely what is desired. Work out with him any foreseeable problems. The event is to occur tomorrow at midday."

"Will I . . . must I . . . be present at the time?"

"Absolutely not. You will be elsewhere. And so will I. I shall be with my mother, on my knees, praying at the Church of Our Savior. I would invite you to pray with us, if you, too, were a Christian. But since you are not, I suggest you go about your ordinary routine. And you will speak of this to no one—not even that clever son of yours."

Zenobius swallowed hard. His mouth was very dry. "I shall be as a mute, Dominus. As a man made speechless. Dumbfounded."

Constantine nodded. They left the tiled room. In the narrow hallway, without a word, Constantine pointed toward the furnace room. Zenobius headed in that direction. After a few steps, he turned and looked back.

Constantine had vanished, though it seemed impossible that he could have departed so quickly. The whole experience was so bizarre, Zenobius almost thought he had imagined it. But he knew that the emperor's request was all too real.

Later, after conferring with the man in the furnace room, Zenobius passed by the tiled room and then through the antechamber and then down a long hallway that led him to a small reception room. No one was present in this neglected wing of the palace. Zenobius paused to steady himself and to catch his breath.

This was one of the oldest rooms in the House of the Laterani, and one of the least affected by the recent refurbishments. The old decorations were still intact. The workmanship was exquisite. Zenobius found comfort in gazing up at the beautifully painted ceiling.

A particular series of images caught his eye. They depicted the tragic story of Hippolytus, son of King Theseus. Gazing at the images in sequence, recalling the tale, Zenobius felt his blood run cold.

Prince Hippolytus was young and handsome. His step-mother, Queen Phaedra, was seized by an uncontrollable lust for him. She attempted to seduce him. Rejecting her advances, pushing her roughly aside, he mounted his chariot in a mad rush to ride as fast and as far away as he could.

In a frenzy of love turned to hate, Phaedra tore her clothes and told King Theseus that Hippolytus had raped her. Theseus believed her. Using magic, he caused the horses of his son's chariot to go mad. Hippolytus was thrown from the chariot, but he did not fall clear. His feet were caught in the reins. As the horses stampeded wildly, he was dragged to a gory, agonizing death.

Wracked by guilt, Phaedra committed suicide, but only after writing a letter to Theseus confessing her lie. The great king realized his error, but only after his son and his wife were both dead.

Gazing up at the images, recalling the story, Zenobius felt a prickling sense of dread, but also a surge of religious exaltation. The story of Hippolytus was only one of the countless stories that made up what the Christians scornfully dismissed as the "old religion." All those stories were interwoven like an endless tapestry extending to infinity in every direction, capturing in its threads every moment of every mortal life already lived or yet to be. Though their meaning was often mysterious, those stories and the people in them held up an uncanny mirror to the very real trials and tribulations of living mortals, offering a glimpse into some ultimate truth about existence. Here Zenobius stood, prompted by these images to recall the tale of Hippolytus, and at that very moment, in that very place, something very like that story was happening around him—and he was being made to play a part.

Something terrible had taken place between Constantine, Crispus, and Fausta—for surely it was Fausta whom Constantine intended to murder in the heated room. How cruel, to roast a helpless mortal in an oven, scalding her hands and feet, scorching her lungs so that each breath became torture, thickening her blood until her heart grew rigid and burst from the strain. Fausta was not to be burned alive—Constantine's preferred penalty for what he deemed sexual crimes—but this punishment was close enough. He would give her a foretaste of the flaming Hell he no doubt envisioned as her ultimate fate.

Constantine mocked the gods. This had to be their revenge on him, this homicidal madness—the murder of his own son, and now his wife. He had fallen prey to the goddess Atë, who brought delusion, folly, and ruin to the heroes of the ancient stories. Hubris was the overweening pride that led the hero into error, but Atë brought the outcome, the horrible consequence. Even the gods were subject to Atë—even Jupiter, her father.

In the ruination of Constantine, Atë had made Zenobius one of her instruments. He left the House of the Laterani reconciled to his role in the drama.

The death of Fausta was reported as an accident, but the gossips of Rome said otherwise. Salacious stories abounded. She had seduced Crispus, but Constantine caught them in the act and ultimately killed them both. Or: she failed to seduce Crispus, then invented a rape, like Phaedra, and tricked Constantine into killing his son, then in the throes of guilt she committed suicide by locking herself in the hot room. Or: Fausta was entirely innocent, because Crispus raped her and then fled, but Constantine went crazy with suspicion and killed her unjustly. Or: like Lucretia of ancient days, she was raped by Crispus and, though she was innocent of any wrongdoing, shame drove her to kill herself.

One of the more twisted variations held that Fausta had orchestrated a coldly calculated hoax: wanting to put her stepson Crispus out of the way so as to advance her own sons, she invented a rape; Constantine believed her and killed Crispus; then it was Helena, Crispus's doting grandmother, who uncovered the deceit and insisted that Constantine put the wicked woman to death.

Yet another rumor asserted that Fausta had deliberately plotted to bring as much pain as she could to both Constantine and his firstborn because she hated both of them with all her might. Why? The plausible catalogue of her grievances was long: her marriage was arranged when she was very young, she had no say in the matter, and she had never loved Constantine; her father had been forced to commit suicide after an alleged coup against Constantine; Constantine had then vilified the dead man with a lurid fiction claiming Maximian was plotting to kill Constantine, in which story Fausta was slandered as betraying her own father; Constantine's attack on Rome had led to the ignominious death of Fausta's brother, Maxentius, a humiliation compounded when Constantine ordered Maxentius's corpse to be desecrated and beheaded, then proudly paraded this gory trophy through the streets of Rome, and even sent it to Africa to intimidate Maxentius's general there. One could only imagine the shame and terror Fausta must have felt, all the while putting on a show of being a loving and loyal wife—lest she be beheaded next! In this version of events, Fausta's return to Rome for the Vicennalia stirred within her a whirlwind of repressed anguish. How could Fausta be in

Rome and not think of her father and brother and their terrible ends, and all the other indignities she had endured?

A particular detail the gossips liked to linger upon was the irony that Constantine, who upon arrival in Italy issued his self-righteous edicts to punish all sorts of sexual immorality, had been made to look a complete fool when cuckolded by his wife and son.

There was even a version of events which involved no sex at all: Crispus, falling prey to overweening ambition, had plotted to usurp his father, was found out, fled Rome, was apprehended and executed—and the death of Fausta was accidental and completely unrelated. From the whispers that worked their way down to him from the inner circles of the court, it seemed to Zenobius that this was likely to be the version Constantine himself would eventually settle on. The official version would show the emperor in the best possible light—a grieving father betrayed by his son and given no choice but to execute him, a loving husband made a widower by a peculiar turn of fate.

Sitting on a balcony of the House of the Beaks, the Pinarii discussed all these differing versions of events, as well as the latest twist, an anonymous couplet in elegant Latin that had been posted on small placards all over the city. The verses made reference to a famous cameo of exquisite workmanship and extraordinary size—almost a foot wide and half again as tall—carved from blue and white agate. It had been presented to Constantine as a gift from the Senate of Rome on the occasion of his previous visit, to celebrate his Decennalia. The cameo depicted Constantine, Fausta, and Crispus as a boy (but already dressed as a warrior) in a triumphal chariot pulled by two centaurs, who also happened to be trampling a pair of enemies meant to represent Maxentius and his young son. Winged Victory hovered over the scene, holding forth a wreath to lay upon Constantine's head. The cameo had been publicly displayed and much talked about ten years ago, during the Decennalia, then had been stored in the imperial treasury, and then brought out again and displayed on a pedestal in the New

Basilica to celebrate the Vicennalia. Day after day, citizens had been queuing up by the thousands to have a look at it.

The little poem that had been widely posted and much talked about in recent days went:

Who still longs for this Golden Age of Saturn?
The memory lingers only on a gem of Nero's pattern.

The references offered a tantalizing puzzle. Everyone took the gem to be the agate cameo, which was still on display. By why "of Nero's pattern"? Nero had never celebrated a triumph—but in common with Constantine, he had killed his wife and child (in Nero's case a child not yet born). "This Golden Age" no doubt referred to the twenty-year reign of Constantine, while the very notion of a Golden Age hearkened back to Saturn, first king of the gods, who reigned at the dawn of time. But the implied comparison was not flattering: Saturn had devoured his own children.

"And so the unknown poet, with great economy, manages not only to dismiss our current 'Golden Age,' but also to equate the emperor to not one but two tyrants who murdered their own offspring," said Zenobius.

"At least he didn't do like Nero, and murder his mother as well," quipped Kaeso. "But leaving poetry and getting back to gossip—after considering all the rival versions, what do you think is the *true* story, Father?"

"We will never know, my son," said Zenobius. *Just as you will never know about your own father's involvement*, he thought, for true to his word he had told no one, not even Kaeso, about his meeting with Constantine on the fateful day before Fausta's death.

A few days later there came to the House of the Beaks another summons, this time to the New Basilica, requesting both Zenobius and Kaeso.

To the great relief of Zenobius, on this occasion their reception was quite formal. The vast hall was filled with courtiers conferring in hushed tones, messengers hurriedly going about their errands, secretaries with dossiers ready to be called on, and scribes recording every official utterance. Wearing purple and gold robes of state and a golden diadem with a double string of pearls—the first emperor to adorn his crown with jewels—Constantine sat on a throne on a high dais in front of the giant statue of himself. He sat so stiffly that at a distance he looked like a miniature version of the statue, perhaps made of painted plaster or wax. But when they drew closer, Zenobius dared to look into the man's eyes, and the eyes of Constantine stared back at him. The rigid figure on the throne was a living man, after all.

"I am cutting short my stay in Rome," said Constantine. "My visit was intended to be longer, and my dear mother urges me to stay, but things here in Rome . . . have not gone to my liking. Frankly, Senator Pinarius, I do not care for the sullen mood of the citizenry, nor for their incessant and reckless gossip, nor for the ill-advised tenacity with which the vast majority cling to the old religion. More now than ever, I can hardly wait for my new city to be built! Toward that end, I am leaving Rome, and you, Senator Pinarius, will come with me. So will your son. Your talents are required for the construction and decoration of the new city."

The emperor fell silent. He nodded to a courtier, who nodded to Zenobius to indicate that he could speak.

"Dominus, is this posting to be . . . temporary?"

"What do you think, Senator? You know the situation at Byzantium. You know how much work remains to be done. It will be a labor of many years. And having built the city, will you not wish to live in it? I suggest that you bring your families with you. Sell or rent out that famous house you live in. Besides that house, what else is keeping you here in this city haunted by demons?"

Not long ago, Zenobius would have answered, "My father." Now the dear old man was gone—his sudden death attributable in some degree to Constantine. But there was so much more that bound him to Rome. This was the city of his childhood, the city of his ancestors, the greatest city in all of human history, a living temple filled with shrines and monuments, layered with the innumerable memories of countless generations. Constantine, the footloose warrior of no fixed abode who had traveled the world slaughtering one rival after another, to whom one fortress or palace was much the same as any other—such a man could never understand how deeply Zenobius loved his native city.

And yet . . . Zenobius was also the son of the queen of Palmyra, and there had always been a part of him that had felt drawn to the eastern half of the empire. The site of Byzantium was a splendid place, and the new city would be stunningly beautiful, all the more so because he and his son would have a hand in building it.

As for Rome, the city was already suffering neglect, and was likely to suffer more, especially if Constantine's sons came to detest it as much as he seemed to. To them, Rome would always be a cursed place, the city where their father murdered their mother.

Zenobius felt torn, uncertain what to say, but when he looked at Kaeso, he saw that his son appeared not at all dismayed or dubious, but excited and eager. Such was the enthusiasm of youth for new vistas and fresh challenges.

"In the new city," said Constantine, "there will be many new opportunities. My new senate will have room for many members, men who have proven their worth to the empire and their loyalty to the emperor. Consider that. There is something else you might consider, very seriously . . ."

Zenobius felt his skin prickle and his heart sink, for he knew what was coming next.

"Consider, I say, becoming Christians, and joining your emperor in the one true religion. The new city will be full of churches, and the most prestigious work will be the building of those churches. I suspect the bishops will chide me if I allow pagans to take a hand in creating their new houses of worship. 'Let the pagans build the sewers and the cisterns,' they will say. In that regard as in many others it will improve a man's prospects, not just in the world to come but in this world as well, if he should become a follower of Christ."

Again Zenobius looked at Kaeso. His son seemed unfazed. Kaeso had always been less religious and less traditional than his father and grandfather. He seemed to have a genuine curiosity about Christianity. No apprehension or anxiety shadowed the excitement on his face. Was the prospect of becoming a Christian acceptable to Kaeso?

Dismissed by the emperor, the Pinarii left the New Basilica. Saying little, they seemed to be of one mind about what to do next. Together they took a long, rambling walk through the Forum, up to the Capitoline Hill, and then all around the city, eventually ascending a stretch of the Aurelian Walls to take in the view.

"When these walls were built," said Zenobius, "all that lay inside was Rome, but all that lay outside was also Rome. Rome owned the empire; the empire belonged to Rome. So it was and always would be, men thought. But the day is coming when Rome will no longer be the capital of the empire—you and I, building Constantine's new city, will help make that happen. Then Rome will be just another city, trapped inside the fortifications that were built to protect it. The city will be a captive of the empire, a prisoner inside its walls. I think that is not the Rome you want your children to live in. The ancestors—all the countless Pinarii since the beginning of the city and before—will forgive us for leaving Rome, I think. They will want their descendants to grow up in the new city, with new traditions, new laws . . . perhaps even a new religion."

"What will I do with *this*?" asked Kaeso. From within his toga, dangling on a chain of silver, he drew forth the fascinum.

Zenobius's eyes grew wide. "You dared to wear it in the emperor's presence?"

"It was I who should have been wearing it the day I watched

Grandfather die at the Senate House, clutching it to his chest. I've worn it every day since."

"But what now? The fascinum will have no place in the new city. People will say it conjures black magic and summons wicked demons. Even to possess such a 'pagan' object may soon be against the law—and the punishments of Constantine are very harsh."

Kaeso fondled the lump of gold between his forefinger and thumb. "Certainly I could never wear it if I . . . if I should become . . . a Christian."

There: Kaeso had said it aloud. The unspeakable had been spoken.

"When Constantine saw your grandfather wearing it, he himself thought it might be a crucifix, from the shape. Perhaps you could get away with wearing it, if—"

"No, Father. I would know what it is, even if others did not. I won't pretend the fascinum is something it isn't."

Zenobius slowly nodded. "The fascinum is yours, son. What you choose to do is up to you. And your descendants, in their generation, will make their own choices. Last night I was reading the meditations of the Divine Marcus, that book in which he recorded his private thoughts. 'For everything fades away and quickly becomes a myth. All is forgotten. Everything is lost in oblivion.' So it will be, even with Rome. So it will be with Constantine's new city, eventually. So with every human life, and with all humanity, with the passage of time. We shall fade away, and there shall be no one to remember us, for those who come after us will have faded away in their turn. It shall be as if none of us ever existed."

Kaeso tilted his head. "The Christians don't think that way. In their scheme of things, everything is planned, everything has a purpose. Nothing is ever forgotten. And no one ever actually dies. No one! Being mortal is not an option. Like it or not, every human will exist forever, some in perpetual joy, others in endless torment."

"What kind of torment?"

"They'll be thrown into a fire that burns the flesh but doesn't consume it. Their screaming agony, and the horror of knowing it will never end, will go on forever and ever."

"What a horrible religion!" Zenobius shook his head. "I shall never be able to accept it."

Kaeso, respecting his father, let him have the last word.

All was packed—all the books and clothes, all the jewelry and mementos and precious keepsakes. Their passage was arranged. Every loose end had been tied up. Except one.

On the night before they were to leave Rome, while the city slept, Kaeso went alone to the Temple of Venus and Roma. He opened the hidden mechanism that allowed access to the secret chamber where his father had hidden the scepter of Maxentius. From its undisturbed state and the musty smell, he was certain that no one had visited the room since then.

Kaeso lifted the necklace over his head. He placed the fascinum next to the scepter. The moment seemed to call for a prayer, but he could think of no words to say. He left the chamber. He closed the secret door. He deliberately broke the hidden mechanism. The room was sealed. There was nothing to suggest that it had ever existed. The contents were as safe as any buried treasure could be.

In the New Rome, he would become a Christian and would have no use for such an amulet. Though he was leaving it behind, Kaeso would make sure that the knowledge of its existence was passed down to the next generation. In his heart he knew that the fascinum still belonged, would always belong, to the Pinarii.

The family heirloom would become a family legend. Perhaps, under different circumstances, a descendant would reclaim it, and the fascinum would be worn again in a future generation.

Epilogue

From the December 2006 issue of the magazine *Roman Archaeology Today*:

> Italian archaeologists have announced that an excavation under a shrine near the Palatine Hill has unearthed several items in wooden boxes, which they have identified as imperial regalia.
>
> These are the only known imperial insignia so far recovered, and thus of tremendous importance. (Up to now, such regalia have only been known from representations on coins and in relief sculptures.)
>
> The items in these boxes, which were wrapped in linen and what appears to be silk, include six complete lances, four javelins, what appears to be a base for standards, and three glass and chalcedony spheres. The most important find was a scepter of a flower holding a blue-green globe, which is believed to have belonged to the emperor himself because of its intricate workmanship.

But which emperor? Clementina Panella, the archae-
ologist who made the discovery, dates them to the reign
of Maxentius. "These artifacts clearly belonged to the
emperor," says Panella, "especially the scepter, which is
very elaborate. It's not an item you would let someone else
have." Panella notes that the insignia were likely hidden
by supporters of Maxentius in an attempt to preserve the
emperor's memory after he was defeated at the Battle of
the Milvian Bridge by Constantine the Great.

Archaeologists hope to restore the items for possible
display at the Museo Nazionale Romano at the Palazzo
Massimo alle Terme.

Reports on the find made no mention of anything
resembling a small gold amulet. The fascinum of the Pinarii
was not among the items recovered.

Author's Note

For everything fades away and quickly becomes a myth; and soon complete oblivion covers them over.

—MARCUS AURELIUS
MEDITATIONS (BIRLEY TRANSLATION)

The past did not generate fixed memories; instead, memories constructed a past.

—RAYMOND VAN DAM
REMEMBERING CONSTANTINE AT THE MILVIAN BRIDGE

The period from the death of Marcus Aurelius, the model of the philosopher-king, to the triumph of Christianity under Constantine the Great comprises about 150 years. No era is more fretted over by later historians, more fraught with insoluble mysteries, or more pregnant with consequence. Sources are missing, fragmentary, misleading, or blatantly fraudulent. Much of one crucial source, the *Historia Augusta,* is essentially a novel, and a very bad novel at that.

Robert Latouche, in *The Birth of the Western Economy,* approaches with a shudder "the third century, a sinister age, the least known in the whole history of Rome. . . . After the reign of the Severi, we plunge into a long tunnel, to emerge only at the beginning of the Late Empire under Diocletian, and when we step out again into daylight, unfamiliar country lies all about us."

In my long-ago college days, these amnesiac years of the Roman Empire were a scholarly backwater. Since then, especially in the last twenty years or so, like particles drawn to a vacuum, historians have converged on the era and found it not entirely vacuous after all. Two wide-ranging works make sense of the chaos: Pat Southern's *The Roman Empire from Severus to Constantine* and David S. Potter's *The Roman Empire at Bay*. Potter expanded my vocabulary as no author has done since Lawrence Durrell.

In the final decade of his life, the great Michael Grant wrote a series of more narrowly focused books, including *The Antonines*, *The Severans*, *The Collapse and Recovery of the Roman Empire*, and *Constantine the Great*. His earlier masterwork, *The Climax of Rome*, is a dazzling foray into the changing thought-world of an empire that produced men as different as Marcus Aurelius and Constantine as its paragons.

Anthony R. Birley's biography *Marcus Aurelius* is especially enlightening when read in conjunction with Marcus's *Meditations*. Olivier Hekster's *Commodus: An Emperor at the Crossroads* offers an evenhanded view of Marcus's detested heir.

The Rain Miracle presents a striking instance where the evolution of a myth can be tracked through time. Péter Kovács examines the incident in *Marcus Aurelius' Rain Miracle and the Marcomannic Wars* and in a later paper, "Marcus Aurelius' Rain Miracle: When and Where?" (freely available at academia.edu). Two other papers of note are "The Rain Miracle of Marcus Aurelius: (Re-)Construction of Consensus," by Ido Israelowich (*Greece & Rome,* Second Series, Vol. 55, No. 1, April 2008), and "Pagan Versions of the Rain Miracle of A.D. 172," by Garth Fowden (*Historia: Zeitschrift für Alte Ges-*

chichte, Bd. 36, H. 1, 1st Qtr., 1987). The counterfeit letter of Marcus crediting the Rain Miracle to Christians can be found in various places online, or in *Ante-Nicene Fathers,* Volume I, edited by Alexander Roberts and James Donaldson.

The plagues that repeatedly devastated the empire during this period have received considerable attention in recent years. Kyle Harper speculates on their profound effects in *The Fate of Rome.*

Tracking down the works of Galen in translation and making sense of them is a difficult and tedious task. But reading Maud W. Gleason's "Shock and Awe: The Performance Dimension of Galen's Anatomy Demonstrations" is a delight. It can be found in *Galen and the World of Knowledge*, edited by Christopher Gill, Tim Whitmarsh, and John Wilkins. *The Prince of Medicine: Galen in the Roman Empire*, by Susan P. Mattern, is a useful biography. Having read a number of his shorter works on Galen, I look forward to Vivian Nutton's *Galen: A Thinking Doctor in Imperial Rome*, which was published after I finished *Dominus.*

Anthony R. Birley in *Septimius Severus: The African Emperor* proposes that the emperor, with his provincial African accent, might have pronounced his name "Sheptimiush Sherverush." I like to imagine Sean Connery saying that.

What do we really know about the emperor now called Elagabalus? First, he was never known by that name in his lifetime. Second, virtually every "fact" about him is disputable. In *The Emperor Elagabalus: Fact or Fiction?*, Leonardo de Arrizabalaga y Prado tackles head-on the epistemological stumbling blocks that most historians sidestep, and strips away the lies, distortions, and false methodologies that surround this particular emperor. It is a difficult, challenging, and superlative work of history.

Jay Carriker's thesis *The World of Elagabalus* (http://hdl. handle.net/10950/370) answers some questions about the emperor Varius while raising others, and boldly asserts that "the religious boundaries that he disregarded reveal a Varian

Moment as a critical period in the Easternization of Roman religion, which makes him one of the most significant figures in Roman History."

Martijn Icks's book published in England as *Images of Elagabalus* was given a more sensational title in the United States—*The Crimes of Elagabalus: The Life and Legacy of Rome's Decadent Boy Emperor*. Much of the book is devoted to what historians call the *Nachleben*, or cultural afterlife, of the emperor. The *Nachleben* of Elagabalus is extraordinarily rich and vastly outsized in proportion to the length of his reign. A particular manifestation of that *Nachleben* was my first introduction to Elagabalus, the novel *Child of the Sun*, by Kyle Onstott and Lance Horner. Published in paperback in 1972, the year I turned sixteen, it was the sort of "trashy novel" a teenager back then would hide from his mother. The novel made a huge impression on me. Now *Dominus,* too, becomes part of the *Nachleben* of Elagabalus, and part of the *Nachleben* of *Child of the Sun*, as well.

Emesa, the home city of Julia Domna and her family, once the center of Elagabalus-worship, is now known as Homs, the site of so much carnage in the Syrian civil war.

About the emperors who follow the Severans, our sources are especially bleak. But among the secondary material I was delighted to find a paper by an old college prof of mine, David Armstrong, "Gallienus in Athens" (*Zeitschrift für Papyrologie und Epigraphik*, Bd. 70, 1987). It was a delight to hear his voice in my head again so many years after the lectures that inspired me as an undergraduate. Someday a good novel will be written about Gallienus, but in this book he is essentially a ghost, offstage.

It is a curious thing that the *Nachleben* of Cleopatra is so rich but that of Zenobia is so meager. The sources are partly to blame; as usual with this period, they are scattered and conflicting. I chose to deal with the final chapter of her life, an epilogue really, which is shrouded in mystery. In the twenty-first century, Zenobia's capital of Palmyra was made world famous even as, indeed because, its ancient ruins were obliterated by ISIS. The Temple of Bel, which Zenobia must have visited many times, is now rubble. It is painful to contemplate the archaeological storehouses of knowledge that have recently been lost across the region, not by decay but by deliberate human action.

Speaking of monotheist religious fanaticism: before the battle outside Rome, what did Constantine see in the sky, and when did he see it—or more to the point, when and how and why did he *remember* seeing it? To borrow a phrase from Tolkien, "this tale grew in the telling." Raymond Van Dam's essential study of the emperor and his vision, *Constantine at the Milvian Bridge*, lays out the timeline, sorts the evidence, and compellingly reflects on the tortuous relationship between history, memory, and reality. History shapes events. But memory reshapes history.

The evolution of the *chi-rho* symbol curiously parallels that of the swastika, an emblem that was already ancient when it was used in America in the 1910s to decorate pillows, brooches, and stationery of the Girls' Club of *Ladies' Home Journal*. Then the Nazis took it over. As the swastika predated Hitler, so the *chi-rho* predated Constantine. In *Money in Ptolemaic Egypt*, Sitta von Reden notes that "the *chi-rho* series of Euergetes' reign" (246 to 222 B.C.) became "the most extensive series of bronze coins ever minted." Thus the image of the *chi-rho* was widespread on coins hundreds of years before Constantine. In *Studies in Constantinian Numismatics,* Patrick Bruun cites the use of *chi-rho* to mark special passages in papyri. Then the Christians took it over.

In like fashion, the words "demon" and "pagan" were subverted and perverted. Adherents of the old religion never called themselves pagans, yet that is the insulting word invariably applied to them even by conscientious historians.

Did Constantine really call Marcus Aurelius "a buffoon"? When I first encountered this detail (unfootnoted) in a book by one of our greatest living historians, now a professor emeritus, I contacted him by email, asking the source. I received a quick reply: "Dear Colleague, I understand your curiosity, it is an odd little fact (if it was a fact), but I'm sorry to say I can't help you. My notes were thrown out, I don't know how many years ago." As a researcher I was disappointed, but as an author I was rather impressed by the nimble elegance of this boilerplate response, to which I may have recourse myself in my retirement. To my rescue, in response to a posting at Facebook, came my fellow novelist Ian Ross, who led me to an obscure source, Peter the Patrician. The original Greek word is καταγέλαστον, which does indeed translate as "ludicrous" or "laughingstock." The insults Constantine aimed at other predecessors come from the same source. No longer as obscure as it once was, *The Lost History of Peter the Patrician* has been published in a translation by Thomas M. Banchich.

(Several years ago, when I thought I should very soon be needing information about the deaths of Crispus and Fausta, Professor Banchich kindly shared with me an advance look at his translation *The History of Zonaras: From Alexander Severus to the Death of Theodosius the Great*. As it turned out, that book was published long before this one.)

The curious case of the cameo of Constantine and the satirical verses (by Flavius Ablabius) that compare him to Nero is recounted by Ruurd B. Halbertsma in his paper *"Nulli tam laeti triumphi*—Constantine's Victory on a Reworked Cameo in Leiden," published in BABESCH 90 (2015).

What are we to make of the early Christians? Robert Knapp's insightful *The Rise of Christianity: People and Gods in a Time of Magic and Miracles* provides much-needed context for the competitive thought-world in which Christianity found a niche, doggedly persisted, and eventually flourished. The new religion aggressively subsumed or obliterated all of its rivals, and in the process became both more and less than it was in the beginning. Once the imminent end-days expected by the first Christians repeatedly failed to materialize (as they still do), the whole raison d'être of the religion had to be retooled, and not for the better. Would Jesus and the first Christian caterpillars have recognized the gaudy but venomous butterflies that emerged in the form of Constantine and his successors? The political rise of Christianity has been explored by Ramsay MacMullen in several excellent books, including the harrowing *Christianizing the Roman Empire*.

Movies and novels have occasionally dipped into this era, with mixed results. *Gladiator* revived cinematic interest in the ancient world, but the movie's portrayal of Commodus struck me as wildly and willfully wrong, hewing to a Hollywood formula that pits a red-blooded hero against an effete emperor. An earlier movie, *The Fall of the Roman Empire*, followed the same formula (with Stephen Boyd as the hero and Christopher Plummer as Commodus). Herodian, an eyewitness and no friend of the emperor, tells us that Commodus "was the handsomest man of his time, both in beauty of features and in physical development . . . inferior to no man in skill and in marksmanship." Commodus was a man's man, into sports, hunting, and hot rods. Imagine if Ridley Scott had subverted the formula and dared to cast Russell Crowe as Commodus, instead of Joaquin Phoenix.

Another Hollywood formula is to avoid novelty and remake whatever worked before. (Some see *Gladiator* as a remake of *The Fall of the Roman Empire*.) So we see Julius Caesar, Cleopatra, Nero, and a handful of others trotted out over and over, but never a cinematic Zenobia, or Elagabalus, or Julia Domna. Perhaps that's for the best.

Novelists have been more adventurous, but not necessarily more accurate. Ramsay MacMullen notes in *Christianizing the Roman Empire*, "The empire had never had on the throne a man given to such bloodthirsty violence as Constantine." That's a startling statement when you consider the homicidal reputations of Nero, Domitian, and several other predecessors of Constantine. At the other end of the spectrum is the Constantine who wouldn't hurt a fly, the fictional character one encounters in works by Dorothy L. Sayers (*The Emperor Con-*

stantine, a play that resembles a Christmas pageant), Frank Slaughter (the novel *Constantine: The Miracle of the Flaming Cross*), and Evelyn Waugh (the novel *Helena*). They are wretched whitewashes; hagiography makes for lousy fiction. At least Waugh's novel is occasionally funny.

What became of the Roman Empire after the end of *Dominus?* Gibbon was the first historian boldly to attempt a survey of the later empire, all the way to the annihilation of its last stronghold by the Ottoman Turks in 1453. With Latin and Greek at his command, Gibbon picked his way through sources that become ever more devious and convoluted—Byzantine, in every sense of the word. Many of those primary texts, long inaccessible to general readers, have in recent years been translated and annotated by historians, so that the curious may examine for themselves the material that so exasperated Gibbon.

In medieval times, the Romans forgot the people they once had been, and the things they once had built fell into ruin and lost their meaning. Bronze statues were particularly vulnerable; the vast majority were melted down so the metal could be reused, often as weapons. But the bronze equestrian statue of Marcus Aurelius survived, in part because the Romans had forgotten Marcus. They thought the statue represented Constantine the Great. (Imagine Constantine with a beard!) It is there no longer, but in medieval times there was still a diminutive, downtrodden figure groveling beneath the horse's raised hoof. Local legend explained that the statue showed the mounted Constantine trampling a dwarf whom the faithless Fausta had received as a lover. This odd little fact (if it is a fact) we learn from Ferdinand Gregorovius's *History of the City of Rome in the Middle Ages,* and from a footnote in the Nichols translation of *Mirabilia Urbis Romae,* "Marvels of the City of Rome," a sort of Baedeker Guide to the city from circa A.D. 1140.

As Marcus himself wrote, "everything fades away and quickly becomes a myth; and soon complete oblivion covers them over."

Before oblivion arrives, let me quickly thank, as always, my husband, Rick, at my side through thick and thin since college days; my longtime editor, Keith Kahla, who knows my work better than I do myself; and my agent since forever, Alan Nevins, without whom I might never have realized the one and only possible title for this book.

Roman Emperors
from Marcus Aurelius to Constantine

A.D. 161–180	Marcus Aurelius, jointly with Lucius Verus until Verus's death in 169
180–192	Commodus
193	Pertinax
193	Marcus Didius Julianus
193–211	Septimius Severus
211–217	Caracalla, jointly with his brother Geta until Geta's death in 212
217–218	Macrinus
218–222	Varius Avitus Bassianus (called Antoninus or Elagabalus)
222–235	Severus Alexander
235–238	Maximinus Thrax
238	Gordian I, jointly with his son, Gordian II
238	Balbinus and Pupienus, jointly
238–244	Gordian III

244–249	Philip
249–251	Decius
251–253	Trebonianus Gallus
253	Aemilian
253–268	Gallienus, jointly with his father, Valerian, until Valerian's capture in 260
268–270	Claudius II
270	Quintillus
270–275	Aurelian
275–276	Marcus Claudius Tacitus
276	Florianus
276–282	Probus
282–283	Carus
283–284	Carinus, first jointly with his father, Carus, then jointly with his brother, Numerian
284–305	Diocletian, jointly with Maximian from 286; both retire in 305; Maximian later attempts to come out of retirement
305–311	Galerius, jointly with Constantius until Constantius's death in 306
306–312	Maxentius emperor in Rome; joint rulers and rivals during his reign include his father, Maximian, and Constantine, Licinius, Severus, and Maximinus Daia
312–324	Constantine and Licinius, jointly, until Licinius's death in 324
324–337	Constantine sole ruler